THE OSTRICH RACE

SIMON BIRKS

The Ostrich Race

Second Edition

First Published in the UK by Thoroughly Professional Productions
This edition published by Blue Fox Publishing
Copyright 2012 © Simon Birks
Cover Illustration by Peter Spells

The right of Simon Birks to be identified as the author of this work has
been asserted by him in accordance with the Copyright, Designs and
Patent Act 1988

Blue Fox Publishing does not have any control over, or any
responsibility for, any author or third-party websites referred to in or
on this book.

Visit **http://bluefoxcomics.com** to read more about all our books,
comics and other publications.

For Marielle,

whose belief makes all things possible.

And for Arran, Fraser and Tabitha,

for letting me be their dad.

BIB, BRENDA, AND THE CRICKET MATCH

It was mid-January, and Gordon knew he was already behind schedule for the Race. Although he'd spent many an aching hour amongst the library's dusty, claustrophobic shelves, the pressure he felt from the work left to do was quickly becoming overwhelming.

Since New Year's, his days had consisted of little more than sitting dutifully at the library's lifeless grey tables, trying to concentrate on a dozen or so different books laid out in front of him. Yet, unlike previous years, it wasn't working. He couldn't reach the state of mind that allowed him to block out all of his immediate distractions. Today, his downfall was the drizzle that fell upon the cold, oblong windows, excusing his mind from the quiet, hushed, hall, and letting it wander between distant, cherished, memories.

~

Gordon hunched the coat he wore around his shoulders as the spots of rain touched the back of his exposed neck. This memory was over forty years old, when Gordon had been twenty-three, though, as he sat in the library, he experienced it as though it had happened only last week. He could even taste the country air as he walked with his future bride on that cold January night.

"Now, Gordy," Brenda said with the mischievous smile she'd worn throughout dinner. "There's something I really ought to tell you."

Under normal circumstances, Gordon would have been worried by this sentence, as, in his experience, it was normally followed by the sort of bombshell that left your mouth open and mind awhirl. Whatever the 'something' turned out to be, there would be a very good reason why it had lain hidden till now, purposefully dormant in order to misdirect the receiver's perception of the truth. This time, however, Gordon knew he had no reason to be worried. After all, this was Brenda, the lady he felt he knew everything about.

Then as easily as changing the channel on a television, a second, older, memory appeared in place of the first; a sunny day, some five months previous; Gordon whistling into an azure, cloudless sky, the warm wind tugging lightly at his shirt. Walking briskly, Gordon soaked up as much sunshine as possible; this was an English summer after all, and he knew just how temperamental they could be.

In his head words swam. It had been the same for many years, and he hardly went anywhere without some idea, phrase or half-plot appearing in his mind. In fact, it was one of the reasons he had to walk so fast. He'd left his rented cottage with plenty of time to spare that morning, but then, as he'd strolled along the road next to the fields on the path into town, a thought had sprung from nowhere and he'd had to stop at a newsagent to buy a small pad of paper and a pencil. Once back outside, he'd found a spot on the grassy bank nearby, sat and scribbled down the words as quickly as he'd thought them, becoming lost in their progressive intricacies. When, at last, he'd checked the time, he realised he was already late for the cricket match pre-meet.

Benjamin Brightly, or Bib to those who knew him, was an old school acquaintance, who had, quite out of the blue, requested him to play in the local club side. As the small pavilion came into view, Gordon caught sight of Bib's tall, exceptionally thin, physique, leaning against it, smoke from his cigarette snaking into the warming air. Gordon smiled, pleasantly amused at how well the human psyche could manipulate the past. Here was a man who he'd never got on with, yet somehow Gordon had agreed to spend a whole day in his presence.

"Indeed," Gordon remembered telling one of his friends at school, "If the two of us were ever marooned on a desert island together, swimming for it would be the better option. And I can't even swim."

In a perverse way, Gordon quite enjoyed Bib's company nonetheless, especially when he knew the experience was only going to last for a few hours, and that Bib would, hopefully, be staying a good ball's throw away. They had a way of insulting each other, that was, on reflection, quite gratifying.

As Gordon got within speaking distance, Bib turned from his pose, and looked all the way down his considerably long nose at him. It's like looking into the barrel of a shotgun, Gordon thought. One with hairs in; Gordon stifled a juvenile laugh.

Bib curled his top lip into a sneer, and a little parabolic plume of smoke escaped, whispering up and up, growing thinner and more elongated until, finally, it disappeared. Gordon smiled as falsely as he could, and offered his hand.

"Gordy," Bib said, taking Gordon's hand with little interest. "We thought we'd have to start without you." Gordon smiled again, let go of the man's limp hand, and trotted up the steps without a word.

When it came to sport, Gordon would, at best, describe himself as a bit of an all-rounder, which is to say he wasn't particularly gifted in any one discipline. He could throw and catch, but not very far or consistently. He could run and jump, but neither at speed nor at great height. In truth, Gordon knew the only reason Bib would have asked him to play was because he'd reached the bottom of his social barrel, but he didn't mind, he enjoyed taking part in any sport, even cricket.

When the whole team was assembled, and waiting, Bib appeared and paraded around in front of them as if in deep thought. He was a failed actor, and like all failed actors, rarely passed up a chance to show off just how bad they could be. When, finally, he started his monologue, it was the usual mixture of over-rehearsed clichés and empty battle cries. He talked proudly of being captain, of his plans of shaping the side into a body of men that could rise to local league glory, but then swiftly followed it with a thorough and direct dissection of the team and exactly where he thought the current problems lay. Needless to say, he didn't mention his own name once.

Gordon looked at the expressions of the regular players around him and saw the same boredom written onto their vacant faces as he himself was currently experiencing. It was amazing they were all still awake. Bib, of course, was completely unaware, stuck, as he was, in the glare of the stage-lights that blazed down upon him from somewhere within his own mind.

As Bib broke the ten-minute barrier, Gordon played with the rotting wood of the window frame. His mind wandered, as it often did, and he couldn't have been further from the cool interior of the cricket house pavilion when the wicket-keepers glove hit him square in the chest. It took Gordon a moment to blink away the dreams, after which he looked up, and saw Bib scowling back towards him.

Gordon held up the glove. "Anyone dropped this?" he asked.

Bib slowly closed his eyes. When he spoke, it was controlled and purposeful. "Didn't look like you were concentrating, Gordy."

Gordon put the glove down. "Of course, I was concentrating, Bib," he said, "Just not on you."

If it had been a winter's day, Gordon mused, he might actually have seen steam coming out of the captain's ears. "If you're not concentrating on me, how on earth are you going to know what to do?" Bib spat.

Ah, this is better, Gordon thought, this is what I remember. Bib's fuse was short and unmistakably easy to light. "I thought we were playing cricket?" he goaded, spinning the glove around on its back, like an upturned turtle.

Bib's eyes narrowed. "We are."

Gordon blew the air from his cheeks. "Well, I should be all right, then. Unless, of course, you've decided to change the rules?"

Bib shifted his position, turning his back ever so slightly on Gordon, and spoke confidently to everyone else in the room, "Right, for the benefit of Gordy, I shall start again..."

Gordon stood, as much for the others benefit than for his own. "Oh, no, you can't do that now," he said.

Gordon watched as Bib's open and shutting mouth attempted to find some words. In the end he just frowned, and managed, "Why ever not?"

Gordon tapped on the window. "Because the oppositions just arrived," he explained, and strode confidently out of the door.

~

Bib's cricket team's prowess started and finished with winning the toss. Gordon, playing surprisingly well, made thirty-four before going for a routine catch at square leg. At tea, the atmosphere was subdued, Bib grinding his jaw as he ate his food and watched the pattern on his plate. The inevitable loss was a lacklustre hour away at most, and the ratio of quality-of-sandwiches to subs paid was low. Gordon put it all out of his mind, and tucked in.

Back on the pitch once more, Gordon noted Bib's pained expression with some glee. His jaw was now lined in knots, and he responded to each ball with a depressed sigh, and a subtle change of field positions. Not that Gordon needed to move that much. Bib had placed him at silly mid-on, directly beside the batsman, more than likely due to the earlier disagreement.

At around five o'clock, Gordon's life took a painful turn. He found himself writhing in agony, after a ball he hadn't seen coming, not in the literal sense, anyway, caught him squarely in an awkward place. When he tried to open his eyes, the tears made everything large blobs of colour. Voices came from above, and in the next moment, he was weightless, as they lifted, carried and placed him on the unforgiving floor of the pavilion.

Gordon felt someone's breath near his face. "Don't be long," Bib snarled, before going back out to re-join the game.

Gordon whimpered a little, mainly for his own benefit, and rolled onto his side for some relief. He opened his eyes once more, and felt the tears drain down the creases as he squinted to focus on the forest of chair and table legs before him. He wasn't sure how many minutes he'd lain there before he'd heard the footsteps behind him. "Go away," he said. "I'm not playing anymore."

The footsteps stopped, and the smell of a light perfume fell gently like a veil around him. "Are you okay?" came the bearer's voice. Gordon listened as the words were first echoed, and then swallowed into the lifeless room.

He cleared his throat. "Not really," he mustered, trying his best to be the slightest bit dignified in such a situation.

"Oh," the woman said, "Well, I'm with St. John's."

"Well, tell him to open the gates, I'm coming in."

There was a pause, "I think that's St. Peter," she mustered, a smile in her reply. Then, as surprising and relaxing as anything he'd expected, her cool, soothing hand rested upon his forehead. "Is, er, everything...okay?"

Gordon must have bitten his lip when the ball had hit, for when he licked them, he tasted blood. "Do you have any ice?" he asked.

There was a short, uncertain, laugh. "Oh, no, I'm not here in any official capacity. I was just watching when I saw the accident. I thought you might need some help."

Gordon nodded his head. "That's very kind of you, Miss..."

"Brenda," the lady said.

"Thank you, Brenda. I'm Gordon. I'd like to stay and talk, but I really ought to get back out there."

There was an intake of breath. "I don't think you're in any shape to do that, do you, Gordon?"

Somewhere in Gordon's mind, he noted the sound of his name from her lips. "Well, you are with St. John's," he sighed, with little resistance, "So I can't very well argue."

She helped him up, and as they made their way from the ground, Gordon smiled at Bib, and dipped his head slightly, just to annoy him a little more. Brenda had a car, and, thirty minutes later, Gordon was prone on the sofa in the cottage, sipping some lemonade and feeling just a little bit sorry for himself. Brenda, who'd escorted him in to make sure he was okay, had since disappeared from the room, so he flicked through the newspaper, enjoying the heat of the late afternoon. Gordon felt strange, but wasn't quite sure why.

The door to the lounge opened and Brenda walked back in, her cheeks a little flushed, carrying a vase containing assorted flowers Gordon didn't recognise. "I found these in your garden," she said, "I'd have been quicker but I had to pull up all the weeds to get to them."

Gordon was embarrassed enough not to reply, instead just watching as Brenda danced the vase around the room, first putting it down, then stepping back, then picking them up once more and trying a new position. To Gordon, she looked every bit the angel she'd previously enacted.

In her early twenties, her skin wonderfully smooth, her eyes bright with life, Brenda's movements held his gaze. As the sunlight from the windows fell upon her hair, he saw it was not black, as he'd first imagined, but dark brown, even reddish in places. She wore a summer dress which stopped a few inches above her flat soled shoes, and as she stood on tiptoe to put the flowers on a shelf, Gordon thought she had the finest ankles he'd ever seen.

Throughout all this she was silent, in her own world, focused only on the vase. Gordon suddenly felt a little jealous, and tried to dismiss it as foolishness. He looked at the paper, but he was unable to concentrate on the small writing, and found his eyes repeatedly returning to this new acquaintance. She was better than any medicine he knew.

When, at last, the imaginary music stopped, and the flowers remained static, she turned to him and looked for approval. He nodded, and her smile, which was definitely on the crooked side, broadened.

"Excellent," he said, tongue tied, "They look very, er, nice."

"Thank you," she said. "Now, is there anything else I can do?"

Gordon had no time to think about his next three words. They came from his subconscious, bypassed any thought processes, and jumped straight to his lips. In the years afterwards, when the two of them reflected on that day, they both agreed the words were the real starting point. Their whole lives, and happiness, hinged on what Gordon had squeezed out of his voice-box.

"Stay a while," he said.

~

Five months on and she was still there, walking beside him in the garden, about to let him in on a secret, that no matter what, Gordon knew wouldn't make the slightest bit of difference to how he viewed her.

"Go on then, what is it?" he asked, a smile playing along his lips. He bent his head a little, an attentive listener ready for the worst horror she could come up with.

"Well, it's my family, really," she offered, and fell strangely silent.

Gordon nodded with mock solemnity. "There's no getting away from the fact, they are your family."

Brenda hit him on the arm, playfully. "Well," she sighed, glancing back to the house, "We have this secret, Gordy. Nothing horrible, you understand," she trailed off and was, once more, silent. She sat on a low stone wall, clasping, and unclasping her hands, the skin taught and pale over delicate bones.

Gordon bent down to see her, his knee resting on the ground, aware of the position he was taking with some amusement. He stroked her arm lightly, "What's wrong?" he asked.

"Oh, I'm not sure whether to feel silly or not," she said.

Gordon watched the light of the house reflected in the ring that clasped his little finger. Brenda sighed, an action full of the character Gordon now knew he loved. She looked down, and brought the tips of her fingers to meet his. The sensation was wonderful, he thought.

Brenda shrugged her shoulders and stood. Gordon rose and they walked on. The moon that night was full, and offered ample light to guide them along the back of the lawn, the grass crunching as they walked. They followed the edge of a line of tall conifers, the strong pine smell mixing with the smoke captured in their clothes from the open fire in the cottage. The combined scents reminded Gordon of his younger days, when he and his sister, Mary, would be allowed to camp out in the back garden. Now, with their backs to the house, Gordon felt a hundred miles away from anywhere.

"Well, come on, then," Gordon whispered, "You can't leave me hanging on."

"Before I tell you," she said, "you must promise not to tell another soul."

Gordon's eyebrows dipped, "Sounds like that 'Mouse Trap' play we saw..." he said.

Brenda giggled, and relaxed, "It does, doesn't it?" she said. "Well, rest assured, no-one's been murdered....yet."

Gordon caught the glint in her eye, and played along, "I'm not too sure I liked the way you said that."

A window opened behind them. The noise from the house doubled, and over the din Jack, Brenda's brother, called out, "Are you two coming in? It's freezing out here, and we're just about ready."

Brenda squeezed his hand, and started toward the house.

"Well, aren't you going to tell me?" he called after her.

"No, I've changed my mind," she said. "And besides, I'm sure you'll cope just fine."

BRENDA, UNCLE, AND THE DRAWING ROOM

The sudden report of a book hitting the library floor jolted Gordon back into the present day, unkindly dispersing all of his fond recollections. Irritably, he looked around for the perpetrator, the stealer of his thoughts, but there was no-one willing to step forward from the shelves and take the blame.

Robbed of his past, Gordon thumbed idly through one of the books in front of him, the cool gloss finish of its pages cruelly reminding him of Brenda's fingertips that night. He lingered, eyes closed, hands gently resting on the book, and willed the memories to return. To his relief, they came back, and as vivid as ever.

~

By the time they made it to the large house, the rain was falling harder. Brenda squeezed his hand as he opened the door for her, and in return, he smiled and squeezed it back with equal pressure. It was yet another subtle method of communication, another way of saying 'I love you' which, until recently, Gordon had never dreamed could ever have existed. It was as if he'd been introduced to a whole new sensory world.

Once inside, they crossed a large hallway with dark wooden panelling reaching from floor to ceiling, passed a large oak table with several high-society magazines laid out, and finally entered the drawing room. There, they were guided into the space specifically left for them, on an expensive Indian rug, in front of the fire. Gordon felt the heat seep through his back muscles and chase the cold away the moment they sat down. As they waited, Gordon sensed the pensive mood that enshrouded the rest of the room's inhabitants, quieting them down. Indeed, it would have been a perfect silence, were it not for a grandfather clock which ticked idly off to one side, itself punctuated every now and then by cracks from the fire's burning wood.

Even though he was in a room full of people he'd only just met, the closeness and familiarity of Brenda gave him a much-needed boost in confidence. He stole a look at her, half hoping she might look back, but she didn't. That was okay, just the sight of her in the firelight was enough. Not for the first time, Gordon thought she was the most beautiful woman he'd ever seen.

He was still slightly surprised to be there. In these last few months, the pair had spent almost all of their free time together, entertaining, socialising or just going for walks. They seemed effortlessly compatible, and Gordon found it difficult to remember what it had felt like before he'd known her. He had no reason to want to be anywhere but by her side, and he assumed the same was true for her. Then, out of the blue, Brenda had announced that she was going to a family gathering on Boxing Day, something that had been planned all year, and said it probably wouldn't be his sort of thing.

"Really?" he'd said. "I'm quite adaptable."

Brenda had nodded. "I know you are, Gordy. But there are a lot of people there, and, well, I don't want to scare you off."

He'd laughed, and whilst there'd been more he'd wanted to ask, had left it at that. Life continued. Then, on Christmas Eve, Brenda had changed her mind and invited him after all. Gordon was puzzled, but took this change of mind as he tried to take most things in his life, as a positive sign.

They'd arrived at seven o'clock, had drinks, and then been shown into the dining room, where they'd been treated to a sumptuous dinner. Judging by the constant hum of news and gossip that continued throughout the several courses, Gordon speculated most of his fellow diners hadn't seen each other in several months.

Now, however, they were all strangely quiet, and Gordon shivered as goose-pimples unexpectedly spread over his body. He'd found himself caught up in something utterly beyond his control, something that seemed to have taken on a life of its own. The others around him were in on this secret, and he felt both excited and vulnerable in their midst.

This room, the drawing room, was large. Large enough, in fact, to fit its thirteen occupants without making it look overcrowded. Even the deep red of the walls, and the wood panelling, which only came halfway up in here, couldn't detract from its size. It had a welcoming feeling, comfortable and somehow cosy despite its impressive dimensions.

Gordon looked over the faces before him. The only person missing from the dinner was the house's owner, Brenda's grandfather, who, as far as Gordon could make out, was known to everyone simply as Uncle. This quaint eccentricity hadn't stopped there, either, spilling over to his wife, so that she was known only as Aunt. Gordon had made a mental note to ask Brenda exactly why this was, later.

Several paintings hung around the walls of the room, many incorporating the surrounding countryside including the house where they were all now sat. Above the fire two rifles pointed in opposite directions, and over to his left, tall shelves stood, crammed with books. Underneath the rug, which stretched out to cover a reasonable proportion of the floor, polished wood amplified every nervous twitch of a leg or tap of a foot.

Seating arrangements consisted of two, red leather, three person sofas, two comfortable looking armchairs from the sitting room suite, and several other wooden chairs that had previously been used at dinner. Oddly, the room's windows looked too small to let enough light in during the day, but by night, the inlaid stained glass added to the overall ambience, in which, now, all attendees anxiously waited.

On the sofa opposite Gordon, Cissy, Vee and Frank sat. Cissy was Brenda's mother, a small lady with sharp features, unnaturally dark hair, and a fairly miserable disposition. She knew everyone there, but had not spoken a word to any of them unless she was asked a specific question. It was the first time Gordon had met her, and when he'd mentioned her manner to Brenda, she'd just given him a quick shrug of her shoulders, and said, "That's mother for you."

Next to her sat Vee, Brenda's aunt on her father's side, and the complete antithesis of Cissy. Vee had laughed like a drain for most of the evening, keeping the mood light with her risqué stories, which the others played off of for their own humour. Externally, she was a little heavier than Cissy, still not large, but slightly stockier. Her long blonde hair was tied back off her pretty face, whose whole added up to more than its individual features. She had thin, but not unattractive lips, animated in almost everything she was doing. Her nose would have been forgettable if it had not been slightly upturned at the end. Her eyes were light blue, disconcerting if left looking at you for too long, but quite beholding when averted. She wore little makeup and jewellery, dressed in a slightly far eastern way, and was different to the rest of the assembled, though, at the same time, firmly a part of them.

Frank, her husband, sat next to her, somewhat in her social shadow, but not ignored by it. He was younger than Vee, and quieter, but Gordon knew that was just his way. He might let Vee be the life of the party, but Frank maintained an equal share when it came to their relationship.

Frank was the only other person in the room he'd spoken to before. Two weeks after they'd met at the cricket match, Brenda and he had been out walking over the downs north of the town. They'd walked all morning, stopping for lunch in the shadow of Arundel Castle, and then slowly made their way back home through the trees and fields. At the top of one particularly steep hill, several painters had gathered, pulled there by the various outstanding views it offered.

As they crested the rise, Brenda stopped and let go of his hand. "That's Uncle Frank," she said, and before he'd had a chance to react she was calling out, "Uncle Frank," and walking toward a figure halfway down the patient daubers.

The sun was beginning to wane, and most of the others were packing up their belongings, and making plans for the evening ahead. The man Brenda was walking towards, however, seemed very still, looking at his painting from under the rim of his straw hat.

Gordon caught her arm, "Maybe he wants to be alone," he said.

Brenda frowned at Gordon, and then looked back at the figure of her uncle. "Not Uncle Frank," she said, taking his hand, pulling him along with her. As they approached, it became obvious that Frank was not, in fact, surveying his brush strokes at all, but was, instead, fast asleep, his chest rising and falling in a constant rhythm.

Brenda sneaked around to look at his painting, and as she did, a small boy nearby threw a stick for his energetic dog, let out a loud whoop, and fell onto his back in exhaustion.

Frank stirred, and, sensing someone nearby, looked round.

"Brenda," he said, a broad smile building his face into its own picture of joy. He placed his palette, which had been precariously balanced on his lap, onto the grass, and slowly unfolded his stiff body with several alarming cracks and creaks.

Brenda kissed him lightly on the cheek. "This is my new boyfriend, Gordon."

"Yes. Yes, you mentioned him. Pleased to meet you Gordon," he said offering his colourful hand, "Please call me Frank."

"Pleased to meet you," Gordon replied, "I'm sorry if we've interrupted you."

"Not at all," Frank said, stretching his thin arms into the sky. He darted a disapproving look at the painting, squinted his eyes and shook his head slowly. "I'm not very good at the best of times," he admitted.

Brenda tutted, and held the stretched canvas to the sky. "Stop putting yourself down, Uncle Frank, it's a beautiful picture."

Frank raised both ginger eyebrows, "Really? Well, if you like it that much, you're welcome to have it." Frank smiled easily at Gordon and winked.

Brenda breathed in sharply, "Really?" she said. "I'd be over the moon to own an original of yours."

"Then take it. What time is it?" Frank asked, rubbing the sleep from his eyes.

"About five o'clock," Gordon answered.

Frank slapped his chest with both palms. "Well, in that case, perhaps you two would like to join me for some tea?"

"Tea?" Gordon said, surprised.

"Yes. Vee's forever telling me I always pack enough for ten. She thinks I must supply all the painters here. She doesn't seem to understand just how hard it is sitting around all day."

Brenda skipped to the hamper close by, "Do you have any tea-cakes?" she asked, hopefully.

"You can't say that," Gordon said with a smile, but Frank held up his palms.

"She'll never change," he said, "And I'll never want her to."

~

Before the dinner at Uncle's, Frank had come up and spoken to Gordon at some length, obviously pleased to see him. Now, beside Vee on the sofa, he looked relaxed once more, happy in the awe of his wife.

To Frank's right, on one of the armchairs, sat Aunt, looking pleased and proud to have so many people visiting, and enjoying, her home. Every so often, her eyes would start to flit around the room, from chair to ornament, from ornament to carpet, from carpet to painting. Gordon smiled, his cheeks flushed, as he thought Aunt had caught him looking at her, but he soon realised that she was, in fact, looking over his shoulder, to where a large lamp stood. She cocked her head slightly, as if listening to someone whisper in her ear, and then, when she was happy that the shade was on straight, moved her eyes on to the next focal point.

Two boys, Jack and Phillip, sat between Gordon and the settee, where a coffee table had been moved to one side. They were both in their mid-teens, and had been quiet at dinner.

Jack was Brenda's brother; a thin, ill looking boy, who avoided people's gaze. Gordon had attempted to strike up a conversation with him, but without much luck.

Phillip, his cousin, was Vee and Frank's red-haired, round, slightly spoilt, son, who only seemed to be content when he was demanding all of his parents' attention and praise.

Monty, Brenda's father, sat on the sofa off to the right, positioned at the furthest end from Gordon. Although he was close enough to touch his wife, the pair of them had barely looked at each other all evening. At least he didn't emanate the ice-cold independence Cissy had seemingly perfected. Instead, he tried his best to speak to the people around him, wanting to be a part of the whole secretive occasion. It was a far cry from the man Gordon had encountered before.

In the five months he'd been courting Brenda, Gordon had only seen her father a couple of times. He knew that, whenever he'd called, Monty would retire to his office immediately, only reappearing after he'd gone. Brenda, however, wasn't the slightest bit concerned by her father's unsociable behaviour, as, she said, he'd never particularly spoken to her, either.

Gordon chanced a sideways look at him now, nervously picking at his socks as he did, and instantly regretted it as their eyes met. Monty smiled and nodded at him, and Gordon felt his jaw drop slightly open in surprise. Aware of how strange he must look, Gordon let his own head drop forward to return the acknowledgement. Then as quickly as the exchange had started, Monty was looking elsewhere, twisting his thumbs impatiently over and over.

Next to Monty, in the middle of the sofa, was a man named Colin, who, with his lower lip permanently stuck out, and a posture that forced his neck forward, was the picture of abject misery. Behind his small square spectacles, Colin's eyes were dull and half shut. As they waited, Gordon found himself watching the reflected patterns of flames from the fire on his near-hairless head. Then, every so often, Colin's eyes would fully close, and his head would slowly lower, until, Pat, his wife, would poke him sharply in the ribs, and he'd blink himself awake, sit up slightly and give her a false smile, only to go through the whole tiring process minutes later. Every time this happened, Pat would look apologetically around the room, shrug her shoulders, and look skywards in despair to anyone who'd seen what had happened.

Pat's voice was slightly whiny, and she used it to good effect, finding holes in everything and everyone she encountered. The lights would be too bright, the vegetables too soft, the sauce too rich, the meringues too hard, the plants too leafy. Gordon doubted she was ever going to be satisfied with anything.

For this, Gordon felt sorry for Colin. His life must be one long list of inadequacies too extreme to mention. If she'd been Gordon's wife, he was certain he would have murdered her by now, using a pillow too soft or grip too tight, he thought, stifling a laugh.

The two remaining people in the room, Lawrence and Elizabeth, sat on uncomfortable wooden chairs off to Gordon's left, almost hidden away in the corner. Neither had partaken in the dinner that evening, instead deciding to walk in the garden. Whenever their names had come up in subsequent conversations, the voices had taken on quieter, sympathetic, tones, and it seemed to Gordon that more words weren't said about them, than were.

Both Lawrence and Elizabeth belonged to Pat and Colin, though neither were their own flesh and blood. Three years into their marriage, they'd been told they were unable to have children, and everybody thought it would spell an end to their relationship. To their credit, though, they persevered, and after a couple of years had been able to adopt Lawrence, then four years old. He had been a problem child, taken away from his previous foster parents when he'd got so difficult they'd been unable to cope with him. It had been difficult for Pat and Colin, too, but somehow, in time, Lawrence's behaviour had improved enough to become tolerable.

Then, three years after adopting Lawrence, Pat's sister and her husband had tragically been killed in an accident, leaving their only daughter, Elizabeth, orphaned. Pat and Colin had been quick to offer a home to her, and to their delight, Elizabeth had accepted.

Over the next ten years, the two children had grown close. They 'didn't spoil a pair', as Gordon's mother would have said. Both were intelligent, when they wanted to be, and almost painfully introverted. They gave off an aura that said, 'stay away', so everybody did.

These were a strange array of people, Gordon mused, and as he sat there, wondering what they could possibly have in common, the drawing room door opened, and in walked Uncle, smiling from ear to ear, and carrying something which looked unmistakably like a lectern.

SIMON, ESME, AND THE HOME

Back in the library, Gordon's stomach rumbled, and a quick glance at his watch confirmed it was lunch-time. Outside the rain hadn't let up, but he was still relatively alone for such bad weather. With little relish, Gordon looked down beside the chair, where his sandwiches lay undisturbed in a crumpled carrier bag. Carefully, and with more noise than he'd wanted, Gordon removed the Tupperware box within, peeled off the lid, and balanced the base of it on his lap whilst he made a space in front of him by closing some of the books.

"Hello, Gordon," a man said, slapping him hard enough on the shoulder to make him jump. Gordon watched as the box tumbled off his leg, turned over in the air, and launched his carefully prepared grated cheddar cheese sandwich toward his feet. There would have been a time when Gordon would have tried to catch it, but now all he could do was look on helplessly as the two pieces of bread split, each landing buttered side down on the dusty floor.

"Sorry," the man apologised, pulling out the chair beside Gordon and sitting down.

Gordon looked at him sideways. "Simon," he said, "Could you perhaps restrain yourself a little, next time?"

"I'll try," Simon offered, beaming.

Simon was a harmlessly annoying man who Gordon did his best to like. Married to Gordon's youngest daughter, Pamela, he held a high-powered job at a local insurance firm, which afforded Gordon's daughter and their two children a comfortable lifestyle. Pamela was third out of

Gordon and Brenda's four children. Her wedding, a grand affair indeed, had been the last Brenda had been able to go to.

If only he didn't smile so much, Gordon thought as he looked at him. It wasn't that Simon's smile didn't suit him, or that it looked greedy or nasty. The problem was that it never went away; a permanent fixture twenty-four hours a day, come rain or shine. Gordon wasn't against happy people, he could even be quite happy himself if he put his mind to it, but he had long ago grown wary of the sort of people who did nothing but grin.

"What's this you're reading?" Simon asked, suddenly scooping the book from under Gordon's nose.

Gordon felt the hairs on the back of his neck prickle. "It's for the Race," he said, irritably.

"Oh, right, of course. Forgot. Sorry." Simon pushed the book slowly back to Gordon, who in turned moved it out of his son-in-law's reach.

A couple of awkward seconds passed. With nothing else to do, Simon ran his fingers through his hair, and Gordon noted the flecks of grey in it. Simon must be slipping, he thought, he was usually very careful not to let it show. As he looked at the younger man slouched in the chair beside him, Gordon noticed his son-in-law was putting on a few pounds, too. When he'd first met him, he'd been a keen runner, but it seemed he'd been spending a little too much time in the office than was healthy. Simon sat up suddenly, as if he'd just felt a drawing pin beneath him. "When's the Presentation?" he asked, beaming more than ever, pleased he'd managed to continue the flagging conversation.

Gordon sighed, and although he doubted Simon's interest, he nevertheless felt the need to talk to someone. After all, Gordon considered, it was what the Race was all about.

"January 30th," Gordon replied, "Hasn't Pam told you?"

"Oh, oh, I'm sure she has," Simon said, "But I still rather rely on her to remember things, you know."

Gordon smiled; he'd been much the same with Brenda.

"Don't mind if I get something to read, do you?" Simon asked, index finger waggling carelessly at the rows of books.

Gordon looked about, "Seems as good a place as any," he couldn't help himself say.

Simon nodded, slightly confused, and sloped off, while Gordon set about consuming what remained of his lunch before he returned.

When Simon sat back down, he was holding a large historical fiction book which he placed on the table in front of him. "Always wanted to read this," he said, excitedly. During the next ten minutes, Simon looked about, tapped his fingers, coughed and fidgeted; anything but read the book. Whenever Gordon looked at him, he continued to smile and nod toward him in a friendly manner, and Gordon couldn't help himself get progressively agitated with his son-in-law's presence. Work on the Race required solitude, and this wasn't it.

"Good book?" Gordon asked, through gritted teeth.

"Oh, this," Simon said, holding it up. "I can't really get into it..."

"I noticed."

"Too... historical," Simon replied. He paused for a moment before looking down at the book like an admonished child.

"They let you take them out, you know."

"Pardon?"

Gordon placed his right hand across Simon's open pages. "The books. They let you take them home."

"I know that," Simon said, "It's a library."

Gordon felt the final straw being placed on the small of his back. "Right, that's it," he said, standing, and packing his books away.

Simon looked surprised. "You're not going, are you?"

Gordon bit his lip. "Yes, and it's probably for the best. I've got a couple of things I need to do."

"Anything I can help with?" his son-in-law offered hopefully.

"No, no, no. You've done quite enough already," Gordon said, "for one day."

Simon suddenly looked very alone. "Oh, well. In that case I'll see you on the thirtieth, then."

Gordon didn't give in. He felt guilty, and slightly ashamed that all Simon had wanted to do was spend some time with him, but Gordon just wasn't in the right mood. "Yes, on the thirtieth," he said, and started toward the exit.

"At your place, is it?" Simon called across an otherwise silent room.

Gordon turned slowly, and smiled. "Yes," he said, then waved, and walked out.

~

As it happened, Gordon really did have somewhere to go that afternoon. He had a meeting booked with Esme Culvert, the owner of 'Rose Paths', the rest home he did voluntary work for. He liked his job at the home, it was a place where he could be someone else, just another helper, to sink into the background and forget about everything else going on around him.

He'd been helping there for a little over two years, after reading in the local paper they were struggling to keep the place running. They'd been no interview, just a raising of eyebrows, a shake of the hand, and a roster sheet. It was the sort of 'get on and do it' mentality he liked and he enjoyed working there. The original owner had been a good man, passionate about caring not only for the residents but for the staff, too. The sort of man Gordon knew didn't come around very often. About six months ago, however, he'd been diagnosed with cancer, and had gone downhill rapidly, finally losing the battle at the beginning of November. Now, the home was being run by his widow, Esme, who was a completely different kettle of fish.

Within a month or so of her husband's death, Gordon had begun to feel the full force of Esme's attention. She knew who he was, and wasn't backward at coming forward. Indeed, Gordon had tried several times to put this meeting off, before he'd finally given in to Esme's superior stubbornness.

When he arrived for the meeting at just before two, the receptionist informed him the venue had changed from Esme's office to her first floor flat. That's not a promising sign, Gordon thought. Nor was the cooking he smelt when he knocked on her door, nor the 'Private' tag which hung around the doorknob.

Before he'd had time to heed all of these warnings and make a hasty retreat, the chain was slid across the catch, and the door whipped open.

"Come in, Gordon," Esme said, predatorily.

Gordon resisted the temptation to run, instead walking carefully into the lounge, not wanting to give off any wrong impressions. After all, he was there to discuss some spring gardening work she'd wanted him to do.

Esme took his bag and patted the sofa seat. "Sit down," she said, a shrill tone in her voice. "So glad you could make it. You're only a few minutes late. I bought a new top, especially for today, do you like it?" Esme twirled. Gordon winced. It was a tiny flat, and Esme wasn't a small woman.

"Lovely," he said, and remained standing. Esme trotted around him, and sat herself down in the middle of the sofa. She had short black hair, a piggy nose, and big, doleful eyes. Everything Gordon didn't look for in a woman. That, plus the fact she was also very fond of her money, probably Gordon's, too, if she had a chance.

Gordon fingered his collar, "I didn't realise you were going to lay on any food?" he said, changing the subject.

Esme smiled, and sighed as if to say, 'poor boy'. "Nor did I until late this morning," she explained, "You see, I decided to take a quick walk into town this morning. I was watching the young couples and their children running around having fun, and I thought of your grandchild, Jennifer."

"Jessica," Gordon corrected.

"That's right. I thought of how you do so much for your family, and then I realised you deserved a little something, for all the hard work you've put in here at the home."

"Do I?" he attempted, his dry throat throttling the words. Gordon was worried what the little something she had in mind would turn out to be.

Esme stood, "Oh, you must be thirsty. How about a sherry? I've got some of your favourite."

"Er, tea, please," he said, looking at his watch.

Esme bent her head disapprovingly, her face resting on the chins below. A picture of a walrus appeared in Gordon's mind, and he had to fake a cough to disguise the sudden laugh.

"Are you sure you're all right?" she said, moving toward him.

Gordon was trapped. The situation was spiralling out of control, and he had to do something to get it back. "Actually, I'm not feeling too great," he said.

Esme, unfortunately, had seemed to anticipate this move. "Perhaps you would you like to lie down?" she asked.

"No, no, not at all," Gordon replied. "I think I'm coming down with something, that's all."

Esme stopped her advance. "Something contagious?" she asked, sudden panic entering her voice.

Of course, Gordon thought, she hates being ill.

"Very," Gordon croaked, managing to make his eyes water. He coughed a couple more times.

It was enough. Within five minutes he was out of the flat, the home, and her grasp, with strict instructions to have a rest and not come back till he was better still ringing in his ears. Not for the first time that day, he felt a little ashamed at his behaviour, but only a little.

~

~ 29 ~

He checked his watch, gulping down the air as he did. It was only half past two, so he still had time to return to the library, or maybe even visit the main one in town. It would be the sensible thing to do, but no matter how much he tried to convince himself, Gordon knew his heart wasn't in it.

The top of his leg felt like it was getting a small electric shock, and it took Gordon a moment to realise it was his mobile phone ringing on silent. It had been a present from Christopher, his youngest son, last Christmas. He looked at the name on the display and smiled when he saw it was he who was ringing him, now.

"Hi, Chris," Gordon said, putting the phone to his ear. Chris and his partner Louise lived in a village about ten miles away. They'd been together for a long time, never married, and probably never would, but they seemed utterly content, and Gordon was perfectly fine with that.

"Dad," Chris exclaimed. "How are you?"

"Not bad, not bad. You?" Gordon tried not to sound as down as he felt. Thankfully, Christopher's natural energy helped.

"Oh, still going," Chris replied. It was his usual retort, and it made Gordon smile. 'Still going' would just about sum him up. Christopher was different than the rest of the family. He hadn't been planned, arriving several years after Gordon and Brenda had thought they'd finished having children. But he was a welcome addition, shorter than the others, standing around five foot two, with very blond hair and blue eyes. Whenever Brenda had described him, she'd say the genes had been caught on the hop, and had thrown a few of the unused ones together and hoped for the best. They hadn't done a bad job, either, Gordon thought.

As a child, Christopher had gotten into trouble with the police for such things as riding on the pavement, trespassing, and generally making a nuisance of himself; the sort of things other children would have simply got away with. None of it really bothered his parents. Gordon and Brenda knew all about imperfections, and as long as they stayed on the minor side, they were happy just to let him have some fun.

Then, in his teens, he'd achieved the reverse of most other children, and had calmed down into a pleasant, likeable, easy-going child. While other children were smoking, stealing, and worse, Christopher had matured into a boy who was happy just to float along with life. He'd actually ask to be taken on outings with his parents, and would regularly suggest going for day trips to places he'd heard of on television. It was from these trips his real wanderlust had developed.

"Wait a minute, Dad," Chris said down the telephone, "Louise is trying to say something to me."

Gordon listened as a muffled conversation took place in the background. Chris came back onto the telephone. "Louise and I were wondering what you were doing tonight?"

"Oh," Gordon said, surprised by the question, "I'm, um, well, in truth I'm not doing anything at all. Why's that?"

"Well, we're having a barbecue..."

"A barbecue?" Gordon blurted, "In this weather?"

Chris laughed, "It's an indoor barbecue, just us and some of the neighbours. Jacket spuds, sausages, onions, that sort of thing. Thought you might like to come and join in?"

Gordon's heart leapt. "Are you sure?" he asked.

"Positive," Chris confirmed, "We've done one before. Should be good fun."

"And I won't be too old for you?"

"You've no need to worry about that. This is hardly a young person's neighbourhood. In fact, you'll probably be below the average age, all right?"

"Okay, but only if you're sure," Gordon said.

"We're sure. Louise will pick you up about seven."

"Great. Looking forward to it, already," Gordon told him.

"Good. And shall I get the sherry out?"

"Well, if you don't mind your old man getting a bit tipsy..." Gordon joked.

"No more than usual," his son retorted, "See you later."

"Yes," Gordon agreed, then added quickly, "Oh, and son?"

"Yes, Dad?"

"Thanks for making me feel welcome."

"Our pleasure," Chris said.

Gordon put the phone back in his pocket, and as he did so, Simon's face appeared in his mind's eye; Gordon knew he shouldn't have been short with him earlier. It hadn't been Simon who had truly interrupted his work on the Race, it had been himself, and the bittersweet memories of what had gone before.

TONY, CATHERINE, AND AN ECCLES CAKE

After accepting Chris' invitation, Gordon decided to head towards town, where he could allow himself to be lost within hundreds of people he didn't know. From where he now stood, it was only a short journey to his bungalow where he could pick up an umbrella to protect him, in case the ever-darkening skies delivered the weather they'd been tinkering with all morning. Although he may not admit it, he also felt a need to stabilise himself after his meeting with Esme, and the bungalow was his safe-haven. Once there, it would give him a solid base from which to restart the day, allowing him the confidence to face the melee that would be a Saturday afternoon in town.

It was just after two forty-five, and around him the traffic was beginning to get quite heavy. Even though Gordon could feel the rain coming ever closer, he still took his time to walk back, enjoying the charged atmosphere. When he reached the bungalow, he let himself in, and slowly, almost subconsciously, visited each room, touching a table, or a chair, or a bed, making sure everything was just as he'd left it. He wasn't expecting anything to have moved, but he knew the morning's remembering needed to be put into the context of now, to be brought back into perspective. He knew if he let those memories take him over, any usefulness left in the day would be lost. At just before three, when he was fully satisfied he could continue, he collected his umbrella, and walked out of the front door.

~

To his friends and family, umbrellas had become synonymous with Gordon. Five years ago, after receiving one as a present, he had tried to hide his disappointment by over-enthusiastically thanking the giver. Unfortunately, his imagination, coupled with the effects of a glass or two of alcohol, had got the better of him, and he'd wound up his emotion filled acceptance speech by saying he'd long been thinking of starting up a collection. The upshot of this was that, as Gordon was a notoriously difficult person to buy presents for, family and friends, en-masse, latched onto this umbrella collecting idea, which, in turn, resulted in the unwanted receiving of several new additions with every passing Christmas or birthday. Soon, a new pastime had been created, with everyone doing their utmost to disguise the umbrellas in whatever way possible, causing several unnecessary but inventive hours being spent building elaborate box sculptures to secrete the objects within. Not only that, but Gordon had had to keep up the ridiculous pretence he was collecting the infernal things.

Gordon stopped before he got to his garden gate, and went back to the bungalow. He fetched the longest carrier bag from the cupboard under the sink, and inspected the tags on the umbrellas in the wardrobe in the spare room. These tags were his best before dates. Or rather, they were his safe after dates. Each one bore the day, month and year the attached gift was received, allowing him to hold on to them for just long enough for the giver to have, hopefully, forgotten about the giving.

The two he picked out today had dates of over two and a half years ago. He recognised one of them as a collective present from Trudie and Denise, his grandchildren by Pamela and Simon, and although it saddened him to give such a gift away, he knew he had to do it, for his sanity if for nothing else.

The challenge Gordon now faced was how to share these objects amongst the various charity shops of the town without anyone noticing him. He was all too aware of precisely how unkind fate could be, and knew it'd be just his luck to be seen disposing of one or, worse still, for a member of family to come face to face with a distinctive umbrella they'd previously bought.

With the two he'd chosen in the bag at his feet, Gordon opened his working umbrella in the porch, and smiled. The crazy thing about the whole situation was that the umbrella he actually used had two finger length tears in the material, which, should the rain be falling or the wind be blowing at a certain angle, rendered the object totally useless. Gordon's smile grew at the irony, and at his stubbornness to let go of its sentimentality - Brenda had given it to him on the birthday before she'd been diagnosed.

~

Gordon walked the two miles into town, stopping only momentarily to help a lady, not much older than him, cross the road. Then, once within the confusion of shoppers, Gordon's feet found what Brenda had called his 'regular groove', and he managed to pass an hour or more just going from one shop to the next, looking at books, or music, or, more recently, computers and the gadgets which went with them. Gordon wasn't a technophobe, more he'd just let it all pass him by. Now, as he slowly started to build his life again, he found he was drawn to them, more and more.

Indeed, one of his New Year resolutions, aided by Louise, was to own a computer by the end of the year. It seemed an easy resolution to keep.

However, not even the enticing marketing signs could do anything to lift his interest today, and he merely walked around, touching keyboards and waggling mice in a sort of half daze.

Gordon ended up, as always, warming himself next to the unusually green radiator in the coffee shop of the main department store. It was the only one he regularly visited, and although busy, it always managed to have a couple of seats left over for him and his umbrella. When available, he would take the seat he now occupied, by the window, overlooking the small shopping annex, which curled like a tendril from the main parade further down.

He was such a regular, that, depending on what staff were working that day, he may or may not have to place any verbal order at all, a simple nod of the head and a smile securing his usual request of a pot of tea and an Eccles cake, should any be available. Today, though, was a Saturday, so most of the weekday staff were absent, and the only person he recognised with any clarity was the manager who, considering his position, seemed to display a very dull view on attracting the older person into his establishment.

After several minutes, it became apparent to Gordon that he had somehow become invisible to the entire waiting staff, so he retrieved his current reading book from the pocket of his coat, and opened it at the page marker Jessica had made for him at school. He turned the marker over in his hands, tracing the red and white blobs of paint that, so he'd been told, depicted a very jolly Father Christmas. Gordon smiled. It was these sorts of things that children were made for, he thought, before reinserting it into the back of the book, and concentrating on the paragraphs within.

He read uninterrupted for a further ten minutes, which, under normal circumstances, would have been perfect. Unfortunately, today, he was hungry, as his rumbling stomach was regularly reminding him. In fact, he was honestly surprised the waiters hadn't heard it for themselves. Gordon's temperament, he'd always upheld, was that of a patient man, it was just his appetite that let him down. Some action needed to be taken, and it had to consist of more than just the ineffectual drumming of his fingers.

Gordon calmly replaced the bookmark, now some fifteen pages on, and caught the eye of a quiet, unassuming waiter who was making his way towards him, gingerly holding a jug of freshly filtered coffee.

"Excuse me," Gordon said, as the boy drew level, "I was wondering whether you were available to take my order?" Maybe it had been Gordon's unintentional brusqueness, or the fact that the boys concentration had been given over entirely to not spilling the coffee, but the waiter reacted as if it was the first time anybody had spoken to him for several months.

"Pardon?" he stammered, concentrating on the black liquid as it swirled precariously near the rim of the pot.

"I'm looking for someone to take my order. You looked dressed for it, so I wondered if you could oblige?"

The boy, no more than seventeen, and yet to fill out his gawky body, looked around in search of help. "Um, well, I'm new here. I need to give someone this coffee."

"That's fine. Just as long as you come back when you've finished doing that," Gordon said, and then offered his kindest smile to the boy as a way of an apology.

"Yes, yes. Okay," he flustered, and headed off down the aisle once more.

Gordon moved the book to one side, and concentrated on the scene beyond the window. He was glad to see the rain that had been pouring when he'd entered the store was now finally abating, giving rise to the emergence of various shoppers of differing ages from the entrances they'd been harbouring in. Many looked battle weary, laden down with January sales goods, and Gordon imagined all of them just wanted to get home. He was still watching the throng of people when the waiter returned and hovered at his shoulder. "Can I take your order, now, sir?" he said, two nervous coughs beginning and ending the sentence.

Gordon read the waiter's name badge. "Yes, I'll have a pot of tea and an Eccles cake, please, Jason." he said.

"Of course," the boy replied, a little taken aback at the use of his name. He wrote quickly on his pad. "Is there anything else I can get for you?"

"No, nothing else, thank you," Gordon replied.

Jason moved off, and Gordon turned back to the window. As he waited for his order to arrive, he thought of the Race, but not too deeply. More, he let it sit on his mind as a feather rests on still water, letting the deeper currents twist and manoeuvre it from underneath. Although almost impossible to prove, Gordon was convinced that this sort of 'focused calm' helped his mind to order things in its own way. He could feel his thoughts and ideas slowly moving, stopping, spawning new ideas, as melting snow differs in its course down the side of a mountain, before collecting once more in a pool at the bottom. To the observer Gordon would appear paralysed, just his eyes twitching, as he let the cascade take effect.

Indeed, close by, someone was watching, their features fixed on the white-haired man sitting still and alone by the window. They'd been watching him since he'd left the bungalow, keeping a safe distance as they'd followed, and now, as Gordon sat and thought, they finished their coffee, paid the waiter, and left, unseen, via the side stairs.

To his annoyance, Gordon's food arrived before any thoughts had taken a firm shape, but as he finished the reasonable Eccles cake, a decision appeared, fully formed in the forefront of his mind. Gordon stopped and waited, approached the idea from all angles, and although it was not the one he had been expecting, it had no flaws, so he knew it must be right. At least it made sense of his recent unease.

Gordon paid at the till and left. Even though he agreed with the decision, Gordon was too experienced not to live with it for a few hours, mull it over, try and take it by surprise. The best way to do this, he'd found, was to talk to someone, to divert his mind, and he knew exactly who he wanted to see.

~

Once outside, in the cold, he headed back through the centre of town, into the outskirts where the shops were little more than adventurous dreams meeting stark consumer reality. Gordon was looking for a specific flat, but not one he'd visited before. The buildings he now passed had all seen better days; days when, Gordon remembered, they'd been highly sought after, a prize for any middle-class couple.

Now, however, they, like many other things, had been split up, two or three times over, into tiny, unkempt flats, which weren't homes at all. People floated into them, rented for a few months, and then moved on. They had no character, for nobody loved them.

At four o'clock, after a ten-minute walk from the department store, and after quickly and surreptitiously disposing of the two umbrellas to a very thankful assistant, Gordon found himself standing outside the communal door to number 62 Windsor Parade. He looked behind him at the front garden with its foot-high weeds and other twisted metal objects, before turning back and finally pressing the button marked 'B'.

Gordon waited ten seconds, then carefully stepped back and looked at the second floor of the three-storey building. Doing his best to ignore the places where the paint was flaking off the walls, he pinpointed the windows he thought might be Flat B's, and saw all the curtains were open.

Gordon stepped up to the door and buzzed once more, waited a few seconds, then looked through the letterbox for no reason he could readily justify. Tony isn't in, Gordon thought, sighing. Sad at his failure in finding his quarry, Gordon turned to leave just as a white Ford van pulled up across the road. With his gloom slightly lifted, he smiled, raised his hand, and was pleased when the driver did the same.

"Gordy," Tony said, as he got out. "What brings you over?"

"I was just passing," Gordon lied, and shook the man's outstretched hand. "And I thought, 'better look in on Tony'. It's been a while."

"No, it hasn't," Tony replied smiling, fetching his keys from a pocket deep within his overalls. When he brought his hand back out, Gordon noted it was covered in the same blue paint that was splashed on his overalls, and grinned.

"I did actually manage to get some on the walls, believe it or not," Tony said, and ran his empty hand through his dark, wavy hair.

Last year this painter and decorator, originally from London, had won the Ostrich Race. When Tony opened the door, Gordon was pleased to see the certificate hanging on the wall. Good old Tony, he thought, he wouldn't let me down. Tony pointed to it himself.

"Looks good, eh?" he prompted.

Gordon put a hand on his ex-son-in-laws muscular shoulder, "Yes, looks great," he said, "You did well."

No one had been more surprised than Gordon when he'd won. At the beginning of last year, Tony had been his son-in-law. By June, Gordon's daughter Catherine had filed for a divorce and was living with a man from work she'd been having an affair with for over a year. Tony had been well and truly kicked out, staying for a while at Gordon's, where there was practically no chance of seeing Catherine, such was the scarceness of contact between her and her father.

Of course, Gordon had gratefully taken Tony in, and could only apologise for his daughter's behaviour. He did everything in his power to help, and, although he wouldn't have admitted it, he was happy to have the extra company to lift his own spirits. They had always got on well.

When Catherine first told him she'd met a man on holiday in Turkey, he'd been very cautious, and advised her not to rush into anything. At the time, Tony had been out of a job, with no real direction. The money he'd had left from his redundancy payment he'd spent on the holiday, and when she'd met him at that Turkish bar he was so broke Catherine had had to buy the drinks. In later years, it was conjecture within the family that Tony's complete reliance on her was the thing that had most attracted Catherine to him; he was something she could own and manipulate how she saw fit.

As Gordon followed him up the stairs to his rented flat, he remembered Tony's utter devastation at Catherine's decision. When she'd come home early from a weekend away with an old school friend, interrupted Tony and Jessica's game of Ludo, and announced in front of the pair that she wanted a divorce, he'd initially taken it as a joke. It was only after she'd picked up Jessica and walked out that he'd realised she'd meant it.

Like the gentleman Gordon knew he was, Tony had complied with Catherine's wishes, so as not to aggravate the situation, or Jessica's fragile emotions, and moved out of the marital home, an action that had broken both his and his daughter's heart. Now, with his dampened umbrella in his hand, Gordon wandered around Tony's makeshift accommodation somewhat depressed.

"Would you like some tea?" Tony called out from the sliver of a kitchen.

"Love one," Gordon replied, making his way back through. The flat wasn't cluttered at all, far from it. There were few personal possessions, and it dawned on Gordon that Tony was drifting now, between the life he once knew, and the one still to come. Gordon was as worried for him as ever. "Now, I don't want this to sound bad," Gordon started, "But, are you sure you wouldn't be happier in the bungalow for a while? It's going to get freezing in here."

Tony smiled, "It's a kind offer," he said, "And I know this place is a real dive, but it's probably best if I stick it out here for a while. Try and find my feet. The only thing that matters at the moment is Jessie, anyway, and I don't bring her here."

"Well, the offer's there anyway," Gordon said. "How's business?"

Tony poured the boiling water into the pot. "Not so bad. Not brilliant. Better than same time last year, I suppose. I reckon I'll have enough money together for a better place about March or April. Then the landlords won't see me for dust."

Gordon went and looked out the grimy lounge window, onto the street below. "I could always lend you some money," Gordon said, "Hell, I could give you some money."

"I know you could, but, well, that's not the point, you know?"

Gordon nodded, and let the curtain fall, "Yes, I know."

Tony poured the tea into the mugs and carried them to the coffee table. "Come on," he said, "These things go cold pretty fast in here."

Gordon sat down, added some milk from a carton, and two spoons of sugar, while Tony crouched down and lit the gas fire. "It takes a while to warm up," he admitted, "About two months."

Gordon smiled and sipped his tea. It was good to hear Tony still had some humour left. "Did Jessica enjoy her Christmas?" he asked.

Still crouching, Tony looked up, "I think you probably saw more of her than I did," he said, and then added, "I didn't mean it to sound like that."

"It's fine, I understand. You saw her on Boxing day as planned, though, didn't you?"

Tony sat opposite Gordon. "Yes, I took her to my mum's. Poor little thing, doesn't really know if she's coming or going. She had to go back that evening."

Gordon cleared his throat. "If you'd like I could try and talk to Catherine? Get her to let you see Jessica more often, or something?"

Tony circled the tea round in his mug, pondering. "Yes," he said eventually, "I'd love you to try. I miss her so much, and everything seems dead against me seeing her."

"I'll see what I can do."

The two men sat, drank, and talked for another hour, by which time the rain had eased, and Tony's spirit seemed a little restored. "Come round next Sunday," Gordon said, as he was leaving, "I'll cook you a roast."

"Sounds good," Tony smiled, "Are you sure?"

"Of course," Gordon replied, "I never cook them anymore. No point for one, is there?"

"I suppose not. Next Sunday, then," Tony agreed, and shook Gordon's hand. "I'll send Jessica your love," he continued, "If I see her first."

"Likewise," the older man replied. "Keep your chin up, eh?"

"Of course, Gordy. You too."

The two men parted with a firm handshake, and Gordon set off heading west once more, toward Graeme, the son that Tony reminded him so much of.

GRAEME, CHRIS, AND THE INDOOR BARBECUE

As Gordon walked further into the afternoon, towards Graeme, his mind wandered once again, back to far more painful memories. With each step he took, his feet felt heavier, as if his energy were being sapped through the soles of his shoes and into the salmon pink paving slabs below. Finally, he felt he could move no more, so he stopped, catching his breath, and calming his pounding heart.

Graeme had been Brenda and Gordon's first child, and of everything that had happened to Gordon in his eventful life, his son's death was by-and-far his biggest regret. It was the mistake that had left a gaping hole inside of him, had undermined all he'd once thought of as stable. It hung over him, around him and beneath him, tarnishing everything he'd held dear, including his marriage.

Graeme had been at University in London, in his second year, and loving every minute of his course. Neither Gordon nor Brenda had been particularly religious people, but Graeme had been a Christian since the age of ten after attending a religious after school club. After that, and to his father's pleasant surprise, his faith had continued to grow, until it was woven into the very fabric of his actions. He cared about people, really cared, and would regularly write to and phone his parents, just to give them an update, and to get all of the home gossip, of which there was always plenty. When he'd rung on the morning of the day he'd died, Gordon had been in the garden, pruning one last time before the winter really set in. Brenda had picked up the telephone, and spoken with him for a while about the ins-and-outs of his current set of friends and circumstances.

As Gordon unhooked himself from a rosebush, he heard Brenda call out to him. "Gray's on the phone, he'd like a word with you."

Gordon straightened his stiff back, and looked round.

Annoyed at having been interrupted, he shouted back at her, "Can't it wait? I've nearly finished." Brenda gave him a disdainful look, but went back inside and conveyed the message to Graeme.

"He asked if you could ring him later," she said, when he came in from the freezing garden.

"Yes, that's fine," Gordon answered, still in a mood, disappearing into the study.

That evening, as the two of them sat down to dinner, Brenda asked, "Did you ring Gray?"

Gordon sighed. "I forgot." He put his cutlery down. "What did he want?"

"I don't know. Sounded like he wanted to tell you something."

Gordon looked at Brenda and felt guilty. "Is it too late now?"

"Not at all," she replied. "You know how late he studies."

Gordon put his knife and fork down on the plate, and was about to rise when the phone started ringing. "That'll be him now," Brenda said. "You stay there, I'll bring it in." Gordon watched his wife get up and go into the hall to answer it.

Gordon heard her talking to someone for a few seconds, followed by a gasp and then an almost silent wail. When Gordon reached her she was slumped against the wall, the phone held limply in her small hand. When he'd gone to her she'd been unable to stand, so he cradled her in his arms as he'd listened to the news from the police on the other end.

His funeral had been a small affair, attended mostly by family, but including a small nucleus of Graeme's friends from school and college. By then, of course, all the children had been born, and even though the youngest, Christopher, had only been eight, they'd gone to church as one unit, each relying on the other, all compressed together. Even Gordon's mother had attended, as had Monty, both frailer than they'd used to be. On that day, Gordon thought, we'd all been frail.

There'd been hymns, and, with the wind howling outside, Gordon had stood and read Graeme's favourite passage from the Bible. Afterwards, after they'd placed his body in the earth, everyone had returned to the house for the wake. Brenda and Gordon had simply stood, still shell-shocked, not knowing whether they wanted everyone to stay or to leave, still half expecting Graeme to appear at the door, larger than life.

Even till this day, Graeme had been the nicest man Gordon had ever met, his patience and forgiving running so deep he would have given any Archbishop a run for his money. From a quiet boy, he'd developed into a likeable, affable man, with an inner strength borne from listening, thinking, caring and resolving. If there was ever a person destined to make a difference in the world, Gordon thought it would be Graeme.

During his teenage years, the two of them had had the inevitable run-ins. When Graeme believed in something, he believed in it with a passion, and it was this passion that would sometimes overtake him. But as he finished school and started his A-levels, he calmed, and he and his father had become strong friends, enjoying their times spent together. They were both keen walkers, and would spend the school holidays hiking up into the nearby countryside. Gordon fondly remembered one particular outing, when, unplanned, they'd ended up staying overnight in a hotel, where they'd set the world to rights, Graeme reaffirming his noble ambition to go out into the world to teach religion in schools.

But his God hadn't let him. At the age of twenty-one, at five thirty-three on a cold, dark, January afternoon, Graeme, Gordon's wonderful son, had been cycling home from a friend's house, back to his digs. Maybe he was thinking about ringing his father as he'd rounded a corner to meet, full on, a car that was over the wrong side of the road. Maybe Gordon had been the very last thing that Graeme had been thinking about.

The police told them, again and again, there wasn't anything Graeme could've done, that he'd died almost instantly. It was a tragic accident. They said he'd have felt very little pain.

Gordon, however, hadn't been afforded that luxury.

Gordon had felt pain like he'd never felt before. A pain that surrounded him, enveloped him, became part of him, so that it sat on the tip of every nerve, in the lining of every muscle and organ of his body. Brenda managed to put a braver face on it, and Gordon knew he should've been bigger and stronger than he was, that his wife probably needed more help than he, but he was unable to think straight.

He nearly let go of everything.

Gordon shuddered against the cold as he continued towards the churchyard. There were few other people on the pavements as he walked, but the roads seemed as busy as ever. The church they'd chosen as his resting place was only around the corner from where they had lived, though its ease of access had not been the reason for its close proximity. They chose the location because they never wanted to forget; every time they came home or went out, in some unspoken punishment for losing a cherished son, they would pass by where his body lay.

It had been the main reason moving from the house to the bungalow had been difficult, but, in the later years, Brenda had been able to see the benefit it would give. A fresh start, in a home with no memories, good or bad, for either of them. She'd always been aware her husband had never stopped grieving, and that time was only distilling, concentrating his feelings into a bitterness that would bubble to the surface on a regular basis.

There was a convenience store on the corner before the church. Gordon bought a bunch of whatever flowers they had, and carried them, all heads hung low, as he trod lightly between the graves, making his way to where his son now rested. The wet grass soaked through his shoes and socks as he walked, adding to his discomfort, pulling it from a mental state to a physical one. In the years he'd been coming here, he'd walked all around this expansive graveyard, reading the names, where possible, on the other slabs, trying to imagine the person within, and the pain their death would have caused others that knew them. He felt guilty that he did not feel for their loss as he felt for his own, and was worried that, like those graves, one day Graeme's would be read by strangers and nothing more.

The headstones here were all sorts of shapes and sizes, this being one of the few local graveyards which didn't have strict rules on their appearance. Several, belonging to the graves of young children, sported footballers, aeroplanes, teddy bears and other similar childhood designs. Gordon took a few moments to read them before moving on.

Then he was there at his son's side. Seeing Graeme's name carved into the stone still cut through him, still made him catch his breath. How could it be his intelligent, handsome boy was buried in the earth? Fresh flowers were already laid at its base, and again, Gordon felt guilty at his selfishness to think that he was the only person who missed Graeme, that still missed him. He knew Chris and Louise made regular visits, as did Pam and even Catherine. Two or three of Graeme's friends also laid flowers, especially around the anniversaries of his birth and death.

The flowers there now were more expensive than the bunch he'd picked up, but that didn't matter. To Gordon, how things looked had never been above what they actually meant. Mary, his sister, had always been the vain one.

Everything was still the same, the grey marble set stark against the deep green of the pines behind. The grass, about an inch high, shifted with the erratic breeze. The sky, black and angry, looked down from above. Gordon took all of this in, and then, as was now tradition, he placed his flowers down, and with head bowed, stood back, and thought about how much he loved his son.

Of all of Graeme features, Gordon remembered his eyes most of all. They'd been dark eyes, a deep, chocolate brown that had melted hearts, and opened bonds between people no amount of talking ever could. They were an asset to his work, and he'd used them wisely. Gordon used them, too. If ever he panicked because he couldn't remember Graeme's face, his eyes were the feature he'd concentrate on, and then, quickly, the rest would fall into place. He'd been the perfect mix; a lot of Brenda, a bit of Gordon, with a good helping of originality, too.

Graeme's hair had been dark blonde, and long enough to rest on his shoulders. His face, should he be unknowingly observed, rested in a position of inquisitiveness; yet another gift that made complete strangers suddenly start to tell him secrets they wouldn't dare tell anyone else. He'd had Brenda's nose, Gordon's mouth, and all the height that Chris had lacked. He'd overtaken Gordon when he was just seventeen, although his weight remained constant, giving rise to a tall, thin, good looking boy.

Gordon moved the flowers he'd laid so they were in a neat parallel to the ones already there. Then he crouched, though he knew he shouldn't, for a long while, just holding the stone, and looking into his son's eyes.

The epitaph under Graeme's name was from a poem his son had written whilst still at school. As Gordon slowly recounted the words, the cold wind abated, and he could hear the sound of a young Graeme opening the back door, running into the kitchen, through the hall, and appearing at the study door, flapping a piece of paper in his hand and smiling so hard it looked painful.

"I won, I won," he'd declared, shifting from one spot to another.

Gordon looked at his son, "What did you win?"

"The competition," Graeme replied. "My poem won."

"Read it to me, then," Gordon said, "I can't wait to hear it."

Then, the two men had sat on the wooden floor in the hallway, while Graeme read it aloud. As he spoke the final words, the rest of the family arrived.

"Let me always be happy, so I can do my best, at home, at school, at work, at rest."

In the graveyard, quite alone with those same words now, Gordon crouched, and wept.

~

At seven o'clock that evening, Louise pulled up outside the bungalow, and waved at Gordon, who'd been hovering near the window. He waved back, checked his pockets for his wallet and keys, and left.

"Hello, Gordy," Louise said, as he opened the passenger door of her beaten up saloon car. "You look very nice."

"Do I?" Gordon said, pushing his tie up. "Good. It's been a while; I thought I may have lost my touch."

"Never," Louise laughed, and then waited for Gordon to put his seatbelt on, before putting the car into first gear, and moving off.

"Is that a new, um...?" Gordon asked, generally pointing in the direction of Louise's face.

"Nose stud? Had it a couple of weeks," she touched the diamond. "Do you like it?"

"Well..." he started, uncertainly.

"Give it an hour, and you won't notice it," Louise said, smiling. She had a pretty face, petite, but quite stunning. Her eyes twinkled when she laughed. Her mother's family originated from Nigeria, her father's from Sweden, and she radiated such a simple beauty that Gordon felt like a million dollars whenever he was near her.

"How's Christopher at the moment?" he asked as they turned onto the main road.

"Oh, Chris? 'Still going'," she said, dropping a gear and flooring the ailing car. "Hold on a second," she told him.

When they'd passed the surprised lorry, Gordon asked, "But what does 'still going' mean today?"

"Well, it means he's not working," she said, with a small sigh. "Well, not getting paid anyway. It means he's healthy, and he's happy, too."

Gordon watched the fence posts zip by the window. "Is he looking for other work?" he asked.

"Gordy, there's no need to worry. We'll be fine. Things have been worse than this. I'm still in contract. Please, just come in and relax. He's really looking forward to seeing you."

Gordon tried to sit back, let his shoulders drop, but Louise's assertive driving did nothing to help him relax, and he was pleased when she pulled into their parking space around the back from their flat. They crossed the dark car park, and Gordon felt concerned at the lack of security lights.

"Do you feel safe here?" he asked.

"Safe? Yes, it's not as bad as it looks."

They walked up the flight of stairs, turned the corner, and stopped in front of their door, the painted number '5' dull in the drab light. As they entered the hallway to the flat, Gordon was again pleased to see the two Ostrich Race certificates on the wall. They had won one each, Christopher when he was eighteen, and Louise four years ago.

"Good to see the certificates," Gordon noted, as they headed toward the kitchen.

"Only thing I've ever won," Louise joked.

"Dad!" shouted Christopher behind him. Gordon turned to see his youngest child, now twenty-seven, approaching him on crutches.

"Louise just told me you were healthy," he said, taken aback.

"Well, apart from the crutches, I am!" Chris and Gordon hugged, lighter than normal. "You're looking good, Dad. What pills are they giving you?"

Gordon scoffed, "When you get to my age, Christopher, you're just pleased for any pills they can offer."

The evening passed quickly in Chris and Louise's warm companionship. Gordon spoke to the other guests, who, on the whole, seemed fairly neurotic. A couple of them even knew of him, and he gave them his usual spiel. By ten-thirty, the others had left, happy to lock themselves safely away behind their own numbered doors, and the three of them sat around the fire in the lounge, freshly brewed coffee within the mugs in their hands.

"You have some interesting neighbours, don't you think?" Gordon asked.

Christopher nodded. "Oh, yes. A little strange, but they're too close not to get on with."

"Wise words indeed," Gordon commented.

Chris cleared his throat, "We're going to see Graeme tomorrow. Would you like to come with us?"

Gordon put his hand on Chris's knee, "That's a very kind offer, but I went there today."

They all nodded in unison, quietly aware of the toll it took.

Gordon frowned. "They weren't your flowers, then?"

Louise shook her head, "No, not ours. Was there a card?"

Gordon raised his eyebrows, "Do you know, I didn't look."

"Well, we'll see if there's one tomorrow, and let you know," Louise said, tousling her long dark hair. A silence briefly descended on the trio. Louise said, "We're looking forward to the Race this year."

Christopher sat up slightly higher. "Wow, almost forgot about that. How's it going? All to schedule?"

Gordon cleared his mind. "Sort of."

"Is everyone else still in?" Louise asked.

Gordon breathed in his coffee. "As far as I know, it's the usual crowd. Tony's still in."

Chris sighed. "He's had a bad year. I suppose Catherine won't show up if he's there."

"As far as I'm concerned," Gordon explained, "If she doesn't come, then she doesn't come."

The entry-door buzzer went off, surprising them all. "That'll be the taxi," Gordon said, draining the mug.

They exchanged a thank you and goodbye at the door, and Gordon trudged out to the cab, his heart heavy with disappointment.

"Where to?" the taxi driver said, and to be honest Gordon didn't really care anymore.

Gordon, who, like most people, avoided change, now knew the decision that had presented itself in the cafe, namely that this year would see the last Ostrich Race ever, was inevitable, and that it was a decision which would ultimately change everything.

"Where to?" the driver asked again.

Gordon sighed. "Home," he replied, "There's no rush."

FRANK, PHILLIP, AND THE LEAD ROLE

"Phone," Brenda called out.

Gordon came out of the study, his reading glasses perched on the end of his nose. "Who is it?" he asked.

Brenda brushed lightly past him, and the smell of bleach invaded his drowsy senses. "Couldn't tell," she said, although Gordon thought he caught just the hint of a smile as she headed into the kitchen.

Gordon picked up the receiver and cradled it under his chin. "Hello," he said, "Gordon here."

"Gordy," came the raspy reply, "It's Frank."

"How are you?" Gordon asked before thinking. Frank was now seventy, and for the last few years he'd been plagued with ill health.

"I'm fine, thanks for asking, but it's not me I want to talk about."

"Uh oh. What've I done now?"

"No, no, no. It's not what you've done, my lad, it's what I want you to do."

Over the next ten minutes, Frank explained the reason for his call. By the time he finished, Gordon felt decidedly weak at the knees.

"Are you sure?" he finally asked.

"Everyone is," Frank said, coughed, and then continued, "It's about time you got your chance, wouldn't you say? Of course, Vee reckons I've got another couple of Races in me, but, well, I'm not so sure. So what do you think? Are you going to accept or not? We're all looking forward to it, eh?"

Gordon hesitated. "But, er, I'm not even a blood relation," he said.

On the other end of the line, Gordon heard Frank wheeze, and realised he was laughing. "Well, nor am I, lad, but that never stopped me."

Brenda was standing in the kitchen doorway when Gordon came off the phone.

"Well?" she asked before her husband had said a word.

"He wants me to be the Race organiser," he said, a mixture of pride and worry in his voice.

Brenda beckoned him into the kitchen. "Did you accept?" she said.

"I said I'd ring him back and confirm."

Brenda turned, confused. "Why did you say that? What's stopping you?"

Gordon was speechless for a second. "I just needed to be sure you were all right with it?"

Brenda smiled. "Well, come on," she said, "Who do you think suggested your name in the first place?"

Slightly crestfallen, Gordon slouched on a stool. "Well, I assumed, that, well, I'd got the job on merit."

Brenda went over to him. "You did. I just thought they needed a little direction. Otherwise who knows how long they'd have taken."

Gordon thought quietly to himself as he held hands with his wife.

"Thank you," he said, eventually, "Thank you for thinking of me."

"It's not very easy, you know," Brenda told him, breaking away and going back to the sink.

"What? Thinking about me?"

"No," she laughed, "The Race. You know Frank spends most of his free time doing it."

"Yes, I know," he agreed. "But, in truth, ever since you got me involved I've wanted to do it. I reckon I could do a good job."

Brenda turned and put her arms around him. "I know you can," she said. "Now hurry up and accept before they find someone else."

~

Gordon opened his eyes and he was back in the bungalow. Outside the sky was still dark, though he could feel it was morning. He'd had a restless night, the decision to end the Race rested like the proverbial pea underneath his mattress. He knew if Brenda had still been alive, he wouldn't have been giving up so easily. She'd still be driving him forward, as she had always done, tackling the problems, finding the workable solutions. If Brenda were with him now, everything would be different, but she wasn't, and without her support Gordon knew it made it harder for him to carry on.

The problem wasn't that he was unable to do the work, for he could, more that he felt the participants interest had faltered over the last few years. Whether this was to do with the speed with which life was now being lived, or the fact the Race had become outdated, he didn't know, but as time moved on, events outside of his control had taken over, and he'd watched, frustrated as his family had somehow drifted apart.

Whilst Catherine's recent actions may not have started the rot, it certainly hadn't helped matters, and Gordon resented her greatly for it. In the last year, he had been twisted from a contented grandfather to a frustrated father, and it hurt him more than he would ever be able to admit. He found it almost impossible to believe that it had only been six months ago Tony had knocked on the bungalow door, asking him for a place to stay, his tall, broad, muscular frame nothing more than a pathetic cage for his shot emotions. It'd shocked Gordon to see him like that, and the moment Tony was asleep in his spare room, he remembered going to the telephone to call his daughter.

~

"Oh, Dad," Catherine had said casually, "Weren't expecting you to ring."

"Weren't you?" he answered.

There was a silence on the other end of the line, then in a cool voice, she said, "I assume you've heard then."

"Of course, I've heard. Didn't you think I would? I don't understand? I thought you were happy."

"Oh, come now, Dad, don't do this to me. Just because you choose not to look too closely doesn't mean everything's all right. But then, you've always ignored the things that don't match your standards, including me."

Gordon was stunned by his daughter's attack. He could just about manage, "What are you saying?" before she interrupted him.

"I can't talk about this right now," she said, "I don't know why you bothered to ring me. It's got nothing to do with you."

Gordon played his ace card. "It has got something to do with me. Tony's here." When no eruption was forthcoming, Gordon prompted, "Well?"

"I don't want to speak to him," Catherine dismissed.

Gordon's heart was burning in his chest. "I didn't mean that," he said, "I meant he's staying with me."

"Fine," his daughter said, "It's no surprise you've turned against me. Not that I care particularly."

Gordon fought the urge to speak what he wanted to say, instead forcing out the words, "This isn't what I expected."

"Of course not, Dad," Catherine retorted, "I've never been what you expected, have I?" And before Gordon had the chance to question her further, she'd hung up.

~

The morning after Chris' indoor barbecue, Gordon pottered around the bungalow, thinking about his eldest daughter, wondering just how much he was to blame. At ten thirty-four, the telephone rang.

"Hello," Gordon croaked, his throat still dry from the previous night's alcohol.

"Gordon," Esme shrilled, "How are you feeling, today?"

"Fine," Gordon said, without really thinking it through. "Is anything the problem?"

"Can't you remember? It's Sunday, you said you'd drop by, help out for a couple of hours. I hoped you'd be feeling better than yesterday. I've been waiting for you. We all have."

Gordon's heart sank further. "I'm sorry, Esme. I don't know how I could have forgotten. Is it too late, now?"

Gordon could picture Esme shaking her head, the chins following just a second behind the rest. For the first time since he woke, he smiled.

"No, of course not," she said, "When can we expect you?"

"About an hour," Gordon guessed.

"See you around eleven, then," she said, and then added, with touching sincerity, "Glad you're okay, Gordon. You really did have us worried, you know."

"Thank you, Esme," Gordon said, and replaced the receiver into its' cradle.

~

When he arrived, the rest home was still adorned with the decorations Gordon had put up before Christmas. Esme called out to him as he came through the door, and asked him if he wouldn't mind taking them down. Gordon didn't mind. It wasn't particularly difficult. What was difficult, however, was having to listen to Esme chirrup away as he worked. She didn't even pause for breath when he went up into the loft space to store them.

"Are you all right up there?" she called to him.

"A little parched, perhaps a cup of tea might help?"

There was a pause whilst she thought about it. "I'll go and make some now. Won't be long."

"No rush," Gordon heard himself say, and hoped it wasn't obvious why he'd said it. Gordon finished off storing the boxes in peace and came down to talk to the inmates.

If it wasn't nice old people, Gordon surmised, it was nasty ones. There didn't seem to be any middle ground. By the time he'd stopped for lunch, at a little after two, Gordon had a list of about half a dozen pensioners he could have quite happily packed into the loft along with the decorations. Still, he thought, tucking into a roast dinner Esme had prepared, he would be one soon, so he ought to try and learn a little patience.

Until now, age hadn't been a worry for Gordon. For the vast majority of his life he'd been content, and that had been enough of a pain killer to dull any anxiety that might have presented itself at the passing of time. Now, however, things weren't looking up. Every passing week seemed to present him with more and more signs he couldn't ignore; heavy breathing after relatively little effort, occasions where he'd forget a job he should've done, and times when 'first thing in the morning' hadn't happened until early afternoon. Life was running down, and it was up to him to make sure it didn't stop altogether.

That afternoon, Gordon served tea and sat and talked to the people who wanted to talk. The ones that didn't either got up and shuffled off, or stayed to continue their solitary diversions. By five in the afternoon, those that weren't already asleep were flagging. As Gordon helped clear the trays of cups, empty the plates of biscuit crumbs and tidy away the unused napkins, he hummed a tune and tried not to think of the Presentation that was now just two weeks away.

Esme sidled up as he stood washing the crockery, and patted him on the arm.

"Are you sure everything's all right?" she asked, picking up a plate and wiping it as if the pattern were simply an impressive food stain. "You don't seem to be your normal self, today."

"Everything's fine," Gordon replied, trying his best to smile, "I just have a lot of things on my mind."

"Anything I can help with?" Esme offered. "I can be quite useful."

Gordon shook his head. "No," he said. "Nothing you can help with. But thank you for asking, anyway."

~

After the rest home, Gordon caught a taxi to 'The Brambles'. He skipped up the steps like the young man he once was, and rang the bell. This house, a solid Victorian edifice situated on the outskirts of town, always brought it out in him. It was a magical place, seemingly larger on the inside, which had been host to Frank's twenty Ostrich Race Presentations. Brenda had always wished it were hers.

When Vee, now in her early nineties, eventually opened the door, she smiled.

"Vee," Gordon said, and gave her a hug.

"All right, all right," she said, "Let's not stand out here all day, it's freezing."

A few minutes later they were sat in the lounge, drinking tea and making small talk. All around the room photographs of her family filled every surface.

Gordon picked up one of Vee's son, Phillip.

"I got a letter from him the other day," she said, placing her cup down shakily.

"Really? How is he?" Gordon asked.

"He's just Phillip. Everything still an adventure. Seems to be happy enough. Did I tell you about his marriage?"

Gordon almost spat out his tea. "Marriage?" he squeaked.

Vee sipped her cup of Earl Grey, and smiled, "Oh, yes," she said, "Nice chap he's met out in America."

Gordon frowned. A lot had happened since he'd last had the chance to talk to Vee alone.

"America?" he questioned, "Last time we spoke about him he'd just finished a run in Bath. How'd he get to all the way to America?"

"He had an offer he couldn't refuse. Friend of a friend of a friend, or such like. Anyway, he was out there in a flash. You know what he's like. Hasn't done too bad, if you can believe his letters."

"Yes, but... who's he married to?"

Vee looked up, smiled, and reached across with a photo in her hand. "Handsome fellow, he is," she said, "Name's Chuck, or something."

Gordon examined the photograph. He could see Phillip and 'Chuck' smiling, obviously holding the camera as they took the picture.

Gordon shook his head, "Am I really getting old?"

Vee cackled slightly, "You're asking the wrong person, Gordy. The wrong person."

Phillip had finished school with good grades, and had then gone on to take an acting course at a school in London. It was what he'd always wanted to be, and although he wasn't necessarily a famous actor, no-one could deny he hadn't achieved his ambition.

On a social level, Gordon had always struggled communicating well with Phillip. Where Gordon was sensible, Phillip was flighty. Gordon practical, Phillip impossible. In short, the two men were a long way from each other, destined to walk on opposite sides of different streets.

Then, of course, there were Gordon's achievements. The times their two paths had met, Phillip never mentioned them. This wasn't a problem with Gordon, who rarely talked about them himself, but what was galling, however, was Phillip's incessant self-adulation.

Once, in London, Gordon had been invited to see a play that Phillip was in. As he'd been there on business, Gordon had watched it alone, a prospect he hadn't been looking forward to. He hadn't seen Phillip since the last Race he'd taken part in, some years previous, and hadn't recognised him at first. Then, in the length of a single syllable, the curtains of his memory had been drawn back, and he was surprised by just how much Brenda's cousin had changed.

Phillip had been a thin and sallow boy, but he'd filled out with age, and by the look of the person who'd stood on stage, his confidence had increased, too. It hadn't been a great play, but Gordon was pleased to have been impressed by Phillip's acting. He'd stood out, and Gordon had told him so when he'd seen him after the show.

"Uncle Gordon," Phillip almost shouted over the din of partying crowds. They hugged, something Gordon hadn't been prepared for, and Phillip led him to the drinks.

"What did you think?" he asked, eyes glazed with adrenaline and emotion.

"I thought you were the best one up there," Gordon said, "Why aren't you playing the lead?"

Phillip threw back his head and laughed. His red hair caught the glow from the lights behind, and for a moment it was as if it was on fire. "Not yet, Uncle Gordy," he said patting his arm, "But I'm looking forward to the day."

Gordon had tried his best to hold a conversation with him for another thirty minutes or so, but it was to little avail. Phillip had been encircled by a small group of friends who seemed to adore him, all sycophantically talking about his wonderful performance. On the few times Gordon had tried to chip in, Phillip had hardly even acknowledged his presence, and in the end, Gordon had politely made his excuses, and left.

~

"Will he ever grow up?" Gordon asked, handing the photograph back to Vee.

"It's hard to make someone what they can never be," Vee said, stroking the picture. Gordon reached out and took her hand. "I'm afraid I won't see him again, Gordy," she said. "I'm afraid he won't come back."

"What about going to America to see him?" Gordon offered, "I'd go with you, if you like."

"That's very kind," she said, "Maybe one day we will. But not right at the moment. Give it time." Vee let go of his hands, and sat up straight. "Now, how's the Race getting on?" she asked.

Gordon shook his head, "Now there's a question."

"Like that, is it?" Vee said.

"Just need a bit of inspiration, that's all."

"A man of your talents, Gordy, I'm surprised you need any inspiration."

"Things change," Gordon said, "And I like to think I change with them. But I don't."

Vee watched the man who sat in front of her. He looked troubled, she thought. He'd looked troubled ever since the day Brenda had died.

"Oh, I'm sure you'll come up trumps, Gordon," she said, attempting to rally him. "Like my dear husband, I have every faith in you."

Gordon nodded and the pair talked about the past some more. When it came time to leave, Gordon asked her, "Are you sure you're okay here on your own?"

"Don't you worry about me, Gordy," she said, "I've been here alone for thirteen years now. I'm quite good company, I can tell you."

"Well, when you write to Phillip next," he said, "Say hello from me, and ask him if he's playing the lead yet, would you?"

They hugged, and Vee said, "I will, my dear. I will."

~

When Gordon got back to the bungalow, he sat at the kitchen table, and tried to pull together all the disparate thoughts and ideas he'd had for this year's Race, but they were nothing more than a collection of strands, barely containing a scrap of overlap. The more he looked, the harder it was to see a way forward, so, when the clock struck seven o'clock, Gordon decided to go for a walk.

The lights along the seafront swayed as the wind blew gustily off the sea. As he moved steadily forward, Gordon concentrated on the ground in front of him, seeking inspiration from the scattered assortment of pebbles that had been washed or kicked onto the tarmac, as if they might hold some mystical or forgotten resolution to the meaning of life. The weather, he noted between thoughts, was turning bad, and the only other people sharing this stretch of the promenade seemed to be dragging either unwilling partners, pets, or both.

Gordon continued thinking. He knew the Race always took something extra; it was never just a case of sitting down and preparing it. The approach had always needed something more than methodical researching; it required a creative side Gordon was finding harder and harder to tap into with each passing year.

Tonight, he was afraid inspiration would elude him once again. He was frightened, as he generally was, that he would fail, and that the Race, its history and its story, would get the better of him. He walked, looking at the people and his surroundings, praying that something would provide the motivation he needed in his darkening mind. At eight forty-five, when nothing of note had come to him, Gordon rang for a taxi to take him home.

Little did he know, but back at the bungalow, that motivation was already there. It had been posted through the door that evening, and now rested against the radiator, out of sight. When he got home, Gordon's feet passed within inches of it, but he didn't look down. He resumed his position at the table, and wrote up as much as he could, his fine writing looping between each line. As the night wore on, the temperature lost a degree or two, and at around ten fifteen, he switched on the radio to give him some company, barely noticing the rain which had started to splash against the window.

Work as he might, his thoughts kept returning to Vee, to her big house, to her lonely life. Now, he realised, the two of them led similar lives, and the loops became tighter.

When he next surfaced from his thoughts, the eleven o'clock news was being read, and he was yawning. There were only a couple of weeks to go until the Presentation, and time was quickly slipping away. He rose, got himself a drink of water, and stretched his legs. It was a bad night to be outside, he thought, and a bad night to be in. Still, it wasn't thundering, so he had something to be thankful for.

At eleven-twenty, Gordon got into his dressing gown, and went on his nightly tour of the bungalow. He checked all of its windows and doors were securely fastened. It was only when Gordon turned off the hall light that he noticed the envelope sitting up against the radiator. A shaft of light from the bathroom picked it out, a stunning white against the dull grey of the carpet. He went and retrieved it, at first thinking it was something he'd dropped, only realising otherwise when he turned it over and saw the single word 'Gordon' on the front. In this light, he didn't even recognise the handwriting.

Gordon went to his bedroom, turned the night light on, and took the letter knife out of the drawer. Even before he'd sliced through the paper, before he'd heard the rip of the fibres and felt their rough edge on his fingertips, Gordon knew this letter was important. A feeling stirred within his stomach, but he kept it down, denied it the rush of blood it demanded.

Then, carefully, Gordon removed the envelope's contents as if the very paper might crumble before him, and read the whole thing, without pause. As he did so, he felt his excitement start to evaporate, replaced by a disappointment and a sadness. He read it all again, making sure he hadn't misinterpreted the words, knowing full well he hadn't.

Gordon put the letter down on the bedside table, and closed his eyes. Overall, things weren't going well. He had enough on his plate without this. The Presentation was in two weeks, and this was to be the last Race.

Now, of all times, Esme decides to propose.

Gordon sighed, shook his head, and turned the light off.

Then, a few minutes later, he turned it back on, sat up, and spent the next few hours finishing off the preparations for the Race.

BRENDA, CISSY, AND A SAFE RETREAT

That night, snow fell. Gordon slept soundly, his anxiety over the Presentation completely dispelled now he had found the theme for this year's Race. There was still plenty to do, however, so when he rose around lunchtime the next day, he left his mobile in the bedside drawer, packed a small suitcase and headed off before anybody had the chance to interrupt him. He knew if he didn't shut himself away, closed the door on the rest of the world, the time would be taken up with a hundred and one other jobs he'd find around the bungalow to do.

The haven he headed for was a hotel about twenty minutes away, a place he'd often gone to if he'd wanted complete privacy. If anyone grew worried about his whereabouts, all they would need to do was look for an upturned plant pot near the back door of the bungalow to know he was safe.

Gordon arrived by taxi, and crossed the crunching gravel of the driveway deep in thought. He was pleased to be back, and before he entered the imposing white building, he took a few moments to take in his surroundings, basking in their early afternoon hushed tranquillity. He was in the heart of green nature, dusted white with the snow, and while its shape changed with every moment, there was still enough here for him to recall past times. The formality of the gardens had changed little over the years, and the great trees acted as markers from which he obtained sentimental bearings.

Behind him, the hotel manager coughed and interrupted his thoughts, but even that was forgivable today. Gordon smiled, turned, and took the man's clammy, outstretched, hand.

"Good day, Mr Paige," he said, his thin arm moving limply in his tightly fitting shirt. "It's nice to have you back."

Gordon smiled, and let him take his bags into the hotel. The previous manager had been a close friend of his, and Gordon had come to rely on him to make his frequent short breaks as relaxing and as comfortable as possible. Unfortunately, the new people left a lot to be desired, but Gordon knew to ignore their ineptitudes by keeping well out of the way. After picking up his room key, Gordon sought refuge for the day in his suite, occasionally ringing down to reception for a tea or a coffee whilst he worked, asking them to leave it outside his door.

That evening, Gordon couldn't help but feel exquisitely happy, unable to remove the Cheshire cat grin that was making his cheeks hurt. He sat in the sumptuous lounge, an after-dinner glow warming his heart, the fire in the hearth warming his toes.

On his lap lay the Race folder, closed. Gordon's fingers lightly tapped its' top, a habit which, over time, had caused a mottled effect on the hard, black cover. He hoped the folder's contents would do the last Race justice.

Throughout the day, he'd been remotely checking the messages on the answer machine at the bungalow and hadn't been surprised to hear Esme's voice on a couple of them. The messages weren't long winded; there were no outflows of emotions or eternal affection, just a simple, 'Call me when you can.' He couldn't help but feel sorry for her. Esme could be the life and soul of all around her, and, whatever her motives might be, he didn't like the thought of upsetting her.

Gordon hoped he hadn't inadvertently given out any signs she'd misinterpreted. He couldn't think of any, yet the guilt remained there in his mind, returning to him every so often as if his train of thoughts were stuck on a circular track. He knew he couldn't accept her proposal, but he hadn't yet built himself up enough to refuse. He had to keep her at arm's length, and hope she wouldn't come looking for him. He decided he would call first thing tomorrow and leave a message with Katie, Esme's daughter, who manned the office in the morning. He would say he was unwell, and unable to work the shifts for the coming week.

There was a large mirror above the lounge fire, and in it he watched the ornate clock's second hand glide swiftly round, surreal in its anti-clockwise sweep. When it reached the top, it triggered nine dull bells which lulled him, unexpectedly, towards sleep. He shook his head and opened his eyes wide. He'd already taken a couple of unplanned naps that afternoon.

Gordon was blissfully alone in the lounge with his thoughts, having told the waiter that if he required another drink he would seek him out. On the table beside him, within arm's reach, sat his single malt scotch, the light from the fire making the liquor inside dance to its staccato cracks. Gordon yawned widely, stood, and stretched himself out - from his warm hands to his snug feet.

He walked over to the window, where the continuing rain danced a light tap, and brushed back the curtains. The light in the lounge was too bright to see anything outside, so Gordon made an arch against the glass with his hand and peered out from underneath. It didn't help much, with the muted moonlight showing nothing but the small strips of snow which still hadn't thawed. Gordon closed his eyes, and remembered.

~

The hotel was bathed with bright sun. Gordon stood on the stone veranda that stretched the length of the back of the hotel, next to the balustrades which bracketed the steps that led down to the lawn. It was almost a year to the day after he'd met Brenda at the cricket match, and she stood beside him as he prepared to say something he never thought he would.

He cleared his throat, nervously, took a couple of seconds to compose himself, and then, in one swift movement, bent one knee and said, "Will you marry me?" He heard Brenda's intake of breath, and realised it was suddenly hard to look at her. He looked away, unwilling to see the possibility of rejection in her eyes, towards the lawns that arced over the landscape.

Then he heard Brenda laugh, and at the same time realised they had become the centre of attention for three other couples and two small children who stood watching from the grass, quite unabashed. One had even stopped halfway through their croquet swing. Gordon had wanted the moment to last forever, but he'd only thought the two of them would be sharing it. While Brenda settled herself, Gordon gave the onlookers a weak smile. He was beginning to worry he might have to give a bow at the end.

The moment stretched. It could have been the light, or just the occasion, but, to Gordon, Brenda seemed more radiant than ever. She wore a pale green summer dress that he particularly liked. Her shoulders were bare, and her skin, slightly tanned and without a single blemish, was perfection. Not for the first time, Gordon counted his blessings.

Brenda opened her mouth, and Gordon tensed. "Yes," she said, quickly followed by, "What on earth took you so long?" And with that Gordon smiled, the small crowd clapped, and Brenda laughed again. He kissed her hands, and they walked on further.

~

Gordon opened his eyes and the January dark descended onto the gardens once more. The tick of the clock continued as he returned to the chair, lifted his whisky glass, and silently toasted his late wife. When Gordon woke twenty minutes later, the rain had abated, and he had an urge to go for a walk, to let the cold air blow the cobwebs away. He got his coat, and, to the strange looks of the staff that saw him, passed through the revolving doors, out into the night.

Gordon breathed the air deep within his lungs.

~

The sun shone again. Now twelve months on from his accidentally public proposal, the gardens were crowded with guests attending their wedding reception. Over a hundred people spilled out onto the lawn, where a band played light music, and waiters busied themselves with drinks orders.

Gordon wandered alone through the gardens, the attention of the wedding guests focused either on Brenda or on each other. He only knew a few of the faces in the crowd; the guest list was primarily Brenda's family and friends, and that suited him.

Gordon sipped his champagne.

"It's a wonderful day," a woman said nearby, and he almost choked.

When he looked around, the only person close enough was Cissy, Brenda's mother. Surely it hadn't come from her. "Pardon?" he asked.

"I said it's a wonderful day, that's all." She bent to smell a rose.

Gordon chose his words carefully. "Couldn't ask for more," he replied, attempting a smile.

Ever since Brenda introduced Gordon to her family, Cissy had discreetly ignored him. She would flutter on the social edges whenever he was there, not being rude, but not being involved either. On the occasions he were stayed for dinner, she would invariably float in before the appetiser, talk to her husband, Monty, about the papers during, and excuse herself before dessert was served, for some errand that she 'just had to run'.

As far as Gordon could make out, and as much as he cared, Cissy ran a life involving a completely different circle of friends than those he'd been introduced to. Names that neither Gordon nor Brenda had ever heard of would often crop up in her conversations, and it soon became apparent that Cissy revelled in playing the mysterious character. Gordon left her to it. In all honesty, it was easier to pretend she wasn't there.

Now, however, here she was, on his wedding day, attempting to have a conversation with him; it was quietly disconcerting.

Gordon scrambled for something to say. "That's a nice dress," he managed, without looking at it.

"Oh, this. Monty bought it for me," she said. "Well, by that I mean I bought it with his money," and she let out an unnerving girlish laugh.

"Oh," Gordon grunted.

Cissy bent down again to smell another of the roses. "These smell divine, don't you think?"

"I'm sure they do," Gordon said, without moving. He wasn't going to pretend he was enjoying the exchange.

With a simple, swift, movement, Cissy snapped the flower off. She smiled once more at Gordon, and then approached him, twirling it in her hands.

"Do you have any money, Mr Paige?" she asked, without breaking her smile.

Gordon frowned, "I'm not sure I understand the question, Cissy? Do you mean, do I have money on me now? Or perhaps, do I have money in the bank?"

"You know perfectly well what I mean, Mr Paige."

Gordon smiled slowly, "And what if I haven't?" he asked. "Would you try and have me banished, or perhaps my name rubbished with your so-called friends?"

Cissy looked angry, her cheeks a deeper red than the rose, "Well, I wouldn't want you to have any misconceptions about marrying into our family."

Gordon shook his head in genuine pity. "Cissy," he said, calmly, "I have no misconceptions, do not worry about that. Your family's money will remain as safe as ever, within your tight, nasty little grip."

Cissy's face hardened and she turned in rage to Gordon. "Mr Paige," she hissed under her breath, "How dare..."

But Gordon was already walking away from her, heading back towards the marquee. When, at its entrance, he turned back to look at the place they'd been talking, Cissy was no longer there. "Good riddance..." he whispered. As Gordon entered the marquee he immediately laughed as Vee sped past holding on to some poor relative, impossibly trying to keep up with her dancing. She waved and winked when she saw him, and then continued head down, bolting towards the edge of the dance floor.

He saw Brenda, beautifully adorned in her ivory dress, chatting to some friends, and started to make his way between the tables towards her. When he was halfway there, Monty appeared at his daughter's side, and she took his arm as they started to waltz. Gordon smiled, and as he did, he found himself alone once more, in the middle of the grounds, on a dark January night. He turned, saddened but happy, back toward the hotel.

~

Gordon walked up the carpeted stairs slowly, twisting the key fob over and over in his hands. He'd toyed with the idea of staying in the same room that he and Brenda had spent their wedding night in, but had decided against it, instead plumping for a second-floor room that was comfortable but with twin-beds. Gordon pocketed the key, and put his hand on the bannister, feeling its smoothness underneath his rough skin as it pulled him upwards. As he approached his bedroom door, Gordon removed the heavy fob, inserted the key, and twisted it in the lock. The door swung inwards, and he immediately saw something that made the hairs on the back of his neck stand to attention. Quickly, instinctively, he checked the hallway, retreated into his room, and shut the door.

Entering an Ostrich Race had traditions all its own. It wasn't the simple task of politely asking the organiser and then turning up at the Presentation. Every person wishing to take part had to complete a form detailing information on the coming year, holidays planned, difficulties with workloads, and such like. There was also a small fee, waived or even paid for by the others should any entrant find themselves in financial difficulties. This money went toward the Mid-Year Bash, a midsummer party held at a nearby hotel under the banner of the Ostrich Lovers Annual Convention. If the entrance form wasn't given in before the Presentation, you didn't compete. Of course, even this rule could be bent if extenuating circumstances arose, but generally everyone who was going to take part in the Race would have hand-posted their form between Boxing Day and the Presentation day.

This year, Gordon had only received five forms, from his children, Pamela and Christopher, their partners, Simon and Louise, and Tony. It was a far cry from the dozen or so players there'd been when he'd first started competing. All the current forms had been received in the usual way, sealed in an envelope, a picture of a single ostrich feather drawn on the outside. Five envelopes, five participants. Or so he'd thought. Now, though, as he stood in the doorway to his room, there was another envelope sitting on the floor. Must have been pushed under the door, Gordon thought. His immediate reaction was that Catherine had decided to enter the Race after all, possibly to make up for the problems and anxiety she had recently caused. Maybe, even, to appease her father. But even if she had somehow found out where he was staying, it was unlikely she would have bothered to come all this way out to deliver it.

She was too wrapped up in her own world to do that. No, she would have simply posted it through the bungalow door.

Gordon breathed out, scooped up the envelope, and turned it over in his hands.

This was getting stranger by the minute, he thought.

When the Ostrich Race started, over hundred and thirty years ago, it consisted of two children and their parents. Over the following years, others joined in, and it soon became a victim of its own success. In order to restrict the number of entrants to a manageable number, the parents commissioned ten unique envelopes, to be used only by participants. These envelopes were hand made, and, due to their age and fragility, hadn't been used in the last twenty years. In fact, he only knew the whereabouts of one other, Brenda's, and that was tucked away, carefully, with the rest of her belongings.

Now, as Gordon stood quietly in his hotel room he held another in his hand.

He turned it over, wondering what it meant. Why should someone reuse an original envelope, when a normal one was quite enough? Gordon opened the door, and hung the 'Do Not Disturb' sign on the knob outside. He sat shakily at the dressing table, placed the envelope down in front of him, and took a few moments to calm himself, the mirror in front of him reflecting his aging face.

He still had most of his thick silver-white hair, 'Polar Bear Hair' as Jessica would say with a gentle tug. It was strong to the touch, trimmed at the sides, while on top it's natural wave pushed out from a side parting. There was a small scar at the side his left eye, hardly noticeable, where he'd been knocked down in a brawl in his younger days. As his heart rate slowed, he flicked his blue eyes from one to another in the mirror. They were not light blue and interesting like Vee's; but dark blue and solid. The sort of eyes you could depend on. Dependable Gordon, he remembered Brenda saying about him, and he shut his eyes as another memory surfaced.

~

"Now," Brenda started, in a tone that told Gordon to listen carefully, "Try not to stare at people for too long."

They were travelling to Gordon's first Presentation in charge.

"Stare?" he laughed, not at all sure at what she meant, "I don't stare."

"Yes, you do. And some people find it disconcerting."

"Disconcerting? I thought you said my eyes are dependable?"

"They are," she agreed. "And disconcerting."

"You make me sound like some sort of gargoyle," Gordon mumbled.

Brenda sighed. "Now, I don't want you getting upset by this, do you understand?"

Gordon sputtered a few times, and then gave up trying to say anything reasonable.

"I think sometimes you don't realise you're staring, and it can be, well, a little off putting."

Gordon looked in the rear-view mirror. "Really?"

"Yes. A few people have mentioned..."

"Let me guess, your mother? Well, tell her I don't like her face, and then we'd both know where we stood."

Brenda smiled, "My mother isn't one of them, she'd hardly waste her self-important breath on you, would she?" Gordon remained quiet in what he hoped was a dignified manner. "Anyway, your eyes have this certain way of boring through people. It makes them feel under scrutiny."

Gordon shut one eye, and looked at himself. He couldn't see what she meant at all. "And how long have you known this?"

"Since I first met you," she said. "At the cricket ground."

Gordon shook his head disbelievingly. "And you decided to bring it up now? On the eve of my first Presentation? I need calming influences, not critiques!"

"I'm not critiquing you," Brenda said, dismissing Gordon's complaints, "I just wanted everything to go as smoothly as possible."

Gordon returned his gaze to the road, "Fine," he said, "I'll do the whole thing with them shut."

~

Back in the hotel room, Gordon opened his eyes and smiled at the memory. He may not remember everything, but the important things were still there. Now, feeling far more in control, Gordon looked at himself once more. His cheekbones were not particularly special in any way, but by the same token, were not a bad feature to have. At least Brenda had never accused them of anything. His nose was slightly longer than average, and his lips formed a slight smile when in resting position. It was a face he could still recognise through all the years of damage. If only it didn't have all those lines.

Gordon looked away from the mirror and focused once more on the envelope. There was something about it that made him feel younger, rekindled the mysteries that age had cynically washed away.

There was a sixth entrant, and it was someone who knew about the history of the Race.

Gordon got up, poured himself a drink, loosened his tie, and kicked off his shoes. He propped the pillows up on the bed, took the envelope, and rested back against the headboard.

The original envelopes had four flaps which interlocked, each holding the next down.

Gordon carefully opened it up. Yes, there inside was the form. He looked guiltily around the room, as if what he was doing was somehow forbidden, then bent forward, and pressed the envelope flat.

Inside each flap was a picture of a member of the family. The two parents, father at the top left, mother at top right, and the two children, bottom left and right, each exquisitely painted. The children, both holding what looked like a toy ostrich, were pictured in their nursery, while their parents sat smiling proudly in their study.

Gordon put his reading glasses on, and examined the pictures. It had been a while since he had looked at one of these. The children in the pictures were about ten and eight years old, and were not of the serious nature that children of such period where sometimes brought up to be. On the contrary, the girl had a broad smile, and the boy was outwardly laughing, his head tipping back in glee.

Gordon used a tissue to wipe his beaded brow, and wetted his drying throat with a sip of sherry.

The form inside was folded in the same way as the envelope, as if whoever had sent it had taken their time. The name, much to Gordon's dismay, but not surprise, was left blank. In fact, apart from the money and an indistinguishable signature the form held no other details at all. Gordon scratched his head in confusion.

"Well, I'll be damned," was all he could say. This was not how he'd been expecting the day to end at all. His routine had been twisted away from him at the last.

Gordon arched his fingers and looked at the black folder on the bed. What was inside was still the last Presentation, however what lay in the envelope before him promised a completely different challenge, altogether.

JESSICA, TONY, AND THE BRASS BAND

For the first time in four days, Gordon woke in his own bed. He had a sore head and cold feet, but apart from that, he felt very pleased with his break at the hotel. As he lay there, thinking about the work he'd done on the Presentation, he went through the familiar routine of checking for any aches and pains. It was a morbid fascination which had only materialised in the last few years, ever since he'd pulled a muscle in his leg trying to do too much, too quickly.

"I'm spending far too much time on my own," he said to the empty room.

As per usual, the only problems he found were in his aching shoulders and lower back, but then that was the case on most cold mornings. Not bad for sixty-four, Gordon thought. At first, his eyes resisted any attempt to focus, so he just lay there, breathing slowly and deeply, trying to remember his dreams. He dreamed well, it was one of the few creative things that still functioned reliably.

Gordon reached out, fumbled in the bowl beside his bed and retrieved an imperial mint. He placed it under his tongue and felt the taste fill his mouth. It struck Gordon, not for the first time, that he was man of infinite habits, and he lay contented in this fact, watching as the rising sun stretched the shadows across the bedroom ceiling.

When he'd woken up enough, he turned on his bedside light, put on his reading glasses, and opened his diary, which was nothing more than a book of lined A4. He turned to the next blank page, and, as he lay there, tried to summarise the events of the previous week. He managed three pages before the boredom set in. It had always been the same. Diaries sounded like such a good idea, but when he came to write them, he rarely felt his experiences warranted capturing.

The date on the clock showed Saturday 22nd January. He had a whole Saturday when he didn't have to think of the Race. It was very liberating. He remembered that Tony was coming around the next day for lunch, so knew he had to stop by a supermarket, but apart from that the day was his, and he wanted to make the most of it; he felt he'd been stuck inside for too long.

Gordon showered, shaved, and dressed quickly, and was out of the bungalow and walking into town at just before eight. The cars and pedestrians all moved with purpose at this time on a Saturday. Why else would people be awake? Employees went to work, couples left houses dressed for weddings, parents drove their children to football matches or hockey tournaments or a thousand other competitions. Gordon just strolled.

He remembered a time he'd been walking in a busy London railway station and someone, a girl handing out flyers for something or other, had stopped him just to say how pleasant it was to see someone who wasn't rushing, and he smiled at the girl for pointing it out. He could rush if he wanted to, and there had been many times he'd needed to, but on the whole, Gordon Paige strolled at a leisurely pace.

The route to the shops took him close to one of the town's smaller railway stations. A footbridge for pedestrians wound its way up, around and over the track, and as he passed by Gordon remembered his father taking him there a few times, so that he could note down the numbers on the carriages as they passed underneath on the track. His father had seemed different then, and Gordon missed those moments. Not the man himself, not his father, but the moments where it felt like he was pretending to be his father. Gordon stopped and studied it for a few moments, then passed on; he had no interest to climb the wooden steps now.

There was a parade of shops between his house and the town centre, and he was pleased to see an 'Open' sign hanging on the door to a coffee shop that nestled amongst them. There was another across the road, and a third one a bit further up. Spoilt for choice, he thought, as he pushed open the door and was greeted with a 'Hello' and a smile from the Saturday girl behind the counter. Gordon sat himself down in one of the window seats and waited patiently for her to come over. He was the only customer, so there was no chance he would be missed today.

The sky was a light grey, and the road outside was busy with through traffic. It was hardly a picturesque location, but Gordon didn't care. The girl came over and took his order of a Latte. Gordon still wasn't sure how he should say it, but the girl smiled and said she had the same problem, before disappearing off behind the counter to grind the beans and heat the milk.

The thought occurred to him that this cafe hadn't been here seven years ago. He sighed; however much he tried to convince himself he was living his own life, he found it impossible not to think about Brenda. Would she have liked to sit here with him, drinking a peppermint tea and talking about the family? He hoped so.

"I miss you," he whispered.

The girl brought his coffee over in a tall glass and set it down in front of him with the standard biscuit wrapped in cellophane. How quickly things change, he thought. Gordon sat back in his chair and quietly watched the people pass by. Near the door, today's papers were wedged in a stand, but Gordon didn't want to read them. He'd always found them quite depressing.

All manner of faces breezed by, though none of them seemed to be smiling. He concentrated on each set of features, trying to work out who they were and what they did, and it made him jump when, suddenly, he recognised one of them. It was Catherine. She was walking by with Jessica. No, she wasn't walking by, she was walking into the cafe.

She opened the door and went to the counter without realising he was there. Jessica, who trailed a moment or two behind her, saw him and did a little jump herself. "Grandpa!" she said, and came up to hug him.

"Oh," he heard Catherine say behind him, but he didn't look round. He hugged Jessica.

"And how is my youngest granddaughter?" he asked her.

"Growing," Jessica said, standing on tiptoe.

"And I must be shrinking," he said, hunching his shoulders, and bending over slightly.

Jessica laughed. "Silly!" she said.

"And what brings you here, today?" Gordon asked her.

Jessica shrugged, tilted her head, and pushed out her bottom lip. "I don't know," she said. "I just follow mummy."

Without prompting, Jessica sat down in the chair opposite Gordon and proceeded with sorting the sugar sticks out into their packet colours. Gordon turned and looked at Catherine still at the bar.

"Dad," she said, forcing the pleasant tone into her voice. "You don't usually have coffee here."

Gordon shook his head. "Nope," he said. "Thought I'd stop in nevertheless."

"Oh," she said. "We usually come here before we go to the library."

"I like the library," Jessica chimed in, her gaze remaining on the sugar.

"Good," Gordon said. "Me, too."

"Well, perhaps you'd like to take her?" Catherine said. "If you have the time?"

Gordon did have the time, but he was always annoyed at the way Catherine phrased a question like you'd be a bad person to say no.

"I'd love to," he said. "I'll finish my coffee and we'll both go, what do you say, Jess?"

Jessica nodded her head in an exaggerated fashion.

After Catherine had ordered her coffee, she went and sat at another table. Gordon laughed to himself. That about summed their relationship up. Gordon, unwilling to have to answer any awkward questions from Jessica, drained his glass, paid the bill, and left the cafe, his granddaughter holding tightly onto his hand. The library was only a minute away. They crossed the road at the bollards, and walked up the bleached slabs and through the swing doors.

Jessica took him to the children's section, and the two of them sat on the smallest bench possible, Gordon's knees almost reaching his ears.

They spent a good half an hour with Jessica getting the books from the wooden boxes and then sitting next to Gordon so he could read them to her. They were some that Jessica knew the words to, and it was a complete pleasure to listen to her read them aloud.

After the eighth or ninth book, Jessica started to become fidgety, so, as they turned the last page, he rested his back against the wall. "What do you want to be when you grow up?" he asked.

"Don't know," she said. "What do you want to be?"

Gordon laughed. "Don't know, either," he replied. "There's plenty of time to work it out, I suppose."

"I'd quite like to be a painter," Jessica said.

"A painter? Really? How artistic. What would you paint?"

Jessica frowned at him. "Walls, of course. Like Daddy."

"Wow, that would be interesting," he said. "Have you told your mother that?"

Jessica shook her head, her long hair slapping the sides of her cheeks. "She never asks."

Gordon frowned, but she didn't see him. "Your father's coming round to my house tomorrow."

"For a sleepover?"

Gordon chuckled again. "No, just for lunch. He misses you very much."

Jessica stopped moving so much. She looked out of the window, the way someone fifty years her senior would do. How much children have to grow up nowadays, Gordon thought.

"I miss him, too," she said, before taking the book from his lap and returning it to the others.

"Do you always go to that cafe?" he asked, trying to change the subject.

Jessica nodded. "Yes. Every week. Mummy likes to talk to the man there," she replied. "He makes her laugh."

Gordon walked Jessica back to the cafe at the arranged time, and Catherine was sat in same place. She was upset; her eyes were red. There were two coffee cups on the table in front of her.

"Come on, Jessie," she said, "We have to go now."

Without even a thank you or a goodbye to Gordon, Catherine left.

~

At half-past twelve Gordon was in town. There was a slight breeze, but nothing he couldn't put up with. It occurred to him there was a chance he'd bump into Esme in such a public place, but he accepted the risk. If it was supposed to be, then it would happen, and he'd deal with it as and when it arose.

He went into a couple of the charity shops on the fringes of town, and saw some of his books on the shelves. Someone must have got rid of a collection, he thought, or worse. He picked them up and thumbed through them. One of them was even signed. 'To Polly' it read in his familiar scrawl, 'Hope you enjoy the read, Gordon Paige'. There was a date, April 1982. That was before Christopher had been born. It made him feel old.

Outside, a brass band started up. Gordon replaced the book, and ventured out to see what was going on. He walked thirty yards or so, and stood watching the Salvation Army playing a tune he couldn't quite recognise. There were five of them in all, two trumpets, a trombone, a tuba and a French horn. There was something warming about their playing.

He waited until they had finished and applauded with the half-dozen or so other onlookers. He was about to turn and go further into the centre when he heard his name called out.

"Gordy?" It was an old man's voice, and Gordon looked around to see where it had come from. "Gordy," it came again, and this time he saw the man who'd said it. It was one of the trumpet players. He looked at him for a second, trying to place him. He was tall, nearly bald, with glasses and...

"Bib?" Gordon asked. "Is that you?"

The man smiled. "Gordy. My God, you're still alive."

"And by the same conclusion, so are you."

The two men looked at each other again. Bib looked older than Gordon, but still didn't look bad. He was tanned in a way that suggested he'd recently come back from a hot climate.

"I stopped seeing your novels on the bookstore shelves and thought you'd left us," he was saying, putting his trumpet into its housing.

"Well, at least someone noticed."

Bib stood back up straight again, wincing slightly. "I need to sit down. Have you got time to have some lunch, for old times?"

Gordon nodded. "For old times."

Gordon had lost touch with Bib after he'd married Brenda. There was no more time to take part in cricket matches, and he was vaguely aware of Bib moving out of the area. They walked to Gordon's usual lunchtime cafe, and found a table with the most comfortable seats. Bib placed his trumpet by the side, and Gordon fetched him a menu from the counter.

"So," Gordon started, "What've you been up to?"

"Where to start?" Bib said. "I moved abroad when I was about twenty-five, after being offered an opportunity in Spain from a family friend. Property development. I had the collateral, and was lucky enough to invest in the right areas. Tourism was booming and people needed somewhere to stay."

"I married, had two children, and had a fantastic life for about fifteen years. Then the marriage went sour, my fault entirely, and I went travelling in Europe and Asia, spending some of my money and seeing the sights. I ended up settling in the south of France. The children came to visit, and all was okay. I put some money into films, and had a mix bag of fortunes. But my head stayed above water."

"Anyway, I had a big hit. Small film, one hundred per cent investment, fantastic returns."

The waiter brought the food over to the table and set it down. Bib paused whilst the cutlery was fetched and placed.

"So, everything was going well, and then I... well... I got ill. So, I decided to come back home. It felt like the right thing to do. I was operated on, and now I'm clear. Have been for five years. I still visit the children and the grandchildren in Spain. Just come back from a month out there. So, all is well. How about you?"

Gordon told his own potted history, and Bib listened, commiserating, and congratulating when the need arose. Gordon found himself enjoying the company. Bib had mellowed, and maybe he had to. Life had a way of rounding off those rough edges. After the food was eaten, and the tea was drunk, the pair sat and chatted about the weather and the state of the town. They spoke about cricket and something of football, and there was still plenty of overlap to keep them going.

At two o'clock, they both stood and shook hands. They exchanged telephone numbers and Bib promised to ring him before Easter arrived.

Gordon watched Bib leave, pleased with his day. As he didn't want to be out late, he started the walk back home, stopping at the local convenience store to purchase what he needed for the next day's meal. When he got back to the bungalow, he unpacked the food, and put the kettle on. He got the diary pad from the bedroom, made the tea and retired to the spare room. He could concentrate more in that room. It was something to do with its size, the fact that the window was difficult to see out of, and that the electric fan heater was stationed in there. Gordon switched it on and wrote about what had happened that day.

~

The next morning, he was in the kitchen by seven o'clock preparing vegetables. Tony was due to arrive at twelve and Gordon didn't want it to look like he couldn't cope. Gordon loved to cook. It was something he'd only taken up in the last few years, but he seemed to have a knack for it. When Tony turned up, the food was just about ready and the pair sat down in the conservatory to eat.

"I saw Catherine yesterday," Gordon told him. "By accident, of course."

"Was Jessica there?" Tony asked.

Gordon nodded. "I took her over to the library and we read some books."

"That sounds fun."

"Yes, it was. I told her that you missed her. I hope that was all right?"

"Absolutely. Did she say anything?"

"She said she missed you, too."

Tony went quiet for a second. He looked to Gordon like he was trying to find the right words for something. "What's the matter?" Gordon asked.

Tony sighed and shook his head. "Sometimes it's hard to know what the right thing to do is."

Gordon nodded, "Yes, Tony. And not just sometimes. Is it about Jessica?"

Tony shook his head. "No, not this time. It's something else. I'm unsure about something. About what to do."

"Would you like my advice?" Gordon offered. "You know it's always there if you need it."

"I know," Tony said. He paused, then looked Gordon squarely in the eye. "Do you trust my judgement, Gordy?"

"Your judgement?" Gordon repeated, taken aback by Tony's frankness. "Yes, of course I do."

Tony nodded again. "Then I guess that'll have to do, for now."

They spoke some more whilst consuming the food, neither mentioning Catherine.

"I was thinking," Gordon said. "Perhaps you'd like to do some decorating here. What do you think?"

Tony looked around. "It looks fine to me."

"It is fine. Just thought it might help cheer the place up a bit, you know. A bit more colour."

"Are you sure? I thought you liked it how it was."

"I did," Gordon said. "I mean, I do. But then I guess everything needs to change in the end."

TONY, BRENDA, AND THE THINGS UNSAID

It was the morning of the 30th January, the beginning of the end for the Ostrich Race. Gordon looked at his watch and saw its reliable hands indicating ten minutes past seven. The man with the disobedient dog was a little late passing by on the pavement in front of the bungalow, and somewhere within his mind, Gordon wondered what might have delayed him. This past week, the aging author had woken early and spent the first fifteen minutes writing whatever words came to him. Then, he'd wait and watch the morning start to come alive outside of the window. He had quickly noticed the patterns, and now, by the sixth day, their regularity made him happy. After forty-five minutes or so of watching, he'd revisit the writing, tweaking, and massaging the words where necessary. This would then be followed by a shower and a shave, and then another redraft, as he gradually developed the piece throughout the morning routine. It was like he was re-learning his trade, and it made it both interesting and spontaneous at the same time.

It troubled Gordon that Esme's proposal had still not been resolved. There was no doubt he would refuse, he was just worried that by doing so, he would have to forfeit his job, and without the rest home to keep him busy, he didn't know quite what he'd do.

At around ten that morning, Tony rang and asked whether Gordon needed any help preparing for the evening's Presentation. He didn't, but the two agreed to a fish and chips lunch at the bungalow to cheer themselves up, and, after he'd hung up, Gordon was pleased to find the conversation had managed to rid him of the lethargy he'd had all morning.

Gordon went into his bedroom, and retrieved the Race folder. He turned to the back, where, in a plastic pocket, he'd placed the original envelope he'd received at the hotel.

He put it on the conservatory table, and paced around, considering his next move. The envelopes had still been in use at the time of the first Presentation he'd attended, and had remained so up until a couple of years after Chris had been born. At that point, Frank, who was the organiser then, had distributed them to the players to keep as they'd become too old to use. Over the past few days, Gordon had spent some time looking through the Race records he had in his possession, hoping to find a list of the people they'd been given to, but hadn't been able to retrieve any pertinent information. This left just one person he could speak to, and after a single successful telephone call, he picked up his coat and keys, and caught a taxi to 'The Brambles'.

~

Vee took a long time to reach her front door. When, eventually, she opened it, Gordon was surprised how full of life she looked.

"Sorry about that," she said, "I was busy cleaning upstairs."

Gordon raised his eyebrows. "Bit early in the day for cleaning, isn't it?"

A look of guilt passed over her face for a fleeting moment, until she dispelled it with a flick of the wrist. "Well, usually, yes," she said, retreating toward the kitchen, leaving Gordon to close the door, "But I woke up early today. Must be Race nerves, eh?"

"An experienced Racer like you?" Gordon goaded.

Vee politely refused to be drawn. It had only been five years since, due to ill health, she'd stopped taking part in the Race, though her lack of participation hadn't dampened her enthusiasm for it. Gordon put the kettle on, while Vee sat herself down at the kitchen table. "Now," she said, "I'm not complaining, Gordy, but what do I owe you for this visit?"

"Can't a man simply like visiting his Aunt?" Gordon said.

"Oh, go on with you, Gordy," Vee said, "I only saw you recently. And you never voluntarily make the tea. Something must be on your mind."

Gordon rested against the sink. "Okay, okay. First, a question."

Vee placed her palms on the table. "Fire away."

"Do you still have your original envelope, from the Race?"

Vee thought for a couple of seconds. "Yes, I think I have. I couldn't tell you where exactly, but I know I haven't thrown it away. It's in this house, somewhere."

"Good," Gordon said, playing with a teaspoon.

"Is that it?" Vee teased, "You could have rung me if that's all you wanted to know."

Gordon fished in his pocket and brought out the anonymous envelope. He put it down on the table in front of her. "I don't suppose there's any way of telling who Frank gave this to, is there?"

Vee sucked in her breath. "It's been awhile since I've seen one of those. It's not Brenda's, then?" she asked.

Gordon shook his head. "I don't think so. No."

Vee put her reading glasses on, turned it over, and opened it up. Eventually, she frowned, and looked up at Gordon.

"No. They're all the same, to my knowledge. Where did you get it from?"

"Someone pushed it under my hotel room door."

Vee's face closed into a confused expression, "What?"

Gordon turned to the boiling kettle. "I went to the hotel to finish off the Presentation. I didn't tell anyone where I was, so I'm guessing they must have followed me there. The entry form was blank."

"Oh. Well, it's all very mysterious, Gordy," Vee said. "What are you going to do?"

"Well, there's nothing against anonymous entrants in the rules. I checked. So, I'm happy to let them play. I'm assuming they won't show up tonight, so was wondering whether Frank kept a list of who he gave the envelopes to? If I could find the person who hasn't got theirs, I'm hoping they'd know who it was who'd entered."

Vee thought for a moment. "I've never seen a list, Gordy. That's not to say there isn't one, of course. Were there any other clues?"

"Not really. The entry form was signed, but you can't make anything out. It's in the folder there, at the front."

Vee opened the binder up. After a couple of seconds, she pulled away. "No, I can't see anything either. I'll have a look through Frank's notes this afternoon, if that's all right?"

"Whenever you can," Gordon said, placing Vee's tea down on the table mat beside her. "Are you sure it's no trouble?"

Vee smiled. "None at all," she said, and then leant forward secretively. "In truth," she admitted, "I've been itching for an excuse to go back through Frank's stuff for a while."

Tony turned up at twelve, as they'd arranged. He brought lunch and they spoke about the day's news while they slowly devoured the chips and battered fish. Afterwards, Tony made two trips to the dump with all the rubbish Gordon had stockpiled in the garage, and, by two, everything was mostly done. On the way back, Tony stopped at a parade of shops, and helped his ex-father-in-law choose a present for Jessica, before the two finally took a walk around a deserted triangular-shaped green.

"This is where you met Brenda," Tony said, matter-of-factly, as they stopped for a rest by a tree.

"How do you know that?" Gordon asked, surprised.

"She told me one Christmas afternoon. We were all out on the constitutional, except Catherine who'd fallen asleep on the settee. You and Chris were behind us, talking as usual."

"You make me sound like an old gas-bag."

Tony laughed, "You are when Chris is around."

"Maybe," Gordon admitted, "What did Brenda say?"

Tony looked away, "Oh, nothing much."

Gordon watched as Tony subconsciously fingered his collar. "Well, go on," Gordon said, "You've started, so you may as well finish."

"Aw, she told me not to tell you, Gordy," Tony said.

"Oh, come on," Gordon started nervously, "How bad can it be?"

Tony frowned, sighed, then continued. "All right, but only because you asked."

~

"This is where I met Gordy," Brenda said, looking toward the centre of the green. Tony wasn't sure if she was talking to him, or not. "He was playing cricket, and I was watching him. I'd watched him for weeks. Secretly, of course. Ever since I'd seen him on the bus. We took the same route for a while. He hadn't noticed me in three months, but I thought he was fascinating."

"How did you know he was going to be playing cricket?"

"I knew Bib, and had been with him and a group of friends when Gordon had passed and nodded a hello. I could hardly believe it, so I asked Bib if he could get him onto the cricket team, and, after some debate, he said yes. I don't think Bib liked him that much."

At this point, Gordon and Chris passed them in animated conversation. After they were out of earshot, Brenda spoke once more. "I always told him that I was just passing because it sounded so much more romantic, and I was young. Truth is, though, I was just waiting for a chance to talk to him. I couldn't believe it when he got hit with the ball. I felt terrible. But then I thought, 'It's now or never, girl,' so I went to see how he was. I even told him I was a St. Johns nurse. Anything to speak to him."

Tony looked at Brenda. She was the most confident woman Tony had ever met. She stood gazing at the back of her husband, her slender hands resting upon hips hidden underneath her warm coat. She wore little makeup, she didn't need to, and it brought out her natural beauty. She turned to Tony.

"I've never told anyone that," she said. "Please don't tell him. I wouldn't want him to be disillusioned, not after all these years."

Tony offered a smile, "Of course not," he said. "I won't say a word."

~

"And you kept it to yourself for all these years?" Gordon said.

"It's what she asked me to do."

"Well, good for you," the older man said. He stood, not really knowing what to say. "Are you positive that's what she said?"

"Absolutely. I can remember it word for word."

"Oh," Gordon replied.

Tony put a hand on Gordon's arm. "It's not all that bad."

Gordon pursed his lips, "I suppose not," he said. "It's just funny what people keep from you, isn't it?"

"Tell me about it. I really liked Brenda, Gordy. She knew what she wanted, didn't she?"

Gordon smiled and put a hand on Tony's shoulder. "Yes, Tony, she definitely did."

Twenty minutes later, having refused the offer of a lift back, Gordon waved Tony on his way. He still had plenty of time before he needed to be home, and he just fancied a meander along the roads he remembered from his youth.

He'd hardly started reminiscing before a car beeped behind him, and the whirr of an electric window made him turn his head.

"Need a lift?" Simon asked.

"I was just wandering around," Gordon replied.

"Have you had lunch?"

"Yes."

"Well, I'm sure the kids would love to see you. Come on, I'll take you home with me."

Gordon relented. He always liked to see Trudie and Denise, and Pamela, of course. Not to mention, their house and gardens. Putting up with Simon for the short drive seemed a small price to pay. When they arrived, Simon let him out of the car at the front door, and drove on towards the garage. A first-floor window opened, and Trudie poked her mass of blonde curls out.

"Hi-ya, Gramps," she called down, with an infectious giggle.

"Hello, mop head," he called back.

"Oh, no. Not you as well. Dad's giving me a hard-enough time as it is. I thought you might be a bit more sympathetic."

Gordon smiled; talking to Trudie gave him back some faith in the younger generation. "Oh, I'm certainly sympathetic towards it."

Trudie tried to look upset, but a smirk gave away her real feelings. "Huh," she managed, before closing the window.

As Simon came out of the garage, Pamela opened the front door. Gordon gave her a quick hug. "Wasn't expecting to see you till this evening," she said.

"Nor was I, but Simon offered me a lift."

"You're brave," she said, as her husband approached.

They went into the large hallway. Slightly to the right, the stairs rose, and at their top, Pamela's other daughter, Denise, sat, head in hands.

"Hello, you," Gordon said.

Denise remained where she was.

"Don't worry, Dad, she's been like that all morning."

Simon walked straight on through to the kitchen, and Pamela leaned forward to whisper in Gordon's ear. "Ask to see her Wendy house," she said. "It's a present from Simon. She loves it. I'll make you a pot of tea."

Gordon climbed the stairs and sat a couple of steps below the grumpy eight-year-old.

"Anything I can help you with?" Gordon asked her. Trudie shook her head. She bore the same blonde hair as her sister, though she wore hers straight, which suited her attitude to most things.

"How's your sister?" Gordon continued, knowing it was a topic that would surely illicit a response.

She shrugged her shoulders. "Same," she said.

"Oh. Well, I hear you've got a new Wendy house, can I have a look?"

Denise nodded, but made no attempt to move. Gordon was about to give in, when Trudie ran along the hallway.

"I'll show you," she said, and was past them both before they really knew what had happened.

Denise immediately got up. "No, you won't," she said, setting off down the stairs after her sister, "I'll show Gramps."

Then, when the noise abated, Gordon found himself alone.

"You all right, Dad?" Pamela asked, at the side of the stairs.

"Just thought I'd have a sit down," he replied, with a smile. "I think I'll go and join them, now."

"I'll call you when I've made the tea."

Gordon walked through the kitchen, and out of the back door, into a cold, but bright, day. Their garden was as beautiful as ever, the envy of any green-fingered individual; though Gordon knew it was only that way because of the gardener they employed to visit once a week.

"Where've you been, Gramps?" Trudie said, as he opened the Wendy house's small door.

Gordon stooped to see his granddaughter, "Look at me when you're talking to me," he said, then reached out and parted her hair. "Oh, you are," he kidded, and all three laughed. "Room for one more?"

"As long as it's you," Denise replied, and Gordon could tell she was only half-joking.

Gordon squeezed in, and sat uncomfortably at the plastic table. "I'm never going to be able to get out of here," he said. "It's a lovely place, but could do with some central heating."

"Dad bought it," Denise said, without hesitation or emotion, "So he could get us out of the house."

Gordon's eyebrows raised involuntarily. "Surely not," he said.

Denise opened her mouth to say something more, but Trudie interrupted her.

"Mum and Dad are arguing a lot at the moment," she said, "So we tend to be staying around friends, or shut out the way. They think they're helping us."

"I'm sorry to hear that," Gordon said.

"That's okay," Trudie told him. "It's not your fault."

Pamela had always been the more likely of his daughters to start a family, and she hadn't let them down. Her biological urge had been strong, almost unstoppable, and it seemed, to Gordon, that Simon had simply come along at the right time. Before they had finished their honeymoon, Pamela was three months pregnant, and then there was Trudie crawling around the floor.

There was a knock at the Wendy house door and all three occupants jumped. Gordon hit his head on the slanting ceiling.

"Tea's up," Pamela said.

Gordon frowned and rubbed his temple in mock pain, whilst the girls fell about laughing. When they'd recovered, Trudie helped him through the door and he held both girls' hands as they followed Pamela towards the house.

"Where's Simon?" Gordon asked his daughter as he picked up his tea from the kitchen table.

"He's had to go back to work. Supervising overtime, or something."

"You are still coming tonight, though, aren't you?" Gordon asked.

Pamela looked up from making some sandwiches for the girls, who were back upstairs. "Yes, we'll be there," she said, "But I better warn you, we haven't been able to get a babysitter, so the girls may be there, too."

"The more, the merrier," Gordon said, and then waited for a couple of seconds before asking, "Did Bren..., your Mum, ever tell you things you weren't supposed to tell me?"

Pamela looked at him strangely, and then laughed. "Of course. Do you think us women tell you everything? Do you tell us everything?"

"Well," Gordon floundered, "I'd like to think I tried."

Pam looked at her father, "Well, you go on thinking that. I'll carry on living in the real world." She turned back to the working surface. Her face suddenly went white. "I went to visit Graeme this morning."

Gordon smiled, "That's kind of you."

Pamela shrugged. "I can't forget him," she said, then suddenly burst into tears. Gordon got up and comforted his daughter. "I'm sorry, Dad."

"There's nothing to be sorry for," he said. "It was just one of those things."

"I don't know what I'd do if I lost Trudie or Denise. It must have been so hard."

"The worst," Gordon said, "The worst."

~

When Gordon arrived back at the bungalow, there were three messages on the answer phone. The first was Vee asking if he needed her to get anything on the way. The second was Tony asking if he'd left his mobile phone there, and the third was Catherine. She sounded quite level headed, for once, wanting nothing more than to let him know she and Jessica would be coming to the Presentation after all.

Gordon thought it might be best if he forewarned Tony of her attendance, but when he rang him at the flat, he got no answer. He then tried his mobile, only to hear its tune play in the lounge. Oh, well, Gordon thought, let the battle commence.

Gordon picked up the Race folder and carried it carefully into the lounge, placing it in the centre of the coffee table. He thumbed through the leaves one last time, making sure everything was correct, and was pleased to note it was.

He checked his watch; five forty-five. Gordon had an hour and a half before people would start to arrive. He twiddled his thumbs for a couple of minutes, and when that didn't help, he went to the sideboard and pulled out the photograph albums. As the seconds turned into minutes,

Gordon lost himself within the pictures, until, eventually, he found himself sat in a room filled with his old, dead family and friends, once again.

VEE, CATHERINE, AND THE LAST PRESENTATION

Vee arrived at seven thirty, a little later than planned, and Gordon answered the door to her in good cheer. He held her arm as they made their way through the bungalow, and sat her in the conservatory, while he fixed her a gin and tonic.

"Catherine's coming," he told her, as he made his way back in. "She's bringing Jessica."

Vee looked surprised, "Does Tony know?" she asked.

"I couldn't contact him. I don't know how he'll take it. If Jessica's here then he'll be okay. Problem is I think he still feels for Catherine."

"Oh, well, we'll just have to try and mediate between the two of them as best we can. You've done it before."

"It's not her and Tony I've got to worry about, Vee. It's her and me."

~

The break-up of Tony and Catherine had taken its toll on everyone. Tony had continued trying to reconcile with his wife, until, at last, she threatened to deny him access to his daughter. Knowing Catherine's resolve, Gordon advised Tony to step back, and talk to a solicitor to help him through any potential custody issues. Catherine retaliated by stopping Jessica seeing Gordon altogether.

When Catherine's new boyfriend moved in, most of their friends sided with Tony, cutting Catherine out of her all so-important social circuit. Gordon wondered whether this had been the reason her new relationship had fallen apart so quickly. Within six weeks of moving in, Catherine and her new man had split.

Finding herself on her own and without friends, Catherine soon reappeared on the scene, wanting to see Tony, using Jessica to arrange meetings with him. She even tried to seduce him, but it was too late; he no longer needed her. Catherine was furious, but tried her damnedest not to show it, instead stewing silently alone.

~

Vee looked in the bag she'd brought with her. "I tried to find some information about the envelopes," she said, "But didn't have any luck."

Gordon sighed. "I thought it'd be difficult."

"But I did have a think about it, and came up with my own list of people who probably have them. It might be of some help."

"I'm sure it will be. I'd trust your memory over mine any day."

"Good," Vee said, still searching. "If only I could find it. It's in here somewhere." The doorbell sounded in the hallway.

Gordon whistled his way to the front door. "Good to see the pair of you," he said to Chris and Louise, who held hands on the doorstep.

"We're not too early, are we, Dad?" Louise asked.

Gordon gave them his warmest smile. "Not at all, everything's in place. Vee's in the conservatory."

He took their coats, showed them through, and left them all to talk, whilst he opened a bottle of wine. Tension, Gordon thought, as he fought with the cork, made up the Presentation. People arrived expectant, and the art of the evening was to build on this, to heighten the tension and expectation, to make people understand the game they were about to embark upon had been played for over a hundred years. The players should feel privileged, Gordon certainly did.

The Ostrich Race was simple. The organiser chose a theme for the year, wrote two initial questions, one for February and one for March, for every participant, and handed them out on the night of the Presentation. The participants completed February's question, in the form of a short essay, detailing everything they had learnt, including their views about it. This way there was no right answer, and it forced the entrants to think about topics they may not have thought about before. The first essays were due in by the last day in February, after which they could start on March's question. Then, throughout March, Gordon would mark February's papers, and using ideas the entrants themselves may have come up with, set April's question. This type of marking and setting would go on throughout the year, making the Race's questions grow almost organically.

"It's a bit like my writing," Gordon remembered explaining to Tony, "I rarely know how the Race is going to end when I start it."

The winner, when all was said and done, was the person the organiser thought had progressed the furthest. It was a difficult criterion to explain, but invariably one of the entrants would stand out above the others.

The first two subjects were sat in plain white envelopes on the dining room table. There were ten sets of questions in all, one for each of the six known entrants, plus a few extra ones in case there were any last-minute requests.

Pamela arrived next with the children. "Where's Simon?" Gordon asked.

"He's on his way," she explained, "You know what he's like. I expect he's wrapping the car in cotton wool, in case anybody's racing down your small, quiet, cul-de-sac."

As Gordon poured their drinks, Chris appeared in the kitchen. "Vee mentioned Cath's coming," he said quietly.

"Hmm," Gordon nodded. "She's family."

"Well, if you need any help, Dad, just let me know."

"Thanks, Chris. Let's hope not. Is... Louise okay?"

"She'll try her best."

From the moment they'd met, it was obvious Catherine and Louise weren't going to be best of friends. During their childhood, Catherine had enjoyed bullying Christopher; about his size, his looks, his friends, and whatever else she could find. Unfortunately, this continued, and whilst Chris had learnt to ignore them on the whole, Louise would retaliate. In a strange way, it helped him. Chris may not directly stand up for himself, but he would always back Louise to the hilt, which was, Gordon thought, an encouraging development. To no-one's surprise, Louise had won the first Race she'd taken part in.

Gordon placed a hand on Chris' shoulder. "I won't let your sister ruin anything this evening."

Once more the doorbell rang. "That'll be my husband," Pamela called from the lounge.

Trudie got up and followed Gordon into the hall.

"Hello, Dad," Catherine said, when he opened the door, and gave him a hug before he'd gotten over the shock of seeing her. Trudie instinctively took a step back.

"Catherine," Gordon said, "You're early."

"Well, you know, Dad, I'm not such an old dog, after all."

The two parted and Jessie raised her arms to Gordon. "Hello, Jessie," he said, picking her up, "How's your week been?"

"Busy," Catherine said, "So don't be too surprised if she doesn't stay awake for long."

"Oh, that's fine. She can fall asleep on me anytime. You do know that Tony's going to be here tonight, don't you?"

Catherine smiled at her father, "Yes, I hoped he would be," she said, "Are the others in the lounge?"

"Yes, just through there."

Catherine turned to her father. "I know it's been a while Dad, but I do remember where the lounge is. Now, you must be Trudie, I haven't seen you in a while. My, how you've grown. Such a pretty young woman. We must have a chat later on."

Trudie smiled an uncomfortable smile. "Okay," she said. As Catherine went into the lounge, the girl turned and looked at her grandfather. "Was that really Aunt Catherine?" she asked.

Gordon raised an eyebrow, "Umm," he said, "It looked like her."

"Dad!" Trudie shouted, and ran at Simon who was standing on the doorstep, hopping from foot to foot. "Hello, Trude. Hello, Gordy. Everything all right?"

"Who knows," he said. "Come on in, it's too chilly to have this door open for long."

Gordon carried Jessica into the lounge, and put her down beside Vee. Instantly she flipped her shoes off, and lay in a foetal position, her head on Vee's lap.

"Hello," the old lady said, but got no reply. Jessica was near enough asleep already.

An awkwardness descended upon the room, everyone unsure of what to say next. Finally, Catherine turned to Louise, and said, "I was thinking about buying that dress myself. It's lovely, isn't it? Mind you, it looks far better on you than it would on me."

Louise's expression didn't change for a few seconds. Gordon could see her trying to work out what to say. In the end, she plumped for, "That's very kind," and left it at that.

"How are you?" Chris asked.

"Very well," Catherine answered, "I've missed seeing you. It's all been so hectic."

Pam shifted in her seat. "What brings you here?" she asked, cagily.

"The Race," she said. "I've come to enter the Race."

Tony appeared at the lounge door, having let himself in with the key Gordon had given him. He beckoned to Gordon, who excused himself.

"I tried to ring to warn you, but your mobile's here."

"Oh," Tony said, then added, "Who's looking after Jessica?"

"No-one, she's here, too. She's asleep on Vee's lap."

Tony looked at the floor. "Sorry about this, Gordy."

"Don't be silly. It's hardly your fault. Besides, Catherine seems... different tonight."

"What do you mean, different?"

"Well," Gordon attempted, not convinced with what he was about to say, "She's being... nice. Well, nicer than I've ever seen her. She even said she was looking forward to meeting you."

Tony thought for a moment. "Doesn't sound promising."

"I know, but go and see for yourself. It's incredible."

The unmistakable laugh of Catherine rang out from the lounge.

"Bloody hell," Tony said.

Everyone had now arrived. Catherine seconded Trudie to work with her on the Race. Pamela and Gordon willingly agreed. They all were curious to see just how far Catherine's change of heart would go. At nine-fifteen, Gordon started the Presentation. As normal, everyone remained silent as Gordon spoke.

"Dear all," he said, holding his arms out to them, "Welcome to 'The Ostrich Race'. Welcome to Simon, Pamela, Chris, Louise, Tony, Catherine and Trudie, who are this year's entrants, may you enjoy the challenges before you. Welcome to Denise and Jessica, who, of course, will have their own challenges to face this year, and lastly, welcome to Vee, a friend through thick and thin. May you all meet your goals."

A shiver ran up Gordon's back, as it always did on Presentation night. The Race seemed to be powered by its own electricity.

"I have to admit, the Race was giving me some difficulties this year," Gordon continued, "I was finding it hard to base it on any theme, but then something happened which set my mind going, as, thank the Lord, it always does." Gordon looked at the faces of the children, trying to gauge if they would last the speech without getting too bored. "Now, some of you may laugh, but recently I've been proposed to." Gordon watched the expressions on the faces. Most smiled, some looked surprised. "And while I have no wish to tell you who the lady in question was, it led me to thinking of how things have changed in general."

"We're living in different times. Things I took as the norm thirty, twenty, even ten, years ago are now outmoded," Gordon saw a look of confusion fall over Denise's face, "Old-fashioned," he added, and saw her nod. "When I was growing up, to be proposed to by a lady was rarely heard of. People wouldn't have found it acceptable. But, nowadays, it's seen as pragmatic, and go-getting. With this fresh in my mind, I decided to base the theme of this year's Race on these changes; between the old and the new. Fairly simple, yet extremely relevant." Gordon took a sip of sherry, and continued. "So, the topics are about the comparisons between what was then, and what is now, which all of us will be able to answer."

"Now, there are a couple of other things I need to say. Firstly, and for the first time in memory, I have received an anonymous entry. This is perfectly allowable under the rules, and I have to assume that one of you knows who it is. I have put more than enough question envelopes out, so please feel free to take an extra one. The same rules still apply, whoever it is needs to send me their monthly answers as usual. I will then leave the next question under the front door mat for them to collect."

The gathered crowd eyed each other suspiciously. Before anything could be said, Gordon continued.

"Secondly, and regrettably, this will be the last Race I'll organise, which, I think, only reinforces the theme of old and new. However, this does not mean the end of the Race forever. Moreover, it will simply be a rest, and I will leave it open to be run by someone in the future. I have all the information, knowledge and experience ready to pass on."

Gordon smiled at them all, and they returned a look of understanding. "So, now that that's out of the way, please feel free to pick up an envelope, and let the Ostrich Race commence."

They clapped, and then, as they filed out to pick up their papers, they took turns to pat him on the shoulder and shake his hand. Vee placed a hand on his arm and squeezed. "Don't worry, Gordy," she said, "I'm amazed you've managed to carry on up till now. What with Brenda and everything."

"It was the Race that kept me going," Gordon said. "We both knew it would."

The only time you really got to look at your initial subjects at the Presentation was the few seconds between picking them up in the dining room and coming back into the lounge. As such, people tended to take their time, milling around by the table. The competitive would say things like, "Oh, this seems easy," or "I know the answer to that one," simply to put the others off. Some would return to the lounge smiling and looking confident.

When everyone had reassembled, they sat and chatted about other things; Christmas, New Year, going back to work, resolutions made and broken. The Race was what brought them together, but it was the companionship which kept them that way.

Around ten o'clock, they started to leave. First, and understandably so, were Catherine and Jessica, who'd remained on the settee all evening.

Gordon saw them out, and returned to a room full of people discussing her. "Something's not right," Tony was saying.

"It's strange," Pamela said, "Usually I can pick up on Catherine, she gives herself away. But tonight, she seemed to be pretty genuine."

"For what it's worth," said Vee, "I always stick by the saying, a leopard never changes its spots."

"I'll second that," said Louise. "I don't trust her one bit. No offence, Gordy."

Gordon smiled, "None taken."

When his children and respective families had left, Gordon sat alone with Vee. She was still holding up remarkably well.

"How do you think they took the news tonight?" he asked.

"Well, they were sad, but they understood."

He sipped his tea. "What's going to happen to the Race?" he asked.

"I don't know, Gordy. Maybe in time someone will take it up. Oh, I've got that list for you, now," she said.

"Thanks."

"By the way," Vee continued, taking the paper out of her purse. "Did you accept the proposal?"

"To Esme? No. But I've not had the guts to reject it either. I was leaving it until tomorrow."

"Well, mind you don't leave it any longer," she replied, "A woman doesn't like to be left hanging around."

"Of course. I must. And I will."

Vee unfolded the paper and laid it out on the table. "These are the people that I think have envelopes, or should I say, had them."

Gordon read out the list. "Brenda, well I can get that. Cissy, Monty, Pat, Colin, Jack, you, Elizabeth, Phillip and Lawrence. I haven't spoken to these people for years."

"I never said it was going to be easy, Gordon."

"But where to start?" he asked.

Vee smiled, "Do what I usually do," she said, "and start with the easy ones, then see what falls into place."

"I guess it'll be Monty, then. At least all his stuff should be in the loft, here."

"Well, then, there's your answer."

With that settled, Gordon and Vee sat and enjoyed each other's company. Gordon showed her some of the photographs he'd found earlier.

Suddenly, Gordon got up and disappeared.

"You all right?" Vee asked after him.

"Absolutely," he said, reappearing a few seconds later, some pieces of paper in his hands.

"What are those?"

"Three question papers," Gordon answered, pleased with himself.

"So?"

"They're the only ones left, and that means I was right. Someone here did take one for the anonymous player. Someone here tonight knew who sent the envelope in. That makes the task not so impossible, don't you think?"

Vee smiled. "If you say, so, Gordon, my dear. If you say so."

MONTY, VEE, AND A DOZEN BOXES

Gordon had ten months to find nine envelopes, though he found it difficult to put his finger on exactly why he felt such a strong urge to uncover the identity of the anonymous player. Maybe, he mused, it was because it had been such a long time since he'd taken part in a Race himself, or maybe it was because it was the final Race. In truth, though, neither theory seemed solid enough to justify the depth of his curiosity.

He also needed to speak to Esme, to tell her, once and for all, he was not going to accept her proposal. Over breakfast, he attempted to pluck up the courage by recalling Vee's words of the previous evening, using them to prick his guilt into submission. It worked, too, right up until he lifted the receiver to call her, when suddenly, his mind put across the compelling argument that he could put it off until the afternoon, and still keep his promise with Vee. This blatant "get-out" clause was further vilified by the thought he could then spend the morning fetching Monty's belongings from the loft. He tried to put the picture of Vee waving an accusatory finger out of his mind.

Monty had died only a year after Graeme, and Cissy had immediately asked for all his things to be removed from the house. As Jack had long been non-contactable, Brenda took it upon herself to store his property in the house's attic until such time she could properly sort through it all. In the end, however, the close proximity of her father's death to Graeme's prevented her from finding the necessary enthusiasm to do it. Gordon remembered, with little relish, the back-breaking task of moving the boxes from the house to the bungalow loft when they'd moved.

There were twelve crates to sort through, and he knew he wouldn't be able to go through them all in one morning, even one day. Perhaps if he made a start, though, he could get lucky and find the Race envelope almost immediately.

The loft of the bungalow was far smaller than the one they'd had at the house. Now, as Gordon, climbed the last rung of the ladder, he remembered just how much smaller. In the house attic, he could stand and walk on the temporary floor with ease. Up here, he was forced to crawl around on his hands and knees, bumping his head on the assortment of diagonal support beams the architects had insisted on including. If only the beam from his torch was as strong as its wooden namesakes, he mused, as he shook the black cylinder back and forth with little success. At least it was efficient; if it gave out any less light it wouldn't warrant being called a torch at all.

After many fruitless minutes scampering around the dusty loft, with its splinter-inducing wood and itchy insulation, Gordon was about ready to give up on the whole exercise. It was only then, only when he was on the brink of stopping for the day, that fate took a little pity on him, and the pathetic light of the torch fell upon a box he thought he recognised. He twisted his way to it, and turned it round in his hands. There, scrawled on its side, were the words 'Monty-8. His heart lifted. He knew he'd stacked them all together, so now it was just a case of manoeuvring all the boxes to the hatch. Puffing a little, Gordon dragged a board across and placed it between him and the opening, which projected the bright day through it like a searchlight.

He grabbed the box that said 'Monty-8' from the pile and placed it on his end of the board. He bent his aching knees, lifted the board, and watched as the force of gravity overtook frictions resistance, and it slid slowly towards the hatch. Gordon smiled at his ingenuity, though it was short lived. About three quarters of the way down it snagged on something, and stopped.

"Damn," Gordon said, raising the board higher. When that didn't work, he jiggled it from side to side in an attempt to jump the box over the obstruction. "Damn," he repeated as he watched the box slowly topple off the board, spilling its contents onto the yellow fibreglass matting underneath. Gordon felt annoyed. Instead of going and fixing the toppled box, he grabbed the next six, arranged them in two neat rows of three, and pushed them in unison toward the hatch, before finally lining up the remaining five behind them.

Gordon shuffled precariously along the narrow ridge of the board he'd left himself, and sat down at the opening, legs dangling and quite out of breath. After rearranging the boxes around the lip of the hatch, he brought them down one by one, blindly feeling for each from the top of the ladder. The thought struck him that if he fell, it could be days before anyone found him, but he put it out of his mind. He'd learned such thoughts could all too quickly spiral out of control.

When he thought he'd brought all the boxes down, he realised he'd left his torch up there, and clambered back up to fetch it. As he looked around for its dim glow, he saw the box that had toppled off. That's the one I'll start with, he thought to himself. That's the sort of thing that fate does. Gordon spent a couple of minutes putting the box back together again, before bringing it down and placing it with the others in the hallway. After closing the loft opening, Gordon took a minute to rest against the wall; the whole thing had taken near enough an hour and Gordon was beyond everything except recuperation. He left the boxes where they were, and made himself a strong pot of tea.

As he sat and drank, Gordon started to think about Monty. It was difficult not to. He'd known him for many years, had shared many experiences together, and now he was surrounded by what was left of his life. It made him feel sad. It made him feel old.

When he was ready, Gordon tentatively opened the first box, an upturned glass, and a postcard beside him in case of any creepy crawlies.

Monty had spent his youth in the army. His shiny shoes and glistening buckles had endured into his later life, and were still indelibly marked into Gordon's memories. However, from the state of it, such fastidiousness hadn't been afforded by whoever had packed the boxes. As he went through every item, Gordon made sure he sorted them into piles himself, spread out over the carpet, like large fungi emerging from the floor. Clumps started to grow of letters, clothes, personal belongings, and photographs. He was surprised by the number of pictures Monty had collected. He had never regarded Brenda's father as the sort of person who would care to be photographed, but now, however, he could see he might have been quite a vain man.

He had certainly been a smouldering chap when he was younger. In the photographs Gordon looked through, he was invariably poised, hand in pocket, smoking a cigarette, while the others around him stood in such a way as to convey that Monty was the person it was good to be around.

The letters Gordon found were mainly from Monty's mother, the lady he'd known of as Auntie. He'd never spoken at length to her, but as Gordon read, he quickly formed a picture of someone whose life had revolved around her son. She wrote using only words that praised him, saying how proud she was, and how they all thought he was doing 'such a fine job' back home. She'd tell him about the social gossip and family news. About holidays she was planning, and how she wanted him to be able to go with them. It took a little while for Gordon to notice it, but there was no mention of Vee whatsoever, even though there were only a few years between them. She was completely ignored by her mother's idolising words.

All in all, it took Gordon an hour and a half to complete the first box. He sighed. He wanted to feel more optimistic, but the lack of finding the envelope straight away only seeded more doubts in his mind. That, and the fact that he'd have to go to the home soon, face Esme, and he hadn't even shaved yet. He took a shower, allowed the water to wash over him, and thought about what he would say. He removed the night's white stubble, dressed sombrely in brown trousers and brown jacket, and set off on the five-minute walk, planning to arrive just after twelve.

The rest home had been built on part of the ground where an old cinema had been. When the redevelopment project had first been proposed, Gordon had been one of the local residents who'd opposed it. Brenda and he had gone there throughout their lives, and Gordon didn't want to see yet another part of their life together disappear. His protestations had fallen on deaf ears, however, and the cinema had been demolished and the home built. All this meant he now worked there with mixed emotions. It had become an important part of his recent life, but it was the cinema that truly contained his most worthwhile experiences, the ones he treasured.

He opened the front door, stepped onto the welcome mat, and wiped his feet.

The lobby was carpeted in pink, wallpapered in a soft yellow, with the light beige of the desk cutting across the two at the back. It reminded Gordon of a Battenberg cake, and his stomach rumbled. As he approached the desk, the receptionist stood up from whatever it was she'd been doing, saw it was Gordon, smiled and sat down again.

"Hello, there," Gordon said, cheerily.

"Hi," said the girl in a monotonous tone, turning the page of the magazine she was reading.

"Is Esme in?" he asked, trying to inject a little enthusiasm into the exchange.

The girl sighed. "Nope, she's on holiday."

"Holiday?" Gordon said, surprised and ashamedly relieved. "She never mentioned that to me?"

The girl clipped her pen to the top of the page, and closed the magazine. She moved it to one side. "Well, you've hardly been here, have you? Last few days she's been all gloomy and depressed. Don't know why. Didn't ask. I'm pleased she's taking a few days off."

Gordon drummed the desk, "Oh, dear," he said.

"She left yesterday. Her daughter's coming in to run the show whilst she's gone."

Gordon felt himself descending deeper into a well of guilt. "Did she say when's she coming back? Or leave a number I can contact her on?"

"Don't know when she'll be back. And she didn't leave a number. Not with me anyway. Her daughter might have one. And, before you ask, she's not expected till day after tomorrow. All right?"

Gordon watched the girl become more agitated. She wanted to return to her magazine. "Thank you," he said, "I'd like to say it's been a pleasure," and left it like that. He had other things to do.

Gordon went home irritated. He looked at the boxes and piles on the floor, and decided he'd had enough of them for one day. He made a fresh pot of tea, found his book, and retired to the conservatory, where he read almost continually as day turned to dusk, then to night. Finally, at an hour he dared not even glance at, he submitted himself to bed, and to sleep.

~

Gordon looked through three more boxes in a little under three weeks. He found very little of relevance or interest in any of them, and towards the end of the third week, was feeling very low indeed. Even though he'd tried to contact Esme's daughter on several occasions, she'd been unable to come to the telephone. It was as if she, too, were trying to ignore him. In fact, it felt as if everything he wanted to do wasn't happening, and he felt victimised. It was just his silly paranoia, he knew, but he felt it all the same.

Gordon sat down on the lounge floor with the sun setting, and opened the fifth box with little relish.

Unsurprisingly, as a creature of habit, Gordon had devised himself a regular routine of searching. It kept him going, allowing him to switch off, follow each step, and still reach the end of the box. He'd take out the clothes first, then the pictures, then the letters and envelopes. Every forty minutes or so he'd go to the kitchen and make himself a pot of tea, and, if his guilt would let him, sneak a custard cream biscuit or two onto the side of the saucer.

As he'd drink his tea, he'd sit and ponder over what he'd discovered about Brenda's father. The various bundles of over-familiar letters from women seemed to paint Monty as a bit of a ladies man, and it was a side Gordon had never expected. By the time he'd first met him, Monty's wandering eye had been severely curtailed by Cissy, who'd continued to keep him on a tight rein throughout their marriage. There were also numerous receipts from an exclusive London club Monty often frequented, some amounting to quite tidy sums. It appeared he'd been a very social man in his day.

Gordon settled into looking through the box. As he delved deeper his attention was caught by some old papers with some familiar names. As he flicked through them, he recognised them as old answer sheets for the Race, and his heavy heart skipped a beat.

As organiser, Gordon had access to all previous subjects. What were never passed on, however, were the participants answers, and as far as Gordon knew, they were either thrown away at the end of the year or returned to the Racers who asked for them. Here, however, were the essays originating from the time when Uncle had been the organiser.

Hoping he could have stored his envelope amongst them, Gordon turned each page over separately. Within moments he found himself looking at Brenda's handwriting, on papers from before he'd known her. He ran his hand over them, read her answers, used his fingers to follow the flow of her words. A wave of loss came over him. He longed to be young again. He rode it out, and was pleased to find his spirit rejuvenated. He'd found something of Brenda's he hadn't known existed, and that made him happy. Within minutes, he'd completed the box, yet still hadn't found the envelope, so Monty's name remained on the list of suspects. Gordon rested back on his haunches, and rubbed his stiff neck.

Brenda's father had been quite unapproachable when Gordon had first known him, only ever interested in people of his own age. When they'd announced their engagement, he'd barely smiled, and only shook Gordon's hand when Gordon stuck it out in front of him. Even the speech he'd given at their wedding had been embarrassingly brief and to the point.

But as time had gone on, and Monty's marriage slipped into decline, the two men's' relationship had improved. Monty, perhaps in an effort to avoid contact with his wife, offered to help with jobs around the house, to which Gordon readily accepted. When, at last, Cissy all but left for good, Monty found solace in his boyhood love of fishing, and the two men would often go and sit by the side of a river, Gordon dabbling with his rod and line, and Monty setting his bait, sitting back, and waiting for the bite. On these days, the two would talk about anything and everything as the water hushed by. Brenda and the children would come and visit them, if only for an hour or so, and they'd be a little family, sitting alone by the river, with nothing much else to do than to amuse each other. In the end, Gordon had to admit, he'd grown quite close to Monty, and his sudden death had hit him hard.

Sorting through the boxes reaffirmed a lot of what the two of them had spoken of. Gordon came across names he remembered, places where he'd visited, and he found the work both exhilarating and exhausting at the same time. As he went through, he hived off a collection of pictures and letters he thought Vee might like to see, and was pleased when she accepted his offer to visit her.

He combined the trip with another visit to the home, but Esme still hadn't made any contact. He scribbled a note on a writing pad asking her to contact him as soon as she got back, and left it in her pigeon hole.

It was past mid-February now, and though it was cold, it wasn't a chill that cut through you. Gordon knocked several times on Vee's front door, and when he got no response, he ventured around the side, through the gate, and found her, wrapped up, reading a book on the patio.

"You all right out here?" he asked, sitting down in the chair next to her.

She looked at him over the half-moon spectacles that rested midway down her nose. "All right? God, yes. I always believe you've got to get out as much as you can. Feel the sun on your face. Never did me any harm. Is that my brothers stuff?" she asked.

He placed it on the table. "Yes."

"Found his envelope, yet?"

"No. But I'm not even half-way through. Plenty of time."

Vee smiled, "What's taking you so long?"

"I don't know. It's hard not to stop and read everything. It makes me feel very nostalgic."

"Of course it does," she exclaimed, "You're the organiser of the Race, remember. The whole things nostalgia, isn't it?"

"Maybe."

They went inside, where the heating, thankfully, was on quite high, and looked through what he'd brought.

"I expect he took you to that club?" Vee asked, holding up a photograph of Monty shaking another man's hand in front of its grandiose doors.

Gordon looked up, "Yes," he said.

Vee smiled, "Thought he would. He took most men he knew there at least once. It was a bit of one-upmanship, I always suspected."

Gordon grunted, "If it was," he said, "It didn't work on me. Far too stuffy for my liking."

Vee sighed. "He was a good-looking man, my brother," she said, "If it hadn't been for the excesses, he'd have kept his looks." She ran a hand over his picture, then pulled it away. "Who's next on your list?" she asked.

"Next?" Gordon said, surprised, "I don't know. Haven't been able to think past the next box just lately. Got any suggestions?"

"I'd be lying if I said I hadn't given it some thought," she said, "I reckon it should be someone we know is still alive, hopefully it'll be a bit less depressing."

Gordon smiled. "You might be right. How about Phillip? Can you get hold of him?"

"I can try, though knowing him, he's probably moved on. I'm due a letter, soon. His address will be on that. Lawrence or Elizabeth may be a safer bet. You might even get them both at once."

Gordon thought about it for a second, and then nodded. "It makes sense," he said.

"I've got an address for Lawrence. Its a few years old, but, who knows, he may still be there, or even have left a forwarding address. It's got to be more exciting than looking through Monty's old things."

"Oh, I don't mind Monty's stuff."

"Even so," she said, standing up, "I'll get it for you."

~

With his hopes raised slightly, he returned to the bungalow. He looked at the boxes he had left to do, and found that he wanted to finish them before moving on to anyone else. He'd never liked loose ends. Besides, he almost had a whole year still to go. There was no need to rush.

He knew he shouldn't take as long with the remaining boxes as he had with the first five, so he honed his attentions solely towards finding the envelope. Within a couple of hours, he'd emptied three more, and would have soldiered on had his tiredness not overcome him.

At ten o'clock that evening, Gordon wrote a letter to Lawrence's old address, and laid it carefully on the low table beside the bed. He could finish the remaining boxes tomorrow, post the letter, and pay a visit to Pamela and Simon to catch up with Trudie and Denise. With these predefined tasks to complete, Gordon drifted off to sleep, happy and content and not the least bit aware of the secrets his investigations were about to uncover.

LONDON, CISSY, AND A WOODEN CHAIR

The next day, Gordon was woken early by the ring of the telephone. His head felt fuzzy, and it took him a few seconds to realise he was no longer dreaming. He turned and noted the time, 07:18.

He popped an imperial mint and swung his old legs out of bed, straight into his slippers. He reached the telephone halfway through his answer phone message.

"Hello, Dad," Pamela said.

"Pam," he replied, wiping the sleep from his eyes, "What's happened?"

"Sorry about the time. I was wondering whether you could look after the kids. Can I come round?"

"Now?"

"If it's all right?"

Gordon looked at himself in the hall mirror. "Of course, love," he said, "Come as soon as you're ready." He replaced the receiver, went into the bathroom and splashed water onto his face. "Great," he said. "Cold, tired and wet."

He had time to brush his teeth, shave and make some coffee before Pamela arrived.

"Dad, I'm so sorry about this," she said. "But I don't know who else to try."

"Coffee?" Gordon asked.

"Please. Just a small cup. Black, one sugar."

"Are you on your own?" he asked.

"Yes, I've left the kids in bed," she answered, "Didn't want to alarm them. Simon's there."

Pamela ran her hands through her hair and sighed. "I need you to take them, just for a few days. Me and Simon need some time alone to try and sort things out."

Gordon paced the floor slowly. "Of course. I'll be happy to take them. What's happening?"

"A lot of things. Too much to try and sort out with the kids around as well. Are you positive you're up to it?"

"Up to it? Who knows? It's been ten years since I've looked after any children. But I'm sure I'll manage. There were four of you, remember."

"I know, but children are different, nowadays."

Gordon smiled, "Of course they are. But then so am I. Don't worry, I'll be fine. Now, is there anything I can do for you and Simon?"

"I don't think so," Pamela said. "Looking after the kids is heaps."

"When are they coming?"

"Today, if that's any good," Pamela said.

"No time like the present. Do they have school?"

"Half-term," Pamela said.

Gordon handed Pam her drink, and they discussed the children's routines, likes and dislikes. Pamela coached him to tell them Mum and Dad were enjoying a short break away.

"What are all these boxes for?" she asked as she was about to leave. "You're not moving, are you?"

"No, No. I'm just sorting some stuff out, too," he replied, "Maybe it's something in the air."

With the imminent arrival of the children, Gordon suddenly had a deadline to meet. He washed and showered with purpose, ate a small breakfast, and set about finishing the last boxes before the girls arrived.

Three hours later, he'd managed to empty the last box. He'd sifted through all of Monty's debris, and except for one intriguing ticket, it had been to no avail. Monty's envelope had not been found. Gordon sat disgruntled on the floor, knowing the only thing left to do now was to put it all carefully back in again.

When that was done, Gordon moved the boxes out into the garage. They'd be far more accessible there, should a need arise to look through them again. Besides, the garage was nearly empty, their last car having been sold shortly after Brenda's death.

As he placed the final box against the back wall, he heard a familiar beep from outside. Gordon opened the garage door from within, summoned the biggest smile he could find, and waved at the two children, who, from what he could make out, were doing exactly the same to him.

By the time they'd reached the door, Simon had pulled away, and the three of them were together. They stood around as if they'd just been shipwrecked.

"Good morning," Gordon said.

"Hello, Gramps," Trudie replied, and then added, without hesitation, "Mum and Dad are going to split up, aren't they?"

Gordon's words caught in his throat. Pamela had been right, children had changed.

"I don't honestly know," he said.

Silence descended once more.

"Now," Gordon rallied, "I thought the two of you might like to plan our day out," he said.

He watched as both children's eyes lit up. Gordon figured it must be a real relief not to be caught in the crossfire of their parents. "Day out?" Trudie asked.

"Oh yes," he answered, "Tomorrow we're going to London."

"London," Denise repeated, with such an awe that Gordon wanted to get on the train there and then.

He had two reasons for the trip. Obviously, it was a great place to entertain the children for a whole day, and secondly, he wanted to go and see Monty's club. He'd already rung Chris and Louise that morning to ask whether they were up to going, and although Chris said he'd already arranged to do some work, Louise had jumped at the offer. He'd rung the club to confirm with them his validity in going, and with only a little persuasion, they'd agreed.

For the rest of the day, the girls found it near impossible to keep quiet. He'd given them a tourist map, and told them to decide where they wanted to go. Many debates ensued, until Trudie came to him with their list.

"It's going to take you all week to see this lot," he said. "But then that was my fault for not tying you down enough. You can have a maximum of four places to visit, two from you, two from Denise. Okay?" Gordon waited for the tantrum, or at least a little foot dragging.

Instead Trudie took the paper back from him and said, "Okay, Gramps," and trotted off for the next bout of negotiation with her sister.

Gordon felt relieved. Both children seemed to be giving him an easy time. He wasn't sure if they'd be doing the same with their parents. Pamela rang him that evening, told them they'd ended up in Cornwall, and spoke to the children for nearly an hour. Gordon wondered if she was speaking to Simon for as long.

The next day, the taxi drew up outside their house with Louise already in it. It was raining, so all three ran from the bungalow, threw their bags in the boot and got in. "Hello," Louise said, "Sorry about being late, we can still catch the train, can't we?"

Gordon looked at his watch. "Plenty of time," he said.

Gordon had bought them first class tickets, and now the rush hour was over, they had the whole compartment to themselves.

When they'd settled down, and the train was pulling off, Louise brought out some puzzle books for the children. One each, no quarrelling. Gordon smiled at Louise, and closed his eyes, letting the motion of the train lull him into a blissful semi-consciousness.

He wasn't altogether looking forward to going back to the club. As he'd told Vee, Monty had taken him there on a single occasion, and Gordon had felt like a fish out of water. When it came to it, he simply hadn't come from the sort of people who did such things. His parents had been altogether different.

The train arrived a little late. From the station, they took the tube to the Natural History museum, where they spent an enjoyable couple of hours, before going to a park and then onto a restaurant that Gordon had pre-booked.

After lunch, they travelled on to the Planetarium, and while Louise and the girls went inside, Gordon visited the club. He walked in the drizzle, stopping every now and then to look into shop windows at whatever caught his eye. He'd told them he'd be there around three, so he still had another half-an-hour to fill.

He stopped at a small bookshop he'd found many years before. Gordon had read a lot of books in his youth, in his room when he should have been asleep.

He'd never thought one day it'd be his profession.

Even now, as he stood browsing, hidden in the rows, he found it strange to see his name on some of the spines. He flicked through one, stopping and reading with the usual distant feeling his own words gave him, as if he hadn't been the one who'd written them at all. In his later years, Gordon's work had slowed. After Brenda's death, it had all but disappeared. Whatever he wrote he found empty, however many times he had tried to rewrite it, and this had given rise to a great deal of despair within him. If he couldn't find solace in his work, he had little but the Race left to do.

As usual, time in the bookshop passed quickly, and when he next looked at the clock above the counter it read five past three. Gordon smiled and put the book back in its space.

Luckily, he thought to himself as he approached the club, his name still opened doors, even if nowadays he had to remind people of exactly who he was. It was his name that had allowed him into the club. That and the ticket he'd found in Monty's belongings.

It had a number on it, and the club had told him it was the ticket to a locker Monty still had in his name. Gordon had explained Monty had passed on, and given Vee as a reference. They'd rung him back and said he could indeed open the locker, if he attended in person with the ticket and some identification.

When he arrived, he gave his name and showed them his passport, and within a minute, a small diminutive man appeared and asked Gordon to follow him. Silently, they descended some steps and entered a room which contained hundreds of metal lockers. Gordon stuck close to his guide's side, which wasn't easy considering the man's pace and manoeuvrability, dodging in and out of the aisles like a rat in a maze.

Abruptly, the man stopped, causing Gordon to bump into him. He apologised and took the key he offered. The man showed him which locker it opened, and Gordon slid the key into the lock, and turned it until there was a definite click. Gordon held his breath. In his mind, he pictured opening the door and the envelope sitting there, dusty, but recognisable.

As the drawer opened, a musty smell wafted up which made Gordon's heart quicken, and when it would go no further, he bent down to see what was within.

Initially, he could see nothing, and he cursed as he thought of all the time and expense he'd gone through to get there. But then, as his eyes adjusted to the dark inside the locker, he realised there was something in it after all, flat against the base. Gordon reached a trembling hand in, fumbled along the metallic bottom, and slowly brought it out into the light.

The man beside him stirred a little as he watched Gordon hold it up.

Gordon's frown deepened. He wasn't prepared for this. He had, as he'd intended to do, found an envelope. The problem was it wasn't the one he'd been expecting.

~

After leaving the club, he walked for a full five minutes before deciding to open the envelope. At first, he thought it might be empty, some leftover from a hurried departure many years previous. Certainly, the locker looked as if it had been totally cleaned out. He mentally kicked himself when he thought that he should've asked the man if he'd known when Monty had left, but he wasn't going back in there now.

He found a tree lined square, sat down on an empty bench, and opened the envelope. Inside, two photographs were lightly stuck together. Unsurprisingly, Cissy was the centre of attention in both. The first depicted her kissing another man, nothing controversial, just a peck on the cheek of old acquaintances.

The second showed her walking down the steps of an apartment block. It was the classic modern day 'revelation' photograph - a young woman sneaking out of her lover's house early in the morning. Whilst it wasn't the result Gordon had been hoping for, the two pictures revealed something darker. Left there in that locker, they had been a story just waiting to be found.

Gordon looked at the first photograph again. He noted Cissy was still wearing her wedding ring, something she'd given back to Monty when she'd moved out. Her own face obscured the man's, but Gordon wasn't interested in him. It was knowledge enough to know she'd had an extramarital affair, and that Monty had known. Who it was with was irrelevant.

Gordon met the others outside Madame Tussauds, and all four had an indulgent afternoon snack in a fast food restaurant of the girls' choice. He toyed with the idea of showing the photographs to Louise, just to share his findings with somebody else, but thought better of it. Louise had never met Monty, and however impatient he was feeling, he knew he ought to show Vee first.

The trip back home was quite sedate. The children had obviously worn themselves out, and sat, quietly, looking out the window towards the pattern of lights emitted from the various towns passing by. Gordon was still feeling troubled, and as he sat opposite them, he turned the envelope over and over in his hands.

"Why don't you get some rest?" Louise said, smiling at him. He was obviously looking as tired as he felt.

"As long as you're okay?" he asked.

"We're okay, aren't we girls?" The two girls sucked on their lollies and nodded.

Gordon closed his eyes, and smiled to himself. He'd expected to have less questions to answer by the end of the day, but now, as they all headed home at some speed, he found he had more.

~

The next day, Chris volunteered to look after the children, whilst Gordon went to visit Vee.

She answered the door brighter than ever, taking Gordon's hat and coat, and ushering him through to the dining room. Tea was made, including two pieces of her homemade chocolate sponge. Gordon breathed in the smell of the baking that hung in the air.

"This place takes me back," Gordon said, as he wandered around the room.

"I don't use it for much nowadays," she said, "But it makes me smile whenever I come in here."

When Frank had become organiser, he redecorated their dining room in homage to that room in Uncle's house where Gordon had first learned about the Race. The result was an old fashioned, beautiful room, with plush carpets, and a large grandfather clock. He'd even opened up the brick fireplace.

"I don't know why he was so fanatical about it," Vee continued. "He just got this bee in his bonnet one day, and off he went. I tried to tell him no-one would have minded what the place looked like, but nothing was going to stop him."

Gordon joined Vee at the table. "I found an envelope in London."

"Oh, that's good..." Vee started, then seeing the look on his face, added, "Isn't it?"

"Not really. It's not a Race envelope."

Not knowing quite how to continue, he pushed the white oblong across the deep brown of the mahogany table. Keeping an inquisitive eye on Gordon, Vee opened it and retrieved the pictures. She turned them over, and put on her glasses. For an instant, Gordon saw an expression of pain on her face, but it quickly melted into one of contempt, and she placed the photographs face up on the table.

She took her spectacles off, but didn't look at Gordon. "That's Cissy for you," she said, almost as a sigh. "The lady was a tramp, and nothing more." Gordon waited a moment. The force of her response was surprising; he couldn't remember Vee ever disliking anyone. Vee sensed it, adding, "Believe me, you don't get to ninety-two managing to like everyone, Gordon."

"So, you think he knew about her affair?" he asked.

"Affairs," Vee corrected. "Oh, yes, he knew. He turned a blind eye. He loved her too much not to. Don't get me wrong, my brother was no saint in his younger days, but when he met Cissy there was only ever her." Vee paused for a second, and then picked up the second photograph again. "She was an awful woman, still is for all I know. An absolute tramp. Nothing more. I shall dislike her till the day I die." Vee went quiet. She put her glasses in her case, sighed, and looked out of the window. "She killed him."

Vee stopped. Gordon could tell she wasn't going to offer any more explanation unless he asked.

"How do you mean?" he prompted.

"Just what I said. If it were not for her, Monty may still be alive today. But he had no more reason for living after she'd gone. He tried, but it was no good."

"Brenda said he died of a heart attack," Gordon said, confused. "He'd been gardening at his house. How was Cissy involved in that?"

Vee looked at him, and shook her head in preparation for what she was about to admit. "I'm afraid the heart attack was just a deceit, Gordy.

One we were both hoping to conceal forever. But I don't see why she," Vee spat that word with venom, "should get away with it."

Gordon rubbed his temple with his left hand. "Please... explain," he said.

"Monty was found in a garden, that much was true. Hell, I found him, I should know, but it wasn't his garden, Gordy, it was mine.

"I came home after a visit to a friend, and started to settle in as you do after some time away. Frank had stayed there to do a commission, so I had the place to myself. I spent a couple of hours in the house before I sensed a change. It was little things, but they added up to the fact that the house was not exactly how I'd left it.

"That was when I went to check the doors. It didn't really occur to me that whoever it was may still be in the house. I guess I've always just survived. The back door was unlocked, which confirmed my feelings. There were no broken windows, though, and in a way, that was the moment I first thought of Monty. Not that I thought he still had a key, but just that leaving things unlocked and undone was a trait of his. Maybe his spirit was in the house."

Vee's chin started to tremble. She took a deep breath, smiled to herself, and tried to carry on.

"I went outside and saw him immediately. It was late in the evening...and frost had started to form...on the grass."

The memory was too much for her. Vee signalled for Gordon to get the box of tissues from the top drawer of the sideboard. As he passed them over, the waft of lavender invaded the air. She took a tissue and held it shakily under her eyes. Gordon found it hard to see her so upset.

"He was sitting in a chair, one from the shed I'd earmarked to throw away. He used to sit in that chair, when he was a lad. We used to have one each and we'd sit in the garden and he'd pretend to be a King and I'd be his daughter, the princess... I knew he was dead before I reached him, the way his head was tipped back, but I kept walking, anyway. It's not something you're ever warned about. Never prepared for. No-one ever says, one day, you may find your brother, the man with whom you spent so many years with, dead.

"I felt for a pulse, but found none. I bent and said a prayer. I was already crying. Then I turned, retreated into the house, and rang for the ambulance."

"For a few days afterwards, we thought, hoped, he'd had a heart attack, but, let's face it, no-one has a heart attack sitting in a chair in the garden in the middle of February. I think Brenda had some misgivings about the situation, too, but neither of us said anything.

"Then the results were back, and it was hypothermia. In his pocket they'd found a note to Cissy, confessing his love for her, and saying he would be waiting to comfort her in the next life. I never gave it to her. Never gave her the pleasure of knowing that's what had happened."

"Is that why you kept it a secret, too?"

Vee nodded. "Yes. If what had really happened became general knowledge, and that awful woman had found out... both Brenda and I decided to keep it under wraps."

"What about his will?" Gordon asked.

"He never made one," Vee explained. "Everything went to Brenda and Jack. Cissy didn't want to get involved with us again, anyway. She'd found a new man, a new well to empty."

"I never knew," Gordon said.

"No. You were never supposed to. As for me, I can never forget the image of Monty dragging that chair out into the garden, and just sitting himself down, waiting for death to take him. He must have felt desperate. From that day, I've wondered what might have happened if I'd been home. I wonder whether he'd gone there because he'd wanted to talk to me first."

Gordon sat with Vee a while longer, until he saw her steely resolve return. Then he got his coat, showed himself out, and returned home, full of sadness and doubt about everything he'd held dear. Gordon hadn't picked up on Monty's anguish, either, and as a result a person he thought he knew had died alone. Vee had lost her brother, which in turn had cemented a hatred he would not have thought possible in one with such compassion. And Brenda, yet again, had lied to him. He understood why the two women had wanted to keep people in the dark; he just didn't know why his own wife hadn't felt she'd been able to trust him.

When he opened the door, he was pleased to see that at least the bungalow appeared tidy. He found a note from Chris explaining he and the girls had gone to the bowling alley, and before too long, the happy crowd returned, full of tales of the strike that got away, and it cheered Gordon up to listen to them.

Chris stayed and cooked a delicious dinner which they all enjoyed. Then, just when Gordon was beginning to smile with ease, the phone rang, and Christopher went to answer. "Trudie," he said, when he returned, "It's your Mum."

Trudie frowned, and then shrugged her shoulders. She dragged herself out to the hall, and Denise followed dutifully.

"She sounded very downbeat," Chris told Gordon.

"Oh, dear," Gordon said. He wondered how much more bad news he could take in one day.

They listened to the tone of Trudie's voice, and it did nothing to raise any hopes. They heard the phone go down in the hall, and Trudie came back in with a face of misery. "Everything all right?" Gordon asked.

"Don't know," she said, "Mum's going to pick us up tomorrow, and we're going away for a few days, she says."

"That sounds all right," Chris said.

"Dad won't be coming though."

"Oh."

Tears started to well in her eyes, Gordon's heart fell an eternity down. "It'll just be the three of us." Without a word, Denise went to Trudie and the two girls hugged. They both knew what it meant.

"Forgive me for saying so, Dad," Chris whispered, "But I don't think I ever want to get married."

"You know," Gordon started, "I'm starting to think you may have a point."

SIMON, TONY, AND A BLACK STUDDED EARRING

When, the next morning, Pamela parked the car in the bungalow drive, the girls still hadn't finished packing. She told them to hurry up, and then had a chat with Gordon about how they'd been. No effort was made to divulge what had happened between her and Simon, and at this moment, Gordon didn't want to know. So much was going on in his own life that he was happy not to get involved. He waved them off at ten-thirty, with Pamela's parting remark still in his ears.

"Simon may come to see you," she'd said, as he'd closed her door.

"Why me?" he'd asked.

"He thinks you like him."

As the car had disappeared out of sight, he remembered how once he'd hoped families got easier as time went on. "Silly old Gordy," he said to himself, and retreated inside.

It crossed his mind that what he'd really like to do today was to close all the curtains, defrost a loaf of bread, and spend the rest of the day in isolation, eating buttered toast, and not answering the door to anyone.

At eleven o'clock, the letterbox banged, and Gordon went to answer it, before remembering this was the normal time for the postman to deliver the mail. On the floor, he found the assortment of letters which he flicked through on his way back to the bedroom. Apart from the heating bill and some junk mail, there was a letter addressed to him in beautifully scripted handwriting. Compared to the cold typeface of the other correspondence, it felt like a breath of fresh air. He opened it, and inside found a letter in the same handwriting, with an address at the top he thought he recognised. On further reading, he realised the writer, a lady by the name of Margaret, was now living in the house he'd sent Lawrence's letter to. She'd received Gordon's correspondence, and wanted to tell him what she knew.

The letter explained that she had a son in a town nearby, and would be down in around three weeks to visit him, if he had some time available then. Gordon was intrigued. Is this another mystery in the making? he thought as he read, and then, Can I handle any more?

"Of course, I can," he said to himself, and wrote a quick reply detailing a time and a place to meet. He balked at his own handwriting, spidery and illegible in places. He had become lazy with it, so he rewrote it again, a little better, and placed it by the foot of the front door so he wouldn't forget to take it with him. At last, some progress, he thought. He would like to have another go at finding Monty's envelope, but the only person he could think of to help him with Monty's would be Cissy, and right now, he wasn't ready to face her. This, overall, meant he had absolutely nothing to do, so he fell back on what he used to do so well, writing.

The hours went by. Gordon no longer wrote for other people and had dropped his agent many years ago, though the two kept in touch with the odd phone call. Now, whenever he wrote, it was no longer the smooth stream of words that used to come to him, but a constant battle with a little pessimistic voice inside his head that constantly suggested his work was not worth the paper it was being written on.

He stopped at two o'clock, made himself some beans on toast, and relaxed watching some old family home movies. They starred Brenda and the three younger children, and he found himself wishing he'd bought the camera a little earlier so he could have captured something of Graeme's earlier years. The tapes were always a menagerie of pictures, blended together with little deftness. One point, you'd be looking at a party for one of the children, then, the screen would flicker, and there'd be Brenda, in the garden, or Gordon himself, relaxing in a chair. He listened to the old voices, and smiled at the jokes and the little sayings that were thrown back and forth.

When he woke up, it was three fifteen. He splashed cold water on his face, and quickly popped down to the local post office with the letter. When he arrived back half-an-hour later, Simon was on his doorstep. Gordon dredged up a little guilt from his depleted stock of emotions, and invited him inside. As Gordon made the tea, Simon sat uncharacteristically quietly.

There was a pause for the best part of a minute, as both men sat at the table stirring their drinks. Then Simon said, "Sorry about this, Gordon," and the genuineness in his voice brought a sudden lump to Gordon's throat.

"Can you explain to me just exactly what you're sorry about, Simon? Between the pair of you, I've been kept completely in the dark." Though you're not the first, he added, silently.

"Of course, it's the least we..., I, could do. How were the girls?"

Gordon, aware he'd just changed the subject, said, "They were a pleasure to look after. They obviously missed you."

"Did they?" Simon said, surprised.

"Yes, I'd say so," Gordon comforted, knowing it was what Simon needed to hear. "Now, tell me what's been happening, and don't spare me any details."

Simon spoke. He was nervous, depressed, confused. At times, he spoke in riddles, at others, he barely spoke at all. The hands on the clock swung round, and by the time they reached seven o'clock, Simon had given him most of what he needed to know. It hadn't been what he'd expected. Nothing is, he thought.

Gordon agreed to talk to Pam on his behalf, and even offered him a temporary room at the bungalow, which he declined. He left saying he would ring Gordon tomorrow.

It was dark outside and the wind had gotten up so as to make walking anywhere unpleasant. Gordon went around the bungalow checking the windows and pulling the curtains. One by one, his eyes on the outside world were shut out, bringing intimacy into the bungalow, intimacy for one.

When he reached the kitchen windows, he didn't even bother to turn the light on. As he bent over the marble effect work surface, where shadows from branches were thrown from the night's half-moon, he thought he saw a movement outside, and stopped, his famous paranoia kicking in. Gordon looked behind him. He'd turned every light out in the bungalow, so whoever it was couldn't see he was there. Gordon stood still and waited, cursing that he'd not taken better care of the back garden last summer. There were too many overgrown bushes, too many evergreens overrunning the edge of the garden. Anybody could be hiding out there. God, they could even get to the edge of the house without him seeing if they were careful. And why hadn't he fitted that security light like he told himself he'd do? Christopher, good old Christopher, was even willing to do it for him, but, stubbornly, he'd refused.

A thought crossed his mind that he ought to check the telephone line, to make sure it hadn't been cut, but he dismissed it as craziness, and convinced himself it was more important to stay by the window.

Then another light gust of wind tugged at the bushes on the right side of the garden, and for a moment, silhouetted, the shoulder and arm of a person appeared, and was then pulled back. It was there - he'd seen it. Gordon had proof, nothing he could show anyone, but someone was there. He was more frightened than he'd been in a while.

Bushes moved against the direction of the wind, and he realised whoever was out there was on the move. Then a noise, heard through the partially open window, a crack of wood splintering. It sounded like the fence - something else he'd intended to fix. Then nothing, and Gordon knew they'd gone. He went to the phone, and rang the only person he felt he could depend on.

~

Tony's van pulled up fifteen minutes later, and Gordon felt immediately at ease. Tony met him at the back door, gave him the spare torch he was carrying, and the pair walked into the back garden.

"Whereabouts?" Tony said.

"Just over there," Gordon replied, "Behind the bushes."

Gordon watched as Tony trod carefully to where he'd pointed. He squatted down, moved methodically up to the fence, the palm of his hand sweeping as a blind man's cane, using touch where his eyes were lacking. He reached the fence, and stood up. Gordon went to him.

"Nothing obvious," Tony said.

"There was a noise like the fence breaking," Gordon explained.

Tony stepped back, and followed the level of the top of the fence. "Here we go," he called back.

Gordon flashed his torch to where Tony stood, saw the broken fence panel, the piece of wood splintered upwards.

"Was that there before?" Tony asked.

Gordon shook his head. He let the torch beam drop, and as he did so, it hit upon something reflective on the muddy ground. Gordon bent and inspected. There was a dull piece of paper, balled up with some silver foil. He put them in his coat pocket.

"Well," Tony said, "Your fence has definitely been broken, but it'd be impossible to prove that someone had only just done it."

"I know," Gordon said, and both men turned towards the bungalow.

~

"Sorry Gordon," Tony said as they stood in the well-lit kitchen. "That was a bit fruitless."

"Maybe not entirely," the older man replied, putting two cups of tea on the side, and holding out the objects he'd found.

Tony looked at them carefully. "What's this?" he asked.

"Hopefully more proof. Though how useful it is, I don't know."

Gordon gave the two pieces of paper to Tony, who turned them over a few times. "It's just a chewing gum wrapper and a receipt," he said, confused.

"But the receipt has today's date on it, and the chewing gum is one of its items. Which probably means..."

"It must have been dropped today," Tony finished.

"Exactly," Gordon said.

"But it still doesn't tell us who it is."

"And I never really expected to find out, I'll leave that sort of thing to Sherlock Holmes, but it does prove I wasn't seeing things."

"I never thought you were," Tony told him. They finished their tea in silence, and then Tony turned and walked towards the front door.

"You all right?" Gordon asked.

"Yes," Tony said. "I'm certain you've nothing to worry about, but I'll fetch my stuff, anyway. Best if I sleep here tonight."

They had a supper of vegetables and tinned ravioli, sitting quite openly in the conservatory, so as to ward off the watcher should they return. They talked to the sound of rain hitting the conservatory roof.

"I don't know what Catherine's up to," Tony said, stretching his body till his shoulders popped. "But I don't want to spoil it by asking, if you know what I mean."

"Yes," Gordon agreed, dabbing his mouth with a paper napkin.

"I've managed to see Jessie three times already in the past week. I know it's rubbish, but somehow I feel more like her dad, the more I see of her."

"Well," Gordon said, "perhaps you're both able to learn more about each other. That level of contact has been missing for a while."

"Tell me about it," Tony said, "What about you? Anything going on?"

Gordon sighed, "What isn't?"

They talked until Gordon grew tired, and he left the younger man up watching the television.

When Gordon rose the next day, Tony had already left, tidying the spare bedroom to a higher standard than he'd found it. When Gordon went into the kitchen, Tony had prepared some breakfast, too, and left a note thanking Gordon for his hospitality, saying that he'd try and organise him and Jessica to come around one evening in the coming week.

Gordon ate breakfast, wrote until there were enough passers-by to feel safe, and ventured back into the garden, where the broken fence panel conveyed less menace than it had done the previous night.

After checking the neighbour's curtains were still closed, Gordon erected his stepladder over the fence and climbed in. Their garden was in a similar state to his own, maybe it's an age thing, he thought. Gordon bent and searched around the tall grass, expecting to find nothing but a couple of juicy slugs. Then he felt a sting in his finger that made him recoil his hand. Just his luck to find a bee at this time of year, he thought. However, it wasn't a bee that had done it. Instead, sticking from his right index finger was a small black plastic ball. He brought it closer, then took it out with his left thumb and forefinger, and inspected it. It was a black stud earring, not rusty. Gordon scratched his head. It was the sort of thing Louise would wear. Maybe it was another fragment left by last night's prowler. Gordon pocketed it, and climbed back over the fence before his neighbour reported him to the police.

When he got back inside, he rang Pamela and left a message on her machine, then donned his coat, and left to do some shopping. Fresh coffee was top of his list.

On the way, he passed the police station. He stopped outside and wondered whether it was worth reporting the previous night's incident. He didn't like the prospect of involving the police, but, against his own judgement, Gordon pushed open the heavy doors and walked inside. The small, uninhabited, square reception was as sterile as a hospital outpatients, with the only noticeable difference being the crime prevention posters and leaflets pinned to the notice board. It had always been difficult for Gordon to face the fact that crime was there in his town; perhaps it was a side effect of his paranoia that he didn't like to accept he had it for a reason.

He rang the bell, and, from the small office behind the reception desk someone called, "Won't be a moment."

Gordon waited patiently, and the receptionist appeared less than a minute later. She took down the details of who, when, and where, and said they'd send someone round to try and ascertain exactly how and why. Unfortunately, she explained, they were very busy at the moment, so he may have to wait for up to five days. Gordon shrugged his shoulders and left, as disillusioned as he'd entered.

On his way into town, a passing car beeped, and he just caught a glimpse of Chris and Louise waving at him before they rounded a corner. Gordon raised his arm and waved, though he doubted they'd have seen it. He smiled, just seeing them made him happier.

Gordon popped into a newsagent and bought a computer magazine, stopping off for his morning tea and Eccles cake in the department store to read it. It was Friday, so Jason, the waiter he'd first met in January wasn't there. The usual full time staff were, though, and their familiarity helped lift his spirits further. Gordon leafed through the magazine looking for anything he might have heard Louise tell him about, but after ten minutes he'd exhausted every possible word he understood, and still knew nothing more than when he'd started.

On the way back, slightly dejected and feeling all of his sixty-four years, he stopped off at the home, and learnt Esme had at last reported back by phone, but hadn't seemed the slightest bit interested in taking Gordon's message. She wasn't coming back for at least a fortnight. Expecting nothing to happen for the next few days, Gordon booked himself in for some shifts, and the harassed looking receptionist gratefully accepted them.

When he got back to the bungalow there was a message from Pam asking him whether he'd like to come over for lunch. He rang back and accepted, and she came and picked him up. There was just the two of them as they sat down at Pamela's kitchen table to a ploughman's salad. The girls were at a friend's, and Simon hadn't returned home since Gordon had last seen him.

"I assume he's okay," she said, with alarming indifference. "I haven't heard anything."

She poured her father a shandy. Gordon could tell she was happier. "Well, I don't know what he's been telling you, Dad, but I thought I'd let you know my side."

Gordon broke into the warm bread. "He came round to see me yesterday," he said.

"I thought he might." Pam pulled her long blonde hair back and secured it with a elastic tie. "I expect he told you he thought I'm having an affair," she didn't wait for Gordon to agree, "Well, he's wrong, but however much I try and convince him otherwise, that's the only way he can justify it."

This time Gordon cut in. "So, what has happened?"

Pamela looked at her father for a moment. Then she looked down at her plate. "Last year, Simon had a fling with some woman at work. He did his best to deny it, but he had to come clean in the end. He's no good at keeping secrets. We nearly fell apart then, but instead went through the standard stuff. He said he'd change, I gave him another chance.

"But soon after I could sense it had been the wrong thing to do. He'd abused the trust I had in him, and there was no getting away from it. He wouldn't change, and I couldn't ignore what had happened. Before long, we'd just slotted back into the old way of things. The bickering, the arguing, the mistrust.

"So, I'm calling it a day. I'm giving him the chance he so obviously wanted last year. I know it's going to be tough on the girls, but it's for the best in the long run. I'm sorry if this has put me in your bad books, Dad."

"You're sure..." Gordon started slowly.

Pam held her hand up, "I'm sure. It's going to be a lot of heartache, but it has to stop."

Gordon sighed. There was quiet. At last, he said, "Well, thank you for telling me. Obviously, it's sad, but I agree with what you say. I know how things can go wrong... Rest assured, I'll do everything I can to help."

Pam got up and kissed her dad on the cheek. "Thanks, Dad," she said.

Gordon finished his lunch and then left for home, full of food, but feeling deflated. It was still only February, and so many things were out of his control.

When he got in, there was another message on his answerphone, this time from Chris, asking if he wanted to come over that evening. In truth, he hardly felt up to it, but he rang back and accepted anyway. At least Chris and Louise didn't hold any surprises.

Or so he thought.

CHRIS, LOUISE, AND THE POLICE

When Gordon arrived at Chris and Louise's just before seven, he was promptly handed a generous glass of white Californian chardonnay, and told to make his way through to the lounge. There he found their small glass table laid for three, and an assortment of ten or so burning candles dotted around the otherwise unlit room. The only window in the room looked out over a busy junction adjacent to a parade of shops, and Gordon stood for a minute or so, watching the lights go by, thinking about very little.

After removing the cushions, Gordon made himself comfortable in a chair that used to be part of his old suite, and read the periodicals which were squashed into the wooden magazine rack beside it.

It was the same set-up whenever he came here for dinner. It was immediately informal, and he could relax as if it were his own home. There was something about Chris's tastes that mirrored his own, and some that simply surpassed them. Like the assortment of green and black olives dotted around in quaint glass bowls, with the extraordinarily mature cheese and sundried tomatoes that complemented them. Gordon was unable to stop himself from picking constantly at such food. It was like heaven on earth.

He kicked off his shoes and placed them behind the chair, making a mental note to try and remember their position at the end of the evening. Of course, even with only half a glass of wine inside him, he knew it would be a fruitless exercise, but at least he liked to think he'd tried.

As he relaxed back, eating with one hand, sipping with the other, he could hear the pair of them in the kitchen. That's how they liked to be in everything, he thought. Equal. They prepared their own dishes, working in each section of the small kitchen but not getting in each other's way. It was like watching a ballet. 'The Nut Cutlet Suite', he thought, and laughed aloud. The wine was certainly having an effect.

Chris and Louise left their guests to get on with entertaining themselves, only popping in every few minutes for a quick snatch of conversation before a call or a buzzer from the kitchen would pull them back in.

Gordon sat, a little hazy, within the flicker of the candles flames. He'd been through everything he'd wanted to read in last Sunday's newspapers. He'd come across an article fronted with a picture of a couple who'd have been about the same age as he and Brenda would be now. They were stood, arms around each other smiling happily at the camera, proud of their garden and of their lives, no doubt. For a few seconds, he did nothing else but think about Brenda, and what he would have given to have her there right now.

As people in his position couldn't help but do, Gordon often wondered why Brenda had been the one to go. In pretty much every way, he figured, she would've been able to provide more support to the family than he ever could, yet fate had seen to it he was the one who'd been left to cope.

"So, Dad," Chris said, carrying in a plate of garlic bread, "Where were you off to earlier?"

Gordon looked blankly at his son for a second, the wine slowing his brain, before smiling broadly at him. He was proud of Chris in so many ways. "Earlier?" he asked.

"Down the town? We beeped you?"

"Oh, yes. I was just shopping," he said.

"Only we thought you may have gone to the police station."

Gordon thought for a moment. "Oh, er, well, I did," he said, hesitantly, "How did you, er...?"

Louise came in with the wine bottle, "A-ha," she said, "We know all your secrets."

Gordon laughed, "I hope not."

"Top up?" Louise asked. Gordon nodded.

"Tony's doing some work for us," Chris explained, "A spot of decorating in the spare room. He told us about your prowler when he was here earlier."

Gordon frowned, "He didn't mention he was doing any decorating to me."

The two of them smiled in unison. "We asked him to keep it quiet," Louise said.

"Oh," Gordon accepted, without thinking. When he realised what they'd said, he frowned and added, "Why?"

Chris and Louise smiled together again. It was as if they'd been practising. They stayed silent.

"Come on, you two, what's so secret you can't tell your Dad?"

"Well, as it's you," Chris joked, "Follow me." He beckoned Gordon to follow him.

As he trailed behind his hobbling son, he asked, "How is your foot?"

"Oh, almost better," Chris said, coming to a stop outside the spare room door. "Okay, close your eyes."

Gordon complied. He heard Chris push the handle down, and then listened as the sweep of the door brushed against the top of the carpet. A click signalled he'd switched the light on, and even before he'd taken a step, Gordon could smell the fresh paint. It was as much as he could do to keep his eyes closed.

Louise caught them up, and said, "Take two steps in, but be careful not to swing your arms too much."

Gordon, feeling a little silly for the wine, made a sound like a baboon, and scratched under his arm pits, which made them all laugh. When he settled down, he moved forward, slowly, feeling the comfort of the carpet beneath his socks.

"Stop there," requested Chris. "Now, after three, open your eyes. One, two, three."

Gordon opened his eyes widely and looked. He blinked a couple of times, to try to cut out the glare of the overhead light. When his eyes had finally adjusted, he could make out coloured balloons punctuating the bright yellow walls.

There was no furniture yet, but the floor was covered with a thick beige carpet, partly obscured by a colourful rug decorated with trains, cars and clouds off to the right.

Gordon's subconscious registered it before he'd had chance to, causing the hairs on the back of his neck to instantly stand to attention. Then, as his brain caught up, he turned around to his son and partner, unable to suppress a beam that encompassed his face. "Is this what I think it's going to be?" he asked.

Once again, the two moved in unison, this time nodding their heads. He held out his arms, and they all hugged. "Congratulations," he said, his voice cracking with emotion. "I never thought I'd see the day."

"Nor did we," Louise said. "Nor did we."

"We hoped you'd like the news," Chris added.

"You'll never know how much," Gordon replied.

~

They made their way back to the lounge, and Chris put a slab of juicy lasagne on his father's plate.

"So, how long have you got to go?" Gordon asked.

"Oh, it's very early days," Chris said, "Sometime in October. We've not known ourselves very long, but it's been such a frustrating time. We know people say it's unlucky to talk about it, but we can't help it. We had to tell you."

"Does anyone else know?"

"Just you and Tony," Louise said, "We had to tell Tony because of the decorating."

For the rest of the evening Gordon found he couldn't stop smiling. The three of them around the table shared a secret, and, for once, it was a good secret. Gordon relayed all the recent events to his hosts, who, for their part, listened well and offered sensible advice when asked. They commiserated over Pamela and Simon.

As the candles burned low, they asked him if he had any ideas what he wanted for his birthday. He blinked once more, and admitted, "I'd totally forgotten about that."

Birthdays after Brenda's death were less of an occasion, somehow, and he rarely bothered to give them much thought. Growing old was inevitable, he was his own living proof. Now, in just over three weeks, he'd be sixty-five.

He blew out his cheeks in a way that signified cluelessness, and said that he'd try and think of something within the next few days. This time, he promised himself, he really would try. He couldn't put up with either vouchers or umbrellas again.

When Gordon left at just after eleven, he was full to the brim, all stocks fully replenished. Back home, his answer phone had been called into service once again, this time recording a message from the police, who wanted to come around tomorrow. Gordon saved it for the morning, and went straight to bed, where he slept as soundly as he'd done all year.

~

Some ten hours later, he waited patiently as the purring in his ear signified a less than prompt response at the station. When they answered, he was put straight through to the dealing officer, who was friendly enough, without actually being friendly. Gordon asked whether they could arrange their visit for this morning, as he had a shift at the rest home starting at noon. They said they would do their best.

Forty minutes on and there was a knock on the door. Gordon smiled to himself; even those four shrift raps carried an authoritative tone.

They belonged to a PC Law, who'd added "No joke," before Gordon had even had time to laugh, a tall middle aged man who was starting to lose his fitness. He was accompanied by WPC Cross, a smaller dark haired attractive lady, who'd simply smiled an apology. They both refused any beverages or biscuits, Cross with a polite no thank you and Law with an annoyed shake of the head, before asking Gordon to show them what he'd found.

They looked around in the back garden, at the pseudo-evidence Gordon had discovered, and stretched themselves to obtain a statement from him. PC Law shook his head a lot, and Gordon caught a look from him directed at his colleague which said, 'What are we doing here?'

He was given a 'Safety in the Home' leaflet, but, they said, with nothing to obtain fingerprints from, it was unlikely to go any further. Perhaps he should get a security light, and maybe a burglar alarm, they offered.

They left just before noon, promising nothing, and, though annoyed, he could see it from their point of view. The old man sighed, at least he had the work at the home to look forward to.

~

He'd booked in to work a shift on each of the three remaining days of February, and even though he'd only been away from the place for a couple of weeks, he was amazed, and slightly perturbed, by the number of new residents he saw.

The winter, as usual, had taken its toll. People had either died, grown too ill to be looked after there, or found more suitable accommodation nearer to their relatives.

There had been no shortage of replacements willing to move into their twenty foot square rooms, either. It was a popular residence for the flusher geriatrics in the town, who were attracted to it for its beautiful gardens, and its ideal positioning, just a short car journey from the seafront.

Gordon took the time to talk to the new faces, making them feel at home.

Might be you, one day, he thought.

On the twenty-seventh, the first Race answers started to come in. It was only ever at this stage that Gordon felt the Race had started proper, when he could see the participants had truly spent some of their own valuable time on it.

Catherine's and Trudie's answer came in first, by post, and although Gordon had told himself he should mark them all at the same time, he couldn't help but open it. The answer was good, a pleasure to read, and as he read he made his own notes on how he might approach April's question. It gave Gordon some hope that the pairing could last until December.

Tony hand delivered his on the same morning, stopping in for a cup of tea, and a chat. He mentioned Chris and Louise's impending addition, and Gordon brightened up immediately. He'd forgotten that Tony knew, and it was a relief to be able to talk to someone else about it.

Another round of drinks was made, and Tony told Gordon how well his work was going, as was his relationship with Jessica and Catherine. Jessica was even going to be allowed to help him this coming Saturday, with a job he just couldn't afford to put off. Gordon smiled and told him he was happy that everything was still okay, keeping his doubts over Catherine's deeper motives to himself.

Tony left before twelve, and Gordon went to the home. Pam dropped her answer through the letterbox that afternoon, and while he was sorry he missed her, he was almost certain she'd done it on purpose.

On the evening of February 28th, Chris and Louise popped in on their way to a party, answers in hand. They seemed bright, and full of energy. Louise was looking more radiant than ever. They couldn't stay long, and by the time they'd left, Gordon knew it was too late to try and start any writing; he was too tired and if he tried, he knew the results would only have to be discarded the following morning.

Chris and Louise's visit had given him a little pick-me-up, though, so instead of going straight to bed, he retired to the lounge with a book he'd received as a Christmas present. At ten o'clock, he was woken in his chair by the noise of the letterbox. Another answer; Simon's. He didn't get out of the chair. It could wait. Then, after a few minutes, the letterbox went again. Gordon sat confused. Who else had to hand in their answer? Then it came to him, and he was up and out of the chair and going to the front door. Damn, he thought. There were two envelopes on the mat. One from Simon, and one from the anonymous player. Gordon stood looking at them in frustration. If he'd been younger, and fitter, he could have stayed awake to see who'd delivered it.

Gordon left Simon's envelope where it'd fallen, but carried the other one, simply marked 'First Answer', into the lounge. He found his letter opener, and carefully made an incision along the top edge of the envelope. He sat down in his chair once more, and inspected the contents. Any extra information he had hoped to find on the entrant was not forthcoming, however; the envelope contained nothing more than a white piece of paper with a typed answer.

At first, Gordon couldn't even muster the enthusiasm to read it. He felt hurt by this continuing need for secrecy. He didn't like being kept in the dark. Eventually, though, he calmed down, and unfolded the piece of paper. Gordon read the words, and as he did, he smiled. They were well written, with humour and knowledge, and he found himself nodding and agreeing with the essay nearly all the way through. Gordon spent another couple of hopeful minutes studying it for any clues, but found none. He sighed, and rubbed his eyes.

Half-an-hour later, Gordon was in bed, the sheet of paper on the bedside table ready to read with fresh eyes the next morning. He pondered over the fact that even though everyone's answers had now arrived, he still had none of his own. As he drifted off into sleep, Gordon had the unsettling thought that whoever it was that was testing him, was winning.

LOUISE, CHRIS, AND A BOX OF UMBRELLAS

Relatively speaking, the first week of March started quietly. Gordon slowed his voluntary work, and was more than happy to just potter around the bungalow, trying his best to catch up on the little jobs that caught his eye from time to time. The garden for one thing. He cleared a lot of the overgrown bushes, trimmed the hedges, and planted a few flowers, which, according to the packets at least, should arrive in time for the start of the summer.

Family contact died down, too; the only conversations were over the telephone, and brief. He continued to read the books on the shelves, and kept himself up to date with the newspapers.

Before he knew it, it was mid-March, and there were only four days until his slightly unwelcome birthday. Chris rang to invite him round for a birthday dinner at their flat on the Sunday, and Gordon gratefully accepted, in return asking his son whether Louise was available to accompany him down to the town to help choose a computer to buy. Chris said he was sure she would, and promised to ask her when she got in from work.

On the Thursday, Louise rang back and said she'd be delighted to go on Saturday, and asked him for his technical requirements, so she could do some price checking. Gordon flustered around for a bit, but eventually the two of them managed to agree what he wanted to use it for. With a little trepidation, Gordon accepted her offer of a lift, as well. It was a small price to pay.

On the Friday, Margaret, Lawrence's friend rang up, and left a message asking if Monday would be okay for their meeting, along with a telephone number she could be contacted on should there be a problem. That afternoon the police also rang, letting him know that, as there weren't any new leads, they would close the case.

Louise pulled up at nine-fifteen on Saturday morning, and, not wanting to keep her waiting, he met her by the gate. As they drove into the busy town centre, she told him what computers she'd looked at since they'd last spoken, and he did his best to concentrate on what she was saying. When she finished, she looked at him and smiled.

"I'll tell you what," she said. "Let's go and have a cup of tea and I can talk you through it slowly."

~

Gordon sat in the cafe and listened. Even though Louise made the subject of computers easier to comprehend, there were still many things he simply didn't understand. He nodded and smiled when it seemed like that was necessary, and pursed his lips and shook his head wherever appropriate. He hoped he'd got it right.

"So, it's this one I should get," he ventured, stabbing his finger towards one of the torn pieces of paper. Louise looked at him impassively. "We had finished discussing the options?" he asked.

Louise smiled, "Yes, we had. But I was hoping I'd managed to put across the fact that we didn't want that one at all."

This time Gordon smiled, "You did, I just wanted to make sure," he lied, unconvincingly.

"The choice is between the other three. The main factor separating them is speed, price, and capacity."

Gordon placed his hands behind his head, this was an easy decision. "Well," he said, "When it comes to speed, I just need it to go at the speed I type, and I'm sure that's covered. Price, thankfully, is no obstacle, so, by process of elimination, I think capacity wins it."

"Makes sense," Louise said, gathering the pieces of paper up, and putting them in her pocket.

"That was more painless than I thought."

Their order arrived, tea was poured, and scones buttered.

"You know what I miss?" Louise asked.

"No," Gordon replied, taking a bite of his food, and catching the crumbs with his other hand.

"Your poetry," she said. "Now, I'm not saying I didn't enjoy your books, because I did. But it was your poetry I really liked."

"I still write it, from time to time," Gordon said, wiping the corners of his mouth with a serviette. "You're welcome to see it."

"You could bring it round tomorrow, if you like."

Gordon nodded. "Yes, if I can find it, why not?"

There was a silence. Louise watched the older man with affection. She knew this look well; his mind seemed to be elsewhere.

"Everything all right, Gordy?" Louise asked. "You seem a little distant."

"Just thinking of Graeme, that's all. He was the real poet of the family. Have you read anything of his?"

Louise shook her head.

"Well, I can search it out for you, if you like. Then you can read some real poetry."

"I'd like to read you both."

As they left the cafe, Gordon found his spirits were high. He was very proud of his late son's poetry, and he enjoyed other people reading it much more than his own. Now, Louise had given him an excuse to find it again. Not that I should've needed one, he thought, mentally kicking himself for leaving it so long.

He and Louise had a morning to fill, so they decided to look at the other computers anyway, just to make sure their specifications hadn't changed. "That happens a lot," Gordon heard her say. At twelve thirty-one, the Saturday boy proudly smiled at the sale of the system, deluded by thinking his inferior knowledge had somehow guaranteed the purchase. Louise shook her head, fetched the car, and loaded it into the back.

"What do you say about Chris coming over and we can have some lunch and set it up?" Louise asked.

"That sounds great," Gordon said. "Have you got time?"

"Of course, Gordy," she said, and swung out into the midday traffic.

~

During the short journey home, Gordon thought about where Graeme's poetry might be. He could remember putting it in a folder somewhere, but beyond that, nothing. Never mind, he thought, he knew he hadn't gotten rid of it. He definitely hadn't done that.

He was, and always had been, a hoarder, much to Brenda's annoyance. She'd often tried to make him throw stuff away, but he would argue the papers were his research, and he couldn't do without them. Eventually, he'd compromise, and dispose of some of them, but, in all their years together, he'd never thrown anything of the children's away. The two of them had agreed on that early on, even more so after Graeme's accident, so he was assured his son's poetry was somewhere within the bungalow.

Either there, he thought, or at the cottage.

There were three birthday cards waiting for him on the mat when he got home. He picked them up and recognised Tony's, Catherine's, and Pam's handwriting instantly. Gordon put them on the mantelpiece to open tomorrow. When Chris arrived, he and Gordon lifted the two heavy boxes into the spare room, where Gordon had decided he'd wanted the computer placed. With the recent problems of the prowler, he didn't want anything like this on show, and the spare room window was the hardest to get to.

When everything was unboxed, Louise set about connecting it up.

"I feel like a bit of a spare part," Chris said to his father, as they stood at the door, watching her.

"Go and put the kettle on, then," barked Louise. Both men obeyed immediately.

As Chris warmed the pot, Gordon ventured, "You don't remember seeing Graeme's poetry when I moved in, do you?"

"Um," Chris started, "It's been a while. Was it in a box?"

Gordon sighed, "Can't remember. Your mum did most of the packing."

"Oh," Chris replied, and thought for a moment. "No, Dad, I don't remember. Sorry. It can only be in the bungalow, though, can't it?"

Gordon nodded.

"Well, we can have a quick look while Louise is still setting up. Usually takes her longer than she thinks, anyhow."

"I can hear you, you know," Louise called from the spare room. Chris screwed his face up, Gordon laughed.

They went about finding Graeme's poetry. Chris searched the garage, spare room, and dining room, while Gordon went through the main bedroom, conservatory and kitchen.

"Finished," Louise called. She popped her head round the door to the lounge. "Is there anywhere I can look?" she asked.

"The loft," Chris called from the garage.

"Oh, I shouldn't bother," Gordon said, "I've been up there quite recently and didn't see it."

Louise narrowed her eyes. "Were you looking for it?"

Gordon frowned, and shook his head.

"Perhaps it's best if I do take a look, then," she said.

"I was only joking," Chris said, "Don't forget your condition."

"You're a fine one to talk," she said, nodding in the direction of his leg. "Now, how big is this folder?"

"A4 size, I think," Gordon said. "It's got his name on the front. I think the first poems called, 'Liking you, too'."

"See you in a minute then," she said.

The two men retreated to the lounge.

"She seems a bit...?" Gordon asked.

"She is, though don't let her hear you say that!" whispered Chris, stealing a glance toward the hatch. "Something to do with the pregnancy, I suspect."

Ten minutes went by, and apart from some scrapings and mutterings, nothing else was heard from the loft. "Do you think she's all right?" Gordon asked.

"Do you want to ask her?" Chris said.

Gordon shook his head.

Chris rested back and sipped his tea. "You and Graeme were going on a poetry writing course at one time, weren't you?"

"How'd you know about that?"

"He spoke to me about it," Chris replied.

Gordon sighed. "Like so many things, we never managed to get round to it."

Ten more minutes ticked on. Then they heard her steps on the ladder. She came in smiling.

"Did you find it?" Chris asked.

She nodded. "But not only that," she said. "This was just by the hatch." She brought her hand from behind her. She was holding some papers. "They were tucked in between the rafter and the fibreglass."

"One of Monty's boxes fell over," Gordon said. "I thought I'd picked it all up."

"Well, in that case," Louise continued, bringing her other hand round, "This is likely to be his envelope, too."

Gordon could hardly believe his eyes. She was holding Monty's original Race envelope.

"Can I?" Gordon asked, holding out his hand.

Louise gave it to him.

"I don't believe it," he said. "This is excellent news."

For the rest of the afternoon, Louise showed Gordon the basics of turning the computer on, launching the word-processor, and writing and saving documents. They left at just after four, and Gordon shut the door with a smile on his face. With the discovery of Monty's envelope, everything felt as if it were back on track once again. He'd got one up on the anonymous player. He'd eliminated one of the possible envelopes, and it didn't matter to him that he'd missed it in the first place. That was just fate playing its hand. If he'd found it straight away, he would never have known about Monty's suicide, and as this thought slid into place, Gordon had the unnerving feeling this would be the way of it. He was destined to discover all the envelopes, but with each one he would get a little bit more than he bargained for.

Regardless of this, he decided he should celebrate the find, and booked a table for one at a restaurant in a village not far away. He soaked in a bath, put on a smart pair of trousers and a shirt, and ordered the taxi for eight. As an inspired afterthought, he picked up Graeme's poetry and took it with him.

When he arrived, Gordon let the staff know he was there, and was given a menu and asked to sit for a few minutes while his table was prepared. He ordered a sherry, and picked at the nuts and Bombay mix that were placed on the table in front of him by one of the waiters. He thumbed the menu, picked out a couple of dishes he'd ask more about, and spent the remaining time people watching until they came for him.

They seated him in the large bay window that, during the day, offered wonderful views overlooking fields. He sipped his drink, and read the lines that had long ago dripped like honey from his son's pen.

"Excuse me," the waitress who'd been serving him said, "I'm very sorry to interrupt you, but you are Gordon Paige, aren't you?"

Gordon was impressed. It'd been many years since anyone had actually recognised him in public, and even then, it was only people of a certain age. This girl must have been early twenties. Gordon fluffed himself up a bit. "Um, yes, that's right. Have you read one of my books?"

"Books?" the girl asked, without an iota of recognition, "No. It's just that someone handed this in at the bar," she said, handing him an envelope.

"Oh, thanks," Gordon said, trying to hide his embarrassment. "Sorry about that."

The waitress smiled and disappeared back into the kitchen.

Gordon could see who it was from just by the typed name on the front. "Touché," he whispered, turning it over in his hands. He opened it up, not quite knowing what to expect, and it took him a moment to realise what he was looking at.

Then he smiled. It was only a birthday card. Why should it be anything else? Not a shop bought one, though, but home-made. On the front was a painted Ostrich. Exquisitely done. Gordon took a minute or so to appreciate the time that had gone into creating it. Inside the card, once again typed, was a 'Happy Birthday' message. No signature.

And then a penny dropped. It fell and clattered as it came to rest in Gordon's mind. The anonymous player had followed him to the restaurant and given them a card to give to him. They'd also followed him to the hotel he was staying at to give him the original envelope. So, that meant that the figure outside the bungalow a few weeks ago was probably the same person. It made him feel happy and yet slightly uneasy all at the same time. Happy because he truly believed the player was harmless, and uneasy because, in the end, he was being watched. Gordon raised a glass to the air, in case the player was still at the restaurant, and took a sip. Then he pocketed the card, and ate a fine meal, reading Graeme's poetry as he did so.

~

Gordon was unsure where most of his birthday went. He could remember getting up and opening his cards, having a pot of tea, and then sitting down and switching on the new computer. After that, everything was a blur.

He went back through the things that Louise had shown him the day before. Whilst at the restaurant the previous evening, he'd struck on the idea of writing up Graeme's poetry, so he could show it to Louise when he was there later. That had started at nine-thirty AM. The next time he looked up it was four o'clock, and he wasn't even halfway through. Still, he had learnt more than he thought he was going to, and that could only be a good thing. He was happy with his purchase; it was far more interesting than vouchers.

Louise picked him up on time, and he showed her what he'd done. She was suitably impressed, especially as he hadn't rung her once during the day.

"Ah," he said, "That might be because I wrote every question I wanted to ask you down. Maybe if we have some time later on?"

"Of course," Louise said.

Unsurprisingly, the time to ask her never materialised. Chris and Louise had invited Vee along as a surprise, and the four of them had had far too much fun to start discussing computers.

After the food, Vee brought out a present for Gordon.

"Oh, you shouldn't have, Vee."

"It's my pleasure," she said, "Happy birthday."

He opened it and laughed. Like Frank, Vee had always been very creative. She wasn't a painter, but was able to create three-dimensional art. Sculptures, models, flower arrangements and such like. "It keeps me off the streets," she'd always say.

For his birthday, she'd made him a present. An exquisite glass fronted shallow box, with a clip on the back to hang it on the wall. It was beautiful, but what really tickled him, was what she'd put inside.

Like the butterfly collections often found in antique shops, Vee had made twenty-five miniature umbrellas, in five rows of five. Each was painted in wonderful bright colours, and skewered with a pin to the back of the box.

"This is wonderful," he said, handing it to Chris, and then giving Vee a hug. "It must have taken an age to make."

"Yes, but have you ever seen anything like it before?"

Gordon shook his head. "Never," he said.

"Here's ours," Chris said. "Although after that, it may not seem much."

"Hope you like them," Louise added.

They'd enlarged and framed two of Gordon's wedding day pictures.

"These are wonderful as well," he said, tears welling in his eyes. "I thought they were creased in the move."

"They managed to remove them," Chris explained, "It's really good, isn't it?"

"Breath taking," was all Gordon could say.

He hugged them both, too. "Well, I may only have had two presents today," he said, "But, honestly, I don't think I could have asked for anything better."

MARGARET, GILES, AND A SERIOUS DOUBT

The next morning, Gordon added Vee's and Chris's presents to the wall of his lounge. He started to move Monty's belongings back from the garage into the loft, and as he did so, couldn't help himself from imagining what Monty must have felt like the evening he'd sat out in the garden to die. Desperation, relief, confusion. He didn't know. But the cold which must have slowly crept into his body was enough to make Gordon physically shiver, and by the time the garage was clear of all the boxes, he felt quite low.

The impending meeting with Lawrence's friend wasn't helping either. He'd already changed his clothes three times, from formal, to casual, and now very casual, and he was getting increasingly fed up with each iteration. Diversions from his normal routines always made him feel out of control, and this was no exception. He knew he was not alone in disliking change, but it made him feel no better. Finding the envelopes meant he had to go through with it; the information on Lawrence's whereabouts was too important.

At least he felt more comfortable in what he wore. He checked his clothes in the hall mirror for a final time, then quickly left before he had a chance to change them yet again.

The cafe where they were meeting was situated in one of the offshoot parades of the town, a pedestrianised area with several cafes and restaurants, and he knew it well. Not too busy to be crowded and jostled and have to wait for a table, but not too quiet to feel awkward. At least that was what it had been like when he'd last gone there. Time, however, had not left it alone. When he arrived slightly early, he saw that it had undergone an internal refit, modernising the insides with mirrors and music. No longer was it the semi-formal place he'd expected; now it was adorned with leather chairs, and low coffee tables. Gordon sighed at the new influx of customers the refit had garnered, and pushed the door open.

The sound volume was high, and as he made his way through the crowded tables, he was reminded of his younger days visiting London. Surprisingly, he found himself relaxing into this earlier, carefree, version of himself, and purposefully avoided any of the large mirrors on the wall, so as not to shatter the illusion. As he was about to sit down, a woman's voice close by called out, "Gordon," and he stopped dead. It'd sounded like Brenda. His heart rate felt as if it had doubled, and his palms became clammy.

"Gordon," the voice came again. Now, though, he could pick up the differences, filter out the distortion the general hubbub had given it.

He turned to where it had come from, with something inside of him still hoping it might be Brenda after all, looking well, smiling at him, and asking him to sit down so they could talk about old times. He had, on more than one occasion, thought he'd caught glimpses of her, whilst shopping, or at functions, even at the home, but of course it wasn't her.

The lady he saw in the cafe was not Brenda, but she was smiling at him, so he smiled back as best he could. His initial surprise at mistaking her voice must still have been apparent on his face, as she stood quickly and held his elbow. "Are you all right?" she asked, but all Gordon could do was nod.

"Perhaps you'd like to sit down?" she continued, indicating the empty seat opposite her. "I thought it was you," Gordon could hear her saying as he sat. "I'm very sorry if I caught you by surprise. I didn't mean to. I was just pleased to see you here. Part of me didn't think you were real."

A waiter swiftly appeared at their table. "What would you like?" the woman, Margaret, Gordon remembered, asked.

"Oh, I haven't looked," Gordon managed. He blinked a few times. "Uh, tea," he said, "Definitely tea."

"Tea it is then, pot for two. And I think I'll have another scone. The last one I had was delicious. Anything to eat, Gordon?"

"No," Gordon said, then realising it may have sounded abrupt, added, "Nothing for me, thank you."

The waiter nodded and moved off toward the counter. There was a moment's pause, and Gordon's mind caught up. "I'm sorry," he said, "That's not the best first impression I've ever given, I have to say."

"No, no, no," Margaret replied, "I have a way of putting people out of their stride. Especially when I'm nervous. You're older than I thought you would be. But younger, too, in a funny way. You don't look an awful lot like Lawrence, do you? But then you wouldn't. At least you were on time, Lawrence was nev..."

Margaret trailed off. She looked over Gordon's shoulder, embarrassed, toward the counter were baristas were creating the coffee with practised movements. "Sorry," she said. She took a few deep breaths, and then smiled. He watched as her shoulders dropped and her face relaxed.

"I'm Margaret. Maggie, preferably." She extended her hand. Gordon took it.

"Gordon, or Gordy," he said. "It's a pleasure to meet you."

Maggie was in her late fifties, early sixties, had an almond shaped face, with white and blonde hair, cut quite short. She looked tanned, and her laughter lines were easily seen. Her eyes were the shape of half-moons, similar in colour to Brenda's, and looked full of life.

"Are you all right sitting in here? I mean, you're not a smoker or anything?"

"Oh, no," Gordon said, "Definitely not a smoker."

Maggie nodded. "Me neither. I was. Gave up years ago, though. Sometimes I wish I hadn't."

"It's not easy to give up, is it?"

"Not really," Maggie said. "Especially at my tender age."

The waiter appeared once more with the tea and set it down. Gordon looked at Maggie and said, "After you."

"Thank you," she replied.

Maggie poured her own tea, and set the pot down, turning the handle towards Gordon. "So, you used to know Lawrence well, did you?" Gordon asked, picking the pot up.

Maggie smiled affectionately, "Oh, yes," she said, buttering the scone, "He used to be my husband."

Gordon stopped what he was doing. "I'm sorry?" he said. "Did you just say..."

Maggie sighed, "Yes, I did. I didn't think you'd know. Few people do. He and his family didn't think it was a proper thing to... publicise."

"Why ever not?"

Maggie looked directly at Gordon, as if she were weighing up his trustworthiness. "I think," she said, slowly, "It's because we had a child so early."

Gordon coughed. "Oh," he said. "Perhaps I should have kept my big mouth shut."

"Don't be stupid. I'm not going to pretend it never happened; and I have a lovely son out of it."

Gordon smiled and nodded. "I understand."

"But you don't want to listen to this," she continued, "You must be a busy man."

Gordon shook his head, "Not half as busy as you'd think. Please, tell me, how did the two of you meet?"

~

As they drained the tea from their cups, Maggie recounted how she and Lawrence had been on the same degree course at university in London.

"Initially," she explained "We didn't really notice each other, Lawrence being the sort of man who preferred studying over everything else. We had a few friends in common, but that was it. Then, by a complete chance, we ended up sharing a taxi home from a local pub, and we were in digs only a couple of roads apart. It was funny, I didn't think we would have anything to talk about, but in the end, we couldn't stop nattering. He was as worse a gossip as I."

Maggie took a bite of her scone, and suddenly looked uncertain. "Are you sure you want to hear this?" she asked, dabbing her lips with the napkin.

"Absolutely. It's very interesting. I know so little of him."

"Well, after that evening, we used to say hello, and talk about the work each of us were doing, and about how we found the other students and lecturers. He was a very clever man, a bit intense, but fascinating, too. Then, after a while, we started to see each other more regularly. Conversations started to turn towards family and home life, and the mood definitely shifted."

Maggie continued about their times together, places they'd visited, and it was easy for Gordon to see how fond she'd been of Lawrence. It eased Gordon's nerves too, he knew getting the other person to talk was one of his best defences.

"What about Elizabeth?" Gordon asked when she fell silent. "Did you ever see her?"

Maggie smiled. "Oh, yes," she said. "She'd regularly appear at the weekends to whisk Lawrence away on some errand or other. She never even said hello to me."

"Now that doesn't surprise me."

Maggie looked serious, suddenly. "Then, one day, it happened," she said, "I woke up feeling nauseous, and then the next day, and the next, and I knew what had happened. We'd been very careful. Obviously, not careful enough. I didn't tell Lawrence until I'd seen a doctor and had it confirmed."

"You see, we'd never talked about having children. Not really even talked about other people's children. Something to do with his parents, I thought. Well, when I told him, he went very quiet, and looked at me as if his world had just collapsed. He turned and left, and I didn't see or hear from him for a couple of weeks or more. I thought he was having a breakdown or something. It was during the summer months, and classes had finished. I lived in London, so it was very difficult."

"But he did come back?" Gordon asked.

"Yes, and with him came an engagement ring. He proposed to me on the doorstep, and to my surprise, I said yes. I'd never wanted to get married so young. But, then, I really didn't feel there was much of a choice."

"He moved into my house, left to me when my parents passed away, and a few weeks later we got married at a small church in a small village. No family were invited, and only a handful of friends from university. On the Monday, we went straight back to study. It was as if it'd never happened."

Gordon watched Maggie carefully. He tried to notice any clues to what else may have happened between them. He often explained to people that stories have more than one side, and that he thought it was the author's job to try and tell them all. Maggie seemed quite genuine.

"What happened next?" he asked her.

"Well, it didn't get any better. I should've seen the signs, but I was young and hopeful. I gave birth to a lovely baby boy, who we named Giles, and I did my best to bring him up, and to try and keep Lawrence interested.

"But, it was an impossible task. He was too interested in his studying, and however hard I tried, he still insisted on going back home at the weekends. Within a year, we had decided enough was enough, and we split up.

"I stayed at the house, worked when I could, and brought up Giles. I never re-married, and I've never spoken to any of his family since."

Maggie laid her knife down on the plate, and pushed it toward the middle of the table. Something didn't feel completely right, but he didn't know what.

"What does Giles do, now?" Gordon asked.

"He works as a salesman in a firm down near here. I was visiting him today. I couldn't believe it when I saw your letter addressed to Lawrence. I wanted to meet you and be able to talk about what happened with someone. I hope I haven't wasted your time."

"Not at all," Gordon said. "I've enjoyed hearing about it. Listen, I know it's a bit of a cheek, but do you happen to have Lawrence's current address?"

"Um, yes, and no. I mean, the only one I know is a few years old, and I'm pretty sure he's moved since then. Sorry. I should have asked Giles before I came out. Nerves, again. I tell you what, I'll ask him this afternoon, and then I could give you a ring. What do you think?"

Gordon smiled. "Tell you what," he said, "Why don't you tell me this evening, in person. That is, if you're available for a meal?"

"Oh," Maggie said, surprised. "Well, I know Giles has got something else planned, so, why not? Where?"

"That place across the street, just over there. About eight?"

Maggie turned and looked in the direction that Gordon was pointing in. "Okay. Eight should be fine."

"Excellent," Gordon said, "It's quite casual. No dressing up required."

"Lovely," Maggie said, and smiled. "I'm looking forward to it already."

~

Despite the onset of a rainy afternoon, Gordon couldn't help but grin all the way home. For the first time since his youth he'd arranged a date with a woman, and it left him feeling as high as a kite. He was amazed at just how comfortable he'd felt in Maggie's company. She'd done a lot of the talking, but it had been an interesting conversation, not just anything to fill the gap.

He stopped himself thinking too far ahead. He knew it would be a mistake. She'd agreed to have a meal with him, and now, thinking back, he wasn't sure whether he'd forced her to or not. Maybe she'd accepted out of politeness. Maybe she'd already left a message on his answer machine cancelling everything, but when he reached the bungalow, the display read zero

He had so much to think about before their meeting that evening, he didn't know quite where to start. As he put the kettle on, there was a knock at the front door, and, still lost in his feelings, he went to answer it without giving it a second thought. His guard was down, and he opened the front door with the broadest smile he could muster.

It froze on his face when he saw Esme on his doorstep, wet through and with bags packed either side. She took one look at him, and immediately burst into tears.

Gordon felt sick with the suddenness of seeing her, but he managed to ride the nausea out long enough to help her in the door. "Just calm down," he said. "I'll make some tea."

He led her through to the kitchen, and, once there, sat her on a stool. "Oh, Gordon," she sobbed, "I've gone and done a terrible thing."

With his back to her, Gordon shut his eyes. "What?" he asked.

There was a long pause. Gordon wasn't sure if it was deliberate. Then, with a sigh, she said "I've sold the home."

Gordon turned and looked at her. "Don't be stupid," he said, failing to hide his astonishment, "That's the craziest thing I've ever heard."

Tears welled in her eyes. "Oh, Gordon, it's true. I've blown everything. I thought I could have anything I wanted. But now it's all gone."

Gordon sighed, "Have you really sold the home?" he asked.

"When I realised you weren't going to say yes, I felt bitter. I wanted to go and do something that would hurt you. And I thought the home was important to you. I wasn't thinking straight. The estate agents were very willing to help."

"Well, of course they were." Gordon replied, trying hard to stay calm. "Didn't you consult with anyone else about it?"

"No-one at all," Esme replied, "The rest of the staff only found out today. God knows what'll happen to them, now."

Gordon ran his fingers through his hair. "And there's no chance you can go back on the deal?"

"None. It's gone. I'm without a home."

Gordon pointed to her bags. "I'm sorry, Esme, but I'm afraid you can't stay here," he said.

"But..., I've got nowhere else to go," she said, "It'd only be..."

"No," he said, more firmly. "You cannot stay here. You'll just have to put yourself up at a B&B somewhere. There must be one still open in town. I know this sounds harsh, but I can't help you on this."

"Gordon," Esme said, a sudden conviction entering her voice, "When I said earlier that you didn't want to marry me, you didn't say anything. Was that because I was right?"

"Esme," Gordon said, gathering himself together, "I like you as a friend, but nothing more. I don't think we would get along."

"I could change," she tried, "I don't mind changing."

"Esme, I think we both know we've got to a stage in our lives where we aren't able to change, however much we try and convince ourselves differently."

"Oh," Esme said, "I see."

There was an awkward silence between them. Finally, she looked up. "I think I better go."

Gordon looked at his feet. "It might be best," he said, hating himself for it, but feeling it was right, nevertheless. Five awkward minutes later, she was gone. It was all over so quickly, Gordon wasn't sure whether it had happened at all.

~

He arrived for his dinner date on time. He was shown to the table, where Maggie was already sitting. "You look stunning," he said, and genuinely meant it.

"That's very kind," she replied, "You look very handsome, too."

Flirting, Gordon thought to himself, who'd have believed I still had it in me.

"You're making a habit of being early," he teased.

"Yes, but at least it's a good habit," she retorted.

Gordon nodded, and opened the menu.

"It's a lovely place you've chosen, isn't it?" Maggie said. "Very bright, and open."

"It's great," Gordon admitted, "You can be nosey at what everyone else is eating."

They looked at the menu, and discussed what each might order. Gordon was happy to note the atmosphere between them seemed very relaxed.

"Did you see your son?" Gordon asked when the waiter had taken their order.

"Oh, yes," she said, "I've got Lawrence's new address. Would you like it?"

"No rush," Gordon said, "Let's eat first."

They talked more and more as the evening drew on, she about her time with Lawrence, he with Brenda. They swapped stories of raising children which made them both laugh. They enjoyed their food, too, over which Maggie told him of how she'd dropped out of university, taking up odd jobs to supplement the money that Lawrence paid her. She didn't know where he got it from, and frankly, hadn't asked. She had two mouths to feed, and that was that.

When Gordon spoke of Brenda, Maggie listened attentively, asking questions, and offering comparisons with her own life. As the coffee was served, Maggie said, "Well, that was the best meal I've had in a long time. And you're very good company, too. It's hard to find someone to talk to, sometimes, isn't it?"

"Oh, yes," Gordon agreed, "Just lately it seems to be everyone else's problems I have to listen to."

Maggie suddenly looked worried. "Oh, I hope you don't think..."

Gordon held his hands up, "No, not at all. It's been a very enjoyable evening."

As they got their coats, Maggie turned to Gordon, and he could see she was working out how to ask for something. "Look," she said, "Giles asked what I wanted the address for, and I told him I was meeting a friend of his father's tonight. He seemed very interested, and I was wondering whether you were available to have lunch with us tomorrow, before I go back?"

"Of course," Gordon said.

"Tell me if you're busy..."

"It's fine. Really."

Maggie smiled. "Excellent. He's quite up on books, too. He knew who you were. I think he has a hankering to write one himself, one day."

"Good for him," Gordon said.

"Good. This time it's my treat, though," she said.

They parted outside the restaurant, and it was only in the taxi home Gordon realised he still didn't have Lawrence's new address. Oh, well, I'll see her tomorrow, he thought, and smiled, unashamedly smugly, to himself.

~

When he woke the next morning, Gordon could have been mistaken to think it was summer. The sun was bright, and the clouds scarce. Within the artificial warmth of his room, he felt as if he was deep in the Mediterranean.

He went for a walk before breakfast, stopping off at the home to speak to the receptionist, to see what was going on. She confirmed Esme's story, so Gordon asked for the name and number of the new owner, to find out whether his help was still needed.

On the way back, he passed several couples in the street, and started to think once more about Brenda. He walked through the green where they met, and suddenly there was a doubt in his mind over what he was doing, of how involved he was getting with Maggie. In the cold light of the morning, something didn't sit quite right. What if the children saw it as Gordon forgetting about their mother, in some way making her memory less important? It wasn't as if either of them had had many partners. What if it was a mistake? What would happen if he couldn't handle it?

He quickened his pace, feeling a sudden need to be back at the bungalow. Brenda had been everything to Gordon, still was in many ways, and it was very doubtful that his fondness for Maggie would turn into anything other than flirting. Maybe I should call it off, he thought.

He got home, and rung the number Maggie had given him. There was no answer. He looked in the phone book for her son, but couldn't find him. As the minutes ticked by, frustration further fuelled his doubt, adding to the desperation he felt. The more he thought about it, the more he convinced himself he was doing Brenda's memory an injustice.

Then, just when his anxiety was getting out of control, there was a knock at the door.

"Oh, no," he mumbled to himself, all too aware of what the last one had heralded.

Then, to his relief, he heard Chris's voice saying, "Are you there, dad?"

Gordon opened the door. "Am I glad to see you," he said. Chris stood on the doorstep, by himself. "How did you get here?" Gordon asked.

"Lou dropped me off; she was on her way to her mother's. Thought you might like some company."

"As a matter of fact, I would. Come in, and I'll put the kettle on. How are you?"

"The foot's improving, but I'm a bit hacked off," Chris said, closing the door. "I've had no luck on the jobs front. I'm starting to think I'm unemployable."

"Don't be stupid," Gordon said, "It's just been a while. These things take time. You're a talented lad. One will come up, you mark my words."

"Maybe," his son said, "It's just a bit demoralising. Can't help thinking it's not what you know, but who you know."

Gordon laughed, "Well, you need to know a few more people, then."

"Thanks, Dad. You're being a real help."

"Well, you know, I try. If you need any money..."

"No, no. We're... okay at the moment. And besides, you know how fiercely independent Lou is."

"Oh, yes," Gordon said. "I've noticed."

The two men drank their coffees in the lounge.

"Now," Gordon started, "I have a question to ask. It's a serious one, too. So listen well. I want your honest opinion."

Chris sat cross-legged on the floor. "I'm all ears."

Gordon went through what had happened with Maggie, about their meetings, and over the fears he had at what the family may think.

When he'd finished, Chris got up and sat beside him. He placed a hand on his shoulder.

"Well, Dad," he said, "I think I can speak for the whole family when I say that to have another relationship with a woman would probably be the best thing that's happened to you in years."

Gordon remained silent, waiting for a 'but'. When none materialised, he said "So, are you saying that you don't mind?"

"Don't mind?" Chris squeaked, "We've been wondering why you haven't done it already. You're still a good-looking chap. A bit old, but you've held onto some resale value."

"Thank you, that makes me feel a whole lot better."

"I can assure you everyone would be delighted. Maybe even Catherine."

"Oh, I wouldn't go that far. Are you sure you really don't mind? Really?" Gordon asked.

"Of course not," he said, "I'm very, genuinely, happy. And relieved. A man can only be content with his own company for so long. I should know."

"That's a relief," he said.

"Another coffee?" Chris asked, heading out toward the kitchen.

"Yes, please," Gordon answered. He paused a moment, then said, "And how long have you been discussing my private life behind my back?"

Chris laughed, "We never stopped. We do talk to one another outside of this house, you know."

Gordon smiled. Chris was right. He'd just been too tied up in his own little world to think that anybody else cared about him.

"What are you doing for lunch?" Gordon asked.

"Nothing."

"Good. You can come with me - even the sides up."

~

Maggie was delighted to meet Chris, and the lunch went fantastically well. Giles was pleasant, if not a touch guarded, and Chris seemed to be his usual, open, self.

Between lunch and desserts, the two young men made themselves scarce at the bar.

"Before I forget," Gordon said, "Have you still got that address?"

"Oh, yes, it's just here," Maggie said, and routed within her bag. "Chris seems a nice boy," she commented.

"He is. And Giles, too."

Maggie nodded as she handed the piece of paper to Gordon.

"I know he's a little shy," Maggie said, "But that's just him. Oh, before you open that, I was wondering. How are you set for next week?"

"Next week?" Gordon said, raising an eyebrow. "Nothing planned."

"Good."

"Why?"

Maggie smiled and said, "Just take a look."

Gordon unfolded the piece of paper, and read the address. "Oh," he said, "And are you offering to..."

"That I am," she replied, "it's been awhile since I saw him."

"Well, in that case," Gordon said, "I'd love to." He put the note on the table. "It's been years since I last went to Scotland."

TRAIN, PLANES, AND ADMISSIONS OF GUILT

Gordon booked aeroplane tickets to Scotland for the coming Friday, and set to work trying to find Chris a job. He rang the rest home first, and arranged to meet with the new owner that afternoon. Next, he strode his familiar path into town, but instead of perusing the shops, he bought a local newspaper, and went to the cafe to look through the job section at the back.

Chris wouldn't be happy if he knew what he was up to, but there was no way Gordon could watch him growing more and more depressed, and not try and do something. Still, he'd have to be careful; Gordon knew however much he offered to help, Chris would be too proud to accept. But the lack of a job was not just a problem for his son, it would surely put a strain on his relationship with Louise, and the pair of them had enough to worry about at the moment.

Gordon closed the paper; some of the adverts were possibilities, but none of them were quite right. There must be something I can think of, he thought.

With his writing, Gordon had never felt as if he'd been out of work. Even before he'd been able to take it up full time, he'd managed to hold down several good jobs, good enough to make a decent living for himself. His parents hadn't been poor either, and when his mother had died, the inheritance had only needed to be split two ways, for him and his sister.

Gordon took out his pencil and paper, and jotted down bullet points for his son. Top of the list was 'Music', although if Chris was going to make it, he would have done it by now. Even Chris had admitted he'd never really possessed enough natural talent to make it, but had simply worked hard to learn what he knew.

Next were 'Hard Worker' and 'Dedicated', but Gordon was aware that however true they may be, these were traits everyone would claim for themselves. Gordon put a line through all three entries. The last remaining item was the work he'd done for Mary's magazine. He knew his sister had been very impressed with Chris, and even though she had retired from the business now, Gordon realised she was his primary hope.

Gordon drained his tea, and took a deep breath. Who knows, she may even be able to get him some work at a music magazine? He remembered Chris saying, "It's not what you know, but who you know," and Gordon suddenly felt he owed it to his son to try.

The only small hurdle to overcome would be Mary herself.

Communication between him and his sister had become something of a portent. Nowadays, the only reason they contacted one another was to report the death of a family member or friend they both knew. The last time they had seen one another had been at Brenda's funeral, seven years ago. Mary had been suffering badly with her hip, and hadn't been able to stay long enough to enable a decent conversation. At least she was back in England now, and just under a hundred miles away.

"Hello, Mary," he said, when she picked up the telephone.

"Oh, Gordy," she said, "Who's it this time?"

"No-one," he replied, "I need to ask a favour?"

There was a short silence on the other end. Gordon was about to repeat what he said, when she replied, "Oh, right. Fire away."

"I don't know whether you can, but I was wondering if you still had any magazine contacts that might be able to help Christopher find a job?"

Another pause before her answer. "Well, I might have," she said, "Is he still as keen as he was when he was younger?"

"Oh, I think so. Especially with a baby on the way."

"Really? I hadn't heard. Why haven't you told me? Send him my congratulations."

"I will."

"You know, Gordy, I can't promise I can help. Or if I find one, it'll be what he wants."

"Of course not, but if you can just ask around, that'll be wonderful," he said.

"Consider it done," she said confidently. "Now, how are you?"

They talked briefly over recent news, Gordon omitting to tell her about Maggie, and he was once again struck by the lack of middle ground the two of them shared. Gordon coped as best he could, certain in the fact that Mary did the same.

"I'll give you a ring, soon," Mary said, closing the conversation. "And I'll do my best for young Chrissy. God knows, he always deserved a break after what he had to go through."

She abruptly put the telephone down, before Gordon had time to question her on what she'd meant. He made a mental note to ask her next time they spoke.

That afternoon, he met with the new owner of the rest home. He was a youngish man, named Martin, who possessed an excitable air about him. He said he was more than happy to continue with Gordon working there, if no laws were being broken, and shook his hand vigorously when he stood to leave.

"Oh, one last thing," Martin said, as Gordon was about to walk out the door. "Do you know any good gardeners? The last one's contract was up a couple of weeks back, and no-one's bothered to renew it."

"I'm afraid not," Gordon said, and closed the door.

A second later he opened it again. "Everything okay?" Martin asked.

"Yes," Gordon said. "About that gardening job. I lied a second ago, I know just the man you need."

When he left, Gordon retrieved his mobile phone and dialled. "Hello, Chris," he said, when their answer machine cut in. "I think I've finally got some good news for you on the work front."

~

With that problem hopefully sorted, Gordon was free to look forward to his trip up north. He was pleased that Maggie wanted to go with him. To go back to a place that held so many memories alone would be something of a waste. In fact, if it weren't for Maggie, the chances are that he would just have sent a letter, and seen what had happened.

According to Maggie's address, Lawrence was now living in a town near Balmoral that Gordon had stopped at on several occasions. He booked two rooms at a hotel on its outskirts for the weekend, but made sure they had an option to stay longer if required.

On the Thursday, Maggie rang, and told him she'd managed to speak to Lawrence, who'd said he'd love to see them both, and that he thought he knew where the envelope was. Gordon thanked her, and they arranged a time to meet at the station to catch the train to the airport the next day.

Gordon had always preferred travelling by train over any other mode of transport. He never quite knew what to expect. One day he might be in the midst of a party of wild school children, and the next blessed with peace and quiet. It was a natural place for him to write, though he was mainly confined to poetry; short, sharp, pieces which he could file to work on at a later date. He drew inspiration from people's comments, newspaper headlines, or some situation or reaction. Of course, the upcoming trip to the airport would offer no such opportunities, as entertaining Maggie would be the order of the day.

When he got to the station, Maggie was already sitting on her suitcase, pen in mouth, puzzling over her newspaper's crossword. She didn't hear him approach.

"Everything okay?" he asked her.

She looked up and smiled. "Yes," she said, "Can't wait."

They boarded the train and sat comfortably in the first-class carriage opposite one another. Maggie leant forward, "I hope you don't mind," she said, "but I find it difficult to talk on the train, makes me feel a bit queasy. So, I'll just be quiet, if that's all right?"

Gordon smiled. "No problem."

They both sat back, Maggie closing her eyes, Gordon fetching the scraps of paper he'd secreted away in his jacket, and his pen from his bag. He was about to look around for some inspiration, when he realised she was already sitting right in front of him.

Fifty minutes later, they disembarked at the airport, and took the lift to the airport concourse. As the doors slid closed, Maggie said, "It must be twenty years since I've been on a plane. I expect they've changed a lot since then."

"A few new gadgets, I expect, but not much more. If it's any help, it's been a few years for me, too."

During Brenda's illness, Gordon had travelled up north without her several times. On one such occasion, when she was in hospital, he'd caught the evening plane back from Newcastle, expecting to arrive an hour or so later. Fifteen minutes into the flight, however, the seatbelt sign had come on, followed by an announcement informing them they were experiencing some technical difficulties, and were having to divert to the nearest airport. Gordon, in a window seat, looked out as they'd banked over the runway, and saw the flashing lights of emergency vehicles assembled on the concrete below, waiting for them.

He'd hardly been able to believe it. Throughout Brenda's illness he'd had to try to come to terms with being left alone, and now it looked as if he might die before her. He offered a silent prayer to whoever might be listening, and held his wedding ring firmly within his clasped hands.

As it had turned out, there'd been no reason to worry. The aeroplane landed relatively smoothly, and after they were all given a quick check over by the paramedics, they were coached on to their various destinations free of charge.

He'd never mentioned the incident to Brenda. He didn't think it was a good idea to say anything to Maggie, either. Since then, however, Gordon had not been on an aeroplane. He'd been asked to do a few guest appearances away from the bungalow, but had either opted to travel there by train, or not gone at all. Still, he was glad to see Maggie was just as nervous.

After checking in, they went through to the gate to wait. Maggie got her newspaper back out to finish the crossword, and Gordon started to read a book he'd just bought. After a few minutes, Maggie nudged him. "Why do you think they're going to Scotland?" she asked, nodding in the direction of two men who sat nearby looking miserable.

"Oh," Gordon mused, "That's an easy one. I suspect they're going to set up a small boat touring company on Loch Ness, with money they've earned demolishing buildings."

Maggie frowned. "Oh," she said, "I see you've played this game before."

"It's my job, sort of," he replied.

~

The flight went very well. When, just after lunch, they arrived at Glasgow Airport, they collected their bags, picked up the car Gordon had hired, and were, within an hour of setting foot on the grey tarmac, rolling through harsh mountains and flowing streams toward their destination.

"Still just as beautiful," he said, as they drove along the twisting road beside Loch Lomond. Then, on an impulse, he pulled into a gravel car park. "This is too good to miss," he said, opening the door.

Maggie wandered with Gordon a few metres along the edge. The mist was burning off, and the shapes of the mountains were just beginning to impose themselves around the edges of view. "I never thought it would look like this," she said. "It's hard to believe we've not left the mainland."

They travelled on for another forty minutes before pulling into a small town to look for a mid-afternoon drink. Maggie had been quiet most of the way, though it was more of a contemplative silence than an embarrassing one. They ordered some homemade vegetable soup, and sat quietly in a corner, overlooked by a collection of pictures from local artists.

Maggie stirred her soup. "Are you okay?" Gordon asked.

She looked at him as if she didn't fully know. "I suppose the best way to describe it is nervous, but it's got nothing to do with meeting Lawrence again. It's more..." she trailed off.

"About you and me?" he offered, bravely.

Maggie nodded. "Yes. I've been waiting for it to go wrong, but it hasn't. And now, here I am, sitting with you and with a beautiful view, thinking, well, what's going to happen, next? It's been a long time since I've been in a situation like this, and, believe me, I don't go looking for them. I've always deliberately distanced myself from men. For my own and Giles' sake.

"To tell you the truth," she continued, nervously stirring the soup, "I'd made up my mind that I was going to grow old on my own. But now, well, I can feel things might change, and I'm not in control of it. And that makes me feel nervous. Do you feel anything like that?"

Gordon gently closed his hands around the warm bowl. "Since you ask," he said, "Yes. After Brenda died, I never thought it'd happen again. But I may have been wrong. In truth, I'm trying not to think about it too much, and just seeing what happens."

Maggie looked out the window. "Maybe that's the best thing to do. If only I could be that way. I'm putting pressure on the whole thing before anything's really got off the ground, aren't I?" She turned back to him. "Tell you what," she said, "Talk to me about Scotland. Perhaps that will take my mind off everything."

"Okay," Gordon said, "that's easy."

Maggie ate her soup as Gordon recounted his stories. As he spoke he felt Maggie relaxing more and more. Perhaps, he thought, it was down to the fact that the more he spoke, the more it revealed about himself.

They journeyed up through the country, admiring the scenery, and avoiding the wildlife, until they finally reached the hotel at just gone eight o'clock. They booked in, went to their rooms, and met at nine for a meal in the restaurant.

"Gordon," Maggie said, in a quiet but firm tone. "As we're meeting Lawrence tomorrow, there's something I need to straighten out."

Gordon sat forward in the lounge armchair, raised his eyebrows, and asked, "Yes?"

"It's to do with what I said to you before," she started, "About the pregnancy." Gordon sipped his drink. Maggie changed the way she was sitting, became a little more defensive. "It wasn't a mistake, I planned it and in so doing, I deceived Lawrence.

"You see, as much as I'm ashamed of it now, all I ever wanted when I was younger was to have a baby. I felt it was the only reason for me being here. Once, I'd overheard my mother telling someone I'd been a mistake, and that never left me. I was angry, and sad. I wanted to show them I wasn't a mistake, that I could do something, and then, when I met

Lawrence, I decided I wanted his baby. It was stupid, naive, callous, even, and I make no excuses. I used him."

"Did you get married?"

Maggie looked sad, "Yes. Everything else was the truth. After we parted, it didn't take me long to realise what a stupid mistake the whole thing was. How I'd thrown away a promising future to try and spite my mother, who, quite oppositely, didn't care how I felt. It was too late then, however. Of course, in hindsight, I still wouldn't have changed a thing. But it was a hard lesson to learn."

"How do you feel about Lawrence, now?"

"Well, I ended up resenting Lawrence for the freedom he had. But we never fell out. We were never close enough to really dislike each other."

"And that's the truth?" Gordon asked.

Maggie nodded, "I swear it is. Lawrence was a good man."

"What about Elizabeth?"

"Elizabeth? She was just very perceptive. I think she somehow knew what I was up to, right from the outset. She protected him. Gordon, I'm sorry I lied to you. I didn't think I'd be here, now. I've always said it was a mistake to protect me."

Gordon took a few moments to think over what she'd said. Then he leant forward and held her hand. It was quite cold. "I'm far from perfect, too," he said, "In this life sometimes you've just got to look out for yourself. The important thing is that you were able to tell me."

"Thank you, Gordon. It's important that you knew the truth, and not just because we're seeing Lawrence tomorrow."

"I understand," he said. "Now, let's eat."

As Gordon got into bed that evening, his mind was fixed on Maggie who slept silently in the room across the hall. Her admission this evening, he knew, had been far more symbolic than either of them were brave enough to admit to, and he wondered, not for the first time, where exactly it was that it was all going to end.

LAWRENCE, ANGUS, AND A SURPRISING REVEAL

Gordon rose at six thirty the next morning, and attempted the impossible; to try and make a decent cup of tea in a hotel room. The problem was the ingredients provided were simply not designed to allow such an outcome. He had to spit the mouthful he tried down the sink, and quickly brush his teeth, while trying hard not to gag.

He rang down to reception with a request, before showering and putting on some warm clothes to divert the freezing air outside. He had about an hour before meeting Maggie for breakfast, and he'd decided to spend it out in the open.

As he walked amongst the greening trees, Gordon was reminded of his early days. As a young man, he'd grown an affection for the outside, and often walked for hours amongst the flora and fauna of his surroundings, breathing in the atmosphere, allowing it to invigorate and refresh him.

The grounds of the hotel weren't overly large, but there were enough secluded corners to make him believe he was the only person alive. Some had even been conveniently furnished with crude wooden benches, which Gordon made full use of. He unpacked the flask of coffee he'd asked reception to have made up, and covered the nearest wooden bench with a tartan rug he'd brought from a novelty shop the day before. He sat and surveyed, feeling happy in the cold.

Scotland, he thought. He'd always fancied the idea of packing everything up and moving to some remote part of this northern kingdom. As things had turned out, he'd been too busy with Brenda, then the children, then the Race. And now? Well, now he knew just how much he relied on his family down south. And, of course, the grass was always greener. Still, he thought, maybe a few months a year wouldn't do him any harm, especially as this is the last Race.

~

Fifty minutes later, he met Maggie in the lounge and they entered the restaurant together, where Gordon enjoyed succulent smoked haddock, and Maggie a brace of poached eggs.

"You look full of life this morning," she said.

Gordon wiped his mouth with the napkin, "I have to say, I feel it."

"Was it something to do with your morning's walk?"

"Could've been," Gordon said, surprised. "How do you know about that?"

"Well, you made enough sound to wake the dead. Then, when the papers arrived, I sat by the window and saw you moving around outside."

"Just searching for some inspiration," Gordon explained.

"Did you find any?"

Gordon looked out the window, into the Scottish greens and browns. "In a way, I suppose."

After breakfast, Maggie rang Lawrence on her mobile phone, and confirmed they were going to arrive around ten-thirty. Then Gordon drove them into town, where they parked by a lovely church that seemed to be the centrepiece of the community. They both took a quick walk around, doing no more than offering a cursory look in the shop windows before moving on.

"How are you feeling now the meeting's so close?" Gordon asked.

"Hmm, good question," Maggie replied, "I'm not really sure. He sounded very pleasant on the phone this morning. Very welcoming. So, I suppose he will be."

Gordon smiled at her. "I'm happy to let you see him on your own, if you'd prefer?" he offered. "It's no problem."

"Don't be silly. I didn't come all this way up here to see him alone. We go as a team."

"As a team," Gordon repeated, and laughed.

"Besides," she said, as they reached the hire car. "I wouldn't have bothered if it wasn't for you and this envelope."

Gordon opened the passenger door, "Then I'm indebted for your help."

Maggie got in, and looked up at him with a grin. "Well, in that case," she said "we're quits. We can both go on with a clean slate."

~

They found Lawrence's house on the second lap. It was a modern, simple building; a stark contrast against the scenery surrounding it.

"Why do you think he moved all the way up here?" Gordon asked as he turned off the engine.

"His job, I guess," Maggie replied, "Although I can't see how."

As they approached, the front door opened and a frail man with a thick brown and grey beard offered an outstretched hand to Gordon, who shook it, lightly, in case he hurt him.

"Hello, you two," Lawrence said, "It's a strange place for a reunion, isn't it?"

"My God," Gordon said, dryly, "You're even looking like a Scotsman."

Lawrence chuckled, "And you an Englishman if ever I saw one. And Maggie, as captivating as ever. But then I always knew you wouldn't fade. You had that bone structure that would last. Not like me. Look at me, I'm nothing but a bag of bones, nowadays. But let's not hang about out here. Come in out of the cold. I'll put the kettle on."

Lawrence retreated inside, leaving Maggie and Gordon to exchange a surprised look and follow.

He showed them into the lounge, and then disappeared off to the kitchen. Before he arrived, Gordon hadn't been sure what to expect, but whatever it had been, it certainly wasn't what he was looking at, now.

The room was spotless, and what there was in way of furniture, was in its place. There were precious few ornaments on the shelves to either clutter, or convey personality. The chairs were covered with throws, and carpets with rugs. Where Lawrence was lacking in money, he more than made up for with ingenuity.

Their host returned after a few moments.

"You've managed to keep this place very clean," Maggie said.

"I'm a changed man, Mags," Lawrence replied.

All three sat down. Around the room, several pictures adorned the walls and the mantelpiece. Family portraits, mainly, taken around ten or more years ago. Gordon recognised people in every one of them. It reminded Gordon of something, but he couldn't quite put his finger on what.

"Is that Elizabeth?" he asked, pointing to a woman's face in a faded photograph.

"Yes," Lawrence replied, "It was taken a while ago."

Gordon got up and had a closer look. "How is she?"

"Oh, not so bad. I must admit I've not seen her for a while. You know how easy it is to lose touch. Oh, that envelope you wanted," Lawrence continued, "Shall I get it now?"

Gordon smiled, "Knowing my memory, I think that's a wise idea. Do you need a hand, or anything?"

"No, no. Not at all," he said, standing, and holding his arms out. "It's in the letter rack in the kitchen. Be back in a minute."

As Lawrence left the room, Maggie took Gordon's arm. "Something isn't right," she whispered, "Can you feel it?"

"Yes," he said, "I think I can."

When Lawrence returned, he brought with him a tray with the tea and the envelope. Gordon was pleased to see that it was in a very good condition. He took it when Lawrence offered, and carefully opened it up.

"It feels right that they should be brought together once again," Lawrence was saying, "It's felt like caring for the crown jewels looking after that thing."

There was quiet as Gordon inspected the envelope. "Well, you've looked after it well," Gordon assured, folding it back up. "Thank you."

"May I have a look?" Maggie asked, delicately. "I've not seen one before."

Gordon handed it across to her, and she turned it over. "It's quite exquisite," she said. After a few more moments, she passed it back to Gordon, who placed it in his inside jacket pocket.

After a short pause, Maggie asked, "So, Scotland. Are you up here teaching?"

Gordon settled back in his seat, happy to let them talk.

"Yes. Exactly. Teaching," Lawrence answered, staccato, and sipped from his cup. That reply might not have been a lie, Gordon mused, but it hadn't been the whole truth, either.

Maggie sipped from her cup, too. "Full-time?"

"Yes, full-time. Definitely," he replied, and, again, fell silent.

A question popped into Gordon's mind, "Do you know many people up here?"

It took Lawrence by surprise. "Um, well, a few, I suppose. I speak to the neighbours a lot." He suddenly got up. "Would you like some biscuits?" he asked.

"I'm all right," Gordon said. Maggie shook her head.

Lawrence remained standing, he turned to look out the bay window. "I can see you're wondering what made me come all the way up here? Well, it's an important job I've got," he said, and picked up a cushion from a seat.

Gordon watched as Lawrence held it to his chest and started to sway. Something in Gordon suddenly clicked, and he remembered what it was that had been niggling at him. He looked at the pictures in the room once more. "My mother had a strange habit," Gordon started, breaking the awkward silence. "Well, strange to me anyway. Whenever she had people coming over she'd arrange the house how she thought they'd like it. A sort of Fung-Shui for guests. Sounds strange, but that was just the sort of person she was. They all knew, of course. Everyone who came round. Anyway, one of the things she used to get us to do was to put pictures out of the people who were visiting. Of course, my sister didn't care too much about this charade, and every so often we'd get the wrong pictures in the wrong places. Oh, I can still see my mother's face when we made a mistake." Gordon paused and looked at Lawrence, he was starting to crumble.

Lawrence held up his hand. "You're a canny man, Gordy," he said. "You've got me. I should've known better. I'm sorry. I don't know what I was thinking of. Yes, I do. It was Maggie. I was thinking of Maggie."

Maggie looked blankly at Lawrence, "I don't understand."

"I'm not working up here, not professionally, anyway." Lawrence got up and beckoned them to follow, "Come with me," he said, "And all will be revealed."

The three of them trailed through to the back of the house, where, in a warm utility room stood a cot containing a small baby, no more than six months old.

"Whose is this?" Maggie said, instinctively reaching down, and adjusting its sheets.

"He's mine, Mags," Lawrence said.

Maggie looked at him. "Yours?"

"Yes. He's my son."

Maggie looked back down to the baby, and then to Gordon. "And his mother, where's she?"

"She's working," he said, "She works a couple of days a week, and I do a few odd evenings as a stand-in at the local college."

Gordon remained toward the back of the room. "What's his name?" she asked.

"Angus, would you believe," Lawrence said, proudly, looking down at him.

Maggie looked stumped as to what to say. "Oh," she managed.

"It's a family name. Her family. Not mine."

"And does Giles know?"

"No," Lawrence confessed, "Not a lot of people do. You see, the academia might not look on it lightly. She was one of my students at University."

"Ah," Maggie uttered. "Is that why you came up here?"

"We wanted to be near family, and hers is up here," Lawrence said. "Look, I'm sorry, Mags, I didn't want to upset you. I didn't want that to happen. Really, I didn't."

Maggie sighed, brought her hand to her face. "It hasn't upset me. I'm just surprised, Lawrie, that's all. But it is a lovely surprise. Are you... happy?"

"Yes, I am now. I was a little concerned when I first found out. But now it's... great. I'm experiencing things I missed with Giles; things being what they were. You don't hold it against me, do you, Mags?"

"Don't be silly," she said, and then Gordon saw that the two of them were crying. He imagined the guilt and the selfishness exhibited in younger years being lifted from their shoulders, whilst Angus laid there, asleep and unaware. Gordon retired quietly back to the lounge and helped himself to another cup of tea.

They stayed till one o'clock, now talking freely and unhindered by the past. They were all nostalgic and proud of it. When the baby woke, Gordon and Maggie said their goodbyes, but before leaving, Gordon offered Lawrence, Angus and the mother a room at the bungalow if ever they wanted to come down and stay for a few days.

Maggie and Gordon got back in the car and drove around the corner waving at Lawrence, Angus in his arms.

"Well," Maggie said, "I don't swear often, but bloody hell, I never expected that."

It proved a good topic of conversation all the way past their hotel and up into the hills, where they spent the afternoon. That evening they met once more in the lounge before dinner. They had a drink, and, as Maggie was about to go into the hotel restaurant, Gordon caught her arm.

"Change of plan," he said, "This way. Your carriage awaits."

"What's this?" Maggie said, as Gordon led her to an elegant black Rolls-Royce, parked outside the front entrance.

"You've had a heavy day," Gordon explained, "This is just what the author ordered. Don't worry about a thing, just put your feet up."

"Is this what you were planning this morning, in the trees?"

"Maybe," he said.

"Well, you shouldn't have," she chided, blushing at the same time.

"On the contrary," Gordon said, "There isn't anything I would rather do."

And before she stepped into the car, she turned and kissed him on the cheek.

"Likewise," she whispered.

BRENDA, VEE, AND THE PHONE CALLS

They spent another week in Scotland, touring and sightseeing. The weather stayed calm, and blue skies shone on them more often than not. He and Maggie grew closer together, and as March faded and April arrived, Gordon realised a period of his own life had begun to fade away, and that, more surprisingly, he'd let it.

The day before they left the north, Gordon rang Chris from the hotel. He'd been thinking about the job and whether or not Chris had been happy about it. Louise picked up the telephone.

"Lou," Gordon exclaimed abruptly, then laughed at himself. "Sorry," he said, "it's just I always expect Chris to answer."

"He usually does, doesn't he? Well, I'm pleased to say he's at the rest home, doing some gardening."

"Already? How's his leg?"

"Much better. I think just being actively employed helps the healing process. Besides, he's not doing too much - pruning and tidying. But he was so pleased to get out of the house, you wouldn't believe!"

Gordon felt relieved. "That's good."

"In truth, I'm glad he's out of the way, too. I'm between contracts at the moment, and it gives me a chance to tidy the place up a bit."

"You're not overdoing it?" Gordon asked, concerned.

"No," she replied, "I'm just trying to enjoy this time as much as I can."

Gordon smiled. "That sounds like an excellent idea."

~

The flight home to Gatwick was even smoother than the one they'd taken up to Scotland. Once more, they travelled back on the train in silence, Maggie looking out of the window at the rolling Sussex countryside, whilst Gordon sat and finished reading his book. After he'd turned the final page, he was pleased to discover he'd enjoyed it immensely.

They disembarked and caught a taxi back to the bungalow, arriving at a little after noon. They stood outside, somehow awkward in their familiarity. Neither knew what should be done next. Finally, it was Maggie who spoke.

"I'm thinking I should visit Giles, and then head back home, to make sure everything's okay."

Gordon nodded. "That makes sense. I'd...," he started. He breathed in deeply. "I'd like to see you again. Soon. Is that too much?"

Maggie smiled and took his hand. "No. It's not too much. In truth, it feels like I'm seventeen again, and you've asked me to the dance."

"Doesn't it just," Gordon said.

"Thank you for a lovely time."

"The pleasures all mine," he replied. "Would you like a drink before you go?"

Maggie smiled. "If I do, I may never leave."

"Is that such a bad thing...," Gordon started.

"I'll give you a call when I'm home; to tell you I got back okay."

"Please do." Maggie leant forward and gently kissed Gordon on the lips. He felt almost giddy.

"Thank you," he said, though it was hard to know which part of the last wonderful week he was thanking her for.

~

With Maggie gone, Gordon found himself at a bit of a loss. He unpacked, made some tea, and then finally wallowed in a hot bath. On the table in the lounge March's Ostrich Race answers were awaiting his gaze. At the quieter times in his hotel room in Scotland, in the morning and the last thing at night, Gordon had written April's questions. He'd sent them out to the players on postcards put inside envelopes, with a note saying he would put the mystery players question in 'the secret place' at the bungalow. When he emerged from his bath, it was four o'clock, and Gordon could feel the trip catching up with him. Instead of looking at the answers, he picked out a book from the dining room shelves, made himself some jam on toast, a hot mug of cocoa, and retired to bed for the rest of the day.

He managed to finish the first six pages before his thoughts were drawn back to the Race. He now possessed three of the original Race envelopes, four, if you counted Vee's, which meant he only had six left to retrieve. Not for the first time in the past couple of months, he jotted down the names of the people who should still have one to collect.

Elizabeth, Phillip, Pat, Colin, Cissy, Jack, Brenda

Gordon tapped his pen on the paper. One of these people's envelopes had been given to the anonymous player. But which one?

On the way back in the plane, he'd gone through the same list trying to decide whose envelope he should concentrate on next. He knew where Elizabeth lived, but, quite frankly, didn't want to see her. He toyed with the idea of writing to her, but Elizabeth was too unpredictable to risk it. She would just as easily burn her envelope than give it to him if she knew he was looking for it. A surprise visit, when he felt up to it, would be his best option.

For Phillip's he was relying on Vee to get in touch with him, and he hardly knew where to start with Pat and Colin. That left Cissy, Jack and Brenda. Cissy was a last resort. The last time they'd spoken hadn't gone well, and she'd ignored his attempts at reconciliation at Brenda's funeral.

So, Jack or Brenda? His mind flitted to where Jack's envelope might be, but, with an effort, he managed to push those thoughts away. Jack was just a diversion. His wife's envelope would be the easier to find by far. It would also be the hardest to bear.

He took the last mouthful of his cocoa, and started to prepare himself. He'd been in no rush to find Brenda's envelope. Family's held secrets, it was an almost universal law, and Brenda had been no different. Something inside him resisted, even now, the start of the search. But it would be selfish to stop. Why should he be allowed to ignore the past? Why should he be able to deny what had happened? It would be childish, and he hoped he'd stopped being that many years ago. Gordon turned out the bedside light, leaving the warm glow of the alarm clock digits to illuminate the immediate area. Gordon glanced at the clock, and saw the date which it also displayed. April 2nd - his heart lurched. He knew that when he next opened his eyes, it would be the 3rd, and all the old memories would line up to taunt him yet again.

He'd often wondered whether getting old was just a punishment for living too long, such was the baggage he'd accumulated over the years. He laid his head on the pillow, unwilling to close his eyes. In the quiet moments, Gordon found himself in from time to time, the moments when he was not preoccupied with the Race or some other goal, he mourned. He mourned for the loss of his youth, the loss of interest in the Race, the loss of his wife. But, most of all, in his heart of hearts, he mourned for the loss of his first son. Tomorrow was Graeme's birthday, and he would have been thirty-eight years old.

Gordon thought back to when he'd have been his son's age. At thirty-eight, Gordon had been married for thirteen years, and had just seen his wife give birth to Christopher. Graeme had turned eleven and won the poetry competition the week after his birthday. And Gordon; Gordon had had his tenth novel in a row published, but his success was taking its toll in other areas. With both the new baby and the publisher vying for his attention, he'd had little time to spend with his eldest son. Not only that, but he'd also had to frequently travel away from home on publicity trips.

In turn, Catherine was becoming unruly, answering her mother back, and throwing tantrums whenever she didn't get her own way. Brenda would often ring her husband in the evenings, at the end of her tether, asking Gordon if he could come back early from his trip, knowing what his answer would be. This would lead to an argument which rarely got resolved by the time the call was over.

Pamela, conversely, grew quieter, and kept out of the way. On the odd days he was at home, catching up with paperwork or some such chore, she would sneak into his study, lean over the back of his chair, and give him a hug silently from behind.

Gordon hadn't been a bad man, but at times, he thought, he hadn't been a great one either, and that saddened him. At ten-thirty-nine PM,

Gordon finally managed to shut his eyes, but the images of his family remained as bright as ever, dancing in his mind. He fell asleep holding the extra pillow tight to his chest, and dreamt of insecurity.

~

The next day, he tried to push all the negative thoughts to the back of his mind, and focus on what was right in front of him. He'd have to look through Brenda's belongings, and to do that meant having to go back to the place where he'd stored them.

Three years after Graeme's death, Gordon's mother passed on. In the last years of her life, she'd lived in a cottage Gordon had bought for her with part of the money from his books, and with her death, the cottage had become free again. Gordon and Brenda had talked about moving there, but in the end, they'd used it as a retreat whenever they felt the need for an escape to the country. After Brenda went, Gordon had taken her things there, vowing to return one day and sort them out, and as he lay in his bed on April 3rd, it occurred to him that day had finally arrived, yet still he didn't want to go back. Reopening those boxes meant reopening memories he'd never wanted to face again.

~

He arrived at the cottage by taxi at just after ten, and was pleased to see the gardener was keeping the lawns, flowers and trees in an excellent condition. Gordon paid the driver and stood in front of the gate, dressed in light clothes under a surprisingly warm blue sky. Some of the bulbs were already out, and the borders were slowly beginning to hint at their full potential. The cottage was incredibly picturesque, and whilst he was psyching himself up to go inside, he took a wander around the garden, reacquainting himself with its bends and dips, its hidden places and breath-taking views. When, at about ten-fifteen, he was ready, he opened the greenhouse door, took a step inside and picked up an aerosol can. He popped the lid off, reached into it, and clumsily peeled off the sellotape that had been holding a Yale key in place.

Gordon let himself in and opened all the windows that would open. He took a couple of minutes to check everything was still there, before finally sitting himself down at the oak table in the dining room. He poured himself a cup of tea from the flask he'd brought with him, and surveyed the boxes which were piled high on either side, ready and waiting his inspection.

As he unfolded the flaps of the first one, he started to feel guilty about leaving Brenda's belongings here. A voice suggested it had been a cowardly act, but, deep down, he knew he'd done it for a good reason. He remembered how Vee had helped him pack them all up; it was her handwriting on the side of each box, giving a brief description of what was inside. But, as Vee had told him back then, Brenda hadn't been these ornaments and papers, she'd been his wife, and, as such, it was his memories of her that were important. "And those," Vee had said, "you will never let go."

His mobile telephone brought him out of his thoughts. He was surprised the cottage even had a signal. He dug it out of his pocket and looked at the display. It just read 'Blocked'.

"Hello?" Gordon said, his throat raspy from the dust. He waited for an answer. When none came, he repeated his greeting. "Hello?" Still no-one replied. Before he had time to ask anything else, the line went dead, as if someone had put the telephone down. Gordon shrugged and put the phone down on the side. It rang again. Gordon watched it for a moment, before picking it up once more. "Hello?" he said, again, loudly and clearly. Silence. "Is anybody there?" he asked, but got no more than an empty line. "I'm sorry, there seems to be something wrong...," he started, but then stopped as he heard something in the background. The phone line went dead once more.

Gordon was spurred into action. He packed his bag as quickly as he could, and left the cottage. As he got to the gate, he heard the phone start once again. He dropped the Yale key into his pocket, and moved at some pace through the back garden, passing through a small gate, and taking the path that headed towards the centre of the village.

He was certain the person who'd rung had been quite able to hear him, and that they had simply chosen not to speak. Like an eighties police drama, he had heard a noise in the background that had given away their position, and they were close. If this was the anonymous player, this was a chance to see who it was.

Before he reached the village green, he stopped behind the cover of some bushes, where he could see the telephone box outside the post office, and behind, the church from which he'd heard the peel of the eleven o'clock bells. The telephone box was empty now, but he remained where he was for a few minutes more, until he was sure they were not going to return. Then he went and used it himself, ordering a taxi, to take him to Aunt Vee's.

~

"Come in, come in," the old lady said, when she saw it was him. "What's happened?"

Gordon was surprised. "Is it that obvious?"

"Like a book," she replied.

Once inside, Gordon explained to her about the calls, while Vee drummed the table in thought.

"Are you going to tell the police?" she asked.

Gordon shook his head. "I don't think so," he answered, "They didn't help last time, and I can't see there's much they could do about this, either. Besides, I'm pretty certain it's the anonymous player, and I don't think they mean me any harm."

"Perhaps not, but, and bear with me on this, perhaps you should think about getting a lodger for a while? This sort of thing is very unnerving, and even if there's no malice in it, I think it would be sensible to be with someone whilst you were at the bungalow. To scare them off, if nothing else."

"A lodger?" Gordon asked. He nodded a couple of times, then turned to Vee. "Well, as it happens, there was another subject I wanted to talk to you about."

Vee sat back slightly. "I'm listening," she said.

"Well," Gordon gulped nervously. "I've... met someone."

Gordon waited to see what Vee would say. She looked as if she was deep in thought, then she looked up, and it occurred to Gordon that she'd only just heard what he'd said. "Met someone?" she asked. Gordon just smiled; he couldn't help himself. "Well, knock me down with an ostrich feather," Vee continued, and then laughed. She slapped the table, making the bone-china cups rattle in their saucers. "Thank the Lord for that."

Gordon was pleased and slightly confused all at once. "Am I to understand that you're not upset?" he managed.

Vee clipped him round the head, and they both laughed. "Hallelujah," she sang, pulling out a bottle of Irish cream from beneath her seat. "Care to join me?"

Gordon snorted, and nodded. "Just a small one then. As it's so early in the day."

Vee smiled at him, "Oh, I wouldn't say it's that early."

He stayed and explained all he thought he should and Vee listened, intrigued, attentive and happy. By the time he left, Gordon owed her a bottle of Irish cream.

~

When he arrived home late in the afternoon, there was a single message on the answer phone. He thought for a moment it would be from the silent caller, but when he pressed the button Maggie's voice chimed instead.

"I don't know about you," she said, "but I've checked everything up here, and now I want to come down. I might be being presumptuous, but give me a ring and let me know what you want to do."

Excitedly, Gordon dialled her number, and when she answered, told her he couldn't agree more. Maggie said she'd be there by lunchtime the next day.

By seven that evening, his arms ached from all the cleaning and washing he'd done, but the bungalow looked and smelt as clean as it'd done for a while. It was important for Gordon to try and make a good impression after all these years. He was also pleased to find the effects of Vee's liquor were starting to fade away, too.

When he'd done all that he could, he took a pen and some sheets of paper to the conservatory, placed his watch on the table, cleared his mind, and waited for something to materialise. Predictably, he woke around nine, face resting against a page of nothing but doodles. He'd fallen asleep, his mind empty. He brought his head up, rubbed his stiff neck, and cursed his stupidity.

It was whilst he was cursing himself that the doorbell rang, and he remembered that it was the doorbell that had woken him up in the first place. Slightly afraid, Gordon stood and turned the lounge light off, sending the bungalow into darkness. He stepped, hidden, into the hallway. The front door was primarily frosted glass, and he could see there was no-one on the doorstep. His heart quickened. Feeling scared and yet ridiculous at the same time, he slipped into the kitchen and picked up the bread knife from the block.

He stepped back into the hall, and what he saw made him start. There was an outline of a person slumped on the doorstep, their back to him, leaning against the wall. Gordon waited for any sort of movement, but whoever it was remained still. He didn't want to, but, carefully, he moved closer to the door. Reaching out slowly, Gordon twisted the catch, and inched the door open. Suddenly there was movement on the edge of his vision, and he gripped the knife tightly behind his back.

"Who's there?" he called.

"It's me, Maggie," the figure said, and now he could see her, as she stepped into the light under the porch. "Didn't you get my message?"

Gordon looked around dazed and saw the '1' flashing on the answerphone display.

"I...I've been asleep."

"Oh, I'm sorry. I rang and said I couldn't wait."

Gordon looked down to what he'd thought had been someone slouched against the door. On the doorstep, Maggie's coat was sprawled across a few of her bags, the hood slightly up to give an impression of a head. He smiled to himself, placing the knife on the ledge by the front door.

"I'm so pleased you're here," he said, genuinely. Maggie was slightly taken aback.

"Is everything okay?" she asked.

Gordon hugged her. "It is now."

He picked her bags up and took them inside, while Maggie fetched the rest of her cases from the car. In a short while, Gordon had made them both some tea, and they were sitting and chatting about the past, present and future as if they'd never parted. When the clock struck midnight, Gordon yawned.

"I think it's time for bed," he said.

"Me, too," Maggie agreed. "I'll unpack some stuff."

A few moments later she reappeared at the kitchen doorway. Gordon was rinsing the cups. "Um," she said, nervously, "I can't find my bags."

Unseen, Gordon smiled. "Where did you look?"

"In the spare room?"

"Well, in that case," he said, "You won't find them."

"Oh," she replied.

Gordon dried his hands on the tea towel. "Follow me," he said.

And she did.

PAUL

Gordon and Maggie stayed in and around the bungalow for the next few days, venturing out to get supplies only when necessary. Gordon told her about his visit to the cottage and the calls, and she was suitably concerned. He even told her how happy Vee had been when he'd told her he was seeing someone.

"That's encouraging," Maggie said.

"That's what I thought, too."

Vee rang on the fourth day of their solitude, just to make sure everything was okay. Gordon said it was, and told her Maggie was staying at the bungalow. "In that case," Vee said, "Perhaps you would like to come out to dinner this evening?"

Maggie, sitting nervously beside Gordon, nodded vigorously. "We'd love too," Gordon said. "We'll pick you up at seven."

~

"Hello, Margaret," Vee said, as she sat herself down in Maggie's car.

"Maggie, please."

"Maggie then, but," she said with a smile, "only if you call me Vee."

Gordon, feeling a little left out on the back seat, cleared his throat.

"Oh, hello, Gordy," she said, "Good to see you're in your place." The two ladies laughed. Gordon sulked ever so slightly.

The evening went smoothly, the two ladies ribbing Gordon at every possible point, and, in truth, he liked the attention.

"Hasn't Gordon cajoled you into helping with the Ostrich Race, yet?"

"You know," Maggie said. "He's hardly mentioned it at all."

"Hmmm, unlike him."

"I am still here you know," he piped up.

"Oh, yes, so you are," Vee teased.

When Maggie went to the bar, Vee leaned across and patted Gordon on his arm. "Relax," she said, "She's a lovely lady. Likes you very much, I can see that."

"Oh, good," Gordon said, slightly abashed.

"And she has a lot of energy, which I think will be good for you."

~

When they dropped Vee back, they watched her walk to her door. "She's a strong lady," Maggie said.

"One of the strongest I've ever known," he replied. "She's helped me out so many times over the years."

The drive home was quiet, with Maggie holding Gordon's hand as she drove. When they stopped outside the bungalow, she turned to Gordon. "I've been thinking," she started. "Would you like me to look for the envelope with you tomorrow? I don't mind."

Gordon looked at her. "Yes, of course, if you're sure?"

Maggie nodded kindly. "Yes, I'm sure. Besides, I'd like to have a look at the cottage. The way you describe it, it sounds delightful."

"It is," Gordon said. "It is."

~

The next morning, Gordon directed her to the cottage. When they pulled up outside, the grey clouds overhead started to drop a few spots of rain onto the windscreen.

"Wow, this place is beautiful," she said.

Gordon nodded, "It needs a lot of work."

Maggie smiled, "That's what I meant."

Gordon retrieved the key from his pocket, unlocked the door, and followed Maggie into the draughty hallway.

"Shall I make us a drink?" Gordon asked, holding up the carrier bag of items they'd picked up from the convenience store.

"Yes, please," Maggie said. "Do you mind if I take a look around?"

"Be my guest," he said.

As he unpacked the travel kettle and a bottle of water, she called to him, "Wow, this place just gets better and better."

By the time Maggie appeared in the kitchen, Gordon had made the tea and was already sifting through one of the boxes. "What would you like me to do?" she asked, gently.

"Oh, just pick a box, and start looking," he replied.

They searched quietly and methodically. It felt strange to Gordon for them to be so close yet not talking.

"I've got another batch of letters here, Gordon," Maggie said, waving some faded pieces of paper in his general direction.

"Who are they from?" he asked.

"Let's see," Maggie said. "Paul, no surname. Just Paul."

"Oh," Gordon said, with a sigh, "We've got to him, already, have we?"

"Why? Who's Paul?" Maggie asked.

Gordon looked at his hands. "He's the man Brenda had an affair with."

~

Gordon had first found the letters when he was sifting through Brenda's paperwork, shortly after her death. He remembered simply not being able to believe what he was reading. He'd felt completely detached, at a distance from the words on the page, as if they had been sent between two total strangers, and not Brenda, the woman he'd lived with and known for most of his life.

He knew the man named Paul, too. He had originally been a friend of Mary's, back when she'd left university. The first time he'd met him, Mary had driven him up from their town to a very chic detached house in the west end of London. Initially, Mary had told him and his mother she was going to stay with a lady friend she'd met from college, and had kept up this facade until they'd reached the house. Gordon had been angry that he'd been lied to so easily, but Mary dismissed his complaints with a disdainful look and the words, "So, you've never lied, then?"

She'd given her brother a quick tour of the impressive house, and by the time they'd finished, Paul was outside, unloading her belongings from the van. He was a tall, broad, man. Not outright handsome, but with a quirky face, which he used to good effect when reciting his many stories. Still stinging from Mary's deception, Gordon tried for the best part of an hour to dislike him, but eventually, conceded defeat, and, by the end of the afternoon, all three were in stitches from Paul's jokes and anecdotes.

Mary had shared Paul's house for just over a year, and it was a real purple patch in the siblings' friendship. Gordon would visit at least once a month, more if they threw any parties, and she and Paul would come down when they'd had enough of their own social circle.

Over this time, Gordon learned that though his sister and Paul were close, he already had a girlfriend. In fact, it was the girlfriend Mary had known first, an old-school friend who had asked his sister to keep an eye on Paul whilst she was away touring Europe and then Australia. Gordon sometimes wondered how easy it had been for Mary to accept.

When she'd earned enough funds to get a flat of her own, Mary had moved out and Gordon had lost touch with them both. It had coincided with him meeting Brenda, so, in truth, he hadn't had a lot of time to miss them. Over the next couple of years, Gordon learned Paul and his girlfriend had split up, and he had secretly expected his sister to turn up one day with him, engagement ring securely on her finger. To his surprise, it had never happened, yet the pair had remained good friends.

The next time he'd seen Mary was at his wedding. She was on her own, but she enjoyed the day just the same as everyone else. She was an independent lady, and Gordon quite admired her for it.

They lost touch completely after that. Mary's work consumed her time, as did Gordon and his home life. They wouldn't see each other for another twenty years, not until the days following Graeme's death, when Gordon's household was spinning out of control. No-one knew what to say or do. On more than one occasion, Gordon remembered asking for some divine help, but little did he expect to get it in the form of his sister. When Mary turned up, bags in hand, three days after the accident, she told them she was there to help.

It was the last person Gordon had expected to appear, but seeing her face at that time of need had made a remarkable difference. It was like having a mother figure there to soothe him, but it wasn't just Gordon that Mary helped. The whole family quickly grew to rely on her. She seemed to have a skill of working in the background, out of the way, tidying, organising, cooking and cleaning. Then, if one of them needed someone to talk to, she'd be there, listening to whatever they wanted to say. Then, in the evenings, she'd go to Gordon's study and do her magazine work, which she was sharing with one of her colleagues. Gordon wondered if she ever slept.

Mary had stayed two months in all, and within that time, Brenda and his sister had become very close. Even after Mary returned to London, Brenda would continue to visit her, and she quickly became Gordon's liaison with his sibling. Gordon often wondered if it was during one of these visits that Brenda had first met Paul.

He only had the content of the letters to develop a picture of how their relationship had grown, and even then, it was only Paul's side, but in a way, they were the best ones to have. He knew that to have read his own wife's words would have been too painful a burden to bear. His writing side had wanted to know more about the man, so he'd begun to do some research. He'd discovered Paul had achieved much in his life, retiring at the tender age of forty-five, after being a finance director with a London investment firm. He'd even been quoted in several Financial Times articles.

Paul had then moved to Bath, and gotten involved with some charity work, but otherwise kept himself busy doing personal things. He'd managed to remain a bachelor and seemed, on the surface, to have enjoyed this lifestyle. From the letters, it was obvious that Brenda had made the initial contact between the pair. The first few replies Paul sent her were nothing more than friendly. He sympathised with Brenda over the loss of Graeme, and tried his utmost to offer words of encouragement.

Paul likened their situation to some friends of his who'd also lost a child, and who'd never been able to fully accept what had happened. He warned that, as a consequence of this, the couple had soon split, and implored Brenda to get some professional help.

The next few letters told her she should be more patient with her husband, however unapproachable he was becoming. He offered a few addresses of counsellors he'd managed to find for her.

In the next, he questioned whether it was a good idea for the two of them to meet. It hadn't been his idea, Gordon could tell, and he respected his prudent words. Unfortunately, Brenda had persisted, and a meeting point had been arranged.

When Gordon thought back, he could remember the time all too well. After Mary had left, their relationship had deteriorated, culminating in several months of near isolation from each other. He would often sleep in his study, or in the chair in front of the television; anywhere, but next to his wife.

When they spoke, it was full of short, sharp sentences, and they avoided direct eye contact. Gordon wrote a disastrous book, full of remorse, which never saw the light of day. He barely spoke to the children. It felt to him as if they were on their mother's side. At some point during this time, Gordon could remember Brenda telling him she was attending a rest and relaxation weekend with Mary, and though he'd been curious about it at the time, he hadn't wanted to ask any questions. When she'd returned a different person, he was so pleased he hadn't dared bring it up again.

After that weekend, the letters were a mixture of guilt and love. Although angered by the deceit, Gordon could feel the anguish Paul had gone through, and in some respect, he felt sorry for him. He knew, in the end, Paul would not be the one who grew old with her. The pair met several more times, before, eventually, in the last letter, Paul told of how he had to let her go. He wrote he could feel her returning to her husband, and that that was the right thing to do.

Gordon was relieved he hadn't known about the affair at the time. He knew back then the situation would have been almost impossible to resolve, and that they would have divorced. In retrospect, he could see how it had happened. He had been very unreasonable, and he'd been ashamed of himself. That Brenda should have found an outlet like Paul, though somewhat devastating, had probably saved their marriage.

~

"And what of Paul, now?" Maggie asked, "Have you seen him since you found out?"

"No. I thought about contacting him, but I didn't think we had much to say to each other."

"And you don't feel any anger towards him?"

Gordon frowned, "I don't think so. It's been seven years since I found out. I've kind of accepted it, now."

"Well, perhaps that's a good thing, considering," she said.

Gordon gave her a sideways look. "Considering what?"

She passed a letter to him. "Considering the post script on this letter."

He read it. "Oh," he said.

"Oh, indeed. That's the last letter, too. It seems some skeletons just won't lie still."

Gordon felt a little cold and a little excited at the same time. At the bottom of the letter he now held in his hand, Paul had written "PS. I found that envelope of yours, the pretty one you lost, with the laughing children on. Where shall I send it too?"

"Of course," Maggie said, surveying the remaining boxes, "There's a chance he may have sent it back."

Gordon nodded. "I agree," he said, looking at the boxes. "But the way this year's going, I'm not about to hold my breath."

MARY, CHRIS, AND AN UNEXPECTED CALL

It took them a week to be sure the envelope wasn't at the cottage. They'd search a box in the morning, and then go out in the afternoon to clear the air, and give Gordon a chance to talk about the things they had uncovered. He made a few attempts to contact Chris, but there was never any answer. Pam and Simon were just as difficult to find, as were Tony and Catherine. It was almost as if they were all giving them some breathing space before visiting. Thankfully, Vee was available, so they dropped in on her a couple of times. Gordon was pleased to note that the arrival of Maggie had brought out an old forgotten side of her.

In the evenings, he caught up on the marking for the Race, as well as planning the next month's questions, while Maggie sat and eagerly listened to his nostalgic ramblings. When they finished the last box with no evidence of Brenda's envelope, Gordon suggested they might leave hers till last. Maggie listened quietly, but suggested it was something he shouldn't try to ignore. There was unfinished business with Paul, and whether or not he had the envelope, Gordon could do worse than to try and speak to him. She even offered to ring Paul herself. "Although," she told him, "I don't think I'd be the right person to do it."

"But where should I start? I don't even know his number." Gordon asked.

"You could ask your sister," Maggie replied. "If you're up to it."

Gordon thought for a moment, before letting out a long sigh. "I am," he said. "As it happens, I wanted to speak to her, anyway."

"Does she know about the affair?"

"I don't think so, and I'm not about to ask."

"Oh, it's you, Gordon," Mary said when he rang her later that day. She sounded slow, as if she were preoccupied with something else. "What do you want?"

"Um, well. Do you remember that man, Paul? The one you lived with in London?"

"Oh, yes. Has he died?"

Gordon stifled an inopportune laugh. "I don't think so. I wondered whether you knew where he lived, now?" The line went quiet. "Are you still there?" Gordon asked.

"Of course," Mary said abruptly, "I was just trying to think if I knew. I haven't spoken to him for years. What's it about?"

"Oh, I'd just like to talk to him, see how he's doing."

"Liar," Mary said, but not nastily, "You always were a bad one. Look, I think I may have a phone number somewhere, I'll try and find it."

"Thank you," Gordon said.

"Is that all?" Mary asked.

"Well," Gordon said, "Have you had time to find out anymore about a possible job for Chris?"

The line fell silent once more. Gordon, not wanting to be chastised again, waited. "Young Chris?" Mary said, uncertainty in her voice.

"You were going to ask your friends to see if there was a possible job at a magazine?"

"Oh, yes, that's right," Mary said, recovering, "No, I've not had a chance to yet. But leave it with me, and I'll see what I can do."

When Gordon put the phone down, he turned to Maggie, who was sitting in the conservatory listening in on the extension. "It sounded like she'd forgotten," he said, and shrugged his shoulders.

~

The next morning, Maggie went off to do, what she called, some real shopping. Gordon wasn't sure he liked the sound of that, but he knew better than to ask too many questions. Instead, he gave her the letters with the new questions in, and she said she'd post them on the way. He went out to the secret hiding place, and placed the anonymous entrants question under the pot. The previous question had been picked up early last month. It struck Gordon that with everything that had happened, he hadn't really had much time to think about the Race.

As he walked back into the bungalow, the telephone started to ring. "Hi, Dad." It was Chris.

Gordon was glad to hear his voice at last. "You're a hard man to get hold of. Everything all right?"

"Not really. Can I come round for lunch?"

Something in the tone of Chris' voice made Gordon's stomach lurch. Please, not something wrong with Chris, he thought. "Is that okay, Dad?"

Gordon pulled himself back to his senses. "Yes, of course it is."

~

Maggie got back just before his son arrived, and seemed happy for Chris to be joining them. Gordon explained he'd seemed worried on the phone, and so, when he arrived, Maggie said her hellos and then made herself scarce in the kitchen so the two of them could talk.

Gordon and Chris went out into the back garden, where they pruned and weeded. It had been Chris's idea, and Gordon wasn't about to argue. Anything that helped Chris was fine by him. As they worked, the smell of the Maggie's cooking seemed to search them out, making their stomachs growl.

"Do you remember when we used to have bonfires back at the house, Dad?"

Gordon laughed, "Considering it was me who built them, yes."

"I always remember the aroma of those nights, of the fireworks, the smoke, the jacket potatoes and onions. It was an idyllic time. Before there were any worries in life."

"Yes."

Chris threw a branch down onto the stack. "Do you remember the boy that used to live near us, at the house? The one who was always around?"

"Young Jamie," Gordon said, "Gosh, yes. How could I forget? There were still his dirty footprints on the carpet when we moved out."

"That's the one. We were good friends, for a while." Chris straightened his back.

"What's happened, Chris?" Gordon asked, putting his hand on his son's shoulder.

"Well, up until a few days ago, Aunt Mary was the only one who knew about my problems, and she didn't even know the half of it."

"Your problems?" Gordon said. "You know you can talk to me. I'm not here to judge, just to help."

"I know. That's why I came."

"Did you tell Louise you were coming?"

"Sort of. Well, no. We've not really spoken in the last few days. Not since she found out."

Maggie appeared at the conservatory doors. "Food's ready."

"Come on in," he said, "and tell us what it's all about."

When Maggie saw the looks on their faces, she asked, "Would you like me to leave the two of you alone?"

Chris shook his head. "Please, stay," he asked. "Any friend of Dad, is a friend of mine."

Maggie wanted to immediately reach out and hug the boy. She stopped herself, but only just.

When all three had settled at the dining room table, Chris said. "In a nutshell, I've been the victim of a blackmail ever since I went to Spain."

Gordon's mind whirled. "Spain? When you were working for Mary? That was eight years ago." Then, somewhere in his mind, memories linked together. "When I sent you the money?"

"Yes, when you sent me the money. That's when it started."

Throughout his journeys, Chris had tried to find time to send postcards back to his friends and family at home. Though seldom received, they would be a breath of fresh air to Gordon and Brenda, who always had him in the back of their minds. Chris would write about his travels, admitting to them that they hadn't been all that he'd hoped they'd be. In fact, he said, he'd been very homesick indeed.

Chris was nineteen when he'd reached Spain. Mary had met him at the airport, where he'd been all smiles and happiness, but behind it all he just wanted to go back to England, have a cup of tea, and maybe watch some football on the television. Yet, he persevered, maybe out of pride, and he was glad he did.

"At least staying with Mary helped," he said to Gordon. "She was very positive, and I loved the work. Then I received a letter from Jamie, saying he'd like to visit. Well, I hadn't seen him for years, so I said fine, and three weeks later I was meeting him from the plane. He originally said he was on a week's holiday, and asked whether I could put him up."

Gordon pictured how he remembered Jamie. He'd been a gangly youth, completely unable to stand still for five seconds, with a mop of reddish blonde hair. He'd been quite a shy boy, certainly not as quick as Chris.

The two of them had made a bit of an odd couple really, brought together because neither had many friends. Each filled the others gap, and for a couple of summers it had been difficult to move without the pair of them getting under your feet. Then, with little warning, Jamie's family had moved across town, and Jamie was seen no more.

"Well, the Jamie I met at the airport was not the one I remembered. Gone was his infectiously happy persona, replaced with sullenness, and a feeling that the whole world was against him. He frightened me as soon as I saw him."

"He didn't endear himself to Aunt Mary, either. He'd mope around her house, leaving everything untidy, and hardly recognising anyone else was there. Then he'd go out till the early hours of the morning, invariably returning drunk. Mary wanted him out, and so did I, especially when the week grew into two weeks, and he hadn't even mentioned leaving. I had a bad feeling he'd never had any intention of going."

"Why couldn't you just kick him out?" Maggie said.

Chris smiled. "Because of what he'd shown me. He had a hold over me, and I couldn't see a way out. At the beginning of the third week, Mary gave me an ultimatum. Him or the both of us. She said it was breaking the law to keep him there."

"He'd already told me what he'd do if I asked him to leave, so I had no choice but to·tell Mary what was going on. I couldn't tell her everything, but she was brilliant, nevertheless. She told him to go herself, when I wasn't around. And he did."

"But he waited outside, and when I returned, demanded money for his silence. I was desperate. I gave him what I'd earned, but it wasn't enough. So, I had to ask you. I didn't want to."

Gordon patted Chris's arm. "I understand."

"But the demands didn't stop there. He's just kept asking me for more ever since. All these years I've been giving him money. And of course, it hasn't just been my money. As it's gone on, I've had to use some of Louise's money she put aside for the savings."

Gordon looked at the bottom of his teacup. "Oh, dear," he said, "And you didn't ask her?"

"No. She found the building society book while cleaning up the house. She confronted me, and I told her everything. She hasn't spoken to me since."

Chris' eyes filled with tears, which fell silently onto the tablecloth.

"Oh, Chris," was all Gordon could say.

"What has he got on you?" Maggie said. Both men looked at her. She was strong, and it was what they needed.

Chris wiped his eyes with a napkin. "It doesn't get any better," he said.

During the second summer Jamie was around, he and Chris had made a rare visit to Jamie's house. His family were out, and while they were hanging around, Jamie produced the keys to his brother's motorbike. It was only a small thing, less than 50cc, and pretty beaten up. They drove it round the back garden a few times, and when that had become boring, Jamie suggested they take it out onto the downs in search of more demanding terrain.

They'd spent an afternoon whizzing up and down pathways, and Chris' confidence on the bike had grown quickly. Then, gradually, his adrenaline started taking over and he was going faster and faster over tougher terrain.

"So," Chris said, "I decided I'd ride up this grass bank. It was only a few feet high, but it was enough for me not to see the man who was walking his dogs on the other side. There was nothing I could do. I hit him square on. Knocked him out cold. Jamie screamed "leg it", so we did, with the bike. We put everything back as we found it, and agreed to go our separate ways."

"And that's how it was left, up until he came out to Spain. As I drove him back to Mary's, he produced a newspaper clipping which described how the man had been paralysed from the waist down, and that the police were pleading for any witnesses. I felt terrible. Still do. It's always been in the back of my mind."

"Wow," Gordon couldn't help himself say. "You didn't go to the police?"

"I was scared, Dad. I was stupid. I don't know what to do."

The table was quiet. Gordon and Maggie looked at Chris, who in turn looked at his plate. "There's only one thing I think we can do," Maggie told them. "We have to try and heal the wounds. And I don't just mean Louise."

By the time Chris left, they'd agreed to meet again, the next evening. Maggie told Gordon to arrange a meeting with Louise, and he met her that very afternoon. Louise was upset and angry, and Gordon did his best to reassure her that everything would be all right.

"Can it ever be again?" she asked him, tears in her eyes.

Gordon nodded. "Of course it can. I guarantee it."

She seemed slightly better when they parted, and Gordon said they should meet again, soon.

When Gordon arrived back at the bungalow, the telephone was ringing. Gordon opened the door as Maggie picked it up.

"Hello? Oh, right. Yes, he's here." Maggie turned and offered the phone to Gordon. "They didn't say who it was."

"Hello," he said.

"Is that Gordon?" a man's voice asked.

"That's right," he replied. "And who's this?"

"It's Paul. Your sister said you wanted to speak to me."

Gordon's throat dried. He coughed, twice, loudly into the earpiece. "Hello, Paul," he croaked. "I wasn't expecting you."

Maggie, who'd been hovering on the periphery, moved forward, concerned.

"Are you all right, Gordon?" Paul was saying. "You don't sound too good."

Gordon didn't feel too good, either. His heart had started to pound in his chest, and his legs felt weak. He'd never expected this day to arrive. It had lain hidden in the back of his mind, coiled up and asleep. Now it barked at him with a ferocity he didn't like.

"I'm... feeling a bit strange," Gordon said, "But I'm okay."

He suddenly had the urge to put the telephone down, change his number. Pretend it never happened.

"Glad to hear it," Paul was saying. "It's been a long time, hasn't it?"

"A lifetime," Gordon said.

"I couldn't believe it when your sister called. Brightened me up no end."

"Good," Gordon replied, trying to sound interested.

A little voice had started inside him. He didn't know where it came from, but he knew where it was going.

"Anyway, how can I help?"

"Well, there's just one small question I needed answering," he heard himself saying, in a detached tone.

"Well, fire away," Paul chirruped.

Now the inside voice was booming, and Gordon listened to what it was saying. "I just wanted to know...," he managed to push out, "why did you have an affair with my wife?"

VEE, LOUISE, AND THE TRUTH

Gordon felt a sweep of goose bumps encase his body. He could hardly believe what he'd just said. There was silence from the other end, and then, if he needed any more proof of what he'd just accused him of, Paul hung up. Gordon leant against the wall, and feigned a small smile at Maggie.

Maggie sensed he needed to sit down. "I'll make you some tea," she said, taking his hand and leading him into the conservatory. "Won't be a moment."

"I obviously touched a nerve," he said.

"That you did."

Gordon sat, somewhat shakily, listening to Maggie making the tea, and he found it made him relax. When she brought it in, she put it down on the table and asked, "How are you feeling now?"

"Better," he replied.

"Do you think he'll ring back?"

Gordon thought for a moment, "Yes," he said, "He's too polite not to."

~

That evening, Paul did. Gordon was asleep in his chair, so Maggie answered it. She woke him gently. "Paul wants to know if you'd like to meet up."

Gordon looked up at her through sad eyes. He nodded. "Somewhere mutual," he said. "Can you ask him?"

She nodded, and went back to the phone. She arranged to meet in a pub Paul said was about halfway between the two of them. When she put the telephone down, it rang again, immediately.

A few seconds later she woke Gordon up for the second time that evening.

"Gordon, get up, quickly," she said, and disappeared.

Gordon closed the reclining chair, and shuffled into the hall, pushing a hand through his hair. "What's going on?"

"That was the hospital on the phone," Maggie said, pulling clothes from the wardrobe.

"Hospital?" exclaimed Gordon, the word bringing him spinning into the conscious world. "What's happened? Is it the baby?"

"No," Maggie said, "It's Vee. She's taken a fall."

~

Vee had been taken to the same hospital that Brenda had spent her last days in. As he and Maggie approached, Gordon felt a growing reluctance to go back inside, though he knew there was no other choice. There was something else, too, a growing feeling that he was unable to shake; he was afraid that like Brenda, once admitted, Vee would never get the chance to leave.

Maggie drove into the new car park, and Gordon noticed with some relief that at least some of the old grey concrete buildings had been pulled down, replaced with red-brick exteriors.

"It's been a while," he mumbled to himself.

Gordon and Maggie walked through the corridors with walls and floors coloured with warm peach and light brown hues. There were bright pictures fixed to the sides and large windows with views onto enclosed courtyards beyond. It felt quite unlike the hospital Gordon remembered.

The pair of them held hands, worried at the seriousness a fall could bring to someone of Vee's age, even of their age. Anxiously, they followed the signs that guided them to where the receptionist had said Vee was located.

They opened the heavy door leading down to the wards, took a left at the end and walked into the unmanned reception area. They waited until a nurse appeared, who then directed them to Vee's private room, and advised that she had been slightly sedated because of the pain.

Gordon knocked on the partially open door. "Come in," Vee's voice struggled weakly.

A dimmed reading lamp lit the room, and it took Gordon's eyes a second to adjust.

Vee lay in the bed, propped up slightly by a couple of thin pillows. She looked tired. Slowly, she lifted her head, and her eyes, which had been so full of life just a few days ago, were now glassy. "Who is it?" she asked.

"Gordon and Maggie," he replied, moving forward slightly so he could touch her hand.

She sighed deeply, "Oh, Gordon, I'm sorry to have troubled you at this hour. It's so late."

"Don't be silly. There's nowhere else I'd rather be. How do you feel?"

"Well, I've felt better, and certain parts of me are a shade of blue I never knew existed. But, as you can tell, they've given me some pain killers, so it's not too bad. They tell me I've not broken anything. It's just my pride that's been put out of shape."

"Is there anything we can bring you from home?" Maggie said.

"My glasses, dear. That's what I need the most." She let out a weak laugh. "That's what got me here in the first place. Take it from me, when you reach my age, don't assume you can do everything you could when you were younger. Please, if you have time, sit down."

They did, Gordon on the bed, Maggie on the chair next to it.

"So, what got you into this fine mess?" Gordon asked.

Vee smiled. It looked to Gordon like she was made of paper. It was something being in hospital did to people.

"Well," she started, wincing from the pain, "I'd just got into bed, when I realised I'd left my reading glasses downstairs. Well, I've done it hundreds of times before, so didn't think twice about going back down to get them. I left the lights off - as usual. Well, next thing I know, I'm coming-to at the bottom of the stairs, unable to move for the pain. Luckily, I was wearing my panic button, that's all I can say. It was all my fault."

"The important thing is that you're all right," Gordon told her. "I can remember Frank saying you were indestructible. And I believed him."

"I thought he was, too," Vee said, sadly.

"Have you got your house keys?" Maggie asked.

"Yes, there should be a set in my bag. You don't mind getting them out?"

"Not at all." Maggie took the bag out of the cabinet, and looked in the top. "Here they are," she said. "Now, we'll bring your glasses in tomorrow. I imagine you'll need a change of clothes, too?"

"Yes, please, dear, that'd be lovely. A nightie would be nice. Oh, I'm sorry to have to put you through all this trouble, really I am. I feel so foolish."

"Vee," Gordon chipped in, "Whatever you need, we can get it for you."

Slowly, Vee's eyes began to clear, and she looked straight at Gordon. "Do you really mean that?" she asked.

Gordon squeezed her hand, "Yes, I really do."

"Then, please Gordon, get me my son," Vee said, "Get me Phillip, however long it takes."

~

As they left the hospital, Maggie said, "What did she mean, 'however long it takes'?"

Gordon thought for the best way to word his answer. "Well," he said, "As her husband, Frank, would say, Vee and her son have always had this on-off relationship. I think the problem's the pair of them are too much alike to get on well. Stubborn and demanding were two words Frank used to describe them. Lovable, was the third." They got into the car, and Maggie turned the engine on. Gordon suddenly felt very sleepy. He blinked himself awake, and started to tell Maggie what he knew.

As far as Gordon had been aware, Frank and Vee had only ever wanted one child, and when Phillip had come along, Vee had quite doted on him. He quickly became a mother's boy, hanging around her legs, or in her arms, and inevitably, the two of them came to share the same passions for crafts, music, and the theatre.

Then, as Phillip grew older, he became increasingly jealous of any friends his mother had, including his father to a certain extent, causing mother and son to be at loggerheads. Gordon laughed as he remembered that, during this time, Frank had suddenly found a liking for painting outdoors.

As his teenage years progressed, Phillip and his parents became mutually exclusive. If Frank or Vee entered the vicinity of their son, he would leave. They didn't specifically argue, but that was only because there simply wasn't enough time where they could actually disagree.

"But then," Gordon explained, "as soon as Phillip turned eighteen, he was off. I think he stayed for a while with Lawrence and Elizabeth, before you knew them. The three were quite inseparable."

"So, what's he doing in America?" Maggie asked.

"He's an actor," Gordon said, "At least, that's what he was when he left."

~

The next morning, they got up early, and after a quick breakfast, went to Vee's. As Maggie set about looking for her glasses, Gordon went to her bureau to find Phillip's address that Vee had told him was there.

Maggie found her quarry first. She tapped him on the shoulder, and said, "There's a little bit of washing up to do. I'll do that before we go."

"Thank you," Gordon said, and they kissed.

Gordon found the bundle of Phillip's letters, and went through looking for the latest one. A few minutes later, he appeared at the kitchen doorway. Maggie was drying the last of the cups.

"Any luck?" she asked.

"Yes," he said, "I found the latest letter, plus this." He held up an Ostrich Race envelope, and was beaming from ear to ear.

"It's good to see you smiling again," Maggie said. "And it's another one off the list." Maggie dried her hands. "Let's go and cheer her up."

~

Thankfully, Vee was brighter than the night before. She instantly recognised them, smiled warmly, and asked them to sit down. Maggie gave her the glasses, and she took them gratefully. "I didn't know what breakfast looked like," she said, "But I didn't eat it on principle. Now at least I can see what I'm missing."

"I found the most recent letter," Gordon offered, taking it from his pocket. "But it's dated December last year."

Vee took the letter from Gordon, put her glasses on, and started to skim down it. "Five months and not a single word. Was there ever such a man? You do suppose he's all right?"

"I can't imagine Phillip not being all right," Gordon said.

"There is that," Vee agreed. "Ah, yes, here's the place. Ocean Boulevard, Los Angeles. He does say it might be a temporary address, and you know Phillip. Maybe this thing down here will help."

Vee handed the letter to Maggie. "Oh, it's an e-mail address," she said, "Giles has one of those. I'm not ever so sure what to do with it, though."

"Maybe you could ask Louise," Vee offered. "She's into computers, isn't she?"

"She is," Gordon agreed. He fidgeted in his seat.

"What is it?" Vee asked him.

"I found this," he said, showing her the envelope. "In the bureau. It's yours, isn't it?"

"It is," Vee said. "And it saves me looking for it."

~

After leaving the hospital, Gordon suggested they have a roast lunch in a pub somewhere, and talk over the issue with Chris and Louise.

"I don't think Louise wanted any help with the money," he said. "I don't think that's what she's most upset about."

"Well, as far as I can see," Maggie offered, "Chris needs to repair the trust, which will take time."

"And, of course, he needs to find and apologise to this man, whoever he is."

Maggie sighed. "He does."

Gordon hung his head low, "I'm worried he'll press charges. I don't know what I'd do if Chris goes to jail. He's a good man."

"I know, Gordon," Maggie said, stroking his hand.

"I'll find out everything Chris knows, and see where we can go from there. Maybe the library will have something on the newspaper article this Jamie showed him."

"Maybe. What should we do about Phillip?"

"Phillip won't be too hard to track down. We'll deal with him later. For now, let's concentrate on Chris. Oh, and Paul."

~

Gordon used the pub phone to make a call to Louise. He arranged to meet her at the library, and Maggie dropped him off there fifteen minutes later. Gordon waited for Louise, and the pair went in together. Fortunately, Louise already knew all the information about the incident, so they were able to look through the data held on the library computers. About an hour into their research, Louise called him over.

"Have a look at this, Gordy," she said. She got out of her chair, and let the old man sit down. Gordon took a minute to read the words on the screen.

"Is this right?" he asked.

"Looks like it."

"Well, I'll be blown," he said.

~

Two more phone calls later, and the scene was set. After Chris left work, Louise picked him up and took him straight to the bungalow.

"What am I doing here?" he asked.

"Just wait and see," Louise replied. Chris looked at her for a moment, and then thought better than to pursue any more answers.

Gordon met them at the door and took Chris around to the back garden, while Louise went inside.

"What's this about, Dad?"

"Good news, of sorts," he said. "Louise and I did some research on the man you paralysed."

Chris stopped. "You did what?"

"We found out some information on the man you ran into. And it turns out it's not as bad as it sounded. In fact, he's fine."

Chris looked dazed. "You're joking," his son said. "Fine?"

"Fine. I've spoken to him, and explained who I was."

"Was that sensible?"

Gordon smiled. "There wasn't really any other choice. He said he wanted to meet you."

"Did he?"

"Yes. Would you like to meet him?"

Chris stopped and looked at his father. "I have to," he said, simply.

"Good. He's in the bungalow. I'll send him out."

Chris looked panicked. "Is he going to be okay?"

"I think so. Tony's here, anyway, so that should act as a deterrent, just in case."

Gordon went back into the bungalow, and a few seconds later, a man in his fifties came out. Gordon watched as the two of them met, shook hands, and sat on the bench by the pond.

Tony stood beside him. "Looks okay," the big man said.

Gordon breathed a sigh of relief. The body language between his son and the other man seemed to say everything would indeed be fine. "I hope so."

At the library, Gordon and Louise had found the same article Jamie had shown Chris when he'd arrived in Spain. What Jamie had neglected to mention, however, was the apology the paper printed the following week, explaining that the man wasn't paralysed after all, and even though he had suffered two broken legs, a full recovery was expected.

"All these years," Tony said, "Chris has been paying for a crime he didn't, to the full extent, commit."

"That's right."

Thirty minutes later the man shook hands with Chris again, and left. Louise went out to speak to Chris in the garden, and the pair hugged. When they came in, Chris turned to his father and gave him a hug as well. "Thanks," he said.

"Don't be silly," Gordon replied, "You're my son, and I'll always, always be here for you."

MAGGIE, VEE, AND THE SURPRISE GUEST

Soon after Chris and Louise's reconciliation, Gordon asked Louise if she could send Phillip an email on Vee's behalf, and she agreed. The following Saturday, Louise rang and told them she'd received a reply, and that it'd probably be best if she came around and showed it to them. Gordon agreed, and by eleven o'clock, she was on his doorstep.

"No Chris?" Gordon asked speculatively.

"He's doing some private gardening work," she explained. "He's just out till two. No Maggie?"

"She's popped over to see Giles."

Louise rummaged in her bag as she followed Gordon into the kitchen. "I've got the email in here," she said.

Gordon opened the fridge. "Excellent. Do you mind reading it out?"

"Not at all." Louise unfolded the piece of A4 paper, cleared her throat, and read. "Hi, Gordy, exclamation mark, there's quite a few of those."

Gordon smiled, "There would be, he's quite an excitable chap."

"It continues, 'It's great to hear from you! And over e-mail! You techno-devil, you! Your correspondence finds me in Las Vegas, of all places, seeing the sites. I can't believe I've never been! Health is adequate, temperament extraordinarily good! How are you coping? Is the Race as good as ever in your capable hands? Isn't it about time you let ol' Uncle Sam entertain you for a while? God knows, there's enough Americans who need cheering up. And I heard you weren't doing any more books? Why's that? Surely, you're still inspired by life? Sorry to hear about Mum, will write her as soon as I can. Please respond ASAP. Once again, lovely to hear from you, Much love, Phillip'."

Gordon handed her the drink. "He can do more than bloody 'write her'," he said. "I'll have to play the trump card. Have you enough time to help me put together a reply?"

Louise nodded and within half-an-hour it was finished. Gordon had been polite, yet firm, offering to pay for Phillip's flights here and back. He knew Phillip couldn't resist a gift horse.

"When will you be able to send the reply?"

"As soon as I get home. Who knows, we could have an answer in a couple of days."

~

That afternoon, Gordon went to see Vee with Mags. He was finding it easier each time he went to the hospital.

"It's a lovely day," Vee said, when they arrived. She was back to normal. A good recovery, one of the doctors had told him. "But I do feel guilty about the both of you coming in like this. You shouldn't worry about me now. I'll be all right."

"Stop it," Gordon said, "I won't hear any of it. Anyway, I have news of your son."

Vee seemed to perk up even more, and Gordon felt guilty for getting her hopes up. "Oh, yes?" she asked.

Gordon explained to Vee about the email, omitting both that Phillip had hardly mentioned her in his reply, or that Gordon had offered to pay for his ticket.

"So, hopefully he'll be here soon," he finished with.

"Have they told you when you're due to get out of here?" Maggie asked.

"Wednesday, I think."

"Good," Gordon said. "I was hoping we could have a meal with Chris and Louise."

Vee nodded, though was slightly guarded. "Would you mind," she started, "if we had it at mine? I'm not sure I'll be up to going out for a while."

"Of course," Gordon said.

"I can cook it," Maggie chipped in. "All you'd have to do is eat and talk. Though not at the same time."

The three laughed together in the hospital room.

When they left, Gordon turned to Maggie, "I may have to put off this meeting with Paul."

Maggie nodded, "Good idea," she agreed. "There's too many other things to worry about. Perhaps you can ring him when we get home."

Gordon smiled. He liked it when Maggie used the word 'home'.

~

Vee was let out of the hospital on the Wednesday as they'd told her, so Gordon arranged for himself, Maggie, Chris, and Louise to go around on the Saturday for a meal. Nothing more was heard from Phillip, and Gordon could feel himself starting to get annoyed with him.

When Saturday came, Maggie went to Vee's early to prepare the meal, leaving Gordon at the bungalow with Louise, connecting the computer up to the Internet.

"You look nice," Vee said, as she opened the front door to Maggie.

The younger woman smiled, "Thank you. As do you. How are you feeling?"

"Sore, but happy," she whispered, then leaned in closer. "I've been looking forward to you coming round."

Maggie hugged her gently, and said, "So have I."

As Maggie stood and prepared the vegetables she'd brought, Vee sat in a comfortable chair in the kitchen and spoke. Maggie's own mother had died ten years previously, and she missed her, missed those long chats where the two of them would talk about anything and everything.

"I hope you don't mind me asking," Maggie said. "But I was wondering what your late husband was like? You mention him often."

Vee smiled. "Well, now there's a story," she said.

~

Vee and Frank had met and married when they were still quite young. Some of the family had frowned upon it, but Vee had always been sure of what she'd wanted, and Frank had been it. He was desperate to become a painter, and Vee thought he had the talent for it, even though at the time they met, his paintings weren't selling at all.

"He needed encouragement," she told Maggie. "Encouragement and nurturing. I didn't know whether it'd work, but I was willing to try." Whether or not Vee's attitude and actions were the impetus he'd needed, but within a year of them meeting, Frank's work was starting to sell.

"He was so pleased," Vee said, a light gleaming in her eyes. "With his growing success, we were able to spend more time around each other. Frank was worried it might be too much, but as it turned out, our relationship thrived."

They spent several years moving around the country, Frank doing exhibitions, his work continuing to grow in popularity, until they finally settled in London, where they wanted to set up a permanent studio and raise a family.

"Children didn't come easily to us," Vee said, ruefully. "In fact, several years passed by without any luck whatsoever."

When, eventually, Phillip arrived, Frank could afford to cut down on his painting, and he concentrated more on helping with the family. Having accumulated enough money to enjoy several work free years, the pair were able to give Phillip their undivided attention.

"Did he miss his painting?" Maggie asked.

"Whenever I asked him that," Vee said, "He'd point to his temple and say, 'I'm always painting, in here.'"

Then, as Phillip grew older, Frank did start to paint again, his style subtly changed by the years.

"Of course, it surprised us both when Phillip announced he wanted to be an actor," Vee admitted. "But we were both quite artistic, so were behind him. Then the next week he told us he was... homosexual. That was less of a surprise."

Frank always enjoyed going to watch him wherever he was. "He was concerned about what would happen if Phillip was ever without work for a period of time, and I understood why. Phillip could get depressed very quickly. Fortunately, he earned enough to get by."

"And what about the Race?" Maggie asked. "Did Frank enjoy it as much as Gordon?"

"Oh, yes, he did. The Race was such a large part of his life. He loved it, and let it fill his spare time. He enjoyed the knowledge it gave him."

"He sounds lovely," Maggie said.

"He was. I'll always remember him as a man who enjoyed everything he did. He was easy to love, and I always felt loved. It was the best time of my life."

The doorbell went, and the two ladies exchanged a frown.

"It's too early for the others," Vee said.

"I'll see who it is."

Maggie walked out, and Vee got up slowly behind her and stood at the entrance to the kitchen. She watched as Maggie opened the front door and the older lady's hand immediately went to her mouth.

"Oh, my God," Vee said.

~

The evening was pleasantly warm, and as they pulled up to the "The Brambles", Gordon saw Maggie waiting outside. She came over to the car as it stopped. Gordon could see something wasn't right, and got out of the car as quickly as he could.

"What's happened?" he asked her.

"We have guests," she said. "I tried to ring, but couldn't get you."

"Sorry," Gordon said, "The mobile's dead."

Chris and Louise got out of the car, and the three greeted each other.

The front door opened and a booming voice erupted behind them.

"Gordy, how long have I waited to see you again? Come and give Phillip a really big hug."

Gordon turned around, stunned for a second. Then he rallied himself. "Phillip," he said, putting on the biggest smile he could, "You made it."

"Of course," Phillip replied indignantly, "I could hardly have left my wounded mother all alone at a time like this."

Maggie squeezed Gordon's hand as she felt him tense. Gordon managed to keep smiling. "When did you arrive?" he asked.

"Today," he said. Phillip walked over to Chris and Louise and extended his hand. "Pleased to meet you. Chris and Louise. Congratulations."

They shook his hand warily but politely. "Thank you," Louise said.

Phillip turned to Gordon. "And, I must say, Gordy, you have the most exquisite taste in women. Maggie is simply delightful."

Gordon smiled on. "Isn't she?" he said.

"Now, talking of taste, my stomach is simply chewing itself into tiny little pieces. Let's go and feast ourselves on the succulent delights inside."

~

Throughout the meal, Gordon did his best to ignore Phillip and his backhanded compliments and face-on barbs. It was a shame he hadn't mellowed with time. Thankfully, Maggie acted as a go-between, and seemed deftly able to diffuse the troubled atmosphere.

Towards the end, when Gordon could finally see the finishing line in sight, Phillip stood up and tapped his wine glass with a spoon. "I'd just like to say thank you to you all," he said, with well-acted sincerity. "Thank you for inviting me over, it's a real pleasure. Of course, the timing couldn't be better. Although I know I'm not a participant, I am still looking forward to my invite to the Mid-Year Bash. I do get an invite, don't I, Gordy?"

Gordon's smile remained on his face, but inside, he went cold. The Mid-Year Bash, he'd totally forgotten about it. "Of course," he said, "We're sending them out soon."

Gordon offered to get everyone a drink after the meal, and took Phillip into the kitchen with him.

"I was wondering," he said. "Did you find out whether or not you had an envelope?"

Phillip took a second or two to focus on him. He'd had quite a bit to drink. "Envelope?" he asked.

"In the email I sent, I asked whether you had one of the Race's original envelopes. You know, the Ostrich Race?"

"Oh, God, yes, I remember," Phillip said, with a derisory tone, "Well, I searched the flat where I was staying but I couldn't find it. And I would've found it if it'd been there. I haven't got much stuff anymore."

"Oh," Gordon said, "So you don't think you had one?"

Phillip leaned forward, the smell of alcohol and cigar smoke following a second behind. "On the contrary," he said. "I'm almost sure I did have one. Daddy gave it to me. I can remember it now. Beautiful, weren't they?"

"Very," Gordon said. "Any ideas where it might be?"

Phillip sighed deeply. "I expect," he said, "That I left it behind when I fled to America. It all happened so quickly, I only had the time to pack a minimum. The rest of it I left with rat-face."

"Rat face?" asked Gordon.

"Oh, you must remember him. Andy. The bastard. I expect that's where I left it. But God only knows what's happened to it now. That man had no morals at all. I wouldn't be surprised if he's sold the lot, and his granny with it."

"I don't suppose you have his number?"

"Humph," came the reply. "I'm sure I can find it out. But I don't want to. It'd be a big favour."

"I understand," Gordon said, biting his lip against the over-riding sensation to list all the unpaid favours he'd done for Phillip in the past. "Can you do it?"

With a big sigh, Phillip said, "Oh, yes, all right. If I must."

~

As they pulled away from Vee's, Maggie said, "So, the Mid-Year Bash?"

"Yes," he said, "The Mid-Year Bash."

Gordon had always enjoyed the name 'The Ostrich Race'. It was mysterious, intriguing, unique. However, since its inception, the actual Race, apart from the entrance form and the certificate's, had had very little to do with Ostriches. According to its history, this was also an omission which had troubled the previous organisers, until, around a hundred years ago, someone had hit on the idea of throwing a party mid-way through the Race, and so the Mid-Year Bash had been born.

Of course, it had been a more sedate occasion back then, taking the form of a sit-down dinner attended by the participants. Then, as the years had worn on, the stiffness had been slowly lost.

"Nowadays," Gordon said, as they got into bed that evening, "We play some games, drink some wine and eat plenty of buffet food. It's really just an excuse for a get-together."

"Sounds nice," Maggie said.

"It is. But it's something else I have to organise."

"I could help?" Maggie suggested. "I wouldn't mind."

"Really?" Gordon said.

"Really. I can organise, and it'll take the burden off you. Deal?"

"Deal," Gordon said. "You don't have to ask me twice."

~

At the breakfast table the next morning, Maggie asked, "So we just have to hire a hall, and lay on some food, right?" She had her pen poised over a pad of paper. "That shouldn't be such a big deal."

"There are also the costumes to think about," Gordon said.

Maggie looked at him over the rim of her glasses. "Costumes?" she inquired. "Surely you don't mean Ostrich costumes?"

"Mm," Gordon offered, feeling slightly awkward.

"Oh boy, oh boy, oh boy. And you've never found this sort of behaviour strange in any way?"

Gordon smiled, "I used to," he said. "I used to."

~

In what felt like a previous lifetime, Gordon remembered Vee picking him and Brenda up from the station, all wearing long coats, and being driven to the big house, where, in a part no longer used, the Mid-Year Bash would be held.

"Don't look so nervous, Gordon," the younger Vee had said, as they'd pulled into the driveway. "There's nothing to worry about."

"Apart from these feathers," he said, shifting in the seat. "They're very uncomfortable. And I'm not totally convinced I'm not allergic to them."

"Oh, you'll get used to them after a while. Forget you have them on by the end of the evening, you mark my words."

And whilst he might not have forgotten he had them on, it did become easier when he saw everyone else looking the same.

~

"And where do I get these ostrich feathers from?" Maggie asked.

Gordon screwed up his face. "Would I sound facetious if I said the ostrich feather shop?"

MARY, SIAN, AND THE PHOTOGRAPH

Over breakfast the following day, Gordon told Maggie he planned to speak to Paul. "Best to get it over and done with," he said gravely.

Maggie offered her help should he need it, but he knew this one was up to him. However much Maggie was now a part of his life, this came from a time before Maggie, and now Brenda had gone, he was the only one left to deal with it.

"Is there any particular date for this Bash?" she asked him.

"The Friday nearest June 21st. Around then."

"I'm on it," she said, and kissed him on the forehead. He watched as she grabbed a piece of toast from her plate, and disappeared into the spare room, to start looking for venues and suppliers on the Internet.

Gordon finished off his own toast in peace. It was May 1st, and there were less than seven months left for the Race. He was keeping up with the answers and the questions, though he hadn't been able to give it as much attention as he'd hoped. Not for the first time, he wished there was a way to slow the days down, to savour them.

He summoned his courage and rang Paul around ten. As he stood listening to the telephone ring at the other end, he could feel himself winding tighter and tighter, until he was worried he wouldn't be able to utter a single word should Paul pick it up. Thankfully, the answer phone cut in, and Gordon managed to push out a polite message. He put the receiver down feeling relieved, yet somehow cheated, as if Paul should've been home, waiting for his call. This, in turn, made him restless, and he didn't know quite what to do.

"Why don't you go out into the garden," Maggie suggested after listening to him huff and puff around the bungalow. "Take a cup of tea and relax."

Gordon agreed, especially since the weather was so agreeable. He brewed a pot and took it out into the back garden. Every so often, Maggie would secretly check on him, to make sure everything was okay. Whilst Maggie stood at the conservatory door, the doorbell rang. She thought about calling to Gordon, but then decided he had enough to worry about and answered it herself. On the doorstep stood an oddly attractive man, who smiled with a relaxed charm.

"Is this where Gordon Paige lives?" he said, his voice a mixture of accents. He brushed a few locks of his curly hair away from his brown eyes. He looked young, but the grey of his hair hinted at his real age.

"And you are?" Maggie asked.

"Paul," he said. "I believe I've spoken to you on the telephone."

"Did you get his message?"

Paul shook his head, "Message?"

"Gordon rang you this morning and left a message."

"Oh, no. I've not been at the house for a few days. I thought I'd come and see him, talk things over face to face. Is he in?"

"Yes, he is. If you wouldn't mind waiting a moment, I'll see if he's okay."

When she told Gordon who was at the front door, he stopped pacing, gathered himself up and went inside. Maggie waited in the garden.

"Good to see you," Gordon said, accepting Paul's outstretched hand with more confidence than he'd anticipated. "Come and sit down."

~ 278 ~

Maggie looked on from outside as the two men talked. She made them drinks a couple of times, but apart from that, she left Gordon to it. He looked as if he was dealing with the situation admirably, and after an hour or so, she saw Gordon give him back the letters he'd written, and in turn Gordon received the Race envelope. It was a strange exchange and one she knew she wasn't a part of.

As Paul left in his car, Gordon held Maggie's hand tight. "Well, that was easier than I thought," he said. "Another chapter closed."

"And another envelope," Maggie added. "I wonder how Phillip's getting on with finding his?"

"Knowing Phillip," Gordon said, "I suspect he may have forgotten about it already."

~

Considering the first four months of the year, May went particularly smoothly. After his confrontation with Paul, Gordon felt both relaxed and exhausted. Both he and Maggie put it down to the fact that he'd lived with the secret of the affair for so long, that now it was finally finished, his body was saying 'no more'. He felt slightly unwell, too, so confined himself to the bungalow, mainly lying on the bed in the spare room whilst Maggie organised the Mid-Year Bash on the computer next to him.

The only two doubtful guests for the event were Simon, due to business, and Catherine, due to her just being Catherine. Gordon wasn't overly worried about either. Maggie managed to book a function room in a restaurant nearby, found a supplier for the ostrich feathers, and sent out the invitations. There was still no communication with Phillip.

In the first week of June, Gordon received a telephone call.

"Hello?" he said.

"Hello," came the reply, a woman's voice. "My name's Sian. We've not spoken before, but I care for your sister Mary."

"Care?" Gordon questioned, confused.

"Yes. I'm a nurse, Mr Paige. Mary employs me to look after her."

"She hasn't said anything to me about a nurse?" he asked.

"Well, she doesn't want people to know. She still wants to be thought of as independent. But now her condition has worsened, well, I thought I ought to at least let you know."

"Condition? What condition?"

"Mr Paige, I'm afraid your sister has Alzheimer's. She's been diagnosed for the last three years."

Gordon felt numb. "W-what? Um, is she there? Can you put her on the line?"

"She's asleep, Mr Paige. But I assure you it's true. I know the two of you don't speak together much, but I thought you ought to pay her a visit before things... deteriorate any further."

"I understand," Gordon said. "Thank you for letting me know." Gordon put the telephone down feeling sick. He desperately wanted to talk to Maggie, to ask her what he should do, but she was at the restaurant talking through everything she wanted for the Bash.

Gordon waited as patiently as he could for her to return. When, at last, he heard her key in the lock, he went to the front door.

"What's the matter?" she asked.

"It's my sister, Mary. Her nurse rang and told me she's got Alzheimer's."

"Oh, no. It never rains but it pours," she said.

Gordon looked at the ground. "I feel so guilty. I've neglected her…"

"Don't punish yourself for this. She's got an illness which is nothing to do with you. At least, you'll have the time to speak to her, to make amends if needed."

Gordon nodded, "Yes, I will," he said, "I will."

~

One week later, Gordon travelled to see Mary alone. Maggie stayed at the bungalow to finish off the last-minute preparations for the Bash, and for that, Gordon was thankful. Although he didn't want to say it, he was unsure how Mary would take to a completely new face. He didn't even know if she'd still recognise his own.

The nurse, Sian, had given him directions, and he arrived at the house in a little under two hours, with just an overnight bag for his luggage. He'd never been to Mary's before, and when he pulled up to the house, he was surprised at just how much it resembled their childhood home. He wondered whether it had ever crossed his sister's mind.

Before Gordon had the chance to knock, the door was opened, and the nurse, who Gordon had imagined as a brunette but was actually a blonde, immediately smiled and said, "Hello, Mr Paige, it's good of you to come. Mary's in the back garden."

"How is she?" he asked.

Once again, he received a warm smile, "Come and see," she said.

The nurse took his bag and led Gordon through the house to the patio doors which opened out onto the garden. As they walked through, Gordon nosed into the rooms through half open doorways, to try and build some sort of background around Mary, this sister he hardly knew. There wasn't an awful lot to see. The sitting room had been the most used, presumably because she spent most of her time there. The furniture was well worn, photographs filled the sides and hung on the wall, and an antique wireless stood in one corner. Gordon had wanted to stop and look around, but he was out the doors and into the garden before he'd had the chance to ask any more questions.

Gordon could tell the garden was large, even though most of it was hidden behind high hedges.

"I call it the labyrinth," the nurse was saying, "But Mary seems to like it."

Sian led Gordon through the hedges, and as he rounded yet another corner he saw Mary seated by a table. The first thing that struck him was how old his sister had become, and it felt as if his breath was being sucked out of his lungs. He wondered what he looked like to her.

"Mary," he called, "It's been a long time."

She looked towards him, and for an awful moment, Gordon thought she might not recognise her own brother. But then a small smile started to twitch at her lips, and she said, "My God, Gordy, I thought you were dead! Come and sit down. Sian can get us some drinks."

"What would you like to drink, Mr Paige?" she asked, her hand subconsciously tapping her watch.

"Please, call me Gordon. A cup of tea would be great. But only if you have time. Don't make yourself late because of me."

Sian looked surprised, and dropped her arms to her side. "No. Not at all. Milk and sugar?"

Gordon replied, "Yes, and two."

When Sian had gone, Mary leaned closer and took his hand. "What do you think of her?" she asked.

"She seems very pleasant, why?"

"Just wondered, that was all. I'm thinking of asking her to help me full time. Until I become too much. Good help is harder to get, nowadays."

"I'm sure it is. Well, if she makes your life easier, Mary, that's all that matters."

They sat and talked while Sian served tea. She then excused herself, and went to do some shopping, leaving the two of them alone, like old times. When his sister put on some sunglasses and leaned back, Gordon was pleased to see he could still recognise the woman of old.

"Do you smoke?" Mary asked him.

"Not anymore."

"You don't mind if I do?" she asked, getting the cigarette out. Gordon shook his head, but she wasn't looking. "Only bloody vice I've got left. Apart from the booze, of course."

When the temperature went down, they moved inside to the sitting room, where they looked through Mary's photograph albums, and Gordon had a good look round. He even noticed some of his books on her shelf.

"I remember this photograph," he said, pointing to a picture of his father leaning against a big black car, the local train station in the background.

"Do you want it?" his sister asked immediately. "There's no point in me keeping these things now."

"I'd love to have it," Gordon said. "Are you sure?"

"Feel free. They don't mean anything to me, now."

"Thank you," he said.

~

When Sian returned at around five o'clock, she cooked them all some tea. The three of them ate at the dining room table, and Gordon was pleased to see how much the two ladies got on.

As the evening progressed, his guilt at not seeing her for so long slowly ebbed away. Although as siblings they'd got on well, it was a simple fact that neither had felt the compunction to be around the other all the time.

At just before eight o'clock, whilst Sian was helping Mary take her bath, Gordon's mobile rang. He looked at the number on the display, and for a moment didn't recognise it. Then he realised it was the bungalow's number. He'd never had a need to put it against his name.

"Gordy, it's Maggie," Maggie said when he answered it. "How's it going?"

"Okay," Gordon said. "It's nice to hear your voice."

"Thank you. I hope I'm not interrupting?"

"Not at all."

"I wondered if you knew if you were staying up there tonight?"

"Um, yes, if that's okay? I'll be home tomorrow."

"No problem," Maggie said, "I'm looking forward to seeing you."

"And you."

When Mary came down again she was in her pyjamas, looking more youthful. She had gained a spring in her step. Perhaps it was something to do with the sherry Sian was holding for her.

"I've been thinking," she said, "Wouldn't it be nice to have a game of Scrabble or two to pass the evening?"

Gordon smiled, "Yes," he said, "I'd love to, as long as you promise not to beat me too badly."

By the time the last tile was drawn, both senior citizens were quite tipsy. Mary and Sian had won one each, Gordon none. It was the right way around. When they parted for their rooms, Mary hugged him.

"Thank you for visiting," she said. "I know I may seem cold, but I do think about how you are."

~

Sian arrived early the next day. Gordon was already up and dressed, and the two of them shared a pot of tea whilst they talked.

"Does she treat you well?" he asked.

"Very. She's a bit of a hard nut to crack, but inside she's fairly kind. She talks about you a fair bit."

Gordon raised his eyebrows. "Does she?"

"Oh, yes. Well, you are her famous novelist brother. And your son, Chris. She likes him a lot, too. Which is quite something, when you listen to all the people she doesn't like."

"How bad is her illness?"

"Oh, it's manageable, at the moment. You've got to admire her, she's trying to fight it every step of the way. It'll be a shame when she has to go into a home."

They all had breakfast together, and then walked as best they could round a public garden nearby.

At noon, Gordon was ready to go. He hugged his sister for the second time in two days, and shook Sian's hand. "See you both soon," he said.

"That'll be nice," Mary replied. "Keep in touch."

~

Traffic was bad on the way back, and Gordon got caught in a tailback on the motorway. Fortunately, he was in no rush, so he drove into the nearest service station, and went to have something to eat.

Before entering the restaurant, he bought a book of matches in the newsagents, and went to the male toilet, where he pulled the photograph of his father from his pocket, struck a match, and watched as the flames licked about his father's smiling face. He'd hated the photograph, and everything it reminded him of. He dropped its smouldering remains down the toilet and flushed.

~

When, a few hours later, he arrived back at the bungalow, Maggie was there to greet him. She looked as lovely as ever, and Gordon tried to convince himself that everything was okay, but it wasn't. There were still some secrets only he knew.

PHILLIP, JOEL, AND THE MID-YEAR BASH

The Sunday before the Mid-Year Bash was Father's Day. During the day, Chris, Pamela and even Catherine dropped in, with their partners and children in tow. Judging by the intervals, it occurred to Gordon they may have organised it, but he didn't mind. It meant there was a steady stream of visitors, and that made both Maggie and he happy. Catherine came first, around ten, and stayed for half an hour with Jessica. Pamela and Simon arrived around eleven and stayed for an hour with the children. Just after lunch, at about two fifteen, Chris and Louise arrived, and they stayed until six.

When they went, Gordon looked at Maggie and at the presents he'd been given.

"I might have known," he said, looking at the three umbrellas on the hooks inside the door. "I thought I was lucky not to get any for my birthday!"

Maggie laughed. "Well, if it's any help, I could do with a new one," she said.

Gordon smiled, and swept his arm along them. "Was there ever such a choice?"

At seven PM, there was a knock at the door. Gordon took his reading glasses off, looked at Maggie, and then got up to go and see who it was.

"Tony," Gordon said, pleased to see him on the doorstep. "Please come in."

"I hope you don't mind," Tony said. The big man came in and wiped his feet on the mat. "I meant to ring and check but didn't get the chance."

"You're always welcome round here," Gordon soothed.

They went into the lounge, where Maggie smiled, and said she'd make them a drink. Gordon went through to the conservatory, and the two men sat down.

Tony fished around in a carrier bag he'd brought with him, and produced a card and a present. "Here you are," he said. "Happy Father's Day."

Gordon had to pause to let the feeling of tears die down. "Thank you," he said.

Maggie arrived carrying a tray with three coffee cups on.

"I thought of getting you an umbrella," Tony said, "But then I decided not to."

Gordon took the present that Tony held out for him.

"You really shouldn't have," Gordon said.

"Yes, I should."

Gordon unwrapped the present, and found inside a set of silver cufflinks, in the shape of a quill.

"They're lovely," Maggie said. "How thoughtful."

"Oh, Tony, you don't have the money for these," Gordon said.

"Yes, I do," he said. "It's the least I could do. Do you like them?"

"They're fantastic," Gordon enthused. "Where did you find them?"

"Oh," Tony said, a little embarrassed. "A friend saw them, and mentioned them to me. And I thought they'd be perfect."

"They are," Gordon replied. "Just perfect."

Tony left a little after eight-thirty, looking tired. As they watched his van pull off, Gordon said. "He didn't mention Catherine, at all."

Maggie nodded. "I noticed that," she said, and they both went inside.

Gordon woke early on the 24th June, knowing the day was going to be a blur of last minute preparations for the Mid-Year Bash, which was taking place that evening. Maggie was already up being busy somewhere in the bungalow, and he got ready as quickly as he could to help her.

"What would you like me to do?" he asked as she looked over papers in a folder.

She turned and smiled at him. "Nothing. I'm in charge of this. Take the day off, see some old friends."

"Really?" Gordon said, frowning. "There's nothing for me to do?"

"Nope, not a thing. Why don't you speak to that friend of yours? Bob, wasn't it?"

"Bib!" Gordon exclaimed. "My word, I'd forgotten about him. Yes, I'll give him a call."

~

"Gordy!" Bib said, when he answered his phone. "Sorry I haven't rung before. So much going on, you know?"

"Oh, yes, I know," Gordon agreed. "Have you got any time today to go for a coffee?"

"Of course," Bib replied, "Let me sort a couple of things out, and I'll be right with you."

Gordon walked into town, and met his old friend at a cafe Bib had recommended.

"You're looking good," Bib said to him. "You must tell me how you do it?"

"If only I knew," Gordon joked. "Besides, you don't look too bad yourself."

They ordered lunch and Gordon filled Bib in on what had been happening in his life. Bib listened, smiling and nodding.

"And this Maggie, she sounds like a keeper," Bib said.

"She is. And what's been happening with you?"

Bib set his cup down and looked at Gordon. "Had a bit of a scare earlier in the year. That's my excuse for not calling. Thought the... illness had come back. Was a scary six weeks or so. But everything came back benign. Anyway, scared the hell out of me, so I decided that I didn't want spend my last few years in this dreary place, so I've been sorting out moving back onto the continent. South of France."

"Sounds lovely," Gordon said.

"Bloody is," Bib agreed. "It's all sorted now, just ready for me to move in. I thought I'd spend one last summer here, and then go. A kind of farewell tour."

"A winner's lap?" Gordon offered.

Bib laughed. "Yes, a winner's lap. I like that idea a lot more. You always were good with words."

"It's what I did." Bib looked at Gordon. "Everything all right?" Gordon asked.

"I'm just trying to work out if it's something you want to do again, Gordy?"

"Writing? I think my time has come and gone, Bib. I had a good innings."

"You did. But what about a second innings? What about another chance to get out there and bat. You still seem very sharp to me. I'm certain you could write something good."

Gordon nodded. "That's very kind. But my problem isn't with ability, it's with substance. Stories used to come to me ten a penny. But now? Now I just sit there and get frustrated. I've spent too long on my own. I've no ideas anymore."

"So, you're telling me, Gordon Paige, that after everything you've said to me today, about your Ostrich Race and family issues, you have no stories to write about? I think you're forgetting the first rule of writing."

Gordon looked at his friend. "Write what you know. I see what you're saying."

"If writing is what you love, then write what you love."

"Has my agent put you up to this?" Gordon asked, with a smile.

Bib sat back, "Oh, how I'd have loved to have been your agent."

After the meal, they took a stroll along the promenade, and sat on a bench in the sunshine.

"We've both had good lives," Bib said. "But there's still more in store for us. That's what I believe."

When they came to part, the two men shook hands.

"Good luck in France," Gordon said.

"Good luck in Blighty," Bib said. "I'll invite you over when I get settled. But if I don't, just make sure you ring and remind me."

"I will."

~

Gordon got back to the bungalow at five o'clock. Maggie seemed to have coped perfectly well without him. He showered and shaved, and emerged from the bathroom an hour later.

"Your costume is on the bed," Maggie said, passing him in a blur. "Feathers and all!"

~

They picked Vee up on the way there. She too, was wearing a suspiciously long coat.

"Still no Phillip?" Gordon asked.

"No," she said, disgruntled, "Don't mention that name. It's been over a month now since I've seen him. He was supposedly trying to get the envelope from his ex. If you ask me, he's found an awful lot more than he was bargaining for. Still, I was expecting to see him this evening. He gave me his word he was coming. Things don't change."

"You never know," Maggie said, "he might have gone straight to the restaurant."

When they arrived, they were shown into the function room, accompanied by some strange looks from the other, less dressed, visitors. All three of them looked in vain for Phillip.

"Sorry, Vee," Gordon said.

Vee shook her head and shrugged. "You can't tell them what to do, I suppose."

Maggie took Gordon on a tour of the room. "It's very nice," Gordon told her. "I've not been here before."

"There's even a log fire," Maggie said, walking ahead.

She took off her coat to hang it on the pegs along the side of the wall. She was wearing a blue dress, with the feathers hanging in the middle at the back.

"You look wonderful," Gordon said, taking off his own coat. His feathers were on the back of his suit jacket arms. "I think the feathers always suited the women more!"

Chris and Louise arrived next, Louise's bump now showing.

"It's lovely to see you looking so buoyant," Vee said to her, "You must be having a wonderful time."

"Oh, it's had its ups and downs," she said, with a smile to Gordon, "But hopefully we're over the worst."

Vee nodded. "You just wait till it's born," she said, "That's the bit no-one ever warns you about. Oh, and the fifty or so years afterwards, too."

Maggie escorted Chris and Louise to the self-service mini bar the restaurant had set up at the side of the room. She'd given strict instructions that no-one was allowed in without an invite, including staff. The food was already laid out on the table furthest away from the fire, covered over to keep it fresh. Gordon's stomach rumbled just looking at it.

Next to arrive were Pamela, Trudie and Denise, all dressed in black, with the feathers attached mainly on their backs.

"Lovely to see you," Gordon said as he greeted them. "No Simon?" he whispered in his daughter's ear as they hugged.

"How would I know?" she said.

"Hello, Gramps," the two girls chanted together.

"Do you like my feathers?" Denise asked, giving the adults a quick twirl.

Vee smiled, "Splendid," she said, "The best feathers I've ever seen."

Lastly, Tony arrived carrying Jessie. The two looked very happy.

"I'm afraid Catherine isn't very well," Tony explained. He seemed upset, but Gordon didn't want to push it.

"Oh, not to worry," Gordon said with an ease he hoped wasn't noticeable. "Get yourself a drink, and relax."

They all talked, played games, ate, and, most importantly, laughed. As organiser, Gordon made sure he walked round and spoke to everyone personally about their answers so far, whilst, in the back of his mind, his thoughts remained with his sister.

He caught up with Tony at the drinks bar.

"Hi, Gordon," Tony said, with little enthusiasm.

"I don't like the sound of that. What's wrong?"

Tony checked to see that Jessica was suitably out of earshot. "Catherine wasn't ill tonight, she just didn't want to come. She's gone all icy again. I think she's going to... well, end it again."

Gordon wanted to scream. Instead, he sighed, and said, "I'll talk to her for you."

Tony shook his head. "No, it's nothing you can help with. I know the signs. It'd be easier if you didn't."

"Are you sure?" Gordon replied.

"Sure," Tony agreed. "There are some things that can't be fixed. Talking doesn't work with Catherine. Sometimes you have to..." but then he trailed off. "Nothing," he said. "Don't mind me."

By ten o'clock, the children were becoming tired, huddling close to their parents who sat near the fire, talking. At ten-fifteen, they took their feathers off, and placed them on the fire. Everyone fell silent, and Gordon offered a prayer up to any deity who might be listening, asking for an easier end to the year. When he finished, there came a knocking at the door.

"That's personal service for you," Gordon joked to himself.

Maggie got up to answer it, but Gordon caught her arm, "Let me do it," he whispered.

Slowly, he opened the ornate door, and smiled at the young waitress who stood looking worried on the other side.

"I'm ever so sorry," she said, "But there's someone outside who wants to see you."

Gordon stepped through the doorway, and saw the figure slumped in a beige patterned chair. "Phillip," he called, "Is everything all right?"

Phillip looked up, his face a mass of cuts, bruises, and blood. He tried to say something, but his lips were too swollen to shape the words.

"Oh, my God," Gordon replied, "I'll get Vee."

~

Two hours later, at half past midnight, Maggie, Vee, Gordon, and Phillip sat in Gordon's lounge. Phillip still held his face in his hands, and periodically would burst into tears, much to the distress of his mother, who sat looking anxiously on. Maggie, to her credit, kept out of it, only offering encouragement if needed, while Gordon did his best to try and wheedle out of Phillip exactly what had happened.

The actor had sustained cuts on his hands and face, and bruising as if he'd just been in a boxing match. Even though he'd barely been able to walk, Phillip had refused any suggestion that he be taken to a hospital.

Slowly, he stopped sobbing. He placed his coffee cup down, looked at the others, and said, very quietly, "Sorry, Mum."

Vee squeezed his hand, but said nothing.

Phillip turned to Gordon. "I'm sorry about turning up like that. I hope I didn't ruin the evening."

"Not at all," Gordon replied, "Everyone was concerned about you."

Phillip breathed out cautiously, wincing a couple of times as he did. "I always seem to bring trouble, don't I?"

"Don't be silly," Gordon said, "Now, please, tell us what's happened?"

Phillip nodded, and said, "Yes. I owe you that, at least."

About a month ago, Phillip had visited Andy, his ex-boyfriend, on the premise of retrieving Gordon's envelope. In truth, it was just an excuse to see him again, especially now both Phillip's relationship and his job in the States had broken down.

Andy and Phillip had lived together for three years before he'd left for America, and Phillip regretted ever leaving, even though it had been his own decision to go. From the outset, Phillip had told Andy that, one day, he'd wanted to go and work in America, and when, quite unexpectedly, the opportunity had arisen, he knew he couldn't let it pass. He'd pleaded with Andy to come with him, but his partner hadn't wanted anything to do with it. Within a week, everything was over, and Phillip had flown alone to the States.

Phillip had turned up at Andy's flat full of worry, though it was swiftly dispelled the moment the front door had been opened. Surely the bag of bones in front of him wasn't the big, healthy man he'd known before, the man who'd lived his life to excesses?

Worse still, the beautiful voice he'd once possessed was now just a painful rasp, punctuated every few syllables with a hacking cough. Andy had let him in, but at first had refused to tell him what was wrong. Then, when Phillip had threatened to call his mother and ask her, he'd admitted to having throat cancer. He'd simply shaken his head when Phillip had asked whether it was treatable.

From that moment on, Phillip had wanted to stay. Andy had initially refused, but Phillip had insisted, and finally his ex-partner had agreed. In that month, Phillip had helplessly watched as Andy's condition worsened. Two weeks ago, he'd been admitted to hospital, and Phillip had gone with him. On June 24th, the day of the Bash, Andy had passed away. Wracked with guilt and sadness, Phillip had gone out to a bar, had a few drinks and started a fight he'd had no way of winning.

"I tried to catch a taxi to the restaurant, but no-one wanted to pick me up. In the end, I walked as fast as I could."

"Are you going to the police about it?" Gordon asked.

"No. I provoked the fight..."

"But this other man," Vee said, "Look what he's done to you. You can't let him get away with it."

"Don't worry, Mum," Phillip said, "I'll heal all right. I'm okay. I'm still alive."

"I'm sorry I made you go," Gordon apologised. "It's my fault."

"No, no, no," Phillip said, "It was totally my choice to stay with Andy. I could've just got the envelope, and left. If truth be known, seeing him again, it was worth the beating, twice over. Here."

Phillip reached into his inside pocket. "It's a little blood stained."

Gordon took the envelope from him. "Thank you," he said, "It means a lot that you got it."

Vee looked up, "What about America? Are you going back there or not?" she asked.

"No," Phillip said, "I don't think so. Anyway, I promised Joel I'd be at his funeral."

While Maggie took them home, Gordon added the envelope to the collection. There were six in all now, leaving a possible four to find off five more people. He updated his list:

Jack, Cissy, Elizabeth, Pat, Colin

Gordon reflected to beginning of the year, to the decision he'd made about this being the last Race. In January, he'd felt sad, almost as if he were letting everyone down, but now, he couldn't wait for it to end, and that surprised him. He went to bed before Maggie got home, and fell asleep only a few minutes after he'd laid his head on the pillow.

He awoke to the sound of the telephone ringing in the hallway. The clock opposite him read 3:06am, though what made him sit bolt upright was the fact that Maggie was not beside him in the bed.

Gordon felt sick to the stomach. He bounded to the bedroom door and pulled it open, where, thank God, he saw Maggie, holding the receiver in one hand, and beckoning to him with the other.

"Who is it?" he asked through the gloom.

"Catherine," she replied.

Gordon took the receiver and placed it by his ear. "Hello?"

"Dad, is Tony with you?" Catherine demanded down the line. "Tell me if he is."

"Um, not that I know of," Gordon responded. He covered the mouthpiece and said to Maggie, "Tony's not here, is he?"

"No," she said.

Gordon took his hand away. "No, he's definitely not here. He left the Bash before we did, saying he was taking Jessie home."

"Well, he's not made it back. I've already rung the police, and the hospital, and they've got nothing. Dad, I think he may have taken her, and I don't know what to do."

"Well, this is Tony we're talking about. He's never going to harm Jessica. There's nothing to worry about on that score."

"I hope not."

"Of course not," Gordon continued, slightly annoyed. "Do you want me to come over?"

"No," Catherine dismissed, "I've got a friend coming round. I just wanted to know if you'd seen them."

"No," he said, "I'll try and think if he said anything more. I'll give you a ring if I come up with anything."

When Gordon put the phone down, Maggie said, "I get the feeling I'm a bad omen."

"What?"

"Surely your life wasn't as complicated as this before I showed up."

Gordon laughed and put a comforting hand on her shoulder. "Oh, you'd be surprised," he replied.

~

Gordon woke at eleven the next morning, and Maggie brought him a cup of tea.

"You spoil me," he said to her.

"It's nice to have someone to spoil," she replied.

Gordon took a sip. The first one of the morning was always the best. "Has there been any news on Tony?"

"I rang this morning, but no, nothing from anywhere. They think they're on the road, but they don't know where. It's getting serious, now."

Gordon nodded, "I can imagine."

~

Gordon rang and left a couple of messages on Tony's mobile offering his help, but didn't hear back. Then, later in the day, Catherine rang and told them Tony had been in touch and had said he'd taken Jessica on a 'holiday', and that they would return in a few days. Jessica had spoken to her mother, and had sounded very happy, so Catherine had okayed it with Tony, before telling the police it had been a misunderstanding. "Better to play along," she'd said to her father. "The most important thing is to get Jessica back." A cynical part of Gordon thought that Catherine was probably enjoying the time to herself.

~

Tony was good to his word, and returned Jessica a few days later. They'd both had a fantastic time, by the looks of it, and no-one said anymore about it. In the week following the Mid-Year Bash, Gordon and

Maggie visited Vee and Phillip a few times, to make sure both were okay. Interestingly, as Phillip's wounds started to heal, a different sort of man emerged. He seemed more caring, and stayed with his mother to help out whenever he could.

"I'm, quite frankly, amazed," he said to Maggie. "I'd have never expected anything to have this sort of effect on him."

"It's a silver lining," Maggie said.

"That it is," Gordon agreed, and as they entered the July of that year, Gordon hoped it would be the first of many.

PAT, COLIN, AND SOME GOOD NEWS

Gordon spent the first two weeks of July sketching out a new idea for a book. He mentioned it to Maggie, who was very supportive, and offered whatever help she could give. It was both an interesting and exciting process, but Gordon deliberately took it slowly. There was no point in rushing into anything, best to let it build by itself.

Around the middle of July, Gordon needed a holiday. He mentioned it to Maggie, who agreed it would be a good idea.

"Do I get to come, too?" she asked, smiling.

Gordon frowned at her. "Of course," he said. "What sort of holiday would it be without you?"

They travelled north again, to the Lake District, and stayed at a bed and breakfast in Windermere. It was a lovely setting, and the pair of them enjoyed walking through the fantastic countryside. They only planned to stay for a few days, but were still there after two weeks. In the third week, they travelled down to Harrogate, and took in the shops and wonderful architecture, staying at a beautiful hotel in the heart of town. After a further fortnight there, they travelled down and stayed at Maggie's house, visiting her friends, and sorting out some more belongings to move down to the bungalow.

"This has been wonderful," she said to Gordon when they got into her car, now laden with objects from her house.

"I agree," he said. "It's been... just fantastic."

~

August crept into September with no discernible difference. Towards the middle of the month the skies started to darken, and the rain fell in unconvincing bursts.

After returning with Jessica, Tony had kept himself to himself, just sending in his answers when required. He was doing well, too. Both he and the anonymous player had edged out ahead of the Race. Not too far, but enough to make a difference, especially at this stage in the campaign.

Gordon was pleased to see the anonymous player doing so well. It was as if they were keeping up their side of the bargain, and it spurred Gordon on to finding the remaining envelopes. In truth, he needed very little motivation; he'd returned from the holiday reinvigorated.

In his conversations with Maggie, he'd discovered she'd remained in contact with Pat and Colin, who, of course, were Giles' grandparents. With only Jack, Elizabeth and Cissy left, they now sounded like the path of least resistance, with the added possibility of gaining two of the envelopes in a single trip.

According to Maggie, the couple had moved into upmarket warden assisted housing, near to where they had lived. It was only a relatively short drive into the country, and Maggie was happy to oblige. She held a great deal of respect for Pat and Colin; they'd been supportive of Giles ever since he was born, and if they'd felt any resentment towards her they'd certainly never shown it.

Gordon talked to her about his experiences with the pair, about how Pat had always seemed to be in control of her husband, and seemed to criticise everything. Maggie had seen it too, but added that Colin was very capable of holding his own when they were by themselves. He was just a quiet, hardworking man, who had a bit of a habit of falling asleep.

All the while Maggie had known Lawrence, she'd felt the resistance he'd had to his parents. Back then, Lawrence had felt angry towards them, with issues arising from of being adopted. He never addressed Pat and Colin as Mum and Dad, instead just using their first names, relishing every opportunity he'd had to remind them they weren't his real parents.

In Maggie's conversations with the couple it became clear Elizabeth had been just as bad as her brother, if not worse. Luckily, Pat and Colin had remained quite philosophical about it. They believed they had made the right decision in adopting them. "Just the thought of them going into care sent shivers down our spines," Colin had once admitted.

When they used to go up and help with Giles, Pat and Colin would make sure Maggie got exactly what she needed; either more time with her son, or more time by herself. As Giles grew older, they'd all go out together and often spent summers at their house; it was one of the reasons Giles had moved down south.

It was midday when they arrived at the place where Pat and Colin lived, and the receptionist, with a mysterious smile, directed them through to the rear garden. Thankfully, the day was better than they'd been of late, and the plush inside was almost empty of inhabitants.

"I've never seen anything this nice," Gordon said, "It doesn't even have that old people smell."

"I don't think it's the run of the mill one we're used to visiting," Maggie replied.

Even after they'd reached the garden, it took them a further ten minutes to find them, not that either Maggie or Gordon complained. The air was warm and the grounds were well-kept and expansive. They had nearly reached the back fence, when Maggie saw their heads poking up and over the top of a hedge. It took Gordon a moment to recognise them.

~

He'd last seen them at Brenda's funeral. They'd helped Gordon tidy up after the wake, and had stayed on to talk to him. He remembered watching Pat finger through the photograph albums that Gordon had laid out on the table of the bungalow.

"We both knew you were an excellent match," he remembered Pat saying. "From the moment we first saw you together at the Race. Didn't we Colin?"

Colin had smiled, "We certainly did. It was as if someone had lighted a fire in Brenda suddenly. She'd always been full of life, you understand, but it always seemed to be one way. You were different though. It went both ways with you two."

No-one had ever spoken to Gordon like that. So much of Brenda and his early relationship had been spent on their own with little outside contact.

"Before you arrived," Pat had continued, "She used to come around to our house, more out of loneliness than anything else. You knew how hard it was for her to see eye-to-eye with either Cissy or Monty. So, she stayed around our place keeping herself busy. Then, one day, she said she'd met this man, playing cricket, wasn't it? And that she thought he seemed different. She thought you were interesting, quite eccentric. We could immediately see how fond she was of you, and I can remember Colin and I exchanging just two words."

Colin nodded, remembering. "We said 'Sound's promising', didn't we? And it was."

The two had stayed the night, talking into the small hours of the morning, and at the time, it had been exactly what Gordon had needed.

~

Now, seeing them again, seven years on, brought an overwhelming sense of comfort for Gordon. He hadn't really thought about them since that day, and it was good to know they were still going strong.

"I'd stop where you are, if I were you," Colin called out, waving his arm in the air. Gordon could now see that they were actually working on the hedge, cutting it into a shape, though, from this angle he couldn't make out what it was.

Maggie and Gordon did what they were told, and looked at each other. "Everything all right?" Gordon asked.

"Won't be a second," Pat said, her head disappearing from view.

"I didn't know you were into topiary, Colin," Maggie called out.

His head, too, had disappeared. "Well, you're never too old to start something new, that's what I always say."

Pat appeared around the side, tying up her dressing gown.

"What have you two been doing behind there?" Maggie asked, laughing nervously.

Pat took her hand, "Let's go and sit down, and we'll tell you all about it. Colin will be along in a minute."

Pat shepherded them across the garden, where a table was set-up for afternoon tea. All around it were high hedges, and Gordon was briefly reminded of his sister.

"Nice and quiet, here," Pat said, "It's good for meditation." She closed her eyes for a few seconds, and took a few deep breaths. "The air's so good," she said to neither of them.

"You two are just a couple of hippies," Maggie joked.

"Oh, yes. But there's nothing wrong with that. Now, so we don't have any awkward conversations, I'll ask you now, are you two an item, or merely friends?"

"An item," Gordon said, without hesitation.

"Oh, that's lovely. Colin will be pleased. Now, shall I be Mum?"

They both nodded, and Pat poured. "This place must cost a bit to stay in," Gordon couldn't help himself say.

"It does. But we've come into a little bit of money." She placed a cake on his plate, and passed it over. "You see," she started, "When I first met Colin, he was quite an entrepreneur. He was a partner in a business he'd set up when leaving college. Well, within a few years we'd realised that the work was taking its toll on his health and our life, so we sold out to the partner, and used the money to pay off most of the mortgage on the house. Even though neither of us had any real plans to live this long back then, we still didn't want to have to work all the hours that God sent. And it worked out very well. Colin, as you know, continued to make furniture, but on a very selective and cut-down basis. He found he enjoyed it much more like that. And I made sure I did my bit by working a few hours at the old business, sorting the office out, and the like. We were both very happy. Anyway, by the time we'd adopted Lawrence and Elizabeth, we'd saved enough to live off for a while, so I gave up the work at the business. In time, we'd forgotten it'd ever existed, up until a couple of years ago."

At this point, Colin appeared from behind the hedge, in his own dressing gown. Gordon decided not to mention it. "Not interrupting, am I?" Colin asked.

Pat smiled "Not at all, dear. I was just telling Gordon about when we heard from Harry's solicitors. Perhaps you'd like to take up the story. Oh, and you were right, they are an item."

Gordon felt himself blush. "Excellent news. Well done, Mags and Gordy. God, it's been awhile, eh, Gordon? Well, anyway, stop me if Pat's already told you some of this, or if you don't understand. A couple of years ago, I heard from Harry's, that's my ex-partners, solicitor, telling me that he'd passed on. Well, at first I couldn't believe it, he was such..."

Pat touched him on the knee, "Try and keep to the story love, or you'll bore them."

"Right, sorry. Anyway, he'd passed away, and he'd given all his shares back to me. Well, by then, the company had grown into a large concern employing a couple of hundred work-force. The shares, which had been worth a little less than five hundred pounds when I first sold them, were now worth in the region of six hundred thousand. Well, we made the decision to sell up, invest the money, and live it up a little. We didn't necessarily need to ever live in a place like this, but, well, we'd heard of it, and it's hardly your typical retirement affair. So, for the last couple of years we've been here, and it's been like a holiday. Hasn't it, Pat?"

"It's been better than that," she said.

"We even put a little money toward this area. They were more than willing to oblige us. Makes them treat us very well. Very well, indeed."

"It's nice to hear you doing so well," Maggie said, adding more clotted cream to her scone.

Colin leaned forward conspiratorially, "Now, you're probably wondering why we're wearing bathrobes?"

Gordon smiled, "I did think it was a little eccentric," he said.

Pat leaned forward, too. "Oh, it is, it is. I quite agree, it certainly is a bit eccentric. But you see Colin and I have both taken up naturalism. Now don't laugh, well, not too loudly anyway. As he's always said, it's never too late to learn."

"Don't the others mind?" Maggie asked.

"Oh, no," Colin explained, "As long as we keep paying them the money and we stay down this end of the garden they don't say a word. Oh, we've had a few funny looks, but everyone generally keeps themselves to themselves. It's only a summer thing anyway. Fair-weather naturism, we call it."

This made them all laugh. It was a nice atmosphere, and they enjoyed catching up on each other's gossip. A while later, Pat and Colin went in to get dressed, and Maggie and Gordon put their coats on and wandered the garden.

"You haven't mentioned about the envelopes, yet?" she prompted.

"No," he said, "I thought it would seem a bit rude to mention it too soon. Besides, they're a fascinating couple, don't you think?"

"They always have been. They actually match each other very well."

Gordon nodded. "I know exactly what you mean. Wouldn't it be nice if...," Gordon trailed off.

"Go on," Maggie coaxed.

"Oh, nothing."

"Don't give me that, Gordon," she said, "I know you too well."

Gordon stopped and turned toward her. "Well, what I was trying to say was, wouldn't it be nice for us to be like that."

Maggie took his hands, "There's nothing wrong with that," she told him.

"No, I suppose you're right." Gordon looked to the heavens, "It's been a lovely six months, hasn't it?"

"Yes," Maggie replied. Gordon waited.

"Is there something troubling you?" Maggie asked.

"Yes," he said again. "I feel I want to ask you to marry me," he said. "But don't know how to phrase it."

Even without looking, he could sense Maggie smile. "Let me help you out," she said, and got down on one knee, "Will you marry me, Gordon Paige?"

Gordon was taken aback for a moment, but only a moment. "Gosh, well, yes," he replied. "I'd love to. Very, very much."

~

They decided they should keep the news of their engagement quiet until they got back to the family, and took Pat and Colin out to a restaurant for dinner. As they all sat down, Pat said, "There's something about Lawrence I need to tell you."

Maggie put her hand on Pat's, "Don't worry, I know about Angus."

"Really. Oh, that is a relief. How?"

Gordon took the opportunity to explain about the mystery entrant, the envelopes, and the trip to Scotland.

"We've got those envelopes, still, haven't we, Colin?"

Colin smiled and nodded, "I know exactly where they are. Remind me to get them when we go back."

~

They journeyed home the next day, two more envelopes closer to the end. There were three messages waiting for them on the answering machine.

The first two were from Simon and Chris respectively, both asking to come around. The third was from Tony. They both stopped what they were doing and listened.

"Hi, Gordon, Maggie. I need a favour, and you're the best people to ask. Please ring me on the mobile when you get a spare moment."

Gordon looked at Mags, "Let's go to bed," he said, "And I'll deal with them all in the morning."

~

They got up the next day around nine. Gordon arranged to see Tony in the evening, Chris in the afternoon, and left a message for Simon.

"So much for taking it easy in your retirement," he said. "And I still have answer papers to mark, and questions to set. Oh, does it ever end?"

Maggie smiled, "Only when you want it to, Gordy. Only when you want it to."

Gordon knew Jack's envelope would pose more of a problem than the others he'd already found. Jack had died just a year after Brenda, and as he'd made no will, his possessions hadn't really had anyone to go to. As far as he knew, it had all been auctioned off. He let the problem sink to the back of his mind, to let his subconscious mull it over for a day. Now that there were only three people to investigate, he could afford himself the time.

At two-thirty, they were greeted by the ever-smiling Chris, and ever expanding Louise, at their flat. Gordon and Maggie were fed and watered while they recounted their latest trips, and Louise went through all that had recently happened to her.

When the catching up was over, Gordon asked his son, "What have you got to tell us, then?"

"Well," Chris started, "I was wondering whether you'd like to be my best man?"

"Best man?" Gordon said, surprised. "You're... getting married?"

They both nodded.

"Congratulations!" Maggie said.

"Yes, congratulations," repeated Gordon, before adding, "Really, you want me to be your best man?"

"Absolutely."

"Excellent. I'd be honoured," he said, and laughed.

Gordon looked at Maggie and smiled.

"What's going on between you two?" Chris asked, noticing the look the pair had shared.

"Well," replied Gordon, "I think we have something to tell you, too."

Gordon recounted what had happened at Pat and Colin's, about their engagement, and it was Louise and Chris' turn to congratulate them.

"So, will you be my best man?" Gordon asked.

Chris nodded, "Of course," he said, and the pair shook hands.

"Have you thought of a date?" Maggie asked.

Chris looked at his watch, "Not yet."

"But quite soon," Louise said, rubbing her tummy. "Perhaps if you have some time, Maggie, you could give me a hand with planning it?"

"Wow, yes," Maggie said. "That would be my pleasure."

Soon after they arrived back at the bungalow, Tony knocked on the door. Earlier in the day Gordon had asked Maggie what they should cook for the evening meal, and she had mouthed the two magic words, the ones guaranteed to make Gordon happy. "Take away."

Tony ordered and collected, and when he arrived back, they dished it up and sat down in the conservatory to eat. "What's on your mind?" Gordon said.

"I didn't know whether Catherine had been in touch with you recently," Tony said.

Gordon shook his head. "Not at all. What's happened?"

"Well, the long and the short of it is, she's pregnant. With my child."

"What?"

Tony sighed. "I know. It seems this was the ploy. She wanted Jessica to have a brother or sister, so she decided to use me to get one."

"That's unbelievable," Gordon heard himself say. "Even for Catherine."

"I know. Seems she felt safer with another child being mine. She never had any intention of taking me back."

"Oh, no," Maggie said.

"When did you find that out?"

"The day of Bash. I was so angry. I didn't know what to do, so I took things into my own hands, and took Jessica away from her. Almost as soon as I'd done it, I knew it'd been the wrong thing to do. Luckily, though, Catherine's doesn't want to make an issue out of it because the truth doesn't look very good for her."

Gordon was angry, "That's an understatement if ever I've heard one. Can I help in any way?"

"I need to see whether I've got a chance of getting Jessica back. Or maybe just being able to see her more. From a legal perspective. I wondered if you could ask your solicitor..."

"I can," Gordon said, "And, as fate would have it, I needed to have a word with him, as well."

SIMON, VINCE, AND THE ENVELOPE

The next morning, Gordon received a phone call from Simon.

"Ah, glad to catch you in," he said, in his usual upbeat, positive, sort of way.

"Good," Gordon returned.

"I hope you don't mind, but, as Pam's away, I've got the kids, and well, I was wondering whether you'd like to see them at all. Especially knowing how much you like them."

"Yes, that'd be nice. All day?"

"Well, for as long as you can manage it. They're with my mother at the moment, and I think they might be a bit much for her. And you know how well they get on with you."

"That'll be the attention I give them," Gordon replied, sourly.

His annoyance was lost on his son-in-law. "Be over about ten, then," Simon said, putting the phone down.

A relieved Trudie and Denise were dropped at the gate of the bungalow at exactly ten o'clock. Judging by the looks on their faces, Simon's mother was not the easiest relative to get on with.

"Is there anything you'd like to do?" Maggie asked, walking them in.

Trudie looked up, "Just relax," she said, with a weary look on her face.

After settling the girls in the lounge, Maggie checked with Gordon that it was still okay for her to go and help Louise with the wedding. Gordon nodded. "Oh, yes, you carry on," he said.

The girls joined Gordon at the door to wave her off. "I like Maggie," Denise said.

"So do I," Gordon agreed.

Gordon rang his solicitor's mobile phone at eleven-thirty, and was surprised when he answered. "Gordon!" he said, excitedly. "What a lovely surprise! I didn't recognise the number. Don't tell me you've actually got a mobile phone?"

"Wonders will never cease."

"Evidently. Now, how can I help?"

"Hello, Vince. I know it's a Saturday, but I was just wondering whether you were free for lunch. I've got a couple of things I need to ask you. I'm afraid I'm babysitting, so you'd have to come to the bungalow?"

"Let me just check my diary," he said. The line went silent for a couple of seconds. "No problem at all. I'll move a couple of things and I can be there about one."

Vince arrived dressed smartly in a three-piece suit of expensive means. The children were playing hide and seek in the back garden, and the two men sat in the conservatory so Gordon could keep an eye on them.

"Working on a Saturday?" Gordon asked him. "Business must be good."

"It's okay," Vince said. "I've not seen any new books lately."

"No, I've too many other things to do nowadays. What about you? Still sailing?"

"Keener than ever," he said. "Though, like you, everything conspires against me getting out there. Now, I haven't got too long, I'm afraid, so, what can I help you with?"

Gordon relayed Tony's requirements.

"Should be okay," Vincent said, "Give me his number, and I'll have a chat with him."

"I'll pay," Gordon said.

Vincent smiled, "You always were a softy, weren't you? Now, you said you had two things. What else is on your mind?"

"It's to do with Brenda's brother, Jack. You were his solicitor, too, weren't you, for his will?"

"Yes, that's right."

"Well, I was just wondering if you could remember who his belongings went to?"

Vincent shook his head slowly. "I can't remember off the top of my head, but I can look it up."

"Excellent. Whenever you can get back to me," Gordon said.

The two men sat and talked for another fifteen minutes about past times, and it was good to listen to what Vincent had been up to. Finally, he checked his watch, stood and stretched out his hand. "It's been nice to see you again, Gordon. Sorry, I couldn't stay any longer."

"That's all right, Vince," Gordon said, shaking his hand. "Thank you for offering to help Tony."

"My pleasure. I'll get back to you as soon as I can."

~

When Gordon shut the front door, he felt slightly happier. The information on Jack would get to him eventually, he could rely on Vince to come up with the name. Gordon settled down to reading a book in the conservatory. When, a little later that afternoon, it started to rain, the girls retreated indoors. Around four o'clock, Denise came up to Gordon holding his mobile phone.

"Gramps," she said, "I think you just got a text."

He took the phone from Trudie, looked at the screen, and smiled. "That was quick work," Gordon said to himself. It wasn't exactly the person Gordon had been hoping for, but it did indeed answer his question.

Trudie cocked her head to one side, and asked, "Who is Cissy, anyway?"

Gordon looked at her, "Apparently, the person all roads lead to."

~

Gordon found himself stuck between a rock, known as Cissy, and a hard place, called Elizabeth. These two women held the remaining envelopes and thus the secret that would lead him into discovering the identity of the anonymous player. Gordon blew the air from his cheeks. There wasn't much of a choice between the two; he couldn't remember either of them ever being very civil towards him.

His logic kept reminding him that Cissy, with two envelopes, would be the more rewarding quarry, yet he couldn't shake the sense of unease he felt over having to contact her again. He tried to convince himself he was just being childish and unreasonable, but it didn't work. He had to tackle Elizabeth next.

In Gordon's opinion, Elizabeth had always been an extremely volatile person, whose moods, he would swear, were able to shift mid-sentence. More often than not, she'd just been plain rude to Gordon, often referring to him as a bore while in his presence. He knew she only did it to try and provoke a reaction, but it still took every ounce of patience he had to deal with her. Gordon remembered how Brenda had always kept her distance. "She's no good," Gordon could hear her say, "Keep well clear."

There was no doubt that Elizabeth was bright, possibly even a genius, if she'd ever been bothered to find out. Unfortunately, she hadn't, instead wrapping herself up with her brother's life, worshipping the ground he'd walked on.

At least Lawrence had improved when he'd escaped to university, which said a lot about Elizabeth's influence. In the ensuing years, it was common knowledge that Elizabeth and Phillip's friendship had also faltered, and by her late-twenties Elizabeth was all-but on her own.

Gordon thought about asking Maggie to help him with her, but in the end decided against it. Elizabeth had a way of tarnishing everything with her words, and bearing in mind she already had a history with Maggie, it was probably better if he tried to deal with her alone. At least Maggie had Louise's wedding to keep herself preoccupied.

It was gone five o'clock when Maggie returned. Gordon, against his own judgement, had drafted Elizabeth a letter, requesting the envelope. He'd kept it to a minimum, so as not to arouse her interest or provoke her spite.

It was nice having Maggie back. Whenever she was away, Gordon missed her presence around the place. She'd reappeared full of excitement from her day's adventures, and it was enough for Gordon to do just to make her sit down and tell him how it'd gone.

"At eight months pregnant, the most difficult thing, of course, is finding a dress," Maggie said. "But we managed it. Not your average wedding dress, but wonderfully colourful, and just suits Louise."

Gordon smiled, and held her hand. "What are the plans for tomorrow?"

"Well, we have a venue. Last minute so it was a good price. Catering is all but signed. So, tomorrow we're hoping to get a photographer booked, then, if we get time, a car. What did you get up to, today?"

Gordon explained about the solicitor and his text message, and Maggie duly sympathised. Gordon decided against mentioning Elizabeth.

"How were Trudie and Denise?" she asked, tipping her head toward the two, who were currently sitting cross legged in front of the television.

"I hardly noticed them, to be honest. I think they just needed to find their own space."

"I'll make them some dinner," Maggie said. "Do you know when Simon's coming to pick them up?"

"No, I forgot to ask."

The children just shrugged their shoulders when Maggie asked them the same question. Maggie looked towards Gordon, and imitated the children's gesture. Gordon smiled.

By eight o'clock, Trudie was getting restless. Gordon had always encouraged his own children to love the outdoors, leaving Brenda to cope with them whenever they were inside. As such, he wasn't very well equipped to keep the girls amused for long.

Denise, thankfully, was curled up in a ball on the settee, fast asleep, her head resting on Maggie's lap, while Maggie read the newspaper and stroked the young girl's hair. It reminded Gordon of younger days.

Trudie sat herself down opposite Gordon in the conservatory, and asked, "Are we staying the night?"

Gordon raised his eyebrows, "Not that I was aware of," he replied. "It certainly wasn't the impression your father gave me."

Gordon heard Maggie clear her throat in an attention seeking way. When he looked at her, she had an envelope in her hand. "It's addressed for you," she said. Gordon rose and took it from her. "It fell out of Denise's bag."

Denise had been inseparable from the shoulder bag all afternoon, now it lay horizontally on the settee.

The next few moments Gordon would remember for the rest of his life. The creases he straightened, the smoothness of the paper as he passed it from his right hand to his left, the tearing he caused by lifting the self-sealing gum. He was aware of the concern on Maggie's face, the annoyance of Trudie, the peacefulness of Denise, lying like an angel in his lover's lap.

It was the words on the page that caused the damage. Each one felt as if it had punctured a hole in his chest, and his body was almost overcome with waves of panic.

"Whatever's the matter?" he heard Maggie ask, but he was already heading for the door, calling back to her to get her coat on, bring the children, that there was no time to lose. It was the first suicide note Gordon had ever read. Simon must have given it to Denise to give to

Gordon. Maybe she'd forgotten to mention it. Maybe she hadn't known it was there.

Within two minutes they were in the car, and Gordon watched the lights go by as he drove as fast as he could.

"Why are you taking us home?" Trudie asked.

Maggie made some excuse up, he didn't hear what. He'd already handed her the note, and could see she was one hundred per cent aware of what he was doing.

"Do you have your keys, Trudie?" Gordon asked. He heard the jangle as she brought them out of her pocket, saw the glint as Maggie held them tight in her hands.

They reached the house within minutes. Gordon skidded into the drive, and opened the door. "Stay in here," he said. The look of fear on Trudie's face made a lump appear in his throat.

He slid the key into the Yale lock, twisted it sharply to the right, and pushed it open.

He had to be in the house somewhere. Gordon had staked everything on it. He ran upstairs, and tried the main bedroom first. Gordon flung the door open, and flicked on the light switch. Outside Maggie crossed herself.

Nothing. Gordon cursed under his breath. From the door, he could see the whole room. There were no-signs anyone had been in here. He quickly scanned for en-suite doors, but saw none.

Next, he tried Trudie's room.

Outside, Denise asked, "What's Gramps doing?"

Maggie looked toward where the latest light had appeared, and said, "He's looking for something."

Once more, there was nothing. Gordon quickly checked the other first floor rooms. Inside of him, his senses were far more alert than they'd been in years. It was eerily invigorating.

He took the stairs two, three steps at a time, not stopping at the bottom, but continuing through the open doorway into the kitchen.

He looked out of the window, over the raised back garden, his eyes level with a brown stone wall, but saw nothing. He turned the fluorescent light on, its flickering causing white lines to remain on his eyelids when he blinked. Again, all looked normal. He went into the small annex at the corner which housed another toilet, and a small utility room next to it. Again nothing.

Although he would never admit it, doubts were starting to creep into his mind. They were saying Simon wasn't here, or he'd missed him in his rush. Gordon did his best to try and push them to the back of his mind.

He paused as he switched off the kitchen light, trying to listen to any noises that might give something away. As his eyes readjusted to the dark, he thought he could make out a shape, beyond the window. He went and looked closer.

There, depicted by the upstairs bathroom light shining down on the lawn, lay what had, at first, looked like a football. Now, however, Gordon could make out an arm to one side, and hair blowing in the breeze. His heart thumped like never before. It was Simon.

Gordon shot the bolts on the back door, cutting himself in the process, and threw it open. He darted onto the patio, up the four steps onto the lawn, and reached Simon's motionless body in seconds.

Gordon looked back at the house, checking the upstairs windows to see if he'd jumped, but they were all shut. He bent down, put his hand on Simon's back, and thought he heard a slight noise. Gordon paused for what felt like an eternity, but finally he thought he felt Simon's body breathe in, then out.

"Simon," he whispered, "can you hear me?"

There was no reply.

"Simon, this is Gordon, can you hear me?"

Again, nothing.

Gordon checked Simon's body for bone breakages. When he couldn't find any, he carefully adjusted his son-in-law into the recovery position. He put his face close to Simon's and felt his breath coming out of his mouth. Airway wasn't blocked. "Simon, this is Gordon," he said, "I'm going to ring for the ambulance. I'll be right back."

After he'd summoned the ambulance, he motioned for Maggie and the children to come in. "Get some warm clothes, blankets anything. He's in the back garden."

Gordon went back to Simon's side, made sure he was still breathing, and then bent down close to his ear. "Simon, this is Gordon again. Trudie and Denise are coming. They need you. Do you understand? They haven't got another father. They need you to stay alive. They'll need you to be there for them when they get older. It's no good you leaving them now."

He heard footsteps close by.

"Dad?" he heard Trudie gasp.

Gordon looked at her, "He's okay, he's just fainted," he lied, "But he needs your help, all of our help. Put the blankets over him and keep him warm. And keep talking to him."

A few minutes later, Gordon saw the flashing blue light appear, and in a few more, they were following the ambulance to the hospital. They waited there for an hour before a doctor was able to update them. Gordon took him aside "How is he?" he asked.

"Still alive," he replied, "But critical. It will be some time before we know the full impact. It's probably best for the children to go home. Is there someone who can look after them?"

"Yes," Gordon said, "I can. I'm the children's grandfather."

SIMON, ELIZABETH, AND THE OLD TIMES

Trudie didn't want to leave. Gordon tried to persuade her that her father would be fine, but she didn't want to leave him alone at the hospital. In the end, Gordon suggested, that if Maggie didn't mind, he could stay there for a while longer. This seemed to calm her down.

"Give me a ring when you get home?" he asked Maggie.

"Of course," she answered. "And you'll get a taxi back?"

"Yes. I'll let you know if there's any change."

After he waved them off, Gordon wandered along the hospital corridors by himself, thinking.

There were still some parts of the hospital Gordon recognised from the time of Brenda's illness. Back then, he'd spent many hours by himself, not knowing what to do, trying to come to terms with the future that lay ahead of him, questioning the past that still hurt him so.

It had been heart-breaking to watch his wife grow pale and weak. These were times he'd tried to forget, but cruelly they would never be too far away. When Maggie called him to say they'd got back safely and the girls were already asleep, Gordon was stood looking out at the memorial he'd paid for, a statue he'd had commissioned to commemorate her life.

At some point in the night the police turned up, and Gordon gave them a brief statement and Simon's note. They thanked him and said that if they needed to talk to him again they'd call him at home. Ten minutes later, when the doctors told him there was no change in Simon's condition, Gordon decided it was time to call for a taxi.

~

The next morning the news was better. Gordon rang the hospital rang and they said Simon's condition had improved, although he was not out of the danger zone yet. Gordon tried to be as upbeat as possible with the girls; they'd obviously had a rough night.

Just after breakfast, Maggie managed to get in touch with Pamela, who said she'd come home immediately, though was a few hours away. Trudie and Denise got dressed, ate some breakfast, and then spent the rest of the time restlessly watching television in the lounge.

Pamela arrived at lunchtime. "Are they ready?" she asked, thin lipped, and stressed.

Gordon looked surprised, "I thought you might stay for some food," he said.

"No time," his daughter told him. "Trudie, Denise. Mum's here," she called.

Father and daughter stood in silence for a couple of seconds. Then Gordon said, "Aren't you going to ask how Simon is?"

"He's got nothing to do with me, anymore," she replied. "If he's going to try and commit suicide to get attention than more the fool him. He should think himself lucky someone cared enough to go."

Trudie and Denise came out of the room. "Come on, kids," she said, "Time to go home."

Gordon watched the car pull away, and sighed. Maggie rested a hand on his shoulder. "You're a good man, Gordon," she said. "They don't know how lucky they are."

Gordon waited until Maggie left to visit Louise, and then finished his letter to Elizabeth. After he'd posted it, he made a short detour to the graveyard, where he spoke to Graeme of the recent news. As usual, Gordon asked his son for forgiveness, then asked him if he could have a word with those in charge to try and keep Simon alive. "For his daughters," Gordon said aloud.

Before he knew it, the light was fading, and the toll of the church bell marked out five o'clock. Gordon said his son's favourite prayer, and turned for home.

~

Over the next few days, Simon's condition did indeed improve, and Pamela took the girls to see him a couple of times. Gordon, by now, was getting used to Maggie's highs at the end of each day. Not only did she have Louise well in hand, but she was also whisking Gordon around the shops to look at one thing or another for a second opinion. Gordon tried his best to get it right.

To his surprise, he received a reply from Elizabeth. It was little more than her Race envelope, and Gordon felt strangely cheated by this. He'd quite expected Elizabeth to put up a fight, though he didn't understand why he was sad she hadn't. He didn't want there to be any trouble, did he? No, he said to himself. He really didn't want any of this.

Gordon put the ninth envelope with the others, and mused. The fact of the matter was that Cissy knew who the anonymous player was, and that was a surprise, in itself.

"Maybe it is Cissy," Maggie said over dinner that evening.

"I can't see why," Gordon replied.

"Maybe it's her way of getting to see you, again."

"But she knows how to contact me, surely?"

"Maybe, maybe not. When are you going to see her?"

Gordon shrugged. "I don't know. There's still two months left of the Race. I know I should care more, but I just don't want to face her yet."

~

Chris and Louise's wedding date was set. By some minor miracle, everything had been arranged in record time. Maybe Chris and Louise had inherited Gordon's luck; maybe that's where it had gone, he thought. There were now just two weeks until they got married. Gordon rang Pamela to see how she was, but he could tell she didn't want to talk to him. He put the telephone down wondering where he'd gone wrong.

He found Maggie preparing a bath.

"Bit early for one of those, isn't it?" he said.

Maggie levelled him a withering look.

"What have I done, now?" he said.

Maggie paused for a few seconds. "You've forgotten, haven't you?"

"Um...," Gordon said, playing for time.

"Stag night? Hen night?" she said.

"Oh, is it?" Gordon asked. "I better get ready."

~

He spent the rest of the afternoon and early evening getting washed and brushed up. "I'm not going to know anyone else," he said.

"You'll know Chris, and he's the most important one," she told him.

Gordon nodded. "You're right."

Maggie smiled, "I know."

~

Chris was already in the taxi that picked Gordon up. "Now, Dad," he started, "This is going to be bit noisy."

"I guessed as much," Gordon replied. "I'll give it my best shot." And he did.

~

When he woke the next morning, his ears were still ringing. Maggie was awake beside him.

"I didn't hear you come back," he said.

"I'm surprised you could hear anything above your snoring," she replied.

"Oh," Gordon said, pretending to be hurt. "How did yours go?"

Maggie thought for a second, and then said, "It hurts to think. Try me again later."

They recounted what they could remember over a light breakfast, and afterwards, Gordon retired to the lounge, where he lay prone on the settee, reading the shorter articles in the newspaper.

~

Later that day Gordon went to see Simon in hospital. Maggie offered to go with him, but he told her he wanted to see him alone, and she accepted that.

Even though it was drizzling outside, Gordon still wanted to walk there. He took a black umbrella, put on his black raincoat, and left the quiet bungalow for the busy streets. When, a few minutes later, the heavens opened wide above him, he took shelter in a lonely bus stop.

When he reached the hospital, the same receptionist who had directed him to Vee, now told him the way to Simon's ward, and by three in the afternoon, still feeling a little queasy from the alcohol, Gordon stood at the end of Simon's bed.

His son-in-law looked up from his magazine. Gordon could see the panic come into his eyes. "Oh, Gordon, I wasn't expecting you. How're things?"

Gordon drew the curtains around the bed.

"On the whole, very good," he replied. "More to the point, how are you?"

Simon squirmed in his bed, "Um, better," he said, "I should be out in a couple of days, as long as nothing goes wrong. Would you like to sit down?"

"No," Gordon answered. "I want you to tell me what happens next?"

Simon furrowed his brow, "What do you mean?"

Gordon could feel his anger uncoiling, "I mean, what happens after you come out of hospital? What are your plans? Are you going to try and kill yourself again? Or has the novelty worn off?"

Simon sat in silence. He looked down towards his bed clothes, then back at Gordon, mouth open, with no words to say.

Gordon took a step closer. "Look, Simon, if you didn't notice, you have two lovely daughters to care for, and be a father for. I don't know what you thought you were doing the other night, or who you were doing it for, but they must come first."

Simon raised his hand, but Gordon wasn't going to let him try and defend himself. "I'm not interested in what you have to say. In truth, I only helped you because of your children. Personally, I'd have been happy to have thrown the note away, and left you to suffer the consequences. But I couldn't. I had to try and give them back their father."

Gordon leaned in closer. "And mark these words carefully, if I ever hear that you've tried to do anything like this again, I'll do everything in my power to cut them off from you. I don't want to have to say this to you, but this is your last chance. You better grow up and take on your responsibilities."

Simon tried to say something, but Gordon was already on his way out.

~

When Gordon got back, Maggie was cooking tea. "Hello," he called from the front door.

There was a pause.

"Hi," said Maggie, without emotion. Gordon could tell something was wrong. He put his jacket, gloves and shoes in the cupboard, and went to the kitchen door.

"Everything all right?" he asked.

"No, it is not. Can you please explain why you've invited Elizabeth to Chris' wedding?"

"I wasn't aware I had," he said.

"Well. Best you listen to the answer phone message, then. See what you make of it."

Stunned, Gordon went and pressed the play button. It was indeed Elizabeth accepting an invitation from Gordon to his son's wedding. He got the last number that had called, and confirmed it was hers.

"Now," he started, on returning to the kitchen, "I'd just like to say the only correspondence I've had with that woman was regarding the envelope. I never mentioned you or the wedding. Why would I? I can't stand her."

Maggie leant against the fridge, "Well, if you didn't tell her, who the hell did?"

"I haven't the faintest idea," Gordon said.

Maggie sighed, "I don't want her coming, Gordon, you know that, don't you?"

"Yes, yes, of course. I don't want her there either. And Chris doesn't even know her."

"What are we going to do, then?" she asked.

"I'll go and see her, face to face, tomorrow," Gordon replied, "And find out exactly what she thinks she's playing at."

~

Early the next day, Gordon arrived at the train station and bought a ticket to a part of the past he'd never wanted to visit again. At least it's a return ticket, he thought, trying to cheer himself up.

Elizabeth lived as a recluse in a detached maisonette deep inland, a far cry from her younger days. When she had turned thirty, and no longer saw her brother or Phillip, she'd moved up to London and become a socialite. It fitted her perfectly. At least once a month, when Gordon had to go there to meet his agent or his publishers, he would get to hear about her outrageous behaviour. The attention was all she had ever wanted. Elizabeth thrived on shocking people, pushing the boundaries as far as she could.

If they were ever at the same social function, Gordon would keep the exchanges as brief as possible, knowing full well Elizabeth's ability of twisting whatever you said completely on its head and using it for her own devices. When his children were born, Gordon made a conscious effort not to go to any more parties, and as such, his contact with Elizabeth gradually dwindled until it disappeared altogether.

It had mostly stayed that way up until now.

The God of trains was looking favourably on Gordon, and the forty-five-minute journey was reassuringly uneventful. He arrived just before lunch, and as he knew the area very well, he resisted the lukewarm pastries on offer at the station, and walked, instead, into the village itself.

Even on such a cold day as this, the place had lost none of its charm. The short trip from the station was extremely picturesque. Thatched cottages, the church, a mill pond set back off the road, all greeted him as old friends would. Eventually, he stopped outside the tiny post office come tea shop.

The drizzle had returned to the month, and the place was devoid of customers. A smiling lady stood behind the counter.

"Good afternoon," she said.

Gordon tipped an imaginary hat, "And to you," he said.

"What can I get you?"

"I'd love some tea," Gordon said, leaning against the counter, "And is that a caramel slice?"

"It certainly is," the lady replied.

"Then I'll take two."

Gordon sat and consumed his purchases overlooking the green. When the lady came to collect the plates, she hovered with an air of apprehension.

"Is everything all right?" Gordon asked her.

"Yes," she said, turning a cloth over in her hands, "I hope you don't mind me asking, but I can't help thinking I've seen you somewhere before?"

Gordon smiled, and tapped the old photograph on the wall above him. It was a picture of Gordon and the owner of the cafe.

"Oh," she said, "Did you know my father well?"

"Quite well," he said, with a smile, "I remember you, too. You two were always laughing."

She wiped her hand and offered it to him. "Pleased to meet you, then, at last," she said. "That picture's been up there for..."

Gordon held up his hand. "Let's just call it a while, shall we?"

The girl smiled. "Of course. Now, can I get you anything else?"

"Oh, no, I'm full. Just the bill, please."

"The bill? Don't be silly, you can have this on me. You're obviously one of our most loyal customers."

As he got up to leave, the woman called over to him. "You wouldn't mind posing for another photograph, would you? For old times?"

Gordon smiled, "What a lovely idea," he said. "For old times."

ELIZABETH, HELENA, AND THE SUSPENDED TRAINS

Gordon left a tip that would more than pay for the food he ate, and walked the short distance to where Elizabeth lived. The place was as he remembered it, albeit a little more overgrown.

He stood for a few minutes, psyching himself up for the encounter that lay ahead. Elizabeth was a determined woman, and he didn't really know how he was going to convince her not to go to Chris' wedding. Yet he knew he had to, so, summoning all his courage, Gordon knocked on the front door.

When, after twenty seconds, nothing had happened, he knocked again, a little more firmly. He was conscious not to make it sound insistent or menacing. She was a woman living on her own, after all. When she still didn't answer the door, Gordon got out his keys and found the one that used to work. By the antiquated look of the lock, it still would.

He slotted it in and, with a little force, managed to turn it. The door swung gently inwards. "Elizabeth?" he called, softly. "Elizabeth?"

He walked tentatively into the cramped lounge but no one was there. It was the same in the kitchen, but, unlike the lounge, at least he could tell someone lived there; the state of the pots and pans on the side was enough to make his stomach turn.

As he made his way up the stairs, he was reminded of a previous visit; his first visit. Gordon wobbled a little, took hold of the bannister, and waited for the wave of emotion to dissipate before venturing any further. He wanted to get this over and done with, and quickly. Slowly, carefully, he continued, step by step, moving toward the landing above, where he paused, listening for any noises that might reveal Elizabeth's whereabouts. He heard nothing.

The upstairs was dark, especially with all the doors shut, so he waited until his eyes had adjusted before proceeding to the main bedroom door. As he reached to open it, the memories once again threatened to immerse him, so he stopped and tried to calm himself. All that was in the past, he thought, and he was a grown man now. Involuntarily, he shot a look off to the right. Nothing there.

As the seconds passed, his confidence grew until he was able to push open the door in front of him. It came to a halt against the wall, and Gordon was surprised by how much everything looked the same; the furniture, the smell, the light coming in through the window. He composed himself and peered in.

It wasn't a large room, none of them were. There was a window off to the right, and behind it, hunched on the same wall, a mahogany wardrobe. In front of the window was a small dressing table, its mirror marked with age, and against the back wall, piles of papers were heaped, ready to topple at any moment.

The bed was over by the left wall, and in it he could see an outline of a body. He watched closely, and was pleased when he saw movement from within the covers.

Gordon retreated carefully out of the room, went back downstairs, and started to wash up with what little hot water there was left. After twenty minutes, there was a sound behind him. "I wouldn't bother," said a woman's voice "You're not going to get around me by tidying up, Gordon Paige."

Gordon felt his stomach dip. He knew that voice so well, its sarcasm and sneer. He hoped he hadn't had a wasted journey.

"I was just cleaning up a bit," he said.

"It's no good you talking to the wall, either. You'll have to look at me if you want me to understand you. I'm as deaf as a post."

Gordon looked around. "I didn't know," he said.

"Why should you? I suppose you've come about the wedding invite, have you?"

Gordon felt guilty. It was the last emotion he'd been expecting to feel. He nodded his response.

"You can't stop me from coming, Gordon," she said, "It's a free world. Especially when I know the groom's father and his partner. It's a big event for me. You see, Gordon, it's difficult living this far out, you lose touch with all those people you used to know. And there's not many people living out here to talk to. But then, you'd know all about that, wouldn't you?"

"Yes," he said. "I would."

Elizabeth smiled. It was the one she reserved for being in control of a situation. "It must have taken some serious decisions for you to come out here again," she said, "That must be what love does to you. Although, I never took to Margaret much. I don't think she liked me, either. She was never any good for Lawrence, that's for sure."

"Why have you invited yourself to the wedding?" he asked.

"Why? Let's call it... nostalgia. I wanted to see how your lot turned out. It'll be interesting to meet everyone. Maybe I can swap a few stories about their beloved father."

Gordon smiled now. He actually felt more relaxed with Elizabeth's threats. It'd been what he was expecting.

"Thanks for sending the envelope," he said.

"Huh, you were lucky," she scoffed, "Another couple of weeks and I'd have thrown it out. Worthless piece of junk."

"Why did you bother, then?"

"Because you asked for it. You took the time to write, and I don't get many letters, Gordon, not personal ones. And you must have caught me in a good mood. I know you think I hate everyone, but I don't. You've helped me out over the years, and I appreciate that."

"How's the old place doing?" he asked, gesturing to the four walls.

Elizabeth got up and put the kettle on. "All right," she said, "You paid those bills for the roof work a couple of years back, but apart from that, the two of us seem to get along just fine."

"Good," he said. "Have you spoken to Lawrence recently?"

Elizabeth let out a quick shrill. "How did you think I found out about the wedding? I spoke to the randy old sod when I got your letter. Sort of gave me a good reason to. I knew he'd had an envelope, so I guessed you'd been in contact with him. I still can't believe he's got a kid when he should've been getting a grandson."

Elizabeth went quiet, and for a moment Gordon thought she was struggling with the kettle. Then she turned back, and he could see her eyes glistening with tears.

"Whatever's the matter?" Gordon asked.

Elizabeth tore off a piece of kitchen towel and dabbed them. "All I did was suggest I go up and see him and Angus, but he said he didn't want me there. He's never said that before, Gordon. He's the only person I've ever been able to rely on."

Elizabeth turned away again, and Gordon remained quiet. There was little else he could do under the circumstances. When she turned back, the tears had gone.

"Did Lawrence mention me when you were there? Did he ask if you'd seen me?"

"Yes," he lied, "He wanted to know how you were."

"Well, at least that's something. I doubt he even thinks of me nowadays. I suppose he's staying at yours for the wedding?"

Gordon shook his head. "He's not coming to the wedding, Elizabeth," he replied. "He sent us a letter declining the invitation. I don't blame him - it's diff..."

"What?" she interrupted. "He's not coming to the wedding?"

"No. He's staying in Scotland with his family."

Gordon watched as Elizabeth drew back. "Oh," she said.

Elizabeth was quiet as she finished making the tea. Curiously, the atmosphere within the cottage had completely changed. Elizabeth was subdued, yet slightly hostile all at the same time, and Gordon thought his quest was lost.

"Have you been to see the grave, yet?" she asked, setting a cup down in front of him.

"No," he answered. "But I don't want to talk about that. I need to know how you're planning on getting to the wedding?"

Elizabeth's eyes narrowed. "Don't be naive, Gordon. What would be the point of me going to the wedding if Lawrence isn't there? I don't care about you, or your family. I wanted to see Lawrence. I don't want to see any of you."

Gordon sat at the table, surprised.

"So, you don't want to go?"

"No. Of course not. Now drink your tea, and leave me well alone."

~

Twenty minutes later, Gordon left Elizabeth to wallow in her own bitterness. On the way back to the station, he made a detour and visited the graveyard, tidied what he could, said a few words, and went to catch the next train home. At a quarter past eight the same evening Gordon reached the bungalow. He recounted the trip to Maggie, telling her the news about Elizabeth's withdrawal from the wedding.

"Thank God for that," Maggie said. "Now, tell me what's really on your mind."

Gordon looked at her, brushed her chin with his hand, and smiled. "You're too perceptive," he said.

"Call it intuition," she replied. "I'll get you a sherry, and you can tell me everything."

Maggie poured them a glass each and came back to the table.

"Thank you," Gordon said, taking the drink. "All right. You may have noticed that I don't speak about my parents very much. Or at all. Over the years, they've sort of been a taboo subject of mine, and if people don't ask, I prefer not to tell them. But there's a good reason behind it. One that's important you know."

"When I was ten, my mother called Mary and me into the kitchen and told us my father had died in an accident at work. He'd worked on the railways for many years, and she said he'd been electrocuted whilst carrying out line repairs."

"It was upsetting, but she didn't want us to talk about him in the house, so, naturally, we'd wait until she was out of earshot. Mary and I would try to remember what he was like, but we soon realised there'd never really been that much to miss about him. He was the sort of father who rose early and arrived back late, and if he was ever home, he'd be up in the loft, playing with his model train set."

"Did his death affect your mother?"

Gordon laughed. "Not really. Within a few months, it was as if he'd never been there."

Four years later, Mary moved away to university, and deep down Gordon wished he could have left, too. Neither of the children had any real ties there anymore.

"When my sister left," Gordon told Maggie, "my mother changed even more. She had a new lease of life, one which didn't really involve me very much. One evening, during the summer break, she was entertaining some friends, and wanted me to stay out of the way. Of course, I was more than happy to oblige, and had already decided I'd go up into the loft to have a look around."

~

The family had collectively referred to it as 'Daddy's little place', and up till now, no-one had been allowed up there to see it. As Gordon carefully opened the hatch he knew he'd have several hours of uninterrupted investigation to uncover the treasures it had hidden away all these years. The young Gordon licked his dry lips, and tried to calm the butterflies dancing in his stomach.

As he scrabbled around looking for the light switch, he remembered his mother warning them that the loft was dark and full of spiders. Gordon didn't overly believe her, and even if he did, the moment the lights came on and he first saw the sight of the railway track, all his phobias instantly disappeared. The loft space was large, and the track took up around two thirds of it, supported from both the floor and the ceiling by metal struts which held loops of wood rigid, on top of which the track had been tacked meticulously into place. There were at least three levels, sometimes four, suspended above the ground like some fantastical boyhood dream. Only the lowest level was flanked by the kind of scenery Gordon had seen in other model railway setups.

Gordon crouched down as low as he could, making sure he could clear the lowest track, and shuffled across the floor. Once in the middle, he rose, God-like, into the middle of this double-O gauge world. He fiddled with a few switches, until, at last, he heard the hum of electricity. A network of lights shone dimly for a second, then grew brighter, and Gordon saw the world as if atop a hill at night.

He moved a lever forward, and heard the mechanics of one of the trains starting to move. It was a few seconds before it pulled out of its tunnel, and Gordon watched, in awe, as it moved around the track. He reached over and pulled another lever, and once again, a train appeared, this time from a long shed over on the far side. The young Gordon smiled. He was enjoying this.

He played with the train set for some time, although he was more amused than enthused, and after a while his attention was drawn to the handmade scenery he knew his father had painstakingly built. From the buildings, to the countryside, to the little figurines dotted around, each was made with the greatest attention to detail.

The main railway station bore the local station's name, but looked little like it. Gordon assumed that his father had simply copied blueprints from one of the modelling magazines he'd often receive through the post.

Gordon looked around the attic that lay beyond the train track. In one corner was a desk and a stool his father had used when he built the models. Gordon ducked back under track and moved closer to investigate. He switched on a small lamp, and its light streamed over an array of tiny paint pots, modelling knives, balsa wood and sheets of sandpaper. As the trains continued to circle the tracks, Gordon was overtaken with the notion that this was where his father had spent so much of his life and passion. He suddenly wanted him to be there, to watch him work; he wouldn't have got in the way.

Gordon lifted the lid of the desk, and tilted the light so he could see what was contained within. There was a pile of half-made models, perhaps mistakes, perhaps ones he'd been half way through when he'd died. Whichever, it made Gordon sad to see them. He delved deeper into the desk, moving things carefully aside to see what he could find, but there was precious little of any real interest. Quietly, Gordon sat in the midst of all the wood and noise, trying to make sense of what he was feeling.

The noise from downstairs was getting louder. The wine must be flowing well, he thought. A glance at his watch revealed he'd been up there for three hours already. Gordon put the wood back in, got up and pushed the stool under the table, but as he did so, it caught on a flap of wood underneath the desk. Gordon jiggled the stool to see if he could loosen it, and heard the wood splinter. "Oops," he said, slowly pulling the stool back out. A sliver of wood dropped to the floor.

He bent down and looked underneath the desk, and what he saw made his heart beat loudly in his chest. Half of the bottom of the desk and fallen away, but instead of spilling the contents onto the floor, Gordon could see a space, no more than a couple of inches high, with a package sticking out of it. Gordon reached up and waggled it free.

He placed it on the desk, untied the string and peeled back the layer of brown paper. It was a box, adorned with his father's initials. There was no lock, so carefully he slid the lid towards him. Inside, wood shavings cushioned three separate objects. Gordon delicately removed them, and took them back across to the track.

~

"I knew what they were from the start," Gordon said to Maggie, whose face was a growing picture of concern.

"The first one was a garden gate. A different design and colour than our own, and with a different number. I looked around the track to find the house it belonged to, but all the houses had gates. What I did notice, however, was that the house that bore our number had a gate which came off. It was the only one that did."

~

The young Gordon, alone in the attic, replaced the gates carefully. It made him feel strange.

~

"The next object was a sign, like the one on the train station, but with a different name. I hadn't noticed it before, but the sign at the station had two small hooks that allowed this new station name to sit over the top."

"Had you heard of the station before?" Maggie asked.

"Never," Gordon replied. "The last object was a model of a woman waving. I scoured the board, but I couldn't see where she was supposed to go."

"Eventually, my gaze came to rest on the station platform. There was a cluster of three figures there, each sharing the same base; a woman with a daughter and a son. Even before I lifted them up, I knew these were the people she supplanted. It was a perfect fit, and in three simple moves the whole landscape had changed. Our house, our town and even ourselves had been replaced."

Maggie put a hand on his, "I'll get you another sherry," she said.

With a recharged glass in hand, Gordon continued. "I wondered why my father had wanted to fantasise about replacing us, and whether my mother knew about it. I didn't want to play with the trains anymore. So, I left the amendments there, went back to the desk, and put my family and the gate in the box. When I tried to put it back up, I couldn't, and when I reached in, I felt another package. I broke the remaining wood to get it out."

~

Young Gordon didn't bother with unwrapping it nicely. This time, he ripped it open, and took out a wooden plaque. It looked familiar, for some reason. Then, when he realised why, his heart dropped. The colour and the numbers matched those on the replacement model gate.

Gordon turned it over, and read the inscription on the back. 'To my dear Helena, With all my love'.

~

"Within those few hours, I travelled the road from boy to man, with all the pain that journey entails. When I felt I could stand again, I turned the trains off, and took the evidence downstairs, where, over the next few days, I dwelled over what action I should take. Of course, there was little choice. I had to find this Helena. I had too many unanswered questions."

Gordon convinced a friend to say he was staying overnight at his house, and, by the following Saturday, was on a train to a destination he'd only ever seen in his loft on a model railway station.

"I didn't have the address of the house, but I had the house number and her name, and assumed everything else would just sort itself out. In retrospect, I was being incredibly naive. I hadn't really thought anything through."

When Gordon had arrived, he stopped off at the local post office, and asked the man behind the counter, who held his daughter in his arms, if he knew of Helena's whereabouts. The man was very pleased to help, and Gordon arrived at just after three in the afternoon.

"There was no doorbell, so I knocked as lightly as I could on the door. When no answer came, I listened at the letterbox, and thought I could hear some music within. I ventured around the back of the house and saw the back door was open. Maybe I should've knocked again, but I didn't. I just walked in."

~

There was no-one in either the kitchen or the lounge. He called from the bottom of the stairs, but doubted he could be heard over the music. There was only one thing he could do.

He followed the sound, up the stairs, and came to a stop outside one of the doors. He stood there not knowing what to say, but hoping he was going to be able to say something. He felt the butterflies from the attic flutter back into his stomach, and fought to keep his rising nausea at bay.

Then, with horror, another door opened to the right of him, and someone came out. Gordon didn't dare look, but instead, tried to escape. He shouldn't have come. He'd been stupid, but it was no use. Whoever it was had caught him firmly by the arm, and he was unable to struggle free.

"It's all right, it's all right," the man said, and immediately the fourteen-year-old Gordon stopped. He recognised that voice. He'd last heard it four years ago. Slowly, he looked up.

"Dad?" he said, and, to his surprise, burst into unexpected, unstoppable tears.

CISSY, LOUISE, AND THE JEALOUS PAST

"Your father?" Maggie asked. "How do you mean?"

"Just that. It was my father, with shaving foam around his face, getting ready to go out."

~

The bedroom door opened, and a woman, Helena, Gordon assumed, said, "Call the police, John."

"No, no, no," his father said, "There's no need to panic. Come on lad, let's go downstairs and we'll have a talk."

Gordon walked behind his father in a state of shock. John took a towel from the boiler and dabbed his face, all the while not looking at Gordon. Then he turned to him, a smirk on his face. "I bet you didn't expect to find me here," he said, seemingly proud of his charade. Gordon remained quiet.

"What's up, lad? It's not such a surprise, is it?" his father said. "Your Mum knows I'm not dead. We came to this little arrangement before I left. It really is the best for everyone. Really, it is."

Young Gordon looked at his father closely. It'd been so long since he'd last seen him. His face, tanned and lined, looked weaker than he remembered it. The pair of grey trousers, his white shirt, both hung on him like a scarecrow's clothes, and his arms and hands were heavily scarred.

"You... you were never in an accident?" Gordon asked.

John shook his head, "Although," he said, "That's not to say I haven't had my fair share." Again, he smirked, and Gordon couldn't understand why.

"Why?" he asked the older man.

"I needed to leave. I needed a new life. I didn't need you anymore." His father said those words so matter-of-factly, he couldn't have hurt his son more if he'd beaten him.

Gordon stood numb, and then managed. "What's going to happen, now?"

"Going to happen? Nothing's going to happen. You're going back home, and forgetting any of this ever happened."

"I can't do that."

"You'll have to. You're not a part of my life now."

Gordon started to cry, he couldn't help it. His father placed a hand on his shoulder, and quite firmly guided him toward the front door. "It's the best for everyone," he was saying. "You'll thank me later."

John opened the door, and before he knew it, Gordon was outside the cottage, and the door was shut. He wanted to knock on it again, but didn't know what he was going to say. His father had sounded so sure. There didn't seem to be anything else he could do.

Young Gordon turned away, unable to understand anything that had just happened, and walked, sobbing in big mouthfuls, back to the station. The first part of the train journey home was spent in utter confusion. When that finally passed, Gordon was left trying to work out what he could do next. It was no use telling his mother he'd found out their little agreement. She was just as likely not to care as his father was. He had no friends he could ask, not even a relative. He thought briefly about speaking to Mary, but didn't know what he was going to say. Maybe it had been better when neither of them had known.

His inability to share the secret meant the whole meeting quickly took on a dream like quality, to such an extent that it was hard for Gordon to even recall such important details as to what his father had said or done.

~

Gordon smiled at Maggie. She looked tired. It was good of her to listen to him now.

"Six months went by," he continued, "I celebrated my fifteenth birthday and, to my surprise, he sent me a card, with a letter tucked inside. Only a few words saying that he'd like to see me. He had a few days off coming up, and he'd like me to come and visit him."

~

At first, Gordon ignored the letter. It was little more than a collection of consonants and vowels that a man, who, at times, he hated, had put together. At some point, though, this hatred had given way to curiosity, and Gordon realised he wanted a reason for what had happened. Gordon sent his own brief note belatedly accepting the offer.

That Spring, when Gordon arrived, he found his father weeding in the front garden. "As soon as I arrived I could tell it was different. He was more relaxed, and more in control. Just like with the train set, my father was calling the shots."

~

Slowly, John got up, shook his son's hand, and gestured that they go inside the maisonette.

"I can't stand gardening," his father admitted as he made them both tea, "But, there's little else to do out this way."

Gordon stood defiantly in the doorway. He didn't say a word.

"So, how did you find me?" his father asked.

"Your train set, in the loft," Gordon replied.

He nodded. "I knew I should've taken that with me."

"What's the point," Gordon said, "When you got everything it stood for?"

Gordon's father didn't even turn around. "Now, I don't want us to argue, son. I invited you here to try and patch up what's happened between us."

"You left, Dad, that's what happened. Stop trying to make it sound any different than it was. You had Helena, everyone else was second."

His father stopped and looked at him, sizing up the situation. Eventually, he said, "I should've listened to Helena, she warned me this wasn't a good idea."

The young Gordon stood firm, but he could feel more tears in his eyes. It made him feel angry. "I don't understand, Dad," he said. "Don't you love us?"

"Of course," came the reply, "But what was the point in keeping contact? I wouldn't be doing you or Mary any service if we'd kept seeing each other. This is my life now."

"Then why did you ask me here? Why get my hopes up? I don't understand any of this. You're nothing but a bastard." Gordon turned and headed for the door, shaking his head, and saying to himself, "My father's nothing but a bastard."

John didn't try to stop him.

When he got home, he couldn't help but tell his mother where he'd been. She shrugged her shoulders and told him to tidy his room.

Four years went by without any further contact. Then, another letter from him, this one full of remorse. It told of how Helena had suddenly died of a brain haemorrhage. His father wanted to see him again, and was sorry for everything he'd done.

Gordon had started his degree, but was able to stay with him for a couple of days. He didn't tell his mother, there wasn't any point. The two men talked little, but slowly they found a way to be. Over the next couple of years, Gordon spent the holidays with him, trying to work out the man he called Dad. During this time, he also transported and re-erected the railway track in the unused garage. "Then, just as suddenly as I'd found him," he told Maggie, "He was taken away from me. A heart attack. However hard I'd tried, nothing had really been resolved."

When his father died, he left the maisonette to Gordon alone, and even though he did little with it, Gordon couldn't bring himself to sell it. "It reminded me of him, of the pain he'd caused me, and I wanted to keep that. It did nothing for many years. I was frightened Mary might find out about it, but she didn't. She still thinks, to this day, that our father died in a railway accident. Then, after Brenda died, I let Elizabeth live there."

Maggie frowned, "Elizabeth? Why her? There's got to be far more deserving people?"

"Oh, there is, there is," Gordon agreed. He took a sip of his sherry. "In truth," he continued, "I didn't want anyone else living there in my lifetime, but, somehow, she found out about Brenda and Paul's affair, and threatened to make it public if I didn't help her out."

Gordon sighed, and topped up his glass. "I didn't want Brenda's affair becoming public knowledge, so I offered her the maisonette, rent free for the rest of her life, as long as she kept her mouth shut. It was a small price to pay, and, so far at least, she's kept up her end of the bargain, and I've kept mine."

There was a pause whilst Gordon drank his sherry.

"I'm sorry, Gordon," Maggie said.

"Sorry? What for?"

"For the world being so bad at times."

"That it is."

She placed her hand on his arm. "Thank you for telling me, too. I know it can't have been easy, but, at the same time, I don't want you suffering on your own."

~

One week later, Gordon was feeling better than he'd done in a long time. Maggie was once again on a high, busying herself with one wedding preparation, then another. In fact, the only thing she didn't have under control was the weather. Unfortunately, the outlook was rain for Saturday, but Gordon tried his best to calm her nerves, citing the fact the weather people were hardly ever right, especially when the forecast more than a day into the future.

The Race answers and questions were still coming through, too. With a little over six weeks to go, Gordon was pleased to see no-one had dropped out, especially considering everything that had happened during the year. Still, with the wedding so close, the Ostrich Race could be put on the back burner.

The rest of the week slipped by surprisingly quickly. In between helping Maggie, Gordon continued his work on the novel. It was shaping up nicely, he thought, and come the beginning of the next year, he would be ready to start.

On the morning of the wedding, Gordon's alarm went off at six, by which time he was already awake and sipping a cup of tea in bed.

"You're awake early," Maggie said, blearily.

Gordon smiled. "Just excited," he replied.

Maggie left for Louise's around nine-thirty, and even though there were spots of rain on the lounge window, Gordon was pleased to see some blue in the sky. Hopefully everything's going to be okay. He was just finishing this thought, when the doorbell rang. Gordon looked at his watch. Quarter past ten. It would be Chris, dead on time as usual.

Gordon was smiling when he opened the door, but froze when he saw Maggie looking so serious on the step.

"Whatever's wrong?" he asked.

"It's Louise," she said to him. "She's having the baby."

They drove to the hospital quickly, and waited in the reception area for some news. "She's a month early, isn't she?" Gordon asked, looking around at the other visitors who sat waiting for news on their own sick friends and relatives.

"Yes. She was just finishing having her hair done when she suddenly let out a moan. When I turned around she was holding her belly, and looking very scared. We called for an ambulance, and rang Chris on the mobile. It all started so quickly."

"And Vee's letting people know?" Gordon checked.

"Yes. We had a list of guests and phone numbers, just in case."

~

The light of the afternoon soon faded without further news. Maggie popped out and bought some food to have for dinner.

"It's hardly wedding cake," she joked as they shared out two doughnuts, "But it'll have to do."

Three more hours passed. People changed shifts, new faces filled up, then emptied, the seats around them. Gordon bought one last cup of tea before the cafe shut. The new receptionist called them over. "I've just spoken to the delivery ward, and they said it'd be best if you went home. It looks like it could be a while. We'll contact you if anything happens."

~

It was a restless night for them both. At six in the morning, the telephone rang. Gordon, who'd had the foresight to put the cordless phone next to the bed, reached a sleepy hand over and picked it up. "Hello?"

"Dad, it's Chris."

Gordon snapped awake. Maggie held Gordon's other hand tightly. "Chris, what's happened?"

"We have a little boy, Dad," Chris said, "Born about an hour ago."

"Oh, thank god. Is he all right?"

"Yes, he's okay. Everyone's okay. He's just under seven pounds. Louise had to be induced in the end. At least it wasn't surgery, though."

Gordon sighed, "That's good news. You sound exhausted."

"I am. Louise is sleeping at the moment."

"Then I'll let you go be Dad. Well done to you all. Let us know when you want visitors, eh?"

"Of course," said his son.

Maggie whispered something in Gordon's ear. "Oh, I nearly forgot, does he have a name?"

"Yes. We've called him Graeme."

Gordon was lost for words. He felt a lump in his throat. "Thank you," he whispered, then handed the telephone to Maggie, who said goodbye, and then held onto Gordon until he'd stopped crying.

~

At breakfast, Gordon interrupted Maggie's book reading. "I've got to go and see Brenda's mother," he said.

"What, now?" she replied.

"Yes. I've got to do it now. She should have the last two envelopes. Then this business is finished."

Maggie put her book down, got up and gave Gordon a hug. "Go on, then," she said. "Is she far away?"

"Not at all," he said. "Not at all."

"Be back soon. Hopefully we'll be able to see baby Graeme today."

~

By Gordon's calculations, Cissy should be about ninety-two. She lived in a rest home in the next large town along the coast, and Gordon was able to catch a train there within the hour. He'd washed and shaved, adorned his smartest suit and freshly polished his shoes. Impressions had meant a lot to Cissy, and, just this once, he was happy to oblige.

As he stood outside the home's entrance, he felt something catch on his elbow. He looked down, and saw someone holding it.

"Excuse me," the woman said, "Would you mind getting me a taxi? I can't see too well without my glasses, and I can't be bothered to turn my bag out."

"Of course," he said, and raised his arm.

"Thank you."

He helped her into the cab, and watched it drive off. As he did so, some faint recognition came to him. That was Cissy, he thought. He went to the next waiting taxi and asked if it could follow the first. The driver looked only too pleased to have been asked.

The old woman was dropped off at the gates of the local park, and the driver kindly helped her out, saying a few words as he left her, which, in turn, she nodded to.

Gordon's own cab stopped. He paid for his journey, then followed the woman at a safe distance. It was difficult to see her face, due to her back being bent into a hunch. The woman seemed content to just meander along the path, stopping every now and then. When she rounded a corner, Gordon quickened his pace, only to come face to face with her as he rounded it himself.

"Gordon Paige," she said. "How did you like your walk?"

"Hello, Cissy. How did you know it was me? I thought you needed your glasses?"

Cissy smiled. "My taxi driver was a fan of yours," she said, "He was quite excited when he told me who'd helped me in. Now, since you're here, let's go and get a coffee."

As they sat in the cafe, Cissy asked, "So, what do you want with me?"

"I'm looking for the Race envelopes. The Ostrich Race."

"I know what Race you're talking about. Silly waste of time, if you ask me."

"I've got two envelopes to find. Yours and Jack's."

"Interesting," Cissy said.

"What is?"

"You're not the first person to ask me for them. Someone came to me at the beginning of the year."

"Really, who?"

"That sort of knowledge is going to cost you."

Gordon shook his head, bemused. "Cost me? Cost me what?"

Cissy took a moment to reply. "I want you're forgiveness, Gordon Paige. I treated you badly when we were younger, and I did it for nothing except jealousy. I hated what you and Brenda had together, and I took it out on you. Are you able to forgive me?"

Gordon nodded. "Yes, of course I can."

Cissy paused. "Thank you," she said. "Now, I'll tell you what I know..."

~

Gordon spent the rest of the afternoon with Cissy. They spoke about the years when they knew each other, and they spoke about Brenda.

They parted, maybe not as old friends, but as people who didn't hate each other either. He even invited Cissy to come down to the bungalow at Christmas. "That's nice," was all she said.

That night, Gordon lay awake, smiling. The truth behind the envelopes had been difficult to find. Maybe it had been the Race's death throes. But now it was over. Cissy had told Gordon where her envelopes resided, and he kicked himself for not seeing it before.

JASON, JACK, AND THE WINNING CEREMONY

On Halloween, whilst children trick or treated around the town, Gordon sat and wrote in his diary. This year it had seen more entries than usual, and now he added one each for Chris and Louise's new baby, the meeting with Cissy and the information about the final envelopes.

Maggie had once more thrown herself into preparations, although this time it was for Christmas. "At least that can't be postponed," she'd said, with humour.

In the following weeks, Gordon filled in at the rest home for people taking holidays. He was getting on well with the new management, who appreciated his time and help. They even gave him a small monetary gift, which he asked them to give to Chris instead.

Baby Graeme was out of hospital, and doing well. Both Gordon and Maggie had immediately fallen in love with him the moment they'd seen him. Vee continued to get back to her old self, her fall now a thing of the past. Phillip was still staying with her, and it'd made all the difference. November flew by, and on December 3rd, Maggie, Vee and Gordon went into town. Maggie left the others in a cafe, while she went and got their presents.

"What would you like?" came a boy's voice he recognised.

Gordon looked up, "The usual for me, Jason. And how are you?"

Over the year, the boy had served Gordon nearly every Saturday he'd been in. He was quite up to date with his progression at college, his birthday celebrations, and his holidays.

"I'm very well," Jason replied. "Especially as I've got a few parties lined up."

Gordon laughed, "Parties, eh? What more could you ask for."

When he'd gone, Vee said, "Oh, to be young again, Gordy."

"I think we both had our fair share of parties," Gordon offered, "Especially you, as I remember."

Vee smiled, "Oh, I think you'll find that was Frank," she lied.

Gordon looked out of the window, and sighed. "You know, it's been a busy year," he said. "I don't remember sitting down for very much of it."

"You've never been one to just sit around, Gordy. Unless you were writing, of course."

"That's true," he said, "But it's been retrieving those blessed envelopes that's taken the time."

Vee raised her eyebrows, "Oh, yes, how've you got on with that?"

"Well, I've got nine envelopes now, and I know where the last one is."

Vee nodded. "You have done well."

They looked at each other for a few seconds. "So, where is it?" Gordon asked.

"Ah," she said, "Cissy told you I asked for hers back?"

Gordon nodded, "She also gave you Jack's as well."

"She did."

Gordon poured himself another tea.

"And you let me wander around the country, trying to find them, knowing all along who the anonymous player was?"

"No," said Vee, "I know as much about them as you. Let me explain. Around this time last year, someone wrote me a letter, typed, not signed. They asked me, very politely, whether I would give them some information about the Race. They said they were related to the family, but would rather not say how. Now, maybe I should have come to you, but I thought you'd be too busy planning to worry about this. And besides, I know how it works. So, I wrote back to the post office box number, and within a few days, received a reply saying thank you, and asking whether I could send them one of the envelopes so they could play anonymously. It's in the rules, and they sounded genuine, so I sent one back."

"Why didn't you tell me this in January, when I decided to find out who it was?"

"Two reasons," Vee explained, "Firstly, you seemed so enthusiastic about collecting the envelopes, more enthusiastic than you'd been a long time, and who was I to quash that? Secondly, and selfishly, I, too, wanted the envelopes in one place. I knew once you got on the case, it was just a matter of when. I was right, too, and you can't tell me it hasn't done you any good, can you?"

Gordon agreed. "But if neither of us know who they are, what happens next?"

Vee shrugged, "Wait and see. Though I can't believe anyone would have gone through this much trouble to remain anonymous."

~

A few days later, Gordon received a letter from Esme. He recognised the handwriting immediately, and opened it with the same guilty feeling he'd felt earlier in the year. When he read it, however, his mood changed to one of relief. She explained she'd managed to find another home to run, and was living with its owner, who she was hoping to marry in the coming year. Gordon was pleased for her, and placed the letter on the bookshelves so he could reply, at a later date.

December gathered pace. Gordon and Maggie went to see baby Graeme a few times, and were amazed by his progress. Naturally, Chris and Louise looked like death warmed up, but then Gordon knew they would.

Tony visited with Jessica, and the two were in good spirits. Tony told him the solicitor had been able to convince Catherine to let him see her more, and it was working well. He went on to say that Catherine's pregnancy was going well, and that he was helping her in any way he could. He also confirmed their attendance for the Winning Ceremony, and spoke about what the coming year may bring.

Even Simon and Pamela were getting along. They popped round with the children on the eighth, and all seemed happy and contented. In a quiet moment, Pamela said to Gordon they were trying to sort the marriage out again, for Trudie and Denise.

On the tenth of the month, Gordon marked the final Race answers, and then prepared the last Winning Ceremony speech. He wasn't short of things to say.

As the end of the Race drew near, Gordon started to feel an ache which began at his shoulders, and carried down to his chest. He'd never felt anything like it, but thought that perhaps it was just a withdrawal symptom from the Race. He knew that however much he had tried to overlook the histrionics involved in making this the last Race, it had constantly niggled away at him.

~

Christmas day was a red-letter day to Gordon. He woke early, and, as he'd always done, peeked outside to see whether or not it had snowed during the night. Unfortunately, it hadn't. After that, he and Maggie spent a blissfully uncomplicated morning, opening presents they'd bought for each other and having a light breakfast. Then they got ready and Maggie drove them to Pam's, where the smell of the roast and the nibbles on the table were too tempting to miss.

Chris and Louise looked slightly better, and baby Graeme behaved himself as best he could. Tony, Jessica, and Catherine were very sociable, too. Trudie divided up the presents between their recipients, and much fun was shared by all. When they were all open, the children and the adults played with their toys, respectively.

It had been a good day, but was over too soon. When they arrived back at the bungalow Gordon and Maggie stayed up with a decanter of sherry and talked over what they remembered. It was amazing just how much Gordon had missed.

~

Boxing Day was the Race's Winning Ceremony day. Even though the events didn't start until the evening, Gordon spent the morning psyching himself up. It was always the same. He rehearsed and re-rehearsed the speech, went over the questions and answers, made sure he'd got the totals correct. They were.

He and Maggie then spent a while getting the bungalow prepared, and at just before seven that evening, the competitors started to arrive.

Chris and Louise were first, with baby Graeme tentatively asleep in his car seat. They placed him in the conservatory, closed the door, and watched him like hawks from the lounge.

While Maggie and Louise talked, Chris leant over to his father, and whispered, "So, how's the Race gone, Dad?"

Gordon gave him a sideways look. "Not bad," he said.

Chris shifted his position, and tried a more direct approach. "Okay, how did I do?"

Gordon narrowed his eyes, "Not bad," he repeated.

Over the years, Gordon had learned to deflect such questions whenever they arose, and 'Not bad' seemed to cover most eventualities.

Chris shrugged, and said, "I had to try."

Simon, Pamela and the two children turned up next. The two girls had fallen in love with baby Graeme the previous day, so they disappeared off, with strict orders not to wake him up. Simon, on Gordon's request, had brought his tools along, and went out to the garage to look at Maggie's car which had developed an annoying rattle of late.

"I didn't get the opportunity to ask you much yesterday," Gordon said to Pam, "Is it going okay?"

Pam raised an eyebrow. "Surprisingly well, I'd say. Although it has nothing to do with his ridiculous suicide attempt, I want you to know. I'm not that easily swayed."

"I never thought you were," Gordon replied.

"It's more to do with the children," she continued. "They were suffering, both at home and at school. It really opened my eyes when I took them to the hospital to see him. So, Simon and I had a chat and we agreed that neither of us had been angels, so we ought to put it all behind us and try again. I have to say, it's seems to be working, thus far."

Gordon handed her a drink, and they raised their glasses. "Here's to your continued success," he toasted.

"And yours, too, Dad. The children absolutely love Mags."

Simon came back in, "Fixed it," he said, with a big grin. "Something was caught around the wheel, that's all. Piece of cake."

"Thank you," Gordon said, and slapped Simon on the back. It was an instinctive reaction, and neither quite knew what to make of it. After a moments awkward pause, Gordon asked, "Would you like a drink?"

Simon cleared his throat. "Oh, not at the moment."

Tony arrived alone. "Catherine's bringing Jessie," he said. "Got a beer?"

Gordon fetched him one from the box in the kitchen. "How's her bump?" he asked.

"Very well," he answered, "I think she's going to bring the latest scan picture with her, so you'll see it first-hand. She's back to being nice to me again. I'll just take each day as it comes."

Catherine arrived soon after, and was in a good mood. It was so refreshing not to have to cringe at everything she said. Jessica left her mother in the lounge, and came to see Gordon.

"Did you want to speak to me?" he asked.

Jessica did a little twirl on the spot, and said, "Do you know what I want to be when I grow up?"

Gordon crouched down, "Now that's an important question. How about a writer?"

Jessica wrinkled her nose up. "No," she said, "I'm going to run the Race, just like you."

Gordon felt goose bumps swathe over him. "Well," Gordon explained, smiling broadly, "That would be a very fine thing."

Vee was the last to arrive. Gordon helped her in from the taxi.

"How's family?" she asked.

"Getting along very well, for the moment. How are you feeling?"

"Fine. I just wish it were warmer. Now, I hope you've got some sherry left, I can feel a thirst coming on."

Not for the first time that year, Gordon really appreciated having Vee around. Throughout their friendship, she'd never made any demands on him, and he couldn't remember the two of them ever falling out. They simply enjoyed each other's company.

When everyone had been fed and watered, Gordon sneaked out of the room, and the conversation amongst those left started to quieten. They all knew where he'd gone.

Gordon opened the cupboard in the spare room. Within it was the Race lectern, made of solid wood, with three carved ostrich feathers supporting the top, upon which rested this year's prize.

It was in these moments, before he went back into the room, that the gravity of the Race really came home. Every single year it had been run, someone had gone through this process. Someone had fetched the lectern and the certificate, and maybe, like he, stopped and thought about what the Race really meant.

Gordon bent his head, but knew not where he prayed. He kept the words simple, offering up a prayer of thanks for his family and friends, before returning to the lounge. As Gordon walked through the people parted, and Gordon felt the pride resurge in his veins. He knew he was going to miss it.

When he was in place, he put both hands on the top of the lectern, and said, "Welcome to the Ostrich Race's Winning Ceremony. It's such a pleasure to see all your faces. The Race has had a tumultuous year. There can be no other word for it. I've spoken to many people I haven't seen for years, and found out things about others I always thought I knew.

"Just over forty years ago I took part in my first Race. I can picture it perfectly, as I'm sure Vee can, too. That's what the Race is about. It's about the times when we're all together, getting along, being friends. I know to the young, and maybe some of the old, it's about the competition, but for me, the Race is a vehicle for us all to stay in touch.

"In the time I've been the organiser, the Race has helped me through both the good times and the bad. It's been a rock to cling to, and an ideal to strive for. It has been a challenge, it has been a pleasure. As I said at the beginning of the year, this is the last Ostrich Race, for the moment." He winked at Jessica when he said that, "And I want to wish it well. Maybe it could do with a rest, too.

"Now, I must say you've all done it the justice it deserves. It was a good Race to finish on. Before the prize giving, I shall quickly summarise the action from the year. For the first round, Catherine and Trudie took the lead, and managed to hold onto it through March. Then she was overtaken by Tony, who briefly took it with a perfect April. May saw Simon come to the fore, and after another short spell by Catherine in June, Pam took it for July. August saw Tony sharing the lead, while September was Louise's month, but the final two months were taken by the eventual winner. Now, if I had my own way, I would've made you all winners this year, but the rules are the rules. So, for my last time, I'd like to present the certificate to this year's winner of the Ostrich Race."

Gordon scanned the expectant faces. "And that's where I have to stop," Gordon said. "For the first time ever I cannot tell you who has won the Race, because I don't know who the anonymous player is."

There was a hush in the room that lasted a couple of seconds. Then Tony cleared his throat. "Um, there's something I need to say," he said. Tony approached Gordon, and put his hand on Gordon's arm. "I hope I've done the right thing."

"Don't worry. I'm sure you have."

Tony looked nervous and scared. "Well," he started, "back in January, someone came to me and said they wanted to take part in the Race. They asked me to keep their participation a secret, and I have. I collected their questions, and sometimes delivered their answers."

Tony went quiet. Gordon looked at him with concern.

"Do you know who it is?" Gordon asked.

Tony nodded, not looking up. "Yes, I do. I've had to keep it a secret to everyone. It was difficult. I really hope I did the right thing."

The bungalow's doorbell rang.

Gordon looked at Tony. "It's all right," he said to the nervous man. "I trust you."

Gordon walked through the lounge and into the hallway. There was a figure standing on the doorstep, but Gordon couldn't see who it was. He reached out and turned the catch on the door, slowly pulling it towards him until he could get a good look at his face.

"Oh, my God," was all he could say. "Oh, my God."

There, standing in front of him was a man he'd never met, yet whose face he knew as well as his own.

"How?" Gordon whispered. "How could this be?"

The man held out his hand. "I'm sorry," he said. "I know this must come as a shock to you. My name's James. And your son, Graeme, was my father."

EPILOGUE

Gordon lay alone in the bedroom, unable to concentrate. He'd been there for twenty minutes, ever since he'd seen the embodiment of his dead son.

Graeme had had a child. These words went over and over in his mind.

There was a knock on the bedroom door.

"Gordon?" Maggie said.

"Come in," he replied.

Maggie came in and sat next to him. "Everyone's gone, apart from the boy."

"What did he say his name was?"

"James. He didn't know if you wanted to see him?"

"God, yes. Tell him I do. Don't let him out of your sight."

~

When Gordon entered the lounge, the man stood looking out of the window. Gordon ran his open palm down his face and shivered. It was as if he were dreaming.

Gordon cleared his throat, and said, "Hello, James."

Startled, the boy turned quickly, and Gordon had to look away. It wasn't easy looking into his dead son's eyes again.

"You all right?" James asked.

Gordon nodded, "Sorry, it's still difficult to..., well, you look so much like your father. Please, sit down."

James sat in the chair furthest from the door, Gordon in the nearest. "Firstly," James said, "I'm really sorry about the garden incident. Tony told me you were worried. That's not what I wanted. I just wanted...

Well, I've always wondered what you were like. Having never known my father. Mum talks about him like he was a saint."

"It's a fitting description," Gordon said, "He was highly thought of by everyone who knew him."

"Mum says he was going to be a great man. That he had a certain look in his eyes. She wanted me to tell you he was very proud of his father."

"Thank you," Gordon told the boy. "One moment," he said, getting up and going into the kitchen. He returned a moment later with a small box. "Is this yours?" Gordon gave the box to James, who took the lid off, and smiled.

"Yes," he said, taking the stud earring out. "I'm not much of a criminal."

The boy seemed as nervous and awkward as Gordon felt.

"Where's your mother, now?"

"She's not here. She knows I'm seeing you, but I think she feels guilty about keeping who you were a secret. She felt bitter when Dad died, and moved away while she was still pregnant with me. She said for me to tell you that that was what Dad was ringing to tell you on the day he died, that he was going to be a father."

They sat in the silence for a few seconds.

Gordon put his head in his hands. "Oh, God. What a mess."

"I wanted to sort it out. I wanted to make amends."

"Oh, James, you have no amends to make. It was my fault, and mine alone."

Gordon looked out of the window.

"I've read a couple of your books," the young man said.

Gordon smiled, stole a glance toward him. "Have you?" he asked.

James leant forward, "Oh, yes. They're very good," he said.

"That's kind of you to say," Gordon told him, "but it's okay if you don't like them. Sometimes it's just as rewarding."

Gordon saw James' face frown. "No, I really mean it," he said sincerely. "They were very good. Knowing you'd written them made the words comforting. They weren't difficult to read at all."

Gordon wanted to change the subject. He didn't want to be the object of any praise. James must have sensed this.

"Are the cuff-links okay?" he asked, pointing toward Gordon's sleeve. Gordon looked down and saw the quills that Tony had given him on Father's Day.

"They are. Were you the friend who pointed them out to him?"

James nodded. "Yes, I hope that's okay."

"More than you'll ever know," Gordon replied, his words catching in his throat. Gordon breathed out slowly, then asked, "So, what do you do?"

"Oh, I'm at college," James replied "Doing English. I was hoping we could have a talk about it when we get to know each other better. My university is just a few miles away, and I'm going to be there for another couple of years."

"That's good," Gordon said.

"I was hoping you might like to have a walk in the morning?" the younger man asked, "Then maybe we could put some flowers on Dad's grave?"

"That sounds perfect," Gordon replied, with a smile and a tear.

~

The next day, Gordon, Maggie and James went up to the hills just north of the town. It was a gentle stroll over reasonably flat terrain, and it offered picturesque views down to the sea.

"It still hasn't sunk in, yet," Gordon admitted. "It's the best news I've ever had."

Maggie patted him on the back. "At least no-one will forget it for a long time," she said. "I've never seen a room clear so quickly. No one knew what to do or say. Which reminds me, Chris rang this morning to check that everything was all right."

They stopped at the cafe next to where Maggie's car was parked, and, for what seemed like the first time all year, Gordon talked about the days to come.

~

That afternoon, Gordon and James visited the graveyard. "It was your flowers I saw back in January, then?" Gordon asked.

"Yes, probably."

They stood in silence for a few moments, then James, sensing Gordon's need to be alone, went off to look at the other gravestones.

Gordon bent down to talk to Graeme. "So, son," he said, in hushed tones, "Now I know what you wanted to speak to me about, and in a way it makes me feel more guilty than ever. But I don't expect it's guilt you'd want me to feel, now. Not after all these years. It's strange to think you had a child. It never crossed my mind you wanted them. Although, I don't understand why it didn't. I can't think of a man more suited to the task of fatherhood."

"I remember your Mum and I telling you we were originally thinking of calling you James. It's good to think you might have been listening."

Gordon sighed, taking a moment to collect himself. "I missed you when you went to university. And I was grumpy with you because you'd chosen to go. You were my confidant, and I'd lost you. And then you died, and everything, everything was obliterated. I still don't understand how it could have happened to you. You always seemed so robust, as if you could deflect such insignificant things as cars. It wasn't fair that you were taken away from us."

"But, you have a son, and he's a nice man. And I wanted you to know that. I wanted to thank you for having him, for in him the part of me that's lived in anguish for so many years can be helped. It's what you'd have wanted all along, I'm sure. I love you, son, my Graeme, and I miss you so much. But now I have a chance to know your son, and I thank you, I thank you, for giving me that chance."

Printed in Great Britain
by Amazon

23600887R00219